THE
GUILTY
ONE

THE GUILTY ONE

ANNA KAROLINA

TRANSLATED BY LISA REINHARDT

THOMAS & MERCER

Previously published as *Försvararen* by Bokfabriken in Sweden in 2020. Translation into English from the edition published by Edition M in Luxembourg in 2021 under the title *Auf Tod komm raus*.

Published by Thomas & Mercer, Seattle

www.apub.com

Amazon, the Amazon logo, and Thomas & Mercer are trademarks of Amazon.com, Inc., or its affiliates.

ISBN-13: 9781662505195
ISBN-10: 1662505191

Cover design by Lisa Horton
Art direction by Lisa Brewster

Printed in the United States of America

THE
GUILTY
ONE

1

'One of us will die today,' says Jasmine, wrapping her subtly pink-glossed lips around the straw and sipping on her gin fizz.

Nicolas looks at her across the table. 'Have you been listening to that fortune teller again?'

Jasmine leans back into the cherry-red faux leather upholstery. 'Yes, maybe. But she was right about lots of other things. That I ought to study something with economics, for example, and that I struggle with relationships.'

Nicolas sighs, his eyes travelling from the bushy Christmas tree near the entrance, adorned with red baubles and topped with a large star, to the side wall by the counter, trying to decipher some of the beer labels stuck there for decoration. The siblings are in a corner pub in the part of Stockholm known as Traneberg. To mark the festive season, a Christmas buffet has been set up along one of the shorter wood-panelled walls. The bar is busy with customers who, for various reasons, choose to spend Christmas Eve here rather than somewhere else.

Nicolas loves his twin sister dearly, but sometimes she becomes obsessed by the weirdest things. Like the story with the fortune teller who's claimed that one of them will die before their thirtieth birthday. Normally, Jasmine isn't the whacky or esoteric type, as some may call it, but ever since she saw this clairvoyant woman almost a year ago, she's constantly gone on about it.

'Those people always say things that can be interpreted in different ways,' he offers, raising his Guinness to his lips. 'Nothing but nonsense.'

'Maybe so. But my gut feeling tells me that something is going to happen.'

Nicolas checks his phone. 21.03 p.m. 'You seriously believe one of us is going to die within the next three hours?'

Jasmine brushes a strand of her long black hair behind an ear. 'Okay, maybe I'm exaggerating. But doesn't it creep you out just a little?'

'Not in the least.' He studies her, searching for any sign that there is something else unsettling her. But no; recently, he's been under the impression that she's happier and more stable than usual. 'Okay. We'll stick together until midnight, proving the fortune teller a fraud.'

She shrugs. 'What else are we going to do? Drive home to the Moretti family and wish them a merry Christmas?'

The two of them can't help but grin. Christmas Eve with the parents. No way. He wonders whether he should change his surname to Karlsson or the like. But what would that achieve?

Wishing to be polite, Nicolas raises his glass to a drunk guy sitting a few tables away. The man was trying for the third time to make eye contact. He probably doesn't feel like drinking on his own. And what's wrong with that? It's Christmas, after all.

But when the guy stands up with some difficulty and staggers towards them, Nicolas regrets his polite gesture. The man is wearing a stained T-shirt and, as Nicolas notices on closer inspection, wooden clogs with no socks. Apparently, he didn't get the message about dressing nicely on Christmas Eve.

'It is you, isn't it?' The man gives a gap-toothed grin. 'Nicolas Moretti, the football player?' He sounds like a mumbling Finnish Moomin troll and slaps Nicolas's shoulder in greeting. 'You switched to some Russian team, didn't you? You vanished into thin air, just like that.'

'Yep.'

'What were you thinking, signing with the Russians? Were you on the warpath?' He laughs loudly at his own joke and pushes in beside Nicolas.

Jasmine leans across the table. 'My brother and I have something to celebrate,' she says above the hum of conversation from the other customers and the instrumental Christmas music. 'We would rather be alone.'

The Finn stares at her as if she'd spoken in Japanese, or some kind of extraterrestrial language. Then he punches Nicolas's arm, making him spill beer on the red tablecloth. 'What about that European championship match against Spain – you were completely open. You should have taken the shot rather than pass the ball.'

Nicolas picks up a napkin and dabs at the spill, listening to the Finnish man without much enthusiasm. Another one of those experts.

'And then a while later, two backs were blocking you, but you decided to take the shot.' The Finn runs his hand across his shaved head. 'What the hell were you thinking? Now I'm going to kick at goal because I didn't do it earlier? Moretti took the shot but couldn't get the ball in.'

'Listen, usually I enjoy talking about football, but not right now. Like my sister said, she and I are celebrating.'

'You getting kids or something?' When he receives no reply, the Finn stares at each of them in turn and props himself up with his fists. 'Oh well, merry Christmas.' He shuffles off and joins the table of an elderly couple whose plates are laden with meatballs, herring and potato-onion-anchovy gratin.

The woman shrinks back when the Finn leans over to her, fingering a brooch on her chest. Judging by the couple's facial expressions, the man won't be staying at their table for long either.

'Anyway – what are we celebrating?' asks Nicolas, grinning at Jasmine.

'How about the fact that we both turn thirty tomorrow?' She plays with the slice of lemon in her glass. 'What a crap day for a birthday. Christmas Day, of all days.'

'Can't be helped.'

Jasmine lifts her glass towards Nicolas. 'Well then, merry Christmas, brother dear. And early happy birthday. To us, the only sensible Morettis.'

'And to Douglas,' adds Nicolas once he's taken a sip and licked the foam from his upper lip.

Jasmine sips on her drink and nods. 'To our baby brother. Let's hope he's not as screwed up as us just yet.' She reaches for her handbag. 'By the way – have I already told you? I've been offered a job at the innovation agency where I worked in the summer. Someone's going on parental leave sometime in March.'

'Congratulations. So we do actually have something to celebrate.'

'Sure do! Come with me.' She stands up, waves her handbag suggestively and ambles off.

Nicolas knows what that means. He also knows that he shouldn't do it. Despite himself, he gulps down his beer and follows his sister to the toilets. All three cubicles appear to be empty. The lighting in the white tiled room is dim, and candles on a shelf above the basins exude the scent of cinnamon. Jasmine manoeuvres Nicolas into the middle cubicle, closes the door behind them and places four lines of white powder on the lid of the toilet seat.

'Where'd you get this?'

'As if you cared.' She goes down on her knees, gathers her hair at the nape of her neck, holds one nostril closed with a finger, sucks in the powder through a shortened straw, and repeats the procedure with the other side. Then she gets to her feet and wipes her nose with the back of her hand. 'There you go.' She holds out the straw, and Nicolas accepts it even though he hadn't intended to do coke.

He has been clean for a month. His father offered him an office job at the football club on condition that he stayed away from drugs. The moral dilemma makes him squirm; his whole body itches. Only tonight, just this once. It's Christmas Eve, after all.

He snorts the lines, hard and determined, before he has time to regret his decision.

Sod it! He doesn't even want this job, engineered by his father in some kind of desperate attempt to patch up their broken relationship. Giorgio made a fool of himself, and nothing will ever go back to how it used to be, no matter how hard he tries.

As the drug begins to take effect, Jasmine's eyes sparkle like those of a child who has just unwrapped a beautiful Christmas present. Nicolas thinks of the ice skates he got for Christmas when he was five or six. Back when all was well, when their mother was still alive and they were a perfectly normal family.

Damn . . . Merry Christmas, sister.

They push open the door, gripped by a laughing fit about the toilet brush that has become caught in Jasmine's hair. Nicolas has no idea how it happened; he only noticed when he turned around. And now they find themselves face to face with the Finn, who was evidently waiting for them outside the cubicle.

The guy leans against one of the basins, eyeing them from dull, squinting eyes. 'You got any more of that?'

Before Nicolas has a chance to reply, Jasmine plants her feet directly in front of the man. 'I need to wash my hands.'

His eyes travel down to her handbag.

'Gimme some and I'll keep my mouth shut.'

Jasmine laughs. 'What is it that you think I have?' She gestures at him to make way. The man's expression darkens, making him look intimidating.

'Come on, let's go,' says Nicolas, and he starts to open the door. 'Just forget about him.'

The guy could be a psychopath, and Nicolas knows all too well that Jasmine likes to pick a fight. He's nothing but a drunk, Nicolas wants to tell her, but changes his mind. He'd rather not provoke the man unnecessarily. The Finn looks powerful and has big hands. He probably used them for hard physical labour before he succumbed to drink.

'Damn brats,' he grumbles when Jasmine finally gives in and walks to the door Nicolas is holding open for her. As he follows her out, she suddenly pushes back past him and throws something at the Finn.

What was that?

Oh no – the toilet brush. The Finn roars.

They race to their table, grab their coats and practically run out of the pub. They slip into their coats once they are outside, taking a shortcut across the dark, deserted car park.

'Damn it, my scarf.' Jasmine stops and looks back.

'Forget it.'

'But it was brand new.'

'We are not going back. No way. He can keep it as a Christmas present for all I care.'

She sighs dramatically but carries on with Nicolas through the slushy snow. Hopefully the Finn isn't following them. Nicolas glances over his shoulder. Not a soul to be seen. But he notices movement out of the corner of his eye. He gazes up at the apartment block some way ahead, where advent candles glow in nearly every window. Nicolas spots a cat with thick, fluffy fur in one of the windows – had that been the movement? The longer Nicolas stares at the animal, the bigger it seems to become. At some point he even believes there are two cats.

He closes his eyes and realizes that he is high.

Who cares whether there are one or two cats. Main thing is they've shaken off the Moomin troll.

They cross the street, laughing about the incident with the toilet brush and discussing where it struck the Finn.

'Only on the shoulder, unfortunately,' says Jasmine.

'Where are we headed?' asks Nicolas. Moisture is seeping through his boots, and he notices all of a sudden how cold and miserable it is. 'Yours, right?'

'Sounds good. Mine is closest.' A hint of fear crosses Jasmine's eyes. 'You will stay until midnight?'

''Course,' he replies, even though he thinks she's being silly. 'What have you got on offer?'

Suddenly, there's a crunching sound above them. Nicolas ducks in reflex, shielding his head with his arms protectively. A block of ice crashes to the ground right in front of them, shattering into razor-sharp splinters.

'That was close.' Nicolas peers up at the roof tiles of the house beside them. A second ice block sits precariously close to the edge. He pushes Jasmine to the side.

'I told you.' Her voice is tinged with panic. 'One of us won't live to see their thirtieth birthday.'

'Stop it.' Nicolas wraps one arm around her and turns his head. There is another unsettling sound. This time, however, it does not stem from an ice block but from the Finn's wooden clogs clip-clop-ping on the cobbled street.

Nicolas swears under his breath, elbows Jasmine in the side and nods his head as a signal to run.

They turn into a walkway and keep looking back. The Finn doesn't give up, pursuing them drunkenly but resolutely. He casts long shadows in the glow of the street lamps.

'You shouldn't have thrown that toilet brush,' says Nicolas, breathing heavily. They cross the train tracks, head towards Alviks Torg and race down the steps to the tram. A handful of passers-by stare at them.

Nicolas turns once more. What the . . . The Finn is stamping down the stairs, taking two steps at a time then jumping the last bit.

You stubborn sponger! What do you want?

2

A few minutes later, they burst into Jasmine's hallway and lock the door behind them, gasping for breath. Nicolas leans against the wall, bent forward, hands on his knees. His eyes meet Jasmine's, and he can tell by her puzzled look that they are both thinking the same. What a nutcase!

Nicolas peers through the small window next to the door, relief flooding him when he sees nobody. Perhaps they actually managed to shake the Finn.

As they hang their jackets on the coat stand, Jasmine promises not to get smart with anyone ever again.

'I'll believe it when I see it,' says Nicolas, climbing the stairs to the thousand-square-foot one-room apartment. He likes to say that his sister lives in the coolest maisonette ever, but Jasmine invariably downplays the compliment, stating that her home is just a plain old apartment that happens to have a hallway for a ground floor.

Whatever you say. Want to swap?

Nicolas has been wondering for a while how she, a poor student, can afford the steep rent. Must be around fourteen or sixteen thousand kronor a month. He has his suspicions, of course, where the money comes from, but chooses not to ask about it. If it works for Jasmine, he won't interfere.

Upstairs in the apartment, Jasmine puts on Christmas music, lights candles and dances by herself on a fluffy rug. Behind her, the candlelight illuminates a raised platform that is her bedroom. Two mattresses on the floor are cosily furnished with cushions, blankets and furs. The entire apartment looks as if a fairy waved her wand and decorated everything in white, grey and pink. Tall windows, a kitchen island that matches the colour of the grey cupboard doors, small side tables, stools and beanbags.

Now she pretends she's holding a microphone, duetting the high-pitched notes of 'O Helga Natt' with Tommy Körberg while Nicolas helps himself to two bottles of beer from the fridge. He opens them with his teeth and hands one to Jasmine. Just then, Jasmine's parrot pipes up. Nicolas walks up to the gold-coloured birdcage that hangs from a hook in the ceiling beside the kitchen island. He holds his nose up to the bird.

'Hello, Pelle. How are you today?'

'Screw you,' caws the bird.

'I see. You're in a bad mood?'

'Screw you.'

Nicolas turns his head to Jasmine. 'You have to teach him more than just "screw you",' he shouts over her singing.

'I did.'

'What?'

She dances away from him and joins in the next song. 'Lake and beach lay glistening . . .'

Suddenly he hears a noise down in the hallway and goes 'Shh!' at her. Was that a knock? Jasmine goes quiet, and now they can both hear it. Yes, someone is knocking on the front door.

'Who could it be?' he whispers.

'No idea.' Jasmine treads silently towards the stairs.

'Wait. What if it's him? The Finn.'

Panic flares up in Jasmine's eyes. Nicolas knows what she is thinking, and he inwardly curses the fortune teller who put this idea in his sister's head. Nonetheless, he can't resist a glance at his phone.

22.13 p.m. Less than two hours until the clock strikes midnight and the alleged danger passes. He follows her down the stairs into the hallway and waits as she looks through the peephole.

'It's a Santa Claus,' she says with a laugh. 'I think I know who it is.' She unlocks the door.

'No, wait!'

But Nicolas is too late. Jasmine opens the door to a man in a Santa costume standing in the porch, swaying from side to side like a flagpole in the wind. Two steps back, one forward. He has a fat stomach, or else he's stuffed a pillow down his costume. The eyes behind the metal-rimmed glasses flicker from side to side as he asks with a heavy tongue: 'D'you maybe have some schnapps for me?'

Nicolas pushes past Jasmine and grasps the door handle. 'Looks like you've had quite enough to drink.'

Nicolas tries to close the door but the man places one boot in the opening.

'Hey, no need to be rude. All I did was ask nicely.'

'Sure, but please leave now.'

The Santa Claus stays put. Has the guy even heard Nicolas? He looks pretty wasted, hanging on to the door frame to stay upright. Nicolas kicks the man's foot out of the way and tries to slam the door shut once more, but again something is preventing it from closing.

Santa's fingers. The man curses, forces open the door and shoves Nicolas into the narrow hallway. The two of them crash into the wall amid a tangle of coat hangers and jackets. Jasmine screams. Nicolas doesn't stand a chance – the guy's at least a hundred pounds heavier than him and has Nicolas in a tight grip.

11

Nicolas might get rid of him if he could manage to get him to the porch outside the door. Nicolas digs his heels into the floor, pushes with his football-player thighs, slips in his socks but manages to catch himself, takes one step towards the door, then another one. He grasps the door frame with one hand and pulls, and suddenly the third step comes easily. The two men tumble down the four steps to the pavement. The Santa Claus lands on his back with Nicolas on top. The man exhales visibly through the long beard, then produces a gargling sound as if his lungs were bursting. Then he goes completely still.

Nicolas rolls off him. His shoulders ache but otherwise he's fine.

'What the hell was that?' Jasmine falls to her knees, holding one ear to the Santa's mouth and two fingers on his wrist. 'What have you done?'

Nicolas stares at the scene of destruction – the crooked beard, the cracked glasses. In a daze, he watches Jasmine place her palms on the man's chest, pushing rhythmically and counting out loud: 'One, two, three, four, five, six.'

Nicolas's mind spins. The Santa Claus is dead. He's killed him.

Eleven, twelve, thirteen. He didn't do it on purpose, but still, he . . .

On the seventeenth count, the man wheezes. Jasmine leans back and waits, her mouth open, her eyes fixed on him. Nicolas does the same – waiting, staring at the man's chest. Is it moving? Is he breathing? After a few seconds, the man wheezes once more. Nicolas breathes a sigh of relief and folds his hands in gratitude. The man gasps a few times and pushes Jasmine away from him with his arm. She rushes to Nicolas's side, and he only notices now that his socks are wet and his feet are freezing. Both he and Jasmine are stepping from foot to foot.

The man scrambles to his feet with some difficulty, then pauses, hunched over, hands braced on his knees. He pants, wheezes, sways from side to side, and generally seems as though he hasn't a clue what just happened to him.

'Well, damn . . . I think I . . .' He adjusts his glasses. 'Well, thank you. I think I've had too much to drink, so excuse me.' He staggers down the street, hands pushed into his lower back. 'I'll be off, thank you.'

Nicolas and Jasmine return to the front door and watch as the man trips over a bike rack and eventually disappears behind a juniper hedge.

Yes, off you go.

Nicolas notices movement out of the corner of his eye. In a window across the street, someone quickly retreats behind the curtain. Or was it just his eyes playing tricks on him again, like with the cat earlier? He focuses his eyes and, moments later, sees the face reappear. An elderly woman with wavy grey hair.

Damn! Hopefully she doesn't ring the cops.

They go inside. Nicolas locks up behind them and pulls on the door handle to double-check.

What a crappy night.

'Shit,' mutters Jasmine as they climb the stairs to her apartment. 'Shit, shit, shit.'

Nicolas heads straight for the fridge. 'I could use something strong right now. Do you have anything other than beer?'

'No, but I know what we need.' Uttering another *shit*, she fetches her handbag, which she'd dumped on the kitchen island earlier, and rummages through it. When she turns around, she seems to have overcome the worst of the shock as she's dancing towards Nicolas now, singing along to George Michael's 'Last Christmas', holding out a closed fist.

'What is it?'

Jasmine opens her fist and reveals a few pale-yellow pills. 'Take two.'

'Are those benzos? Roofies?'

'Just take them.'

He washes them down with a swig of beer from a fresh bottle and asks, lips on the bottleneck: 'Who on earth was that idiot?'

'He lives a few houses down. I thought he was all right. We've spoken a few times.'

'Complete moron.'

Jasmine nods, pops a pill and sashays towards the kitchen island like a ballerina. She pirouettes and throws herself on the marble benchtop, writhing like an eel and pretending to make out with someone.

Nicolas sits down on the couch, leans back and wishes he were as relaxed and crazy as Jasmine. They shared the same womb, after all, drank the same amniotic fluid. But they seem to have nothing in common, looks aside – the dark hair and olive skin of their Italian father, their mother's slim figure. They always looked young for their age, much to Jasmine's delight – at least since adulthood. Nicolas doesn't feel the same way. Who wants to be told all their life how cute they are?

She comes to the couch with a bowl of hazelnuts, places it on the table and pushes aside his legs so she can sit down next to him. She picks up a nut and tries to crack the shell with a kitchen knife. Just the thought that the blade might slip sends a shiver down Nicolas's spine.

'Don't you have a nutcracker?'

'I do, somewhere, but this works just fine.' But the shell refuses to crack.

'Let me try.'

Jasmine hands him the knife. Nicolas places the nut on the table and smacks it with the knife handle. The nut skips off the table and rolls across the floor.

Nicolas swears as he puts down the knife and shuffles to the kitchen, rummaging through the drawers until, right at the back between ladles and whisks, he finds a silver nutcracker.

'Here you go.'

She takes the nutcracker, cracks the shell and asks if he wants one too. Suddenly the floor beneath his feet begins to roll. He feels like he's on a cruise ship in a heavy swell. He plants his feet apart to keep his balance and waves his arms about.

'*Titanic*. We're aboard the *Titanic*.'

'What kind of nonsense are you talking? Come, sit.'

'Don't you see it? Everything is moving.'

Jasmine pulls him on to the couch. 'Yes, you're right. We're sinking, we're sinking!'

They burst out giggling, but soon stop as the *Titanic* capsizes.

'What was in those pills?'

'Good stuff, I promise.' She crosses two fingers.

Damn. Nicolas rests his head in Jasmine's lap to stop the dizzy spell. He looks forward to passing a milestone in his life soon. Thirty. Not long now. He picks up his phone and checks the time. 23.37 p.m. When he peers up at Jasmine, he sees that she has fallen asleep. Her head is leaning against the backrest, her mouth half open. Good. She can stop worrying now. After all, there's only a little over twenty minutes left until midnight.

What could possibly go wrong now?

3

When Nicolas wakes up, he feels something sticky on his cheek. Or perhaps it happened the other way around – he felt something sticky and therefore woke up. Whatever the case, he is lying in something damp. When he lifts his head, blinking, there's a smacking sound as if someone had slapped his ear with a wet rag.

Where am I? A zebra-patterned chair, empty beer bottles, grey cupboard doors. Jasmine. At my sister's apartment. Now he can see her hand next to him on the couch – fingers bent so that the red-polished nails are facing the ceiling. That's right, they went to sleep on the couch and he is lying in her lap. He turns his head, his eyes searching for her face, then immediately turns his head away again. Closes his eyes.

What was that? Thoughts are skipping back and forth in his head like a pinball. He obviously didn't see properly. What was in those pills? Why can't he ever say no?

He turns his head again and opens his eyes very slowly, but the hallucination has not vanished.

Jasmine's head is hanging down like that of a butchered chicken, and there is blood everywhere. He bolts from the couch and gapes at his sister, who tilts to the side and comes to rest with her forehead on the seat so that he only sees a small part of one side of her face. Her dark hair hangs down in wet, bloodied strands.

He shrinks back another step and covers his face with his hands. But then he forces himself to look once more. Oh God, please no!

Gingerly, he moves close enough to touch her. He runs the tips of his fingers through her hair. When his fingertips turn wet and red, he rubs them together to make sure. Yes, this is blood.

There's a roaring in his ears, a roaring that paralyses him. The last time he felt this way was at fourteen, but right now it seems like that was only yesterday. The same panic, the same urge to run away yet being unable to move, wanting to flee but not knowing where to go. His face is hot, his body on fire.

An ambulance! The thought flickers past somewhere in his drug-addled brain. I must call an ambulance!

He leans down, touches his sister by the shoulder and shakes her softly.

'Jasmine, wake up.' But he knows she will never wake again.

His sister is dead. Murdered. When she fell face down on to the couch, he saw the cut on her neck. And all the blood. The pink upholstery is dyed red, and there are splatters of blood on the table, the rug, his T-shirt and his jeans. The colour practically screams death.

Realization hits him like a hammer blow, and he stifles an inhuman sound by burying his face in the crook of his arm.

Jasmine is dead. He doesn't know where to turn, can't cope with the situation. The pain is so intense that he feels he might burst into a million atoms any moment.

Suddenly he notices an object at his feet. The knife. The same knife they used to try to crack the nuts. The blade is smeared with blood.

As he wipes saliva from the corner of his mouth, the significance of all this gradually dawns on him.

He will be accused of the murder.

His fingerprints are on the knife handle, her blood is on his clothes. And there is no one here besides him.

His brain switches from panic to self-preservation mode. Jasmine has been murdered and he needs to get out of here as fast as he can.

He slides the knife into the back of his waistband, collects the beer bottles from the table and rushes to the kitchen sink, where he wipes the bottles with a cloth before dumping them in the rubbish bin under the sink. Then he carefully cleans any spot where he may have left fingerprints – the kitchen island, the fridge, the sink. Then he walks to the bathroom, washes his face with water and runs his fingers through his hair. The water in the basin turns pink and disappears, swirling down the plughole like a bloody maelstrom. He dries off with a towel, returns it to the hook and hurries towards the stairs. He can't stop himself from glancing at the couch. The sight of his dead twin sister makes him choke.

Nicolas breathes hard as he runs down the steps to the hallway, slips into his coat, fastens it button by button and searches for his leather gloves. He finds them in his coat pockets and pulls them on. When he is about to open the door, a thought strikes him. The door! A cold shiver runs down his spine and the hairs at the nape of his neck stand on end. He takes one step forward and grasps the door handle. Yes, the door is still locked; no one else has come in. Consequently, it must have been he who— No, it can't be. He would never murder his sister.

The shock fills every part of him. Those pills he and Jasmine took – how everything was spinning – the sinking *Titanic*. What was in those damn pills?

He unlocks the door and wipes the handle and the knob with his coat sleeve. Just when he's about to pull the door shut, he glimpses something red next to the shoe rack. He steps back into the hall and takes a closer look. A Santa hat. It's the fucking Santa Claus's hat.

Nicolas stares at it for a while, then picks it up and pulls it over his head. Maybe there's still blood in his hair that didn't wash out.

He slips out of the door, locks it and jogs into the street. His eyes travel along the neighbouring houses and pause at the window where the old woman was hiding behind the curtain. He knows neither what he is looking for nor where he is supposed to go. Away from here. Perhaps he could catch the tram at Alviks Torg? He reaches into his pocket and feels for his mobile phone, stops, searches in the other pocket. Negative. The phone isn't in his trouser pockets, either. His heart skips a beat. He spins around and stares at Jasmine's front door. Shit! He must have left it inside.

He runs back and rattles the doorknob. Locked, of course. You idiot! He searches for something to smash the side window with and finds a flowerpot with a dead plant. He picks it up and looks around. Not a soul in sight, and most windows are dark, aside from a few electric candles here and there, left burning in the middle of the night. What time is it, anyway? He has no idea. But people should be asleep at this time.

He hits the windowpane with the pot. Shards of glass fall on to the steps, crunching under his feet. The noise is too loud; that much he knows, even though he is high on drugs and alcohol and even though there is a panic-induced emptiness in his head. But he needs to go upstairs and get his phone. Carefully, he puts his hand through the hole in the broken glass, feels for the lock and opens it. When he pulls back his hand, pain shoots through his wrist and he curses under his breath. He inspects the cut between his sleeve and glove and finds that it's superficial.

Up in the apartment, Jasmine is still in the exact same position on the couch – upper body keeled over and forehead on the seat.

Yes, of course she's still in the same position, she's dead after all. Still – he cannot and does not want to believe it, and he feels sick.

His eyes scan the room and stop at the coffee table, where he believes he left his phone. But it isn't there. He searches under the table, on the kitchen island and by the sink. Then he knows where it might be. He breathes deeply a couple of times before lifting Jasmine's legs and feeling between the cushions with his hand, and eventually he finds it. Even though the phone is black, it is clearly speckled with blood, especially the screen. He wipes it clean with a paper towel then slips the phone into the inside pocket of his coat.

Outside, the north wind has a firm grip on the neighbourhood. Snowflakes swirl all around him in the light of the street lamps. Nicolas flips up his collar, runs along the deserted streets, trips and slips on ice. He slows down as he reaches the steps leading down to Alviks Torg. His heart thumps with merciless determination against his ribs. He squints in the direction of the tramline, hoping to take the first one along, but none is in sight, and the underground display is too far away for him to make out in how many minutes the next train arrives. Suddenly he hears the sound of a large engine, turns to look and waves at the bus that is about to drive off the square.

Stop, damn it, wait for me!

The driver slows down and opens the door for Nicolas, who jumps on board. He doesn't care where this bus is going. He pulls out his phone, opens the public transport app and waits for the ticket to download. Ridiculously slow internet! The bus driver glowers at him from underneath bushy eyebrows.

'Just a moment, I need to—' The phone slips out of his hand, but he catches it before it hits the floor. He taps the screen again, purchases a ticket and inspects a tiny dot on the upper right edge. It is blood.

'Sit down before you fall over.'

He nods at the driver and staggers towards the back as the bus drives on. Apart from himself, there are three other passengers – a young couple at the far back and an elderly man a few rows on, who is gazing out of the window. Nicolas takes a seat near the middle exit and rubs the blood spot on his phone with his glove until it's gone. He notices that the driver keeps glancing at him in the rear-view mirror.

Is it obvious what's happened to him? That he's just found his sister dead and is running from the scene of the crime? No, he's imagining things.

When the bus jolts on the kerb, Nicolas's stomach cramps. He presses his lips together and swallows back the bile that fills his mouth. But he can't suppress the urge to vomit for long. He leaps to the exit.

'I need to get out! Stop the bus!'

The brakes squeal. Nicolas clutches the backrest of a seat to stay on his feet. He jumps outside and finds himself near Ulvsundaplan. Doubled over, he makes for the nearest bushes. Vomit lands on the ground, splattering his shoes and trouser legs. Nicolas remains in this position and waits for round two, which arrives a few seconds later. When it's over, he is gasping. He takes a deep breath and wipes the back of his hand across his mouth. Suddenly, a blood-stained white pompom dangles in front of his eyes. Nicolas pulls off the Santa hat and stuffs it under his coat.

How did the hat get blood on it? Probably when he was searching for his phone on the couch. Did the bus driver notice, or one of the other passengers? Before he can follow this line of thought, he hears a car slow down nearby.

A police car.

Nicolas staggers a few steps to the side. You've got to be kidding! Even though panic wells up in him once more, he remembers one thing: the knife! He feels for it in his waistband, grasps the handle, pulls it out and tosses it with a flick of the wrist into the

21

bushes. Then he squares his shoulders and tries to look as upright and normal as possible.

Two officers in uniform climb out of the car and walk towards him. One is a tubby woman with silvery white hair that sticks out from under her cap, and the other is a man around Nicolas's age with reddish hair and freckles that remind Nicolas of the spot on his display. He rubbed it off, didn't he? The ground shifts beneath his feet when it dawns on him that it's all over now. There's blood on his clothes, his hands, his hair. Did he wash it all off in the bathroom? The police officers in front of him seem blurry, the street lamp is on a lean, and the house on the other side of the street keels over. Everything around him collapses.

'Wow!'

Someone catches him. When he comes to a moment later, he is kneeling, a cop holding him on either side. His surroundings gradually take shape – cold slush beneath his knees, the police officers' boots.

'How are you feeling?' The freckled one places a hand on his shoulder. 'Have you had too much to drink?'

Nicolas winces as the nausea returns, but he manages to contain it.

'What's your name?'

'Nicolas. Nicolas Moretti.'

'I thought I recognized you from somewhere. Djurgården?'

Nicolas grumbles affirmatively. He's uncertain whether it's good or bad to be recognized by the officer. Maybe there are bonus points for arresting a celebrity. Although, technically speaking, he no longer is a celebrity; his time in the upper league lies a few years back now, and there aren't many left who know him.

'But then you switched to FK Krasnodar, right?' continues Freckles, helping Nicolas to his feet. 'What's it like there? Were you allowed to pick the colour of your own clothes?'

22

Before Nicolas gets a chance to reply, the policewoman cuts him off. 'Have you consumed drugs this evening?'

Nicolas blinks a few times and shakes his head.

'Looks that way, though.' She shines a torch into his face.

He tries to relax, but what good will it do? He can hardly shrink his pupils through sheer willpower.

The policewoman switches off the torch and slides it back into her belt. Unlike her colleague, she doesn't seem in the mood for small talk. 'Are you carrying anything on you? Drugs? Anything pointy or sharp I could cut myself on?'

'No, just my phone, my keys, wallet and so on.'

'And so on?'

'Well, maybe a receipt or something like that, but nothing sharp.' He glances at the bushes. He knows he shouldn't, but the knife in there draws his eyes like a magnet. He once heard somewhere that liars avert their gaze. Neither of the cops seem to notice, though, and Nicolas tries hard to appear as innocent as possible. Maybe it'll work.

'Take out your items.' The policewoman reinforces her order with gestures that remind Nicolas of a stern general in Nazi Germany.

Once Nicolas has emptied his pockets, the cops lead him to the car and ask him to place his hands on the roof. His hands are shaking, and he presses them hard against the steel so they won't notice.

The General frisks him. She starts at the top, her hands slipping under the coat, into his armpits, across the coat's breast pocket. Nicolas flinches when she squeezes the Santa hat inside the pocket between her fingers. Perhaps he even stops breathing, he isn't certain. It seems to him her hand remains there especially long, but then she moves on to his legs.

Nicolas silently exhales while the police officers talk. Something about drugs and LOB. He has no idea what LOB stands for, but neither that nor a drug conviction sounds good. Least of all now.

'You're coming to the station with us,' says the General. 'We're under the impression that you're too intoxicated to cope by yourself. And then we shall see about a drug test.'

'But I haven't taken anything.'

'Of course you haven't. And I am not a policewoman.'

Nicolas's heart is racing. Is this really happening? Should he run away? No, then he'll make himself look even more suspicious. But he *is* fast. He peers in the direction of the rich quarter a little way up the road and considers running to the lake beyond. He reckons he can run almost as fast as he used to, despite the drugs and booze. He studies the cops' bodies, trying to gauge their fitness levels. The General doesn't stand a chance against him; she is short, squat and probably strong, but definitely not a sprinter. But he oughtn't underestimate the football fan, and besides, both of them are armed. What if they shoot at him? Thoughts are buzzing around his head like a swarm of angry bees. Before he makes a decision, the policewoman opens the rear door of the patrol car, attaches a leather cloth to the headrest, folds it open and covers the seat with it.

Now he's sitting inside the car, feeling like a grubby hobo picked up off the street by the police, his sister's blood on his clothes.

The thoughts in his mind are spinning so fast that he can't focus on a single one. All he can do is stare listlessly out of the window as the car sets off, the General behind the wheel and Freckles next to Nicolas on the back seat. After just a few yards, the radio crackles.

'*Three-zero calling three. We have a suspected breaking-and-entering at Väktarstigen 23B in Alvik. The intruder fled the scene about ten minutes ago. The woman who called it in pursued him as far as Alviks*

Torg and watched him take bus number 112 in the direction of Spånga station. Unit 32-3150, I can see you are at Ulvsunda. Come in.'

The General brings the microphone to her mouth. 'We'll be there in about one minute. Over.' She replaces the microphone in the holder, switches on the flashing lights and makes a U-turn on the empty street.

Nicolas shifts his weight to prevent himself from falling over, while everything else collapses like a house of cards. Väktarstigen 23B . . . Jasmine's address. Evidently someone saw him, followed him even, and watched him take the bus. He pushes the thought aside and tries to focus on the police radio. The dispatcher's voice sends several patrol cars to the address and orders two more to stop bus number 112. The description of the suspect echoes from the radio and causes Nicolas to shrink in his seat, even if the description isn't a perfect match.

'Male in his twenties, slim, about six foot tall. Dark clothing and wearing a Santa hat.'

Nicolas touches his chest. The hat in the coat's inside pocket feels like a huge growth. He is struck by the thought that the hat might be his saving grace. The caller must have focused on this one detail, causing her to overlook others. Dark clothing – that may be true for his coat, but not his jeans. Those are light blue.

The police car runs red lights and races past industrial buildings, the flashing lights casting flickering shadows on their walls. Freckles leans forward to his colleague. 'What are we going to do with the LOB?'

'We drive to the address and find out what's going on. Depending on the situation, we can always change our plan.'

'Maybe we should let him go right away. What if we need to chase the intruder?'

'No, the caller wasn't a hundred per cent certain. Besides, the guy is over the hills and far away. And with a bit of luck, if we have a public intoxication arrest in the car, we may not have to do the report for the break-in.'

While the two officers debate what to do about him, Nicolas's eyes shift back and forth between the pair. Are they going to let him go? Or what do they mean? The football fan seems to be in favour of this idea, because when he leans back, he turns to Nicolas and shrugs apologetically. Unfortunately, it seems the woman is wearing the trousers.

Just his luck.

The General slams on the brakes, turns left, then right, then left again. Behind a tree, Nicolas makes out the green apartment building where Jasmine lives and where her body lies dead.

He is back at the scene of the crime.

4

Despite his dry mouth, Nicolas tries to swallow, as if he might be able to somehow drown his knowledge of Jasmine's death in stomach acid. Doesn't work. Someone killed her. And now, sitting all alone in a police car outside her apartment, the fact of the matter hits him with full force. His T-shirt is stuck to his skin, beads of sweat run down his forehead, and his racing pulse makes him tremble, partly because of the drugs, but mostly because of his present situation. Maybe he should just explain to the cops how all this came about. But no; they'd never believe him.

Meanwhile, another patrol car arrives. Two uniforms inspect the house from the outside, shining torches up the façade and combing the bare courtyard. The General and Freckles had forced the door with a crowbar a moment ago and vanished into the apartment. The police radio is still chattering about the break-in. The most recent update says that the window by the door was smashed with a flowerpot and that there was dirt on the floor.

Nicolas leans forward to get a view of the passenger seat, where his belongings sit – mobile phone, keys and wallet. He focuses on the phone screen to make sure he's got rid of the blood, but he doubts it. It doesn't really look like blood, but as if someone has smeared it with their fingers. But isn't that what all phones look like – smudged with sticky fingerprints, food and various liquids?

He leans back, sitting uncomfortably twisted because his hands are tied at his back. The cops handcuffed him before they left the car. He guesses they don't want to risk him doing a runner. They locked the vehicle, too. Nicolas turns to the side regardless and pulls on the lever when his fingers find it, but in vain.

More chatter on the radio. They stopped the bus, but the description of the suspect matches none of the passengers. However, the driver informed them that a young man wearing a Santa hat had disembarked at Ulvsundavägen.

Nicolas hyperventilates. Now he's screwed.

He eyes the General and Freckles as they emerge from the apartment. Their movements seem more urgent as they gesticulate at their colleagues, and their backs seem straighter. The General talks into her lapel mic, her voice rumbling like thunder from the speakers in the car.

'*We found a deceased woman in the apartment. She's been murdered.*' On the word *murder*, she looks at the patrol car where Nicolas sits. Her expression is serious, possibly accusatory.

The world in front of Nicolas's eyes flickers. Surely she thinks that he murdered the woman inside the apartment. His sister. Do the cops even know that she's his sister? He suppresses a sob and forces himself to return the General's stare, mostly so he doesn't miss what's happening. But instead of walking over to him as he expected, she fishes her mobile phone from her pocket and makes a call.

His stomach cramps persist even though there's nothing left to spew out, apart from stomach acid seasoned with despair, panic and hope. It's the hope that is eating him the most – the teeny-tiny chance that he might get away with it. Because if they really were accusing him of murder, they should be arresting him now, right? I already am arrested, he reminds himself. But not for murder. And they were talking about letting me go.

Moments later, the place is teeming with police cars with flashing lights and uniforms securing the crime scene with tape and talking through the radio and in person. An unmarked car parks as close to the police tape as they can, and out gets a lanky man with a camera, slinking around the scene looking for good angles. A journalist, presumably, because the policemen repeatedly shoo him away. Curious faces appear in several windows around the neighbourhood. A handful of onlookers venture into the street, one of them clad in nothing but a bathrobe and wellies.

Why are they just leaving him sitting here? Nicolas hasn't the foggiest, but perhaps it's for the best. An elderly woman with a tiny dog on a leash suddenly makes her way through the bustle, approaching a plain-clothes officer wearing a green army-style parka and baggy trousers. Nicolas had noticed the officer a moment earlier, gauging him to be around the same age as himself, with slightly darker skin and an inconspicuous beanie. He's holding a mobile phone to his ear and speaking earnestly with someone while at the same time giving instructions to some of his colleagues. His body language exudes confidence. If they were on a football pitch, Nicolas would prefer the man on his own team rather than as an opponent.

When the woman reaches him, the plain-clothes officer slips his phone into his jacket pocket and takes a step closer to her. It seems as though he is struggling to understand her. The little mutt takes a terrified leap away from his boots, cowering at his owner's trouser legs and trembling just as much as the old lady. She's probably cold in her thin cardigan.

With a growing sense of trepidation, Nicolas watches as the cop listens to the woman with great interest, nods repeatedly, and eventually looks in the direction of her outstretched arm.

The same direction Nicolas ran in after leaving the apartment.

Nicolas swallows. Could this woman be the one who called the police, having pursued him? The next moment, she points at the window where Nicolas had spotted the twitching curtain following the incident with the Santa Claus.

Of course! An old biddy with nothing better to do than spy on the neighbours. And evidently she's as sharp as a tack.

Nicolas grits his teeth, accepting the fact that he has lost. He feels as though he's paralysed; nothing matters any more.

Plainclothes scribbles on a notepad during the conversation. The minutes pass by, maybe five, maybe twenty, but to Nicolas they seem like days. What is the woman saying? How much did she see? The two finally appear to be done. The woman drags the dog away and casts a glance at the police car Nicolas is sitting in. He turns away, hoping the windows are tinted heavily. He squeezes one of his thumbs until it throbs with pain, then lets it go and looks outside.

The old biddy is gone. Nicolas inhales and exhales deeply a few times as the worst of the tension eases. He pinches his back where he can reach it to make sure he isn't dreaming, to make sure everything out there is really happening. Pure drive-in cinema, and he has a front-row seat.

Suddenly, a uniformed policeman with a military vibe approaches the car, and Nicolas pulls himself together. The man scrutinizes him with squinted eyes, blinking as if to double-check he has seen correctly. He walks up to the car with a bow-legged gait, leans down to the window and stares at Nicolas. Then he calls for Freckles in a tone that demands a response, pointing at Nicolas.

'Who the hell is that?'

Nicolas catches only part of Freckles's reply. Something about an arrest for drunkenness.

'An LOB! How long has he been sitting in there?'

Freckles checks his watch, shrivelling up beside his colleague, and mumbles something.

'Let him go?' retorts the other man angrily. 'He's been in custody for over an hour. You must realize that we can't simply let him go!'

The General joins the duo, and the ensuing discussion doesn't sound good for Nicolas. The bow-legged one is talking himself into a rage, poking holes in the air with his index finger. Unfortunately, he seems to be the one in charge – he has more gold on his epaulettes – and the other two merely nod.

Nicolas's spirits dwindle, and when the General climbs into the driver's seat and explains that she's taking him to the station, he doesn't make a sound.

Freckles sits down next to him with an apologetic expression. 'You'll have to go to the drunk tank after all and take a drug test. I'm sorry about the detour.'

'Is that really necessary?' asks Nicolas. 'I feel much better. It's been an hour already. I can manage on my own.'

'I'm sorry, it's not as we thought.'

As they drive off, Nicolas looks down at his coat, wondering if the blood underneath has somehow vanished all by itself. He hopes so.

5

Nicolas sees and hears everything happening around him at the desk of the police station custody suite, even though scraps of memories from the night before keep spinning in his mind's eye. Jasmine with the toilet brush in her hair; Jasmine, dancing and singing to 'O Helga Natt'. Her torso tilting to the side on the couch. The blood.

Now he's sitting on a wooden bench in a sparsely furnished room. The inventory is limited to two desks with one computer each, separated by Perspex screens from the area where those arrested wait on benches. Nicolas is one of these. Unlike the others, the cops have left him under the supervision of a guard, informing him he'd need to wait a while longer since they had to take care of other things first.

'You know, the murder and all,' Freckles explained, shrugging apologetically once more. 'We have to report to the chief because we were first on the scene.'

To alleviate his frustration, Nicolas silently empathizes with his fellow inmates. There's a long-haired guy who tapped diesel from a truck with a hose. A druggy couple who got into a traffic check with a carload of so-called Christmas gifts that turned out to be stolen goods. A vociferous Polish woman who spent the night on a park bench. Nicolas assumes she was arrested for the same reason as himself – because she can't cope on her own. But unlike him, there doesn't appear to be blood beneath her chequered hat. Blood stemming from a murder.

A door opens and a woman wearing a skirt and high heels breezes into the room with a policeman who looks too young to have lost all his hair. His facial hair, on the other hand, is abundant. He is tall and powerful-looking and, for office duty, has chosen Birkenstock sandals with his uniform. His epaulettes display just as much gold as the bow-legged officer's. Must be a bigwig, thinks Nicolas, returning his gaze to the elegant woman.

Judging by her sharp and clear manner of speaking, she doesn't belong here. Also, she strikes Nicolas as familiar. Her dark hair comes down to her shoulders in immaculately styled curls and she is wearing a fur coat. If Nicolas understands correctly, she's a criminal defence lawyer or something along those lines, come to the station to meet with a client. The guard leads her down the corridor lined with white doors while the bald-headed cop turns to Nicolas.

'And who are you?'

Nicolas looks over his own shoulder to make sure there's just a wall behind him. The bigwig is talking to him. He moistens his lips, preparing to answer, but a policeman on the next bench gets in first.

'He's an LOB. Tarja and Robin brought him in.'

Tarja and Robin. Are those the names of the General and Freckles?

The bigwig grumbles. Judging by his heavy footsteps as he stamped to the door, he is irritated.

Nicolas shuffles back and forth on his seat. His bladder is going to burst. As he looks around for a bathroom, he realizes this might be the perfect opportunity. He might be able to wash properly at a basin, get rid of most of the blood and maybe even hide his T-shirt in a rubbish bin. He catches the guard's attention when the man returns down the corridor.

'May I please go to the bathroom? I'm about to piss my pants.'

A wide grin spreads on the guard's triangular face. 'You think I'm stupid or something?'

Nicolas grows even more disheartened. He hangs his head, his shoulders drooping, and he struggles to breathe. This time it really feels like he's about to die. Evidently he hides it well, though, since no one seems to notice. Not even Tarja and Robin, who turn up a while later with the bigwig. Now that Nicolas knows their names, they seem more human to him. But none of them seem particularly happy, least of all the bigwig.

'An LOB you say? Serious intoxication?'

'And suspected drug use,' adds Tarja. 'Probably a small amount for personal needs.'

'Did you search him? Was he carrying drugs?'

'No.'

'No to which? Did you search him or not?'

'Yes, we did.' Tarja rubs the palms of her hands together. 'We didn't find anything, but he shows signs of drug abuse.'

'And he has three previous convictions for minor narcotics offences,' adds Robin.

'Okay, but he's been sitting here for far too long—'

Someone appears from behind, interrupting the conversation. When Nicolas recognizes the new arrival, a stale taste fills his mouth. It's the plain-clothes officer he saw outside Jasmine's apartment, the guy he'd rather not have as an opponent on the football pitch. Plainclothes whispers into the bigwig's ear while fingering the police badge dangling from his neck by a chain. The bigwig asks him to wait a moment, then turns to Nicolas once more. The uneasy feeling returns. All this can only end one way – he is totally screwed. The policeman asks him how he's feeling, how much he's had to drink and what drugs he took. Nicolas replies as curtly as possible, on the one hand because he doesn't want to give too much away, but also because there's chaos in his head. How is his life supposed to go on without Jasmine, the only person he could talk to? Who might have wished her ill? Who killed her? Will they convict him of the murder? What will people think? And his fans? Not that there are many left, but he still has a small group of loyal followers. Most importantly – what will his family think? His father, his younger brother. Amid this tangle of thoughts, Nicolas suddenly realizes that the plain-clothes officer is looking at him strangely. The man is studying him in an unpleasant way, as if he knows something. Nicolas avoids his gaze, abruptly replying to his question about what he was doing at Ulvsunda.

'I was on my way home. I live at Solna.'

The bigwig is satisfied with the answer. Seems like he doesn't have the time to listen to life stories. He asks Tarja to take the hand-cuffs off Nicolas and explains which tests are going to be conducted on him, and that he will have to spend the night in the sobering cell.

'Will that really be necessary?' Nicolas tries to not sound overly desperate, rubbing the red patches on his wrists. 'I'm fine now.'

'A few hours' sleep and you'll feel better still.' The bigwig turns on his heels and walks out of earshot with Plainclothes, discussing something with him.

'The murder weapon has been found!'

Nicolas stares at the policeman behind the desk in front of him. The man had shouted out the news as if he'd just hit the jackpot.

'Our colleagues found a bloodied kitchen knife in some bushes near Ulvsundaplan.'

Nicolas clenches his fists.

He notices Plainclothes muttering something to Bigwig, all the while eyeing him up. Then the two men approach Tarja, and Plainclothes asks: 'Did you pick him up at Ulvsundavägen?'

'Yes.'

'Where exactly?'

Tarja swallows and turns red. 'A few hundred yards up from Ulvsundaplan.'

Even though Nicolas is keeping his eyes fixed on Tarja, he can feel Plainclothes looking him up and down, hears the tension in his voice as he continues: 'What time did you find him there?'

Robin fishes a notepad from the leg pocket of his trousers and leafs through it. 'At 2.47.'

Plainclothes takes a step towards Nicolas. 'The call reporting the break-in was made at 2.54, seven minutes after you arrested this man less than a mile from the scene of the crime, at the same place where a knife has just been found. And if I'm not mistaken, bus number 112 drives right past there.'

Nicolas is so cramped up and tense he feels like he's about to have an epileptic seizure.

'Stand up,' says Plainclothes.

Nicolas remains seated. Does he have the right to refuse the order?

'Didn't you hear me? Stand up and take off your coat.'

This time, Nicolas obeys.

He fumbles around on purpose with the top button and eventually undoes it, since he can't draw out the moment for ever. Then he starts on the next one. What else can he do? He'd like to run away, but where to?

Finally, he unbuttons the coat fully and looks down at his bloodstained T-shirt.

Silence. Only a snort from Tarja, who knows that she has done shoddy work.

Plainclothes steps up to him and pulls something from the coat's breast pocket.

The Santa hat.

Now he's deep in the shit. Up to his neck.

Nicolas's brain shuts down as if someone has flipped a switch.

He leaps towards the nearest door and pulls at the handle in vain. When he spins around, a blow strikes him on the chin and he goes down. He feels the weight of bodies upon him, hears roaring voices.

'Lie down! Show me your hands! Your hands!'

6

The next few hours are shrouded in a dull fog – serious faces eyeing him up, policemen dealing with him, policemen he saw at the scene of the crime, policemen arriving with new arrests, policemen who are plain curious.

Plainclothes and a forensic tech take off his clothes and photograph him from the front and in profile. They place his fingers in a fingerprint scanner, take a swab from his mouth and note down his injuries. The cut on his wrist and a bump on the head. The latter must have come from the tussle with the Santa Claus; Nicolas didn't notice it at the time. A handful of grazes and bruises. At some point during these procedures, Nicolas catches Plainclothes's name – it's Simon Weyler. The man is lead interrogator at the major crimes unit and has taken over the case from Tarja and Robin. Apparently, Nicolas's public drunkenness is no longer the priority; instead, he is suspected of murder.

The murder of his sister.

By the time he sits down on a chair in the interview room, the fresh T-shirt they gave him is already soaked with sweat, clinging to his skin.

Simon takes a seat on the opposite side of the desk, clutching a steaming mug of coffee.

'You sure you don't want one?'

Nicolas shakes his head. He doesn't feel like coffee right at this moment. In fact, he feels as though he will never be able to eat or drink anything again.

Of course the cops believe he did it. All the evidence points to him.

Nicolas focuses on the notes Simon writes on a pad. Upside down, they look like the date and time. Then he puts the ballpoint pen aside, fixes his hazel eyes on Nicolas and informs him that he is under suspicion of having murdered Jasmine Moretti.

'Do you admit or deny having committed the murder?'

Nicolas thinks about those words. Admit or deny? He has been asked this question three times already. Do you admit or deny the allegations? At first, they merely suspected him of drug use, which was bad enough. He had imagined the headlines in the media and how it would diminish his chances of finding work. He had felt ashamed about ruining his life over a few lines of coke. But this, now . . . Murder. His future lies destroyed.

You do not have to say anything . . . Anything you do say may be given in evidence. The caution surfaces somewhere in the back of his mind. Maybe he's better off keeping his trap shut.

'Hello? Nicolas?' Simon snaps his fingers in front of Nicolas's face. 'Did you hear my question? Do you admit or deny the murder of Jasmine Moretti?'

'I deny it.'

Scepticism flashes through Simon's eyes. 'You deny it.'

'Yes.'

Simon makes a note on his pad. 'Okay. Before we continue, I would like to inform you of your right to have a lawyer present during questioning. Would you like to make use of this right?'

'Yes, I think so.'

'Would you like anyone in particular?'

Would you like. The policeman says the words as lightly as if the question was which sauce the customer would prefer on his doner kebab. Tomato or garlic?

'If you don't, you will be assigned a public defender,' Simon explains when he receives no reply. He drums on the table with his pen, seemingly thinking about something. 'As it happens, there's a lawyer in the building at present. Angela Köhler. You may have noticed her in the waiting room earlier?'

Angela Köhler. Nicolas remembers the elegant woman with the high heels. Most likely Simon is referring to her. Nicolas matches the name with the face and the long, coiffed hair, realizing the lawyer in question regularly appears on TV, speaking about female victims of crime, rape and such things.

Simon rests his elbows on the table. 'She asked me to tell you that she would like to talk to you.'

'I see.'

'Yes, well, that's up to you. But it could take a while for us to find someone else. As I said, she's already here.'

Nicolas thinks. Is it helpful to him if the questioning is over and done with asap? They'll hardly let him go after. But she's here and she's a public defender.

'Okay. I suppose I can talk to her.'

A few minutes later, Angela Köhler fills the entire room with her presence, authority and elegance. Her perfume exudes an exclusive scent. Her heels make her at least three inches taller than she actually is, and she's about 5 foot 9 already.

Simon leaves the two of them. Angela sits down on the spare chair and crosses her legs. She keeps her back straight, studies him intently and enunciates each word exaggeratedly when she speaks. Tight, thin lines form around her lips, which are painted red.

'You are suspected of murder, but I can help you.' She allows the words to sink in before she continues. 'You may be surprised to hear it, but I knew Jasmine. She came to me about six months ago, looking for help. She had some trouble with a stalker who came into the possession of a few – how shall I put it? – embarrassing photos.'

Nicolas stares at her. Has he heard right? 'You knew my sister?'

'Yes. When I heard that she'd been murdered, my first suspicion was that stalker. I don't suppose you know who he is? Did Jasmine tell you about him?'

He shakes his head, fighting back the feeling that he is disappointed in his sister. It doesn't feel right in this context. Nonetheless, he can't help but wonder why she didn't say anything. They always told each other everything. Well, almost everything.

The muscles on Angela's neck twitch and she gazes at him even more intently. 'Let's get one thing out of the way first: did you murder Jasmine?'

Nicolas swallows. In his mind, he sees the deep cut on Jasmine's neck and the knife, now bloodied, that they had tried to crack nuts with before he fell asleep.

'No,' he says quietly.

'Good. Stick with that statement. I have some background facts that the police don't know about. Jasmine never reported the stalker, she was too afraid. But I know that he exists and I can find him. Only if you want me to help you, that is.'

'As my defender, you mean?'

'That's right. You engage me as your criminal defence lawyer, the state pays my fee, and I will do everything within my power to clear you of the charge. It won't be easy. You've dug quite the hole for yourself, I must tell you. But from the little I've heard so far, the police made mistakes too. The very fact that you were taken to the scene of the crime, for example.' Angela smiles. 'I eat cops like those for breakfast. Believe me, they'll still have nightmares about me long after they retire.'

She shifts her weight and crosses her legs once more. The sight of the pale nylon stockings gleaming in the light of the energy-saving bulb reminds Nicolas of Sharon Stone in *Basic Instinct*. He knows the thought is inappropriate, but perhaps it's some kind of stress management strategy for him, a survival instinct.

'Are we agreed?' asks Angela.

'I think so.'

'Very well. Then tell me briefly what happened.'

Nicolas looks down, gazing at the ring left on the table by Simon's coffee. 'We were at Jasmine's and drank a fair bit. She sang Christmas songs and danced. Then we flaked out on the couch, and when I woke up—' His voice grows sharper. 'When I woke up, she was dead and I was lying in her lap. I must have been off my face.'

'From the drugs you both consumed.'

'Uh-huh.'

'So you believe someone else murdered her while you were sleeping on her lap?'

Nicolas looks up. 'Yes.' Then he looks back down. He knows full well how unlikely that sounds – that he was sleeping on her legs while someone slit her throat. 'I must have overdosed. I can't remember a thing.'

'Better not mention overdosing during the questioning. People can act out of control in such situations, turning aggressive and violent. That doesn't sound good. What did you take?'

'I don't know. Jasmine had some yellows pills. Benzos, I guess.'

'We'll find out from the blood test. Okay, at least we can explain the blood on your clothes. You were lying in her lap when she was murdered. Concerning the knife, however . . . did you hide it in the bushes when you were vomiting?'

'Yes.'

'You could claim you happened to see it lying there and picked it up to see what it was. That would explain your fingerprints.'

Angela stretches her neck. 'But since you're covered in Jasmine's blood, it's probably better to admit that you were there. Yes, that's what we'll do. You admit that you were there and— Why did you take the knife away from Jasmine's apartment?'

Nicolas slumps some more. 'I panicked. I wasn't thinking . . .'

'You just wanted to hide the murder weapon?'

'I guess so.'

'You guess. No, that's not good enough. You panicked. You say that loud and clear. You had just seen your near-decapitated sister and you were in shock. That's how it was.'

'Yes, probably.'

Angela gives him a sharp look and Nicolas clears his throat.

'Yes, I was in shock.'

'Good. Did Jasmine have any enemies that you were aware of? A jealous boyfriend or the like?'

'No, she was single.' Nicolas shuffles nervously on the chair. Why is he lying? He knew his sister frequently had male company, and even though she never told him in as many words, he knew that was how she paid her rent. But he's not going to air her dirty laundry. Jasmine deserves a better send-off.

'All right.' Angela stands and holds out her hand. 'That'll do for now. The police are going to question you again in the morning, and I will be present. Until then, I suggest you go over the evening once more in your mind. Maybe you'll think of something we can use to your advantage.'

They finish their handshake and Angela is about to walk out of the door.

'Oh, by the way,' he calls after her. His voice is so feeble he scarcely recognizes it.

Angela turns in the doorway.

'There was this man who followed us on the way to Jasmine's apartment from the pub. He wore wooden clogs without socks and

Jasmine really pissed him off.' Nicolas tells her about the cocaine they took in the toilet, about the Finn, angry because they didn't give him any, and about the toilet brush that Jasmine threw at him.

'All right, we'll check him out,' says Angela, without any sign of surprise or amusement about the incident with the toilet brush. 'Don't mention the Finn to the police. We want to find him first. This might be a deciding factor for you.'

'But,' says Nicolas, stammering, 'it might be of use for me to tell them? Maybe he is the murderer?'

'That's right. But the police are convinced that you murdered Jasmine, and therefore they won't waste much time on questioning an alcoholic. And once the guy is warned, he'll get himself an alibi that we can't refute. Leave him to me for now.'

Angela gives him a look that makes it crystal clear to him that he ought not to question her decisions from now on. And so he merely nods. Is it normal for defence lawyers to ask their clients to lie? Apparently so. Perhaps bending the rules is part of being successful in the profession.

When the guard walks him back to his cell, Nicolas feels a little better. Despite everything, Angela Köhler seems to believe him – the only person in the whole world to do so. Maybe he's in with a chance. Maybe the Finn killed Jasmine, or the stalker Angela mentioned.

It must have been one of the two.

7

Emma buries her head under the pillow, pressing her face into the mattress when her doorbell shrills for the second time. Who would turn up at hers this early in the morning? Her tongue feels furry and there's a sour taste in her throat. Did she throw up last night?

The doorbell rings again. To Emma, it sounds as loud as a motorbike with a cracked exhaust. She wraps herself up in her duvet and pretends she doesn't exist. Right at this moment, nothing would be more wonderful than that. Everything would be so much easier if she weren't around. Then she wouldn't feel as rotten as she does. She has a nasty hangover and a headache that the persistent ringing is making worse.

Jesus Christ, give it up already!

Emma throws back the covers, swings her legs out of bed and stands up. Immediately the room starts spinning, forcing her to lean on the bedside table.

'All right, all right,' she mutters with irritation when the doorbell goes again. She looks around for her dressing gown before realizing that she doesn't need it because she slept in her clothes – leather trousers and a shirt.

She drags herself down the hallway, running her fingers through her blonde hair before yanking open the door.

'Good morning.' The woman on her doorstep holds out her hand. 'Angela Köhler, criminal defence lawyer. We met a handful of times when I represented Oliver Sandgren.'

Emma's vision flickers at the sound of the name Oliver Sandgren.

She takes in the elegant woman in front of her with growing unease. Fur coat, fancy pumps. Her make-up must have taken an hour. Perfectly styled hair. One of the best lawyers in Sweden.

'I have a job proposal for you,' continues Angela. 'May I come in for five minutes?'

Before Emma can reply, she is overcome by the sudden urge to run to the bathroom and lean over the toilet bowl. The beet-root salad she ate last night speckles the white porcelain like spray paint, while the rest of her stomach contents are difficult to define. As she retches, one question mark lines up after another in her mind. What the devil does Angela Köhler want? And why did she mention Oliver Sandgren? Hasn't she had enough trouble because of what happened back then? After all, that was the reason she'd handed in her police badge.

Emma presses the flush, gargles with a dab of toothpaste and returns to the hallway. The front door is shut; Angela Köhler has invited herself in. The lawyer is standing at a window behind one of the butterfly chairs in the living room, gazing out at the red-dish-brown roofs and the small river Bällstaån, whose cool waters are visible at the foot of the hill. Piled up on the chair are dirty clothes that for some reason never made it to the washing basket. Emma hopes that somehow, magically, Angela hasn't noticed the pile. When she hears Emma enter, she turns.

'I have three minutes left. I want you to work for me as an investigator. This morning I took on a case, a murder that occurred in Alvik last night. The client's name is Nicolas Moretti and he is suspected of murdering his sister. All the evidence points to him, but the police did a shoddy job, to put it mildly. Chances are I'll get him off. Since I have a load of other commitments, however, I can't do it all by myself. That's why I'd like to offer you this job. Following this case, there may be further assignments in the future. What do you think?'

Emma studies the woman sceptically through eyelashes glued together with mascara, trying to digest the words. A job? Her?

'I know that Hellberg tried to lay the entire blame on you,' Angela continues without waiting for Emma to speak. 'But it's not your fault that Oliver jumped in front of the train. Hellberg was the one pressuring the prosecutor with his demand for enforcement measures.'

In her mind's eye, Emma can see the train speeding towards her, just like during the first few months following the incident when the panic attacks were at their worst. The images haunted her dreams the moment she closed her eyes or while she was watching TV. They were images that weren't easily erased. Even though she wasn't there when it happened, she could see it all before her. And now, nearly a year later, Angela says it was the fault of Hellberg – her former boss. She hears Angela speak and tries to focus on her words.

'I was impressed by your work, even if I represented Oliver.' A crooked smile. 'And not only then. I followed several of your cases and consider myself lucky I wasn't the defence lawyer in any of them. I'm not easily rattled, but you are incredibly deft at blocking off any opportunities for the suspect to lie. You ask questions no one else thought of, and in my opinion you deserve better than this.' Her eyes scan Emma's shirt, and Emma realizes that it is splattered with beetroot salad. Maybe some red wine stains, too.

Emma brushes down her shirt, more an automatic gesture than in the belief that it'll help.

Angela takes a step closer to Emma. 'I know what it's like to feel sidelined. I've been in a similar situation before. Perhaps you remember the shitstorm that broke out following a post I put up on social media.'

Emma digs in her memory, thinking she knows what Angela is hinting at – some statement she made about refugee children. But she can't be sure because that happened right in the middle of her own turbulent phase, during which the problems of the world around her seemed like trifles compared to her own.

Angela grasps Emma by the chin with three fingers and gives her a piercing stare. 'The two of us would complement each other perfectly. You know how the major crimes unit works and are well acquainted with the procedures.'

'Major crimes unit?' asks Emma, even though she knows full well that that is where murders land.

'That's right. John Hellberg and your former colleagues are investigating the case.'

Emma can feel the corner of her mouth twitch involuntarily. Her whole body aches at the thought of running into those people again. Angela has just revealed to her that it was Hellberg who . . . Emma is confused. Was it really him who—? No, it no longer matters. She'd been the one who had put so much pressure on Oliver during the questioning that he took his life. She would never be able to face her former colleagues again. Despite herself, she can't resist asking one question. 'Nicolas Moretti, did you say? Isn't that—'

'Former football star at Djurgårdens IF, then professional player for Russia. Most recently drug consumer in varying degrees and suspected of the murder of his sister. Your curiosity leads me to believe that you are interested. You get thirty thousand kronor a month and a bonus if we win.'

'Hold on! I never said I was interested.'

Angela pulls up the sleeve of her fur coat a tiny bit and glances at her watch. 'I must go to sit in with our client for an interview, and then I'll take a look at the crime scene. Meet me there at eleven if you feel like doing something useful with your life. Väktarstigen 23B.' She spins on her heels and walks to the hallway. By the front door, she bends down to pick up a pile of letters and hands it to Emma, raising an eyebrow.

The envelope on top displays the Kronofogden logo, the government enforcement authority.

'I look forward to working with you and hope you'll give serious consideration to my offer.' Angela shoots her a meaningful look before walking out.

Emma shuts the door behind her and leans against the wall, waiting for the clip-clopping of Angela's high heels in the stairwell to recede. Was she dreaming or did that really just happen? Emma has never dealt with a woman as energetic and tenacious as Angela before.

She glances at the clock in the kitchen. Ten to eight. Angela's visit feels more unreal by the second. At ten to eight on Christmas Day, Angela Köhler left Emma's apartment in Mariehäll. Emma has to hand it to the woman – she's ambitious. She'll have to find someone else, though. What is it that the lawyer thinks she, Emma, would bring to the table? After all, she is – or rather, *was* – a policewoman. There's enough policewoman left inside her for her to know that she's not interested in defending a murderer.

8

The interview room isn't big enough for four people. Nicolas is sitting beside the defence lawyer, shuffling nervously in his seat. She must have gone home and changed during the last few hours. In place of the fur coat, she is now wearing a green dress. Simon Weyler and another policeman, the bow-legged officer Nicolas saw outside Jasmine's apartment, took the chairs on the other side of the table. The other man introduced himself as Detective John Hellberg, squeezing Nicolas's hand so hard that his bones clicked.

Once the formalities have been sorted, Simon mentions that he's visited the Morettis to deliver the news of Jasmine's death. Nicolas feels goosebumps on his arms as he thinks of his father. How did he take the horrible news? And Douglas, Nicolas's baby brother. He loved Jasmine. And he loves Nicolas. But now he probably believes that Nicolas killed Jasmine. Nicolas wipes some beads of sweat from his upper lip with his sleeve. His hand trembles, maybe because he's nervous, maybe because the effect of the drugs is waning.

Following Simon's prompt, Nicolas outlines the events of the previous night. How he met up with Jasmine at the pub and, later, went home with her. He mentions the yellow pills and that he and Jasmine fell asleep on the couch. He leaves out the aggressive Finn, even though his tongue is itching to say something. But Angela wants to investigate the man first, and Nicolas has to trust her with this. Even though the policemen try to appear impartial, he can see by their faces that they don't believe in Nicolas's innocence. They've already decided that he's lying; he can tell by their looks. Especially those from Hellberg – the man just sits there the whole time, glowering at him like a prison warden.

'So,' says Simon eventually. 'If I understand correctly, you panicked when you woke up and saw Jasmine. And then you tried to remove any evidence?'

'Yes.'

'Didn't it occur to you to call the emergency services?'

'It did, but no one would have believed me.'

Simon nods. 'And when you left the apartment, you realized you'd left your phone inside. Why did you go back to get it? Or rather, why did you break in?'

'I needed my phone to buy a ticket.'

'That was your reason for breaking in?'

'Yes.'

'Not in order to murder your sister? Because you had an argument with her about something and decided to go back to kill her?'

The thought of his sister's death devours him from the inside like a wild beast burrowing through his innards.

'No, honestly,' he gasps.

'Okay. Then you got on a bus, you say. But shortly afterwards you felt nauseous, and you disembarked. Can you explain to us how the knife ended up in the bushes at the place where our patrol unit picked you up?'

Nicolas gives Angela a questioning look and receives a nod in reply.

'I was in shock. Traumatized, you could say. I'd just seen my almost decapitated sister and was in shock. It was clear to me that I could end up in prison, and so I got rid of the knife.'

'So, you wanted to hide the murder weapon from the police.'

Angela clears her throat discreetly, prompting Nicolas to take his time before answering.

'I don't know if the knife was the murder weapon. But since it was bloody, I assumed it was.'

Simon stares first at him and then at Angela, scribbles something on his notepad and, following an encouraging nod from Hellberg, tries another tack. 'We found a Santa hat in the inside pocket of your coat. What was it doing there?'

Nicolas blinks, trying to keep his composure, considering his reply carefully. The old biddy behind the curtains saw everything, and she spoke with Simon outside Jasmine's apartment. He decides to tell them about the altercation with the Santa Claus. When he is done, Simon leans back with his arms crossed on his chest, accentuating the muscles beneath his T-shirt.

'Sounds like that movie – *Messy Christmas*.'

'Exactly,' says Nicolas when he remembers the film. 'The guy was hammered.'

Hellberg straightens up, fixes Nicolas with his eyes and speaks for the first time. 'And who is this Santa Claus supposed to be? It would be nice if we could question him.'

'I don't know. Some neighbour, I think.'

'Then why don't you describe him to us.'

Nicolas describes the damn Santa the best he can. After all, it might be of help. 'You have to check him out,' Nicolas says in the end. 'Who knows, maybe it was him.'

Simon gives a faint smile. 'We certainly will.'

John Hellberg says nothing. But a soft snort suggests that he doesn't believe a word.

During the remainder of the interrogation, Nicolas answers in as few words as possible. To the question of how Jasmine was able to afford such an expensive apartment, he replies with a shrug. He's been asking himself the same question, and he has his suspicions. He only knows for certain that the apartment is owned by a retired couple, and that is what he tells the cops.

Simon continues to write notes and ask questions. When he is done, he closes the notepad and leaves the room with his colleague.

Only now does Nicolas notice Angela's angry glare.

She pushes back her chair noisily, stands up tall and adjusts her neck scarf. 'Is there anything else you've been keeping from me? Another Santa Claus, perhaps?'

Nicolas shakes his head, swallowing back all that he should perhaps mention, but not now. He wants to wait and see where the thing with the Santa leads.

9

Don't you believe for a minute that you mean anything to me. I'm glad it's finally over. You bastard! Does she fuck better than me? Merry Christmas, you asshole!

With a thumping headache, Emma scrolls down the text messages she apparently sent Jens the night before. Of course she remembers that her effusions weren't particularly intelligent. But so many of them? The final message annoys her more than all the others. I'm sorry. Please call me.

How desperate can you be?

Jens had not replied to a single one.

Emma tosses the phone aside, crawls back under the duvet and closes her eyes. If you can't see me, I'm not there. Unfortunately, reality doesn't work like that. The destructive spiral of thoughts in her mind continues to spin. Is Jens's new girlfriend better in bed? He'd never complained about their sex life. On the contrary – sometimes they did it wildly, trying out positions that would make the most flexible yoga freak turn green with envy. But why else would he leave her? Could it be because her work took up too much of her time? Towards the end it did, she can see that now. The metaphorical baggage she carried home each night for the eight years of their relationship was filled to the top with shit.

'Can we talk about something other than Oliver for once?' Jens had asked her one Saturday morning during a breakfast of jam rolls. 'I can't hear it any longer. If you can't handle your job, you need to quit.'

And that was what she did. But too late – Jens had already been shagging someone else; someone with arms covered in tats and a pierced eyebrow. Emma can't help but wonder whether the slut has a piercing between her legs too. She pushes that disgusting thought away when she remembers something else. She tears the duvet aside and stares into her hallway. This dream she had. Angela Köhler and her job offer. Emma leans on her elbows, visualizing the lawyer in her fur coat and high heels. It hadn't been a dream. Angela had actually been here.

She wedges a pillow behind her back and clicks through the news to make sure she isn't losing it right now. To her relief, she finds that the Alvik murder is the top headline on various news sites.

Well-known Football Player Arrested for Murder, one headline reads. Others declare **Brutal Murder in Stockholm – Djurgården in Shock**.

In a live broadcast from the crime scene, a reporter with a chequered flat cap explains that Nicolas Moretti has been arrested near Alvik, where his sister was found dead in her apartment. The police have not yet announced a motive.

Emma toggles the image to full screen. Strange that the media are giving the full name so soon. But, as usual, that must be down to a leak.

The reporter carries on about Moretti's background and his previous convictions for drug abuse. Then he holds the microphone out to a man, and Emma's stomach turns when she recognizes him.

John Hellberg.

She stares at him, his arrogant expression, the confident smile. Odd, how a person who isn't unattractive per se can turn into a repulsive slimeball merely on account of his personality.

She turns up the volume as he squares his shoulders beneath the designer jacket, looks straight into the camera and reports on the case.

'Yes, it is correct that we found a female body and that there are clear indications of murder. It is also true that we have arrested Nicolas Moretti, the murder victim's brother. No, unfortunately I can't say anything else for reasons pertaining to the investigation. Yes, yes, no. I am one hundred per cent convinced that we will solve this case. We have strong evidence.' He smiles a smile that Emma has learned to hate. 'Let me put it this way: if our suspect is not convicted, I have no business working in the major crimes unit. From a police perspective, the case is solved.'

Emma snorts derisively. Police perspective, solved! How clumsy can you be, deciding on the suspect's guilt from the word go, and on a live broadcast to boot? She continues to click through the news. Of course, Hellberg has managed to make a statement on every platform. '*The case is solved from a police perspective*' is his standard text, as well as '*we have strong evidence*'. The more she reads, the more something inside her is triggered – a kind of buzz she hasn't felt in a long while.

With no intentions of getting out of bed, she clicks on the news broadcast once more and zooms in on the house behind the reporter and Hellberg. A green apartment building. What was the address Angela mentioned? Väktarstigen something?

10

Emma's heart beats faster the closer she gets to Jasmine's apartment. Outside the front door, the blue-and-white police tape flaps in the icy breeze, preventing unauthorized persons from entering the crime scene.

Is Hellberg still here? Or another former colleague? She's about to turn back when she spots Angela Köhler waving at her. She is standing next to the forensic team's black van, chatting to someone. When Emma comes closer, she recognizes the man as Peter Borg, a colleague she had encountered frequently over the years. He looks surprised when he greets her.

'Emma? Are you back?'

'She works for me now,' says Angela.

Even though she is far from having decided, Emma does not respond. She only came to gauge the situation, find out what the job is about and whether it would even be an option for her.

'I see . . . and how are you?' asks Peter with an expression that betrays his puzzlement about the constellation of Angela Köhler and Emma Tapper.

Angela is wearing a figure-hugging green dress, new high heels in which she trudges through the slushy snow, and the same fur coat as earlier. The contrast between the two women could hardly be greater – Emma in her worn-out jeans and quilted jacket, severely hungover even though she downed a hair-of-the-dog beer before leaving her apartment. At least the alcohol is warming her from the inside. She discreetly sucks on a mint, just in case. Emma is fully aware that she can't compete with Angela in terms of elegance. Then again, hardly anyone can.

'Well,' she tells Peter, straining to smile. 'I'm doing well. I'm studying for the bar exam, trying out something else.'

'Really? I had no idea.'

'Yeah. I can hardly believe it either.' Emma hopes he will ask no more questions about her studies, which have begun to gather dust. Why did she even mention it? Well, she knows why. It sounds good, like something she'd been meaning to do for a long time. And a small part of her actually feels that way. After all, she quit policing to make a fresh start, as they say.

Peter doesn't know how she has really spent the last ten months. Drank. Hung out in bars. Got dumped by her boyfriend. Drank. Wasted countless hours on conversational therapy – all for nothing. Drank.

No, this does sound better. Investigator at the Köhler firm.

Angela tightens the fur coat around herself. 'Are you nearly done? Can we go inside?'

Peter glances at the house. 'I'll have to clear that with Lena first. In the meantime, you may look around outside.'

'How generous.' Angela shivers dramatically from the cold and brushes some melting snowflakes off her fur coat. Then she stalks to the tape and lifts it for Emma to duck under. 'I'm glad you came. Together, we're going to go far.'

'The news tells a different story. From a police perspective, the case is solved and all evidence points towards your client as the culprit.'

'Our client.' Angela gives Emma an intense look. 'If the police believe their case is in the bag, they sit back with a pack of

58

doughnuts. You should know that. And as I already mentioned – the police made so many serious mistakes that I scarcely know where to start.'

There is a sudden click behind them when a young man takes their photograph with a camera. Emma pulls the hood of her jacket a little lower; she would rather not end up in the paper. Angela does the complete opposite: she straightens up and arranges her hair, posing as if she were strutting on the red carpet. Emma walks up to the house, and when Angela catches up with her she describes the details of Nicolas Moretti's arrest as they inspect the green wooden façade, the windows and the frost-covered flowerbeds.

'Was he really in a patrol car, here at the crime scene? For over an hour?'

Angela nods. 'I was at the station with another client when they brought him in. I only knew who he was because I'd met his sister. Normally I don't know much about football. Anyhow, Jasmine had trouble with a stalker, and we must find him before the police do.'

'A stalker? You knew her?'

'Yes, that's right. She contacted me for advice on how to get rid of the guy. It started a little over six months ago. He would regularly stand outside her apartment, staring at her window. And then he sent her photos of his penis and similar declarations of love from a prepaid mobile phone. I'll provide you with all the info I have on him.'

'And you think he might be the murderer?'

'He's the ace up our sleeve, but we have two more. A drunk guy who followed Nicolas and Jasmine home from the pub last night, and a Santa Claus who rang the doorbell a while later.' Angela waves away Emma's questions with one hand. 'I'll give you the details later. Let's inspect the crime scene.'

They walk through an arch to the courtyard, shaded for the most part by an old oak tree shielding the area from the neighbouring houses. In the summer, this was probably a leafy garden with vines creeping up the walls.

'Which floor is her apartment?' asks Emma.

'First. But it has its own entrance from the street.'

'So this balcony belongs to it.' Emma points at a balcony with wrought-iron railings directly above a wooden deck, wondering if she could climb up there. Maybe using the outdoor furniture that she suspects is underneath a cover? But no, even standing on a table would leave at least six feet to the bottom edge of the balcony. The downpipe? No. Too far from the balcony for one thing, and too rusty to carry the weight of a person for another.

'The front door was closed and a witness saw how Nicolas broke in,' says Angela. It seems she agrees with Emma's approach.

'What about the balcony door? Was it also locked?'

'No. According to the first police officers on the scene it was shut but not locked.'

Emma studies the surroundings. She can't see any footprints, and if there were any, the wet snow would have obliterated them. Suddenly she spots a small hole in the flowerbed along the wall of the house, below the balcony and a little to the side. She steps up to it, pushes aside a vine with her boot and discovers a second hole a few inches to the side. The distance between the holes could be the same as that between the two legs of a ladder.

Emma peers up at the balcony once more. This time, she notices the end of some reinforcing steel jutting out from the wall of the house. Something is caught on it – a scrap of fabric flapping in the wind. Someone might have climbed up there after all.

She takes a tour of the courtyard, glancing behind a wheelie bin shelter, inspecting the fence, the area around the bike stand, a fire pit and a sandpit. Finally, she finds what she's looking for. Leaning against the back wall of the storage shed, half hidden behind some scrub, is a ladder.

Emma carries it to Jasmine's balcony and holds it above the holes in the flowerbed.

Angela appears next to her and breathes in deeply, as if she can already smell victory. 'It's a perfect fit.' She calls over crime scene tech Peter Borg. 'You need to document this carefully.'

Peter looks impressed and a little abashed. 'I missed that.'

'And look, there.' Emma points at the steel bar a little way below the balcony. 'Can you see something hanging on that bit of steel? Could be fabric from the murderer's clothes, caught there when he climbed up or down.'

Angela and Peter squint up at Emma's find.

'I'll secure the evidence,' he says.

Emma turns to Angela. 'What was Nicolas Moretti wearing?'

'Nothing purple, as far as I know. That is purple, isn't it? I don't see well at a distance.'

'As purple as beetroot salad,' says Emma. She can still taste the vomit she left in the toilet bowl this morning.

How much longer is this hangover going to last? She craves a drink, something strong. Her hands are shaking and she feels lousy. Maybe it's because she hasn't been at a crime scene in a long while, working in the presence of people who are accustomed to checking and scrutinizing others.

All right, I got drunk last night. I might have had a little too much, but doesn't everyone once in a while? And I texted my ex. But I'm the only one who knows that. Apart from Jens, of course, and his new girlfriend. Are they together right now, reading my messages? Are they laughing at them? Laughing at me?

Suddenly her chest tightens, and she eagerly follows Angela into the apartment, grateful to have something else to focus on. The devil take Jens.

'Was she loaded?' asks Emma at the sight of the tastefully decorated apartment. 'I thought she was a student.'

'That is correct. School of economics.'

'Then how could she afford this place? Rich parents?'

'Her father is Giorgio Moretti, former captain of the men's national football team. These days he coaches youths and serves on the board of several companies.'

Emma is impressed. 'You dug up a lot of information this morning.'

Angela smiles. 'One must always keep one step ahead of the police.'

'Perhaps the father pays the rent,' suggests Emma, moving cautiously through the apartment as if she doesn't want to disturb the murder victim's peace, even though the body has already been taken away. A bowl of nuts sits on a coffee table and strewn around the bowl are nutshells and several yellow pills. Benzos or ecstasy most likely; the lab results will tell them more. Congealed blood on the sofa and splatters on the rug testify to the crime that occurred here.

Angela steps beside her. 'They sat here and got smashed, and then Nicolas fell asleep with his head in her lap. When he woke up, she was dead and he was lying in her blood. He panicked and started to eliminate any traces of his presence. Then he fled the apartment, leaving behind his phone. That was why he broke the window by the door. He wanted to fetch his phone.'

Emma thinks about Angela's report for a while. 'And you believe him? You think he's innocent?'

'I get that question all the time. And you know what? I don't care.'

'But you must have a gut feeling?' asks Emma, somewhat surprised.

'No. Because I know that my clients lie, like all humans. How many times have you thought you knew someone, only to realize later that you were profoundly mistaken?'

Again, Jens flashes before her mind's eye. Her wonderful boyfriend who ditched her when she needed him most.

'How well do you know me, for example?' continues Angela. 'You know that I'm a lawyer, and an extremely good one at that. But am I truly the person you think I am? Do I keep criminal contacts? Am I tortured by obsessive thoughts? Do I seek out one-night stands to debase myself? Do I masturbate at home in front of my neighbour? Only one thing matters to me: if we can prove that he is innocent, then he is.' She turns on her heels and continues to inspect the apartment, leaving Emma alone with her thoughts. If we can prove that he is innocent.

So, Angela does not believe Nicolas Moretti – or does she? Regardless, she wants to defend him because she believes she has a chance of winning.

Does Emma share her belief? She would like to, above all for moral reasons. But as a former policewoman, she can't help but agree with John Hellberg.

All evidence points to Nicolas Moretti as the murderer. From a police perspective, the case is solved.

However, no final verdict has been pronounced, and if she accepts Angela's offer, it will be her task to represent the suspect. Is there a chance that Nicolas Moretti isn't the murderer? There's some evidence suggesting his innocence. The ladder that someone appears to have leaned against the house; the scrap of fabric caught on the reinforcing steel.

Could a third person have climbed up to the balcony and entered the apartment, murdering Jasmine while Nicolas lay sleeping in her lap? Unlikely, but at least possible.

Emma walks over to the balcony, inspects the door handle and finds that it opens from outside. The first uniforms on the scene confirmed that this door was unlocked. Someone could have come in this way – someone with purple clothing.

Emma suddenly hears a rattling sound, and when she turns to the kitchen she spots the birdcage suspended from the ceiling. She walks up to it, studying the parrot, whose eyes are as grey as his feathers. Only his tail is bright red.

'Here we have our witness. Our prime witness.' Emma holds her nose up to the cage as closely as she dares. 'Speak up. What happened here? Who murdered your Jasmine?'

'Screw you!'

Emma jumps back. She hadn't really expected a reply, least of all this one.

'Beg your pardon?'

'Screw you!'

Angela laughs from the sofa, where she is examining the seats and cushions. 'I bet he's a sly old devil.'

'But think about it – he saw what happened here. He must have. Just imagine what he could tell us.'

'That's not how it works. Teaching a parrot to speak takes a long time. And they can only learn certain phrases.'

'Really? Maybe this one's a genius, an Einstein.' Emma gazes at the parrot once more, wondering what he might have seen. Does he comprehend what happened? Is he sad because his mistress is dead?

'Who's going to look after him now?'

'I guess he'll go to a zoo, or else he'll be put down. I don't know.'

'Screw you!' The parrot bounces around his cage as if he understands Angela's words.

Put down. The bird's potential fate tugs at Emma's heartstrings. There must be someone who will take him in. Someone from Jasmine's family, someone who likes animals.

For a moment she considers taking the parrot home with her, but she has never owned a pet before and right now she is struggling to look after herself.

She leaves the parrot and walks to the bathroom. She can see residues of diluted blood in the basin, and there is a reddish-brown stain on the mat. Was this where Nicolas tried to wash off the blood? The towels, too, are covered in suspicious stains. Why did he leave so much evidence if, as he claims, he rushed out in a panic?

Angela sticks her head in the door. 'We'll sort out the formalities later. I need to do something else first.'

Emma gives her a puzzled look.

'Your contract. I'm employing you as a legal assistant. That way, you will have limited powers of representation for our clients, but between you and me, you're an investigator. You do the prep work and I act in court.'

Emma draws up her shoulders, trying for a gesture that expresses *okay*. She's not certain of what she wants; she only came to get an idea of the situation. Although, if she's perfectly honest, Hellberg's stupid performance in the live broadcast does have something to do with it. Just imagine how embarrassed he'll be if they achieve the seemingly impossible – a 'not guilty' verdict for Nicolas Moretti. Because then they'll have to release him. Besides, she can't bear the loneliness any longer. She needs a task, even if she doesn't feel like the company of other people.

They walk out to the hallway, and before going their separate ways, Emma receives her first instructions as an employee of the Köhler firm.

'Try to find the Finn before the police do. The one who followed the siblings home from the pub. And the Santa Claus who
rang the doorbell. Only you and I know about the stalker – he can
wait. The other two are more important.'

Emma nods. She is employed once more, this time as a legal
assistant in Angela Köhler's office.

11

Emma is standing outside a corner pub in Traneberg, wiping muddy snow off her boots on the doormat made of fir twigs. When she enters, warm air and a variety of smells hit her face – beer, damp clothing and sweet glögg. Her eyes scan the bar. Dark timber cladding, a wall decorated with beer labels, cherry-red faux leather couches and matching chequered tablecloths create a cosy atmosphere. The pub only opened five minutes ago, but already customers are sitting at the tables. They must have waited outside the door, desperate for a drink. As is Emma. She takes one of the bar stools along the counter and orders a bourbon, eyeing the barman as he pours the liquid into a short glass. His grey hair and weather-beaten face make him look as if he has been running this pub since ancient times.

She drains the glass in one gulp and pushes it towards him for a refill.

'Tough morning?' he asks without judgement.

When the barman returns with the bottle, Emma watches the gold-brown liquid as the first shot burns in her body, slowly suffocating the fear that has been gripping her. Instead of replying, she asks if he worked the previous day.

'Yep.' He bends down to unload a crate of beer bottles into the fridge.

'At night? Till closing time?'

'This is my place. I always work.'

'I'm investigating the murder that happened nearby last night. Perhaps you've heard about it?'

'Yes, I saw something on the news.' He pauses, holding a few bottles clamped under his arm, eyeing her sceptically. Emma knows why. He thinks she is with the police, and a policewoman shouldn't be drinking while on duty.

But he says nothing. Perhaps he's forgiving of human weaknesses, or perhaps he's used to police officers who drink. Or else he's simply content to sell bourbon to a pathetic young woman. As long as she pays, it's all the same to him.

Emma sips on the whiskey. She mustn't drink too much; not enough to make it noticeable. 'Was it busy here last night?'

'Reasonably.'

'A young man was here with a woman, both of Italian heritage. Do you remember them?'

'I know who you mean. The football player. He was arrested.' The barman holds out one of the bottles to her. The label reads *Moretti*. His eyes widen as realization seems to strike him. 'Is she dead? The woman who was with him? Is she the murder victim?'

Emma nods. 'She was his sister. Jasmine.'

The barman places the last couple of bottles in the fridge and shuts the door. 'So she's dead,' he says, as if he's trying to comprehend the fact. 'Strange. I mean, she was here only yesterday and now she's dead.'

'Did you notice anything in particular? What were those two doing? Did they talk to anyone?'

'They weren't here for very long. But at some point there was a kerfuffle in the toilets with another customer, and then they left.'

'Who was the other customer?'

'A regular. Rantanen, his name. Most just call him Ranta, or the barefoot man. He only ever wears wooden clogs with bare feet, you know? Even if it's minus twenty outside.'

'Does he live nearby?'

'I doubt he lives anywhere at all. He spends his days in pubs. I think he crashes anywhere and nowhere.'

Emma raises the glass to her lips, remembers that she needs to take it slow and sets it back down. 'Do you know where else he's a regular?'

'He mostly hangs out in this area, Alvik. Sometimes he goes to the Thai place up the hill, you know.' The barman waves his arm towards upper Traneberg, and Emma knows which restaurant he means. Lots of cops grab lunch there.

'What time did he leave last night?'

'Right after those two, around nine. I don't know the exact time. But you don't think Ranta—'

Emma waves dismissively. 'I don't think anything, I'm merely trying to establish their movements last night. What happened in the toilets?'

'I haven't a clue. Ranta has a short fuse – something minor could have set him off.'

A new arrival waves at the barman. When he leaves Emma, she takes another small sip of her bourbon, relishing the alcohol's soothing effect, which helps her to process her impressions of this morning's events. Usually, she'd only be getting up around this time, eating a rusk spread with cod roe for breakfast while others were already on lunch. Then she'd have a drink to get going, watch some TV series or other, run errands and keep appointments – counselling, pharmacy, yawn, yawn.

Just as well she has a job to go to now.

Another customer draws the barman's attention, a dark-skinned man standing at the counter a few bar stools up from Emma. To her annoyance, he flashes a police badge.

'Simon Weyler, major crimes unit. As you may be aware, there was a murder in Alvik last night. According to our information, the victim, a woman, visited this pub during the evening with her brother. May I ask you a few questions?'

Emma studies him as inconspicuously as she can. Major crimes unit. John Hellberg must have brought him in after she left.

The barman's round, slightly protruding eyeballs dart back and forth between her and Simon. Evidently he is struggling to make sense of the situation.

'You two work together or what?'

Simon looks first at her, then at her glass. 'No, I don't think so.'

'Well, in a way, we do,' says Emma, attempting to sound as confident as Angela. 'I'm legal assistant at the Köhler office, and Nicolas Moretti is our client.' She lifts her glass, only to find it empty. She drains the last drop and plonks it back down. Legal assistant. Sounds odd, as if she made it up. At the same time, it sounds incredibly good. She's working towards a law degree, after all, and lawyers usually look down on cops. She wonders why she still feels inferior. She's probably still getting used to it.

Simon moves closer and takes the bar stool next to her. He is far better looking than the kind of men who usually seek her out in bars. Brown, inquisitive eyes. She supposes one of his parents is of African descent. He's tall, and his posture suggests he exercises a lot. He's dressed in a warm softshell jacket and cargo trousers with many pockets – a practical outfit, typical of plain-clothes police officers trying to go unnoticed.

'You belong to the opposition, then,' he says.

'I guess you could put it like that.'

He holds out his hand. 'Simon Weyler, major crimes unit.'

Emma shakes his hand. 'I heard.' She turns to the barman. 'Could I please have another?'

'Mineral water for me,' adds Simon. 'And you? Do you have a name?'

'Emma.' She swallows. 'Emma Tapper.'

'Emma Tapper.' Simon speaks her name slowly and deliberately. 'Sounds familiar.'

'Also formerly major crimes unit,' she adds quickly. 'I left the force nearly a year ago.'

Simon's charming expression freezes. 'That's right. I've heard of you.'

'Nothing positive, I imagine. Anyway, congratulations.'

Simon frowns.

'On your new job at the major crimes unit. I assume you got my position.'

Simon gives her an intense look. Then he waves at the barman, pointing at Emma's glass. 'One of those for me too, please.'

As the barman serves them, they sit in silence as if they were each brooding over the other. At least, this is true for Emma. Where did Hellberg find the guy? Emma has never seen him before, nor heard of him. Is he fresh out of police college?

'Is it true what they say about you?' Simon's fingers play with the rim of his glass.

'You can't be very busy if you're still talking about me,' retorts Emma.

Simon rests his arms on the bar. 'Okay. If you work for Angela Köhler, like you say, then we'll be seeing a bit of each other.'

Emma bites her bottom lip. 'We will indeed.'

'Not for long, though. The case is clear as day, after all.'

'Don't say that.'

'Oh, really? Do you have any suspects other than Nicolas Moretti?'

Emma thinks she glimpsed an amused smile on Simon's face before he tried to hide it in his whiskey glass.

'Have you found the man in the Santa outfit?' she asks.

'Not yet. Several neighbours gave us a name, but no one's answering at the address we were given.'

Emma raises her eyebrows. 'Perhaps for a reason. Shouldn't you gain access to his apartment and question him?'

'As far as I know, he's not under suspicion.'

'May I have his address?'

'Hold on a second! Are you conducting your own inquiries?'

Emma gives a shrug. 'Naturally, we check all the information we receive. Besides, we're pursuing the same goal. Neither of us wants to see an innocent man convicted of murder, do we?'

This time Simon fails to conceal his smile. 'So you believe he's innocent – that someone else slit his sister's throat while he was lying in her lap, sleeping.'

'He passed out on drugs,' says Emma, noticing in the same moment the small gap between Simon's front teeth, which makes him look more charming than she cares for. 'If it isn't too much bother, I'd like the address now, please.'

Simon nods, more to himself, it seems, than in agreement. But eventually he fishes a pen and a notepad from one of his leg pockets, scribbles an address and hands Emma the torn-off sheet.

'Thanks.' She glances at the note before pocketing it.

Simon nods in the direction of the barman. 'Did he tell you anything interesting? I'm guessing you already questioned him.'

'He merely confirmed that the two of them were here around 9 p.m.'

'And what impression did they give? Were they arguing or in good spirits? Were they celebrating Christmas?'

'No, nothing in particular.'

'Don't you think it's strange they were here on Christmas Eve? Their family lives in Stockholm, after all. Their father is Giorgio Moretti, the football coach.'

Emma indicates with an 'mm' that she knows.

'And his wife, as well as Nicolas and Jasmine's younger brother.'

She nods as if she knows that too, even though she hasn't had a chance to study Nicolas Moretti's family closely.

'I was there, delivering the news of the death,' says Simon, sipping on his drink and staring into his glass.

Emma can imagine what he's thinking. Delivering news of someone's death to the family is the grimmest task in the world. You gaze into their pale faces, watching panic grab hold of them as they realize that the stranger on their doorstep is speaking the truth. Even if this truth is hard to digest.

'How was it?' she asks.

'Well, it was two lots of terrible news at once. Their daughter was murdered and their son is suspected of having committed the crime. You can imagine. Lovely Christmas surprise, so to speak.' Simon takes another sip. 'They were devastated. The boy especially.'

'How old is he?'

'Fourteen. But the family was a little strange. The mother – or stepmother, rather – wanted to hire a good defence lawyer for Nicolas, but the father objected. Reckoned the boy will have to cope with whatever duty solicitor he gets appointed.'

'I see. But they can't really complain about Angela Köhler, can they?'

Simon snorts. 'Perhaps not. But don't you think it strange that the father didn't show more interest?'

'He was probably in shock. After all, his son is being accused of murdering his daughter. Maybe that's why he feels his son will have to cope on his own. How would you have reacted?'

'If he feels that his son has to cope on his own, then it sounds to me like he's not putting murder past Nicolas.'

The implication crashes down on Emma like a wave. She hadn't expected this reply. Could it be true? Does Giorgio Moretti consider his own son capable of murdering his sister? She badly needs to speak with the Morettis herself and form her own opinion about who they are and who Nicolas is. She needs to hear what they have to say about him.

She changes the subject. 'Anything you wish to say about the arrest of Nicolas and the early measures taken by your colleagues at the scene of the crime?'

Simon gives a dry laugh. 'You sound like a journalist.'

'This stays between us.'

'Perhaps it wasn't the most successful operation. Nothing I'd write home about.'

'Who made the arrest?'

'Everyone makes mistakes sometimes.'

'I admire your loyalty, but I'll find out anyway when I read the police reports. You might as well tell me now.'

Simon leans closer, fixing his eyes on her. 'Tarja Lundquist and Robin Andersson.'

Emma lifts her glass, but settles for sniffing its contents for now. She mustn't get drunk. Tarja Lundquist. Emma had been on patrol with her a handful of times. Even back then she was known for taking the easy route, trying to shirk the duty of report writing whenever possible. Emma remembers one incident in particular, where Tarja accidentally on purpose took a wrong turn just so she wouldn't be the first at the scene of a robbery. In the end, their operations manager still chose them to write up the report. Their boss saw right through Tarja, and Emma felt embarrassed, kicking herself for lacking the courage to stand up to her colleague sooner.

She has no trouble imagining that Robin Andersson might feel similarly today. Emma doesn't know him; a newbie, probably.

'If I understand it correctly, Nicolas watched the whole operation for over an hour from the patrol car?'

'Yes, pretty much.'

'And Tarja and Robin didn't notice that the murder victim in the apartment and the drunk in the patrol car shared the same family name?'

'We missed that one.'

We. He lays no blame on his colleagues. What a gentleman.

Simon continues to describe what happened, giving Emma the impression he's searching for an explanation for the mistake. 'It took a while before Jasmine was identified since she was only renting the apartment. And then they missed the name when it was radioed through because they were busy with something else.'

'Yes. The scene of a murder can be a stressful place.'

'That's right.'

Suddenly, the door to the street squeaks open and a tall man enters. The elastic waistband on his trousers underlines his paunch in an unflattering way, but the most notable feature is that the man is wearing wooden clogs with no socks. He plods down the steps and slumps, panting, on to a chair at the first free table he comes to.

Emma's entire body tingles. She eyeballs Simon, wondering when he might leave. He's got work to do, after all. Solving a murder.

The barefoot man hollers something about the Christmas tree getting a good dose of Chernobyl. Emma has no idea who he's talking to; probably himself or everyone, but she does note the Finnish accent. Another clue that he is the man she's looking for.

She smiles at Simon. Go away already.

But Simon stays. Perhaps he thinks she's nice? Or interesting, at least. But then she dismisses the thought. He's probably just curious about her. She can vividly imagine the gossip at the station, can practically hear John Hellberg's irritating blather.

'*How can Emma Tapper live with herself, after everything that's happened? Imagine how she must feel, looking into the eyes of the boy's parents. She was too hard on him, much too hard. This job requires a certain . . . delicacy.*'

Next, he'd throw in something funny, like: '*Remember the guy who shagged a blow-up doll? The one where we stormed the flat because the stairwell stank of grass? Hahaha! He was sitting in the detention cell last night, wearing women's underwear with a rolled-up sock inside to make his willy look bigger.*'

Everyone remembers, and laughs at Hellberg's joke. Their boss makes sure everyone feels comfortable at work. Provided they keep on his good side and don't scratch his ego.

The barman walks over to Emma, tearing her from her thoughts. When she looks up at him, he nods at the barefoot man.

'That's Ranta, the guy you asked about.'

'Who is he?' asks Simon once the barman is out of earshot. 'Why did you ask about him?'

Before Emma figures out what to reply, Ranta rises and teeters bow-legged towards the toilets. She places a hand on Simon's arm.

'Wait here a moment.'

Emma follows Ranta into the toilets, where she hears someone operating the flush in one of the cubicles, groaning as if this basic act were a herculean task. She crouches, peering underneath the door to double-check. Two heels with cracked skin in a pair of wooden clogs. Yep, that's him.

She passes the time by studying her reflection in the mirror. Ew, yuck, she looks terrible! She tries to make the best of it, wiping mascara from under one eye and slapping her cheeks to get some colour into them. Then Ranta opens the door to the cubicle, his eyes fixed on his fly. When he notices Emma, he mutters something about her being in the way, pushes her aside and walks to the door.

'Excuse me!'

Ranta looks back over his shoulder, and Emma introduces herself in roughly the same way as she did to the barman earlier – as someone investigating last night's murder.

'If I understand correctly, you were here last night, just like the woman who was murdered and the man accused of murdering her.' Ranta stares at her as she describes Jasmine and Nicolas.

'Yes, they were here,' he mumbles. 'They were doing coke in here.'

'How do you know that?'

'I wasn't born yesterday.'

No, indeed, you were not. Emma doesn't share this thought out loud, trying instead to prise more information from him. 'Did you see when they left?'

Ranta grasps the door handle with his strong fist and begins to open the door.

'Hey, wait. I need to speak with you.'

'What about?' He turns back around.

'According to witnesses, there was an altercation in here between you and the two siblings. Afterwards, you followed them. Is that true?'

Ranta narrows his eyes. 'What the devil are you saying, girl?'

'I just want to know where you went once you left here.'

'No, you don't. You're saying that I killed her. In your world, it must have been me, and not a famous football player.'

When Ranta continues to open the door, Emma grabs him by the sleeve of his jacket. 'I'm not saying any such thing. I merely want to know what happened, whether you were arguing or whether you noticed anything in particular when you followed them.'

Ranta yanks himself free, turns around and stomps past her and into one of the cubicles. When he emerges, he's brandishing a toilet brush.

'This is how I was treated!'

Emma ducks when he throws the brush, hears a shout behind her and finds that it came from Simon.

Brownish water drips from his face. It seems the toilet brush got him. He wipes off the worst of it, storms towards Ranta and shoves his palm flat into the Finn's face.

Emma would have advised Simon against one-on-one combat with the barefoot man, since Ranta is taller and heavier. But somehow Simon manages to drop Ranta to the ground. Then things get rough. Ranta grabs Simon, wrapping arms and legs around him and rolling around like an experienced wrestler.

Simon gasps for air; he doesn't stand a chance.

When Ranta throttles him with both hands, Emma rushes to Simon's aid by kicking the Finn's arm. Nothing happens. She's about to kick him again – in the head this time – when she notices the pepper spray on Simon's belt. She rips the can from the holster and sprays a good dose at Ranta's face.

The Finn squints his eyes, blinking, but does not loosen his grip on Simon, whose face is changing to a different shade of red every second.

Emma empties the entire can in Ranta's face, tossing it aside when he still shows no reaction. She feels for the Sig Sauer in Simon's holster. There it is. She grabs the gun's hilt and is about to draw it when Ranta lets go of Simon and shoves him aside. Simon rolls around and remains on the ground, wheezing, his hands on his throat. He's in no position to help Emma when Ranta scrambles to his feet, standing in front of her with his feet firmly planted apart. They are alone. Emma and the biggest man in the world. She shoots a glance at Simon and the gun, still in his holster. When Ranta suddenly spins around and makes for one of the basins, Emma is flooded with surprise and relief. He turns on the tap, bends down and rinses his eyes, muttering, 'Bloody women.'

Apparently, the pepper spray worked.

12

A few minutes later, police lights are flashing outside the pub. Four uniforms lead the handcuffed Ranta to one of the patrol cars. One of the policemen places a hand on the Finn's head and pushes him into the back seat. Emma watches from the open door, annoyed that the police have taken the man who may have murdered Jasmine. Now she can no longer question him and find out where he was at the time of the murder.

She returns to the toilets, where Simon has taken over Ranta's spot by the basin.

'Are you feeling better?' she asks, probably for the tenth time. It's not that she feels bad about dragging him into the dirty work – such things are part of the job. But still . . .

Simon turns his head, blinking at her from reddened eyes. 'Why didn't you tell me about Rantanen? I gave you the Santa Claus's address.'

Emma shrugs apologetically. 'I didn't get around to it.'

Simon snorts and turns back to the basin, rinsing his eyes. 'And I thought you said we were pursuing the same goal.'

'Are we, though? Seems to me you've already narrowed it down to one suspect.'

Simon feels for the paper towel dispenser. 'You can hardly deny that the evidence against Nicolas Moretti is overwhelming.'

Emma can't be bothered listening to any more and walks out. Angela is right. The police won't do jack shit to investigate any other suspects. She and Angela will have to do that themselves. And perhaps her contact with Ranta hasn't been for nothing – at least he demonstrated his potential for violence in the presence of a police officer. Now she only has to wait and see what he says during questioning. In the meantime, there are two more people she has to find – the Santa Claus and the stalker.

An unmarked car pulls up outside the window. Emma fetches her jacket, which the barman has been keeping an eye on, and quickly leaves the bar through a side door leading to a beer garden that is closed for the winter. She doesn't want to risk bumping into John Hellberg. Sooner or later an encounter will be inevitable, but she prefers later.

She walks to her car, a blue Ford Fiesta, parked a block away. She pops a mint before driving off, forcing aside the thought that she oughtn't to drive, given her alcohol consumption. But she hasn't really had that much – just a couple of sips.

A few minutes later she enters the stairwell at the address Simon gave her. The man is called Roland Nilsson and lives on the ground floor. Trying to avoid making a creaking sound, Emma carefully lifts the flap of the letter box and listens. She can smell freshly brewed coffee and hear the chinking of china and the sound of running water. Someone is home. She closes the flap, rings the doorbell and waits. When nobody opens, she raps on the door, calling through the slot: 'Hello, this is—' She breaks off. Back when she could call herself a police officer, this was easier. But what can she say now to exude the same level of authority? She sharpens her tone. 'It's about a murder that happened nearby. I'm investigating. We've already spoken with the neighbours. Would you be so kind as to open the door?'

Suddenly the apartment goes silent – the tap stops running and no one moves the china. Nor does anyone open the door. Has she misheard? No, the smell of coffee is unmistakable. Emma presses the bell once more, but when still no one opens the door, she walks around the house into the courtyard. She finds the enclosed terrace belonging to the apartment and enters it through a gate in the fence. She presses her face against the windowpane, shielding her eyes from the blinding daylight with her hands. She starts at the sight of the half-naked man on the other side of the glass. The only thing covering his extremely hairy body is a pair of boxer shorts.

Emma points at the door handle and mouths, 'Open up.'

'Who are you?'

Emma spins around and finds herself face to face with the lined face of a woman.

'Oh, excuse me.' Emma takes a couple of steps to the side so she isn't trapped between the veranda door and the woman, who is wearing a brown trench coat and an expression of displeasure. 'Do you live here?'

'Who are you?' repeats the woman.

Emma describes the reason for her presence as calmly as possible. She remains vague about herself, stating merely that she is investigating the murder that occurred last night, questioning the entire neighbourhood. The woman's grim, heavily made-up face relaxes a little, taking on an expression of surprise paired with a touch of horror.

'Murder? I had no idea! In this neighbourhood?'

When Emma tells her about Jasmine Moretti, the woman seems even more distraught.

'She rents Curt and Berit's apartment, but they're in Portugal at the moment. Curt suffers from psoriasis, and the sun is good for him.'

Once the woman has got Portugal and the sun off her chest, she introduces herself as Eva Nilsson, lights a cigarette and draws on it with thin lips as she processes the news. 'I don't really know Jasmine. We say hello when we pass each other in the street. Discuss the weather, at most. Dear God, I can't believe she's dead.'

'Yes, terrible thing,' says Emma. 'And we're obliged to question all residents in the area, but – I assume the man inside is your husband. He didn't open the door when I rang the bell.'

Eva rolls her eyes and asks Emma to follow her. They walk around the house, and Emma nods at the duffle bag in Eva's hand. 'Have you been away?'

'Um, well, no, I wouldn't say that.'

'What do you mean? It's important for us to know whether or not you were at home. You might have seen or heard something?'

Eva holds open the front door for Emma as she searches for an answer. 'It's a sensitive topic, you see? Roland and I, we're in the middle of a divorce. I'd rather not talk about it at all.' She walks ahead to the apartment door where Emma knocked earlier, unlocks it and leads Emma into a hallway that still smells of freshly brewed coffee.

They find Roland in the bedroom. He is sitting, reclined, on a double bed, his arms crossed on his chest, watching a game of hockey on the television. During the minutes that have passed since their encounter by the window, he's had the decency to put on a T-shirt. It's faded and full of holes, but better than nothing. Eva explains to him that Emma is with the police. Emma smiles at him, unflinching. After all, she didn't say it; Eva did. Finally, Roland seems to comprehend that Emma is here about a murder and tears himself away from the TV.

'Jasmine? Murdered? When?'

'At some point last night,' replies Emma. 'First, I'd like to know why you didn't open up when I rang the doorbell.'

Roland gives a snort. 'I never do. Too many rip-off merchants out there, trying to sell you something.'

'Okay,' Emma says, even though she doesn't believe him. 'Were you at home yesterday?'

'Yes.'

'All evening and all night?'

'Yes.'

Emma takes another step into the room. Now she can smell booze. She has no trouble imagining how hungover the man feels – quite similar to herself. Perhaps he, too, threw up when he awoke this morning and treated himself to a hair of the dog. Her eyes catch something red sticking out from the foot end of the bed. She walks up to the bed and, on closer inspection, identifies a Santa costume with a white beard beside it. She tries to conceal her excitement.

'Or rather, no, I did go out for a bit,' says Roland, correcting himself when he leans over the edge of the bed, realizing what it is that Emma has spotted. 'Dressed as a Santa Claus. The Janssons – they live nearby – wanted a Santa for their little ones and I said yes. And then I called round to another couple of friends.'

'Who exactly?'

Roland runs his hand through his greasy hair. 'To be honest, I don't remember. I was a little squiffy, as they say.'

Eva gives a loud sigh, and Emma has a hunch as to the reason for the divorce.

'Did you call at Jasmine's too?'

'I vaguely remember doing so, yes.'

'Do you remember what time?'

'Haven't the foggiest.'

'Did she open up? Was there anyone with her?'

'Yes, some guy her age. I think there might have been a little tiff, 'cause my back hurts like hell.' He rubs his back with his hand. 'I don't know. Maybe I tripped and fell. In any case, next thing I know I was lying on the pavement.'

'What was the reason for the argument?'

'I don't know. Like I said, I was drunk. But it wasn't a big deal.'

Eva sighs again, a drawn-out sigh of disgust.

'Do you know what time you got back home?' asks Emma.

Roland touches his round chin, his skin shiny from everything his pores have excreted. 'Hard to tell. But I woke up on the sofa around midnight, thirsty as hell.'

Emma bends down to the Santa outfit. Around midnight. She has no way of knowing if Roland is speaking the truth or if he checked the time at all, but regardless, he could be the one she's after – the person who climbed Jasmine's balcony and entered her apartment. She gently tugs at the costume and turns it in her hands, searching for any kind of evidence. But all she can make out with the naked eye is dirt.

'Do you maybe have a paper bag?' she asks Eva.

'Sure. What do you need it for?'

'I'm confiscating the Santa costume.'

'But—' Roland swings his legs over the side of the bed and stands up. 'You don't believe that I—'

Emma takes a couple of steps back. 'Pure routine,' she says, hoping the two of them aren't overly familiar with police procedures. 'Since you were in contact with Jasmine shortly before her death, we need to examine the clothing you were wearing at the time. But we do that mostly to rule you out as a suspect.'

'But what if you find something that . . .'

Emma looks at him intently. 'What do you think we might find?'

'Something.' Roland's eyes dart back and forth between Emma and his wife. 'I mean, like I said, we had an argument and next thing I was lying in the street.'

'Jasmine too?' asks Emma.

'No, I don't think so, but—'

'Then you have nothing to worry about,' says Emma, asking Eva once more for a paper bag.

While Eva goes away to look for one, Emma takes a closer look at the scratches she spotted on Roland's hand. She asks him what caused them.

'I don't know. Must have happened when I fell.'

'Okay.' Emma pulls out her phone and taps on the camera app. 'I need to document the injury. Could you please hold out your hand? Yes, like that.' She takes several pictures from different angles. She would like to examine his whole body, but she knows she has long since crossed the line of the permissible, even if she were still a policewoman. Roland isn't a suspect, after all. Not yet.

She takes the bag Eva brings her, unfolding it noisily. She places the Santa costume inside, along with the fake beard and a pair of muddy boots from the hallway, which, as Roland reluctantly admits, he wore the night before. She studies the soles, annoyed at the fact that the miserable weather destroyed any footprints beneath Jasmine's balcony. But maybe she'll find something else of interest on the boots.

Emma thanks them, goes out to her car and climbs in. She gazes at the bag on the passenger seat holding the confiscated items, wondering how she'll get away with this manoeuvre. She opens the glove compartment, fishes out her hip flask, unscrews the lid and indulges in a swig. Not the smartest thing to do, she thinks, but it's just a sip or two. She needs the alcohol to get through the rest of the day and Nicolas's interview, which is going to take place in just over half an hour. She would much rather forget about it and drive home. She doesn't feel like a reunion with her former colleagues, least of all Hellberg. *Doesn't feel like it* being a slight understatement – she is terrified. But following her blitz at Roland Nilsson's, she doesn't have a choice. She returns the hip flask to the glovebox, pops a mint and drives off. Destination: the Solna police station on Sundbybergsvägen.

13

Emma enters the police station and walks up to reception. It costs her some effort to convince the woman behind the pane of glass that she works for a lawyer now and has come to sit in during the interview of their client. The woman fetches the station chief, who turns out to be Jonas Berg, a colleague with whom Emma had worked now and again over the years. Jonas gives her a surprised look above the rim of his glasses and, in his turn, fetches Simon, who puts in a good word for her while chewing on a protein bar. Emma deciphers the flavour on the wrapper – salted caramel. How can anyone believe those bars are useful?

'Isn't Angela coming?' asks Simon, still blinking frequently. An after-effect of the pepper spray.

'Yes, she is. Isn't she here yet?'

'No, I haven't seen her. What have you got there?' He gestures at the bag in her hand.

'Nothing special,' she replies, unsure of the best way to handle the Santa outfit. 'But I may need your help with something.'

'Okay,' he says with a shrug, leading the way through the reception area and then offices with mostly empty desks. Only those who really have to come into work on Christmas Day. In the hallway leading to the custody suite, she greets two former colleagues in passing. She hurries on as she doesn't feel like explaining what she's doing here.

'You just disappeared earlier,' says Simon, holding his card above the scanner by the door to the custody suite foyer until there's a humming sound. The first person Emma sees when the door opens is John Hellberg.

'I needed your witness statement,' continues Simon.

'That can wait,' mumbles Emma, her eyes firmly on Hellberg. Her former boss is talking to a guard called David Lind, a muscleman with cauliflower ears who used to have a crush on her.

When the two men spot Emma, they fall silent. They greet her, David with a cheerful smile, while Hellberg's is obviously fake.

'Would you look at that? Emma Tapper. I heard you were on your way here.'

Emma forces herself to extend her hand, tolerating Hellberg's rough handshake.

'So you're employed as a legal assistant? I say.' He stares at her, allowing the seconds to pass slowly and ensuring that she feels even more rotten than she already did. 'Then we'll be seeing more of each other. I look forward to it.'

Emma's heart thumps so loudly beneath her jacket that she fears everyone can hear it. Still, she manages to utter, 'So do I,' without a wobble.

Hellberg crosses his arms and comes closer, ignoring the boundaries of personal space. Emma stays put through sheer willpower, trying to suppress her unease, which she despises as much as the stench of nicotine on Hellberg's clothes, as well as her anger about him laying the blame for the tragedy with Oliver at her feet. Even though she still feels guilty about what happened, her boss was at least as involved as she was. If what Angela says is true.

'Has Simon already told you that you're suspected of committing a criminal offence?'

Emma tilts back her head so she gets a better view of Hellberg, putting on a confident expression. A twitching underneath one eye threatens to shatter the façade.

'He hasn't? Simon just filed a report because you appropriated his pepper spray, using it against the Finn during his arrest – Timo Rantanen. You are suspected of assault.' Hellberg places a hand on her shoulder, massaging it with his thumb. 'But don't worry. I'm sure it'll all get cleared up.'

'It was self-defence,' says Simon, looking at the floor. 'You know how this works – we're obliged to report such incidents.'

Emma takes a step away from Hellberg. 'I know exactly how this works. Have you questioned him yet? Does he have an alibi?'

'Maybe,' replies Simon, meeting her eye. 'He claims he did the rounds between Alviks Torg and Traneberg. First he wanted to visit a mate in Alvik, but he wasn't home. Then he went back to the pub before remembering that he was supposed to take the underground to Telefonplan, where another mate of his lives. We'll look into it, and if it checks out, we can rule him out as a suspect.'

'I'm sure we will,' says Hellberg with a grin, exposing a row of bleached teeth. 'We're fully aware of the fact that he did not murder Jasmine Moretti.'

'I see,' says Emma, clutching the bag tightly. Should she mention the clothes now or will it backfire? After brief consideration, she concludes that she might as well get it over and done with. The confiscation is a done deal, and sooner or later they'll hear about it.

'Oh, there's one more thing,' she begins cautiously. 'I got hold of Roland Nilsson, the man you were looking for. He was on his own last night. His wife was out, or staying with a friend, rather—'

'How did you manage that?' asks Hellberg, cutting her off with a suspicious glance at Simon.

'I knocked on doors in the neighbourhood, just like you did,' she replies, not intending to dob Simon in. She needs him on her side, especially now. 'He struggled to explain to me what exactly he was up to last night. It would pay for you to question him thoroughly. And the neighbours too, where he played Santa.'

Hellberg gives a snorting laugh. 'You don't have to tell us.'

'I already spoke with most of the neighbours,' says Simon. 'Apparently the guy was drunk as a lord.'

'Yes, he reeked of booze.'

Hellberg sniffs in Emma's direction, muttering like a clumsy ventriloquist: 'I know someone else like that.'

She ignores the sideswipe but feels rattled. Is the smell of alcohol that obvious?

'I . . .' Emma lifts the bag. 'I confiscated a few items that might be important to the investigation.'

'You did *what*?'

At the same moment, the door to the custody suite opens. Emma breathes a sigh of relief when she sees Angela. The lawyer stalks over to them.

'Forgive me for arriving a few minutes late. Busy day in the office.'

Hellberg takes a step to the side so that Angela can join their conversation. 'Emma's just told us that she found the notorious Santa Claus.'

'Aha.' Angela gives Emma a stern look that soon softens. 'That's good. What did he say?'

Emma moistens her lips and describes her visit once more, up to the moment of the confiscation.

'The Santa costume was lying in a heap on the floor and I thought it might contain evidence. If I hadn't taken it, he might have got rid of it.'

'That may be true,' says Hellberg. 'The only problem being that you have no authority to do so.'

'The most important thing is that we have it,' counters Angela. 'There must be a way of wording it nicely in the report. You needed to go and interview him anyway. And then you would have taken the costume too. Right?'

'Why should we? The man isn't a suspect.'

'But you know that he and Nicolas Moretti were involved in a scuffle. That is called assault and it is a crime, one you knew about at that. Have you reported it? No? Then you neglected your duties. But in the meantime, you were clever enough to secure any evidence that might be relevant to the case.'

Hellberg brushes his hand across his slicked-back hair, shiny with pomade, with an expression as if he wants to strangle Angela. 'Okay,' he says eventually, snatching the bag from Emma's hand. 'Don't do it again.'

Angela gives a strained smile in the direction of the clock on the wall. 'We require five minutes alone with our client before you question him.' She goes to call the guard but Emma gets in first.

'I'll do it,' she says, rushing off in the direction of David, who is sitting in his cubbyhole. She is glad to escape Hellberg for a moment.

She pops another mint along the way.

'I'm guessing they want me to fetch Moretti?' says David when he sees her. He runs his finger down the list of names of arrests, stopping on number fourteen. From the corner of her eye, she reads *Nicolas Moretti*.

David eyes her inquisitively. 'It's lovely to see you, by the way, but I don't really understand what's going on.'

'Nor do I. But as of today I'm working as a legal assistant to Angela Köhler.'

'Oh, nice.'

'I'll tell you more another time.'

'Can't wait.'

Emma follows him to the cell, mostly to keep away from John Hellberg. Even though she hates being here, she can't deny feeling a sense of longing as she walks down the corridor lined with doors, so full of memories of all those years she worked here. But life, as well as Hellberg, had other plans for her.

Outside door number fourteen, David pulls a key ring from his pocket and inserts a key into the lock. But instead of turning the key, he gives Emma a mischievous look. 'Nice photo on Instagram.'

'What photo?'

'The one where you're wearing red undies and one of those push-up bras where you can see everything. And I mean everything.'

Emma's hand shoots to her phone in her pocket in reflex. She wants to find out what he's talking about. But before she has a chance to look, David opens the heavy door to Nicolas Moretti's cell.

14

Nicolas is sitting in silence in the interview room, where the air already feels stuffy, looking at his lawyer Angela Köhler and her legal assistant, Emma Tapper, who fetched him from his cell. Evidently, the latter used to work for the police, a circumstance that worried him at first. Cops, after all, work to get suspects locked up, not discharged. But Angela has been reassuring him for the last few minutes, praising the woman and promising that her experience in her time at the major crimes unit would work to their advantage when it came to proving his innocence.

But am I really innocent?

Nicolas can't stop pondering what happened in Jasmine's apartment. Why was the bloodied knife lying on the carpet just where he was sitting? Why was the front door locked? How did the real murderer get in? The last thing he remembers is sitting on the couch with Jasmine, cracking nuts. Then there is just blackness, up until the moment he awoke in a bloodbath on her lap.

But somehow, subconsciously, he knows that he didn't do it. He would never have been capable of killing Jasmine.

He wipes sweat from his forehead, observing that Emma and Angela are complete opposites. Emma is more like himself, around his age, dressed in regular jeans and a plain T-shirt. Pretty? Yes, for sure. But she also looks quite run-down and seems quiet – she'd merely greeted him and briefly explained her role. Angela had added that she and Emma work as a team, and Nicolas had the feeling that the lawyer is the one who wants to be seen and heard. He guesses Angela is in her early fifties. Her style of clothing and mannerisms make her seem a lot more disciplined than Emma.

When Simon Weyler and the other officer come in and sit down opposite him, Nicolas looks up. They ask him if he wants anything to drink and whether he needs to use the bathroom before they begin the interview. Nicolas says no to both.

'Well then,' says Simon, scribbling something on his notepad. 'First of all, many happy returns, even if your birthday isn't taking place in the happiest of circumstances.'

Nicolas's eyes fill with tears and he blinks rapidly to keep them in check. He had totally forgotten that today is his and Jasmine's thirtieth birthday – though now that applies only to him. The realization causes him physical pain, paralysing him so acutely that he doesn't know what to do. At the same time, a terrible thought takes shape in his mind. He's lost his twin sister, just like the fortune teller predicted. He shudders at the thought. How could this prediction have come true? When he doesn't even believe in such things.

'Are we good to go?' asks Simon. 'Is it all right if I make a start?'

Nicolas wipes an escapee tear off his cheek and nods. Should he tell the police about the prophecy? He glances at Simon, who is leafing through a stack of papers, and at the other cop, who seems arrogant and hostile. John something. No, they would think he's crazy if he came out with a story like that.

He listens as Simon explains what this interview is about and, when asked if he would like to respond to the allegations, once again responds in a faint voice: 'I am innocent.'

'Then I'd like to start at the pub you and Jasmine visited last night. Why did you not tell us about the Finnish man you got into an argument with in the toilets?'

Nicolas darts a furtive glance at Angela, and she gives a nod. She prepared him for this question before the interview.

'I'd forgotten about it,' he says. 'It wasn't even a proper argument to me. He mouthed off at me and followed us when we left the pub.'

'Mouthed off? What about?'

Nicolas accepts the fact that they'll find evidence of drug consumption in his blood. He might as well come out with the truth now. He squints against the bright fluorescent lights on the ceiling. His head is about to explode, and he wishes he could pull something dark over it, anything would do.

'We did a line each in one of the cubicles,' he says. 'And when we came out, he wanted some. He figured out what we were doing in there. And then Jasmine threw a toilet brush at him.'

Amused smiles in the interview room. Only John remains stony-faced.

'And what happened next?' asks Simon.

'We left.'

'And he followed you?'

'It looked that way. We didn't notice right away, but then we stopped because a block of ice hit the—' Nicolas pauses. The ice block. It could have killed one of them – an early omen that something was going to happen. Why hadn't he realized it then? 'Well, a block of ice fell from a roof and nearly hit us. And then we noticed that he was following us.'

'What did you do then?'

'We kept going.'

'Did he say anything? Was he running after you?'

'He didn't say a word. But he followed us as far as Alviks Torg. I didn't see him again afterwards, but it was pretty dark.'

'He didn't catch up with you?'

'No, all of a sudden he was gone.'

'I see.' Simon writes something down on his pad and asks Nicolas to start once more from the beginning, from his visit to the bar up to his arrest. The interview takes at least an hour, not because Nicolas has much to say but because Simon asks at times absurd questions that are difficult to answer. He wants to know exact times, who else was at the pub, what they looked like and what they were doing. Simon writes down all the details while John's task appears to be making sure Nicolas feels uncomfortable. He stares at him the entire time, scrutinizing him as if everything that comes out of Nicolas's mouth is a lie.

When Nicolas reaches the part about the scuffle with the Santa, Simon mentions that they've found him.

'Or rather Emma has,' he says, nodding at her. 'We haven't had a chance to listen to his version of events yet. Do you maintain that he became aggressive when you refused to give him alcohol? That he didn't want to leave, and the scuffle occurred as a result?'

'Yes, but he started it.'

'That's how we will put it in the protocol. Was it his Santa hat that you were carrying on your arrest?'

'Yes.'

'How come you had it?'

'He must have lost it. It was lying in the hallway when I . . .'

'When you what?'

John asks this time. Nicolas mutters something about being in shock and panicking. The guy frightens him. Perhaps it's just a game the two of them are playing. Good cop, bad cop or some bullshit. Nicolas feels as if he's sitting at a poker table – he with a mixed hand, a seven his highest number, while the evil cop is holding a royal flush.

'Why were you panicking?'

Simon resumes the questioning. Good.

'I had just found my sister dead. Murdered.'

Simon pauses as he sips on his glass of water. 'Can you describe your relationship with Jasmine to us?'

Nicolas shrugs. 'It was good. We saw each other often.'

'And what did you do when you met up?'

'All sorts.'

'Did you take drugs together?'

'No, I quit. Well, I—' Nicolas breaks off. He can hear how trite his words sound. 'I was on my way to becoming clean. I've got a job and all.'

'What kind of job?'

'In the office at Djurgårdens IF. My father got me the job.'

'Okay. You and your father get on well?'

'So-so.'

'Can you elaborate? If I understand it correctly, your mother is dead and your father lives with his new wife.'

'Yep.'

'And they have a fourteen-year-old son, your half-brother.'

'His name is Douglas.' Nicolas clenches his fists in an automatic gesture. 'I never call him my half-brother. He is my brother.'

'Did you celebrate Christmas Eve with your family yesterday?' continues Simon without acknowledging Nicolas's comment.

He shakes his head.

'Why not?'

'We didn't feel like it.'

'So Jasmine didn't celebrate with your family either?'

'No.'

'Did anything in particular happen? Something that caused a rift in the family?'

Nicolas closes his eyes and sees Douglas. How he would love to look into his eyes now and reassure him that he didn't kill Jasmine. Douglas mustn't think that.

He replies with great difficulty. 'No, nothing like that. It simply didn't work out like that.'

'Please forgive me for feeling surprised, but in my world it seems strange when a family doesn't spend Christmas together, especially when everyone lives in the same city. Or is there something I don't know about? Perhaps you and your sister celebrated with someone else? Did Jasmine have a steady boyfriend, for example?'

'No.'

'So you simply didn't feel like it.'

'That's right.'

Simon and John exchange a glance before Simon changes the subject. 'Jasmine was a student, and if my calculations are correct, I struggle to see how she was coping financially. The rent for her apartment costs more than she received from subsidies and student loans. As far as I know, she had no other income. Do you know where the money came from?'

Angela shifts nervously in her seat and Nicolas remembers what she'd told him earlier. No more Santa Clauses. He should probably keep what he knows to himself for now. Then again, he wants to help the cops find an alternative murderer and show them that he didn't kill Jasmine.

'I know that someone was paying her rent.' He rubs his hands on his thighs. 'I don't know who he was, only that she met him regularly.'

'Like a boyfriend, you mean?'

'Not really. I don't know.'

'Do you have a name and address? Can you describe him?'

'No.'

'So this man pays Jasmine's rent. What did he get in return?'

Nicolas is seething. And the withdrawal symptoms are giving him a hard time, both physically and mentally. This is precisely what he was trying to avoid – dragging Jasmine through the dirt in front of the police and everyone else who has access to this information. It's not her fault that she ended up in this situation. He could easily have ended up the same way. They both lost their mother when they were eight years old, and once everything went to pieces, nothing was as it had been before.

'You'd have to ask Jasmine. I don't know anything else.'

Simon leans across the table, twisting the pen between his fingers. 'Do you know a Philip Stenhammar?'

Nicolas thinks for a while. The name rings a bell. 'I think he might have studied with Jasmine. Why?'

'Just tell me what you know about him.'

'Only the name.'

'So you know the names of various fellow students?'

'No, but the two of them met up occasionally in her spare time. I don't know any details. Only that she mentioned him every now and then.'

Nicolas notices the look Angela and Emma exchange. Emma nods as if she's making a mental note. *Philip Stenhammar. I'll check him out.*

'I've got enough for today.' Simon turns to John. 'Do you have any questions?'

John declines with the same portentous look as earlier, as if he is trying to say: *I know you killed your sister.*

'And you, Nicolas? Is there anything else you'd like to get off your chest? Is there anything that needs clarifying?'

He can see Angela shaking her head from the corner of his eye, but he does have one question. 'What about Jasmine's parrot? Is anyone taking care of him?'

15

Once the interview is finished, Emma follows Angela back to the foyer, pulling out her phone and opening Instagram. What was this photo David supposedly saw of her? She scrolls down the page, but before she finds anything Angela pulls her aside, stopping out of earshot of two officers who are in the middle of searching an arrest. The lawyer looks grim and angry.

Is she kicking me out? On my first day?

'How could you be so stupid as to confiscate the Santa costume and the boots? I told you to speak with the man and ensure that he doesn't get the chance to prepare an alibi. Which part of that did you not understand?'

'But . . . I had to improvise. The costume was just lying there, directly under—'

'Imagine if Hellberg had reported you.'

'But he hasn't. And if the forensic examination finds Jasmine's DNA on it, that works to our advantage.'

'I know.' Angela is looking at her as if she were scolding an unruly child. 'But then chances are Hellberg will claim that the confiscation was unlawful. And you're already facing a charge of assault. On top of everything else, Nicolas gets another charge added to his list. I bet Hellberg is already crafting it on his computer.'

Emma looks sheepishly to the floor and accepts the fact that her efforts to make a good first impression have failed.

Angela places a hand on her arm and continues in a gentler tone. 'Don't worry, I'll fix it. And concerning the charge against you – I'll make sure the prosecutor is on our side.'

'Thank you. I honestly didn't mean to cause trouble.'

'Now listen carefully. Women must stick together. Nothing else matters to me. John Hellberg is no more intelligent than Jasmine's parrot. I've met lots like him. His sort likes to act the big cheese, but when something goes wrong, they blame others.'

A wave of gratitude washes over Emma. For the first time in a long while, she's working with someone who can see right through Hellberg.

Angela slips into the fur coat she has been carrying across her arm. 'Now we need to focus on the man who was paying Jasmine's rent. Sounds a lot like prostitution to me. But first of all, go and search for Philip Stenhammar, Jasmine's fellow student, and find out why the police are interested in him.'

'Will do,' says Emma. She too is curious about the man.

'I will sort out that charge for you,' repeats Angela with a wink, and she walks towards the exit.

As soon as Angela is out of the door, Emma returns to Instagram, bringing up the profile called *Miss Secret*. There she finds the photo with the red lingerie David mentioned. He was right. You can see everything. Her breasts are practically popping out of her bra and the slip is so thin it doesn't actually serve any purpose. She switches off the display and feels her whole body grow hot.

Bloody Ester.

Normally she doesn't visit her twin sister's profile page, but following David's pointed remark she wanted to know what Ester had thought up this time.

'*Not my fault if people can't tell us apart*' is her standard excuse every time Emma points out that, for her, those pornographic pictures are – to put it mildly – problematic.

In the past, Emma used to change her hair style and colour regularly to make herself look as different to Ester as possible. But in the last six months she hasn't had the energy. Now her hair is the same shade of blonde as Ester's and cut in a bob. Ester's hair is slightly longer, but the length of a woman's hair scarcely matters to men when they jerk off with their smartphone in their hand.

Emma looks at the door when it opens. It's Simon, returning from his conversation with the chief.

'You sure you want to look after the parrot?'

Emma gives a shrug. 'Who else is going to do it?'

'Then you'd better take it right away. It's in the storeroom.'

'Someone already brought him here?'

'Obviously. Seems you weren't the only one feeling sorry for the bird.'

Emma follows Simon to the small room where animals that are taken into custody are typically kept until their owners are ready to take them back. Which, in this case, isn't going to happen.

'Well, I'm just going to fill in until we find a permanent solution,' says Emma. She hadn't expected to receive the animal so soon. Her main motive had been to get in with Nicolas and win his trust. What does a bird like that even eat? Reluctantly, she lifts the cage, the parrot flapping his wings nervously. 'It's all right, it's all right,' she says.

'You can't change your mind,' says Simon. 'He's non-returnable. He's a grey parrot. Do you know much about the species?'

'No, but I can find out.'

'They are social creatures and don't like to be alone.'

Emma responds with a smile and changes the subject before Simon can tell her she ought to get a second parrot. 'Tell me – this

Philip Stenhammar you were asking about during the interview . . .
why are you interested in him?'

'You'll find out soon enough,' says Simon, leaving the
storeroom.

Emma hurries after him and talks to his back. 'I can understand that you're angry because I didn't tell you about the confrontation in the toilets. I only wanted to speak with Ranta first to see
who he is so that you wouldn't simply brush him aside in your
investigation.'

'Fine. If you can do it, I can too.'

'Oh, come on. Give me something on Philip Stenhammar.'

Simon waves disinterestedly. 'This is a police investigation, and
you are not a policewoman.'

'Screw you,' says a croaking voice from the cage.

Emma lifts the cage and studies the parrot, who is shuffling on
his perch, completely unaware that he has just won Emma's heart.
'That's right. Screw you. And what do you think we should do now?
Go find Philip Stenhammar, you say? Yes, that's what we'll do. Stuff
Simon. He can go to hell.'

She leaves the police station with her new friend and walks to
her car, where she places the cage containing Einstein – as she'd
christened the bird, since it appeared fitting for a genius – on the
passenger seat. She starts the engine, cranks up the demister and
pulls out her phone. A search for Philip Stenhammar results in
three candidates that match Jasmine's age here in Stockholm. She
turns to Einstein.

'Which address should we try first? Bergshamra, Fisksätra or
Östermalm?'

Einstein sticks his beak through the bars of his cage. Emma
carefully holds out a finger, but quickly pulls it back when the
parrot tries to bite it. She's about to tell him off when she notices
someone walking to the car park.

Simon. He unlocks a black Volvo with the remote, and Emma notices that he appears somewhat square underneath his jacket. He is wearing a bulletproof vest. So, he's still on duty and on his way somewhere – perhaps to see Philip Stenhammar.

Emma grasps her steering wheel, waiting for the Volvo to pull out on to the road before driving after it.

16

Emma parks a few hundred yards behind Simon on the kerb and watches as he climbs out of his car, gazing up at the whitish-grey façade of one of the tall apartment blocks in the suburb of Gärdet. He walks up to the front door and pushes on it. Then he makes a phone call, probably to headquarters to ask for the door code. But a few minutes later an elderly man comes out of the building and Simon slips through the door.

Emma turns to Einstein. 'Wait here. I'll be right back.' While she locks her car, she notices a young man in a dark blue coat walking along the pavement some distance away, his hands deep in his pockets. A grey scarf is wrapped around his neck, matching the colour of his ribbed beanie.

Could this be Philip Stenhammar? The guy is tall and skinny, and probably around the same age as the Philip who lives here, according to online directory *Eniro* – around twenty-five.

Emma stays on the far side of the street, half concealed by parked vehicles covered in ice, watching him as he enters through the same door as Simon.

She crosses the street and pulls on the door handle, even though she knows it's locked. Her eyes search the ground and she grabs a handful of pebbles, tossing them at the bottom-most balcony. She can see the flickering colours of a TV screen glowing through the window. When nothing happens, she throws more stones. This time, a shadow moves behind the window, and moments later the balcony door squeaks. But at the exact same moment a person appears on the balcony, the front door of the building flies open.

The man in the dark blue coat who had just entered the house runs into the street. Emma hears footsteps racing down the stairwell, trying to catch up with the runaway. She runs after the man, turning a corner and taking a shortcut across a playground. When she's only a few yards away from him, they reach an intersection. While the man pauses for a moment, seemingly deliberating which way to turn, Emma dives at him and knocks him to the ground. The guy rolls on his side and Emma throws herself on top of him just as Simon catches up with them. The young man stops resisting, not even trying to make a run for it. Perhaps that's because Simon is yelling that he is police, and perhaps also because he can see that he doesn't stand a chance.

A few minutes later they're standing underneath the roofed entrance to a minimart, where the curious eyes of neighbours can't reach them. The young man does indeed turn out to be Philip Stenhammar. Simon doesn't ask Emma what she's doing here. Evidently, he is resigned to the fact that they are working together, regardless of which side they're on.

'Why did you run?' asks Simon, still catching his breath.

Philip shakes some dirt off his hat and pulls it back over his longish wavy hair. 'I thought you were someone else.'

'Who?'

'I don't know. You were standing outside my flat and you looked suspicious. What do you want?'

Emma fails to stifle a grin, but makes sure only Simon can see it, not Philip.

'It's about your fellow student Jasmine Moretti.'

'I thought so. I mean . . .' Philip looks at his feet. 'Now that I know who you are.'

'So you know what happened?'

'What do you think? People are talking about nothing else.'

'And what exactly are people saying?' asks Emma. She still doesn't know why the police are interested in Philip Stenhammar, of all people.

'That her brother killed her.' Philip looks at Emma. 'I mean, the police have arrested him, haven't they?'

'Jasmine called you yesterday,' Simon cuts in. 'Just a few hours before her death. What did she want?'

Philip blinks repeatedly, probably wondering what to reply. 'Nothing in particular. She wanted to wish me a happy Christmas.'

'So, you two knew each other quite well?'

'Yes, I guess you could say that. We often see each other in lectures and so on, and sometimes we grab a coffee. Or rather, we used to . . .'

Simon places a hand on Philip's shoulder, giving him a few moments to process the fact that Jasmine is no longer alive.

'Were you just friends or were you in a relationship?'

'No, I'm single.'

'Okay. Just friends, then?'

Philip nods and wipes his nose.

'Can you imagine what motive her brother might have had to kill her?'

'Or anyone else?' adds Emma.

Philip looks from one to the other. 'What are you saying? It could have been someone else?'

'In the early stages we must explore all avenues,' says Simon, asking Emma with a warning glance to keep quiet. 'Anything you know about Jasmine could be of help to us. Did she tell you anything? Was she having problems? Like drug or alcohol abuse, for example.'

'No, not that I know of. I mean, maybe she smoked something every now and again, but who doesn't?'

'I don't.' Simon takes his hand off Philip's shoulder. 'Where did she get the hash from? Because that's what you meant, right?'

Philip looks back down. 'I don't know. She never did anything like that when we hung out.'

'Okay. Have you been to her apartment?'

'A few times.'

'Have you never wondered how she could afford the place? I mean, both of you live off student loans, right?'

'Yes, but I never thought about that before. Maybe her old man was paying the rent. Well, I'd love to be of help, but you already have a suspect. Nicolas Moretti is known for his drug use and, besides, he gambled away all his money. Not that I know his background or anything, but maybe he just lost the plot.'

'Do you know him?'

'We've never met in person, but I know who he is, and Jasmine told me about him. It must have been super-rough for him – first a well-paid professional footballer and now completely broke.'

Simon waits as two teenage girls enter the shop, continuing the interview as soon as the sliding doors close.

'How did you spend Christmas Eve? And what were you doing later that night?'

'Well, what do you do on Christmas Eve? Did the whole family thing. We watched *Kalle Anka* and ate Christmas ham.'

'Where exactly?'

'At my grandparents' in Hässelby.'

'Did you stay the night?'

110

'Nope.' Philip pushes a cigarette butt around with the toe of his shoe. 'My father drove me home just after ten. So I was probably home around eleven.'

'And he can verify that?'

'Absolutely.'

They question Philip a while longer, noting down names of various fellow students who knew Jasmine from the school of economics, as well as his father's phone number. Simon walks a few steps to the side to call him right away. Meanwhile, Emma tries to prise more information from Philip.

'Did Jasmine say anything about her family? I mean, did anything in particular happen?'

'No, she never really spoke about them. But since her brother murdered her, something must have been rotten.'

'Well, like I said, he hasn't been convicted yet . . .' She leaves the sentence unfinished, and Simon returns.

'No answer.' He shoots Philip a stern look. 'Did you give me the correct number?'

'You should be able to check that. Do you think I'm lying?' He rubs his arms. 'I'm getting cold. Are we done yet?'

Simon nods towards the street. 'You're free to go.'

'What do you think?' asks Emma a short while later, on the way back to their cars. 'Was he with his father when Jasmine was murdered?'

'No idea. What a pain, no one answering. I'm trying again.' Simon pulls out his phone and dials, unlocking the Volvo with the push of a button at the same time. 'And now it's engaged.'

They exchange a meaningful look.

'Safe to assume he's talking to his son?' says Emma. 'We should have taken him in.'

'We?'

'Okay,' relents Emma. 'You should have taken him in.'

'For what reason?'

'Any. You're police. Think of something.'

Simon gives her a mock salute. Emma shakes her head and walks away.

'See you later, Tapper,' he calls after her.

Emma turns around and takes a few steps back towards him. 'Want to go grab a drink?' She can see the wonder in his eyes; he is just as baffled as she is. What on earth possessed her? 'Well,' she says, trying to downplay her invite, 'I wanted to check out the pub in Traneberg again. You never know what lead one might find. I mean, the two of them were there before—' She holds up her hands and shrugs. 'Oh well.'

Simon gives her a smile. 'I'm sorry, but I need to be fit in the morning. Another time, perhaps.'

Standing alone on the pavement, watching the rear lights of Simon's Volvo disappear in the winter fog, she feels annoyed at herself. What did she ask him such a question for? He's not even nice. She checks the time on her phone, wondering if she should swing by the Morettis', but it's a little late for that. It will have to wait until tomorrow.

17

Emma parks her Ford in a side street with a view of the white façade of the Morettis' villa behind a snow-capped stone wall. Last night's drunkenness is still in her bones, making her sweat. She hadn't intended to drink when she got home after Simon's rebuff, but her resolve hadn't lasted. Strictly speaking, Simon had doubly snubbed her – he had also rejected any suggestion of digging deeper into the investigation. He was probably scared of finding something that might exonerate Nicolas.

Her hand grasps the door handle, then lingers. She wants to both get out and stay in the car at the same time. Wants to hide from the world outside – from the guy with the dachshund over by the park benches; from the idyllic family meandering past with children on toboggans. Eventually, she opens the glovebox and takes out the hip flask. Feels the whiskey burn in her throat and spread through her veins. Relief floats down upon her like a blurry veil.

She pops a mint and tries for the fifth time that morning to get hold of Angela, but she doesn't answer. When voicemail comes on, she hangs up and glances at the birdcage beside her.

'Ready to meet your grandparents?'

Einstein ignores her.

She picks up the cage, climbs out of the car and walks towards the large house, a nervous knot forming in her chest. How will

Jasmine's family react to her visit? Grieving parents who are probably still in shock.

The metal gate squeaks when she opens it. A fine dusting of snow covers the gravelled path. Steps lead up to the front door. A pink plastic flamingo stands one-legged on one of the steps. Emma lowers the cage to the flamingo's level.

'Check it out, Einstein, a friend.'

No reaction.

'Not your style, is it?'

Emma pushes the doorbell. The shrill ringing makes the parrot jump about in his cage. While she mutters soothing words, she hears footsteps in the house. The solid oak door opens, revealing a grey-haired man whose puffy eyes suggest he had a sleepless night. Giorgio Moretti. Emma recognizes him from TV and other media. The man is tall and impressive, although instead of authority, today his face radiates only tragedy. He gives Emma and the parrot in the cage a puzzled look.

'My name is Emma Tapper and I work for Köhler Lawyers.' She gets the feeling that he wants nothing to do with her, and adds hastily, 'I wanted to ask if you have a moment. It's about Jasmine and Nicolas. I am so sorry about—'

'Köhler Lawyers?' he asks, cutting her off. 'Are you Nicolas's defender?'

'Not really, but I work for Angela Köhler, who is representing your son.'

'Then there's nothing to talk about.' Giorgio pulls the door closed but Emma manages just in time to jam a foot in the opening.

'Please. I brought Jasmine's parrot and wanted to ask you if you were able to look after it. Or else he might get put down.'

Giorgio stares at her through the narrow crack. 'Is that her parrot?'

'Yes, it was in the apartment when we . . .' Emma struggles to find words that aren't too detailed. 'When we looked at the apartment yesterday.'

'Isn't that the police's job?'

'It is, but it was important for us to see the scene of the crime for ourselves.'

'Nicolas murdered my daughter.'

'We're not as certain of that as the police. There is some evidence suggesting that it could have been someone else – a third person who gained access to the apartment.'

Suddenly, someone appears behind Giorgio and places a fine-boned hand on his arm.

'We should ask her in. I'm sure you'll want to hear what she has to say.'

Giorgio hesitates for a moment but eventually relents to his wife's wish. When Emma enters the generous hallway, the woman introduces herself as Vera Moretti. Underneath her loose-fitting blouse she seems to float, reminding Emma of the way a ballerina moves with the weight shifted to her toes. At a guess, Vera is ten years younger than her husband, and even though her eyes also show signs of a sleepless and tearful night, it does nothing to diminish her beauty. Her pale complexion contrasts with her red hair, which is tied in a loose bun at the nape of her neck.

Vera leads the way to the kitchen, speaking over her shoulder in a gentle voice: 'So, what is your theory of the events if Nicolas is not the killer?'

'Yes, like I was saying, there's a possibility that someone else entered the apartment. Additionally, we have spoken with two men who in the course of the evening had altercations with Jasmine and Nicolas.'

'Sounds just like Nicolas,' remarks Giorgio disparagingly.

Vera gestures at an armchair-like stool by the kitchen island, and Emma takes a seat. 'I've only met Nicolas once, during an interview, but do you really consider your son capable of murdering his own sister? Your daughter?'

Giorgio's eyes go blank. He blinks a few times and looks as if he is about to collapse. 'He is a junkie and dragged her down with him.'

'But do you really believe it was him?'

Giorgio holds his clenched fist to his mouth, turns his back to Emma and leans over the sink, his breath coming in gasps. Vera steps up to him and strokes his arm. Emma waits a few moments before asking: 'Do you know if Jasmine had enemies?'

Giorgio and Vera both shake their head.

Emma changes the subject, asking about the man who paid Jasmine's rent.

'Do you know who he is?'

'No. Why should someone be paying her rent? She had a student loan and paid for the apartment herself.'

'Her rent was a little more than fifteen thousand kronor a month. The student loan didn't cover that.'

'What are you trying to say?'

'Nothing. I would merely like to know who was helping her and why.'

'No idea.'

Vera walks around to Emma and takes the stool next to her. 'The situation is extremely difficult for my husband. I hope you understand. For me too, of course – I am devastated.' She wipes a tear from the corner of her eye. 'But it's worse for Giorgio. You probably know that I'm not Jasmine and Nicolas's real mother?'

Emma nods as if she understands, although she has zero experience at being a stepmother. But there's probably a reason why they call it 'my kids, your kids'.

Vera stares into blank space. 'I know what he must be going through. Just imagine if it had been Douglas.'

Emma swallows, wishing she could leave, not wanting to disturb their grieving over the worst possible loss any parent could experience. But she has to ask a few more questions.

'Do you know a Philip Stenhammar? Fellow student of Jasmine's.'

'No, I've never heard the name.' Vera turns her eyes to Giorgio. 'Do you know a Philip Stenhammar?'

He waves dismissively.

Movement in the lounge causes Emma to look to the side. A teenage boy, whose eyes are as swollen as those of his parents, walks into the kitchen. His skin is a lighter shade than that of Nicolas and Jasmine. Evidently, he inherited Vera's pale, freckled complexion.

'Come here, darling.' Vera holds out her arms towards him and he slumps into them. 'We are just talking about what happened.' She kisses his wavy hair. 'Can you please go back to your room?'

'I only wanted to take my antibiotics.'

'Do that, sweetheart.'

'What happened to your arm?' asks Emma, looking at the thick bandage on Douglas's forearm.

'He grazed it and wouldn't stop playing with the scab,' replies Vera as the boy walks to the fridge and fetches a bottle of cordial, pouring some into a glass. 'Our son, Douglas,' she explains with a faint smile. 'He's pretty down.'

'I can imagine.' Since Nicolas's younger brother is in the kitchen, Emma lowers her voice. 'So, Jasmine never mentioned a fellow student named Philip Stenhammar?'

'Not as far as I remember, no.'

'Okay. When were you last in contact with Jasmine?'

'Oh, hard to tell. A while back. Do you remember when we last saw her?' she asks Giorgio.

He shakes his head, reaching into the air to hold on to something that isn't there. Apparently, he is closer to collapsing than before.

'If I understand it correctly, your relationship with Nicolas was strained. Why is that?'

'Oh, that. No.' Vera pins a strand of hair behind her ear. 'We don't see Nicolas much these days. As Giorgio said, he has a drug problem. But Jasmine came by every now and then.' She turns to Douglas, who is running the tap and holding a finger in the stream of water. 'Do you know when she was last here? Must have been a few weeks back, while you were at football practice?'

Douglas looks first at his mother over his shoulder, then at his father, replying with an almost imperceptible nod. Then he turns back to the stream of water and, once he appears satisfied with the temperature, fills the glass with the cordial. It seems as if the last thing he wants to do is talk.

'If we got it right, then Jasmine also took drugs,' says Emma, as diplomatically as she can manage.

Giorgio eyes Douglas uncomfortably – a silent message to Emma, asking her not to discuss such matters in the boy's presence. 'That wasn't the same. Nicolas was an addict. Jasmine might have tried something every now and again.'

'But the night Jasmine died, they both took drugs together.'

No reply, just a tense silence. Emma drops the subject.

'There is one other thing I found a little strange. Christmas Eve. Why weren't you celebrating with Jasmine and Nicolas?'

'It just didn't happen,' replies Vera. 'We were going to celebrate together the following day. It was their birthday, you see, but—'

'Did you buy them something?'

Vera frowns.

'A birthday present, I mean.'

'No, not yet. We had been planning to do that yesterday.'

'On Christmas Day?'

'Plenty of shops stay open.'

Douglas comes to the kitchen island with the glass in his hand and looks at the birdcage.

'What's his name?'

'Einstein. Well, that's what I call him.' Emma tries to hide her surprise at the fact that no one here seems to know that Jasmine owned a parrot. According to Vera, Jasmine visited only a few weeks ago.

Strange. But Emma chooses not to comment. No point making the Morettis feel any worse than they already do.

'Would you be able to look after him?' asks Emma once more, as if it were the most natural thing in the world.

Douglas gives his parents a pleading look.

'I'm afraid that's not possible,' says Vera. 'I'm allergic.'

'Please,' begs Douglas.

Giorgio runs his hands through his grey hair. 'Listen to your mother.'

Douglas's shoulders droop and he plays with the bars of the cage.

Emma slips off the bar stool. 'Okay, I'd better be on my way back to the city. Don't hesitate to give me a call if you remember anything else.' She hands Giorgio one of Angela's cards, having added her own number in pen.

'Like what?' asks Vera.

'Anything that might help solve the case. Maybe the police are right and Nicolas did it. But if he didn't, he will need your help.' She picks up the cage and walks into the hallway, glancing back over her shoulder to say goodbye. But no one has followed her. She opens the front door and steps outside. As she pulls the door closed behind her, her eyes meet Douglas's beseeching look from the kitchen. She feels a pang of conscience. Did she raise false hope

119

in the boy? Did she give him the impression she could actually get his older brother off?

Softly, she closes the door. As she hurries through the front garden, she notices that the Tesla parked in the drive bears slight damage at the front – the right-hand headlight is broken. Someone was in a rush.

Flapping from the cage reminds her of the parrot she failed to get rid of.

'Are you cold?' she asks with mock concern. 'Do you want to get in the car?'

'Screw you.'

Before Emma climbs in, she scrapes the freshly formed ice off the Ford's windscreen. She turns up the demister and straps the cage in with the seat belt. Then she tries again to reach Angela, and this time the lawyer picks up.

'I've been flat out.' She explains her unavailability without giving Emma a chance to tell her about her visit to Nicolas's parents. Instead, she starts to talk about Jasmine's stalker.

'Now that all the other suspects have come to nothing, we need to focus on him. Jasmine came to see me about six months ago and asked me for help about a man who was harassing her. And now it's your job to prove that he is the murderer.'

Emma breathes hot air on the hand holding her smartphone. She considers pointing out that the stalker might also be innocent, but Angela keeps talking.

'He drove a blue sports car, a Honda Civic, and the plate contained an R at the start and a 2 in the middle. And there was a T, but she couldn't remember where exactly.'

'And that was approximately six months ago?'

'That was when it started. Then she contacted me again on 14 October. On that day, he was standing in her courtyard, staring up at her window. And one time she saw him in her part of town with his girlfriend, so it's safe to assume that he lives nearby.'

'Girlfriend?'

'Yes, Jasmine believed the two of them looked like a couple. They were holding hands and the like. But you know what men are like – one woman isn't validation enough.'

'But Jasmine never met up with him? Was he an ex?'

'No, no. Or at least, she didn't say he was. But I suppose we must be open to all possibilities.'

'What did he look like?'

'Slim, ash-blond hair, around thirty, tattoos on his right arm. A skull and a spider web, apparently. I've got nothing else. I truly hope you find him – that might be decisive for us.'

They finish the conversation and Emma leans back against the headrest. Angela said *for us*, but she meant me. Finding the stalker is decisive for me, or else I'm out.

How can she solve this task? The vehicle licensing agency requires the entire plate number, not just parts. An R, a T and a 2. Should she sniff around Jasmine's neighbourhood in the hope that the sports car would turn up at some point? No way; she doesn't have the time. If she had access to the police database she could enter the incomplete plate number, receive possible vehicle suggestions and then investigate their owners. Grudgingly, she brings her phone's screen back to life. She knows who she must call to ask for help.

18

He is sitting on the same bar stool as during their last encounter in this pub. The man who took over Emma's job and probably her desk too. Perhaps he uses the old radio she left behind when she hurriedly packed her things and practically ran out of the office. Hopefully it still produces static noise when a mobile phone rings nearby.

Emma slips on to the stool next to him, waves at the barman and orders the same drink as the one sitting in front of Simon – a bourbon. When she receives hers, she takes one sip, sets the glass down on the bar and traces the rim with her finger. Feels the silent pensiveness floating in the air between them while she glances about the bar. Ranta isn't here today, but there are a few others of his type who seem to be regulars, and a few couples who instead of a Christmas meal decided on pizza or *plankstek* – steak grilled on a wooden board with mashed potato and vegetables.

After another sip: 'You wanted to meet me.'

Simon moves closer and whispers into her ear: 'You should have told me about Rantanen.'

Emma turns her face so that it's only about four inches from his. 'And you should have told me about Philip Stenhammar.'

She keeps drinking. So that was where the shoe pinched when she asked him for a drink yesterday. 'Like I said, I have my doubts whether we're even working towards the same goal.'

'I don't. We both want to see Jasmine Moretti's murderer convicted.'

'Of course. And both of us want to find the actual murderer?'

'Sure. But seriously – do you believe your client is innocent?'

'If we can prove that someone else did it, then yes, he is innocent.'

Simon leans back a little. 'So the guy with the blue sports car, the Honda Civic Type R? Is he your suspect now?'

Emma tries to conceal her eagerness, knowing full well that her eyes are wide with excitement. 'Have you found him?'

'Why is he important? What's his connection to the investigation?'

'So you've found him.'

Simon tries to maintain a serious expression, but his eyes glint mischievously.

'Come on,' she says. 'If you tell me some more about the investigation, I'll tell you why I'm interested in the guy with the sports car.'

Simon laughs. 'Don't forget that I'm the one sitting on the information.'

'Haven't we only just agreed that we're both after the real murderer?' counters Emma. 'Give me something already.'

Simon raises his glass to his lips, appearing to think as he sips on his whiskey. 'The Santa Claus reported Nicolas for assault.'

Emma sighs. 'That would be thanks to me. Hellberg must have called him as soon as he got the costume. Anything else?'

'No, nothing in particular. Apart from the guy with the sports car.'

'How long are you going to leave me hanging?'

'Until you tell me why you're interested in him.'

'Okay.' Emma accepts that she has to give in. She'll deal with the fact that Angela won't be happy later. 'Jasmine was being harassed by a stalker. She got in touch with Angela to ask for help in the matter. Perhaps now you understand why he's important. It's possible that he killed Jasmine.'

'Hold on.' Simon raises one hand, seemingly trying to wrap his head around this news. 'Are you saying that Jasmine and Angela knew each other?'

'Well, they were in contact because of the thing with the stalker.'

'Why didn't you say something? This is an extremely important piece of information.'

'Is it? Listening to you lot, I was under the impression you'd branded Moretti the culprit long ago. And besides, I only just received the info about the stalker.'

Simon props his elbows on the table, breathing loudly through his folded hands. 'From here on, this is how we do it: no more secrets. All right?'

'All right. No more secrets.'

'How was he harassing her?'

'He would stand outside her apartment, staring up at her window. And he sent photos of his penis. I don't know all the details, but Angela documented everything.'

'Why did she approach Angela?'

'I don't know. I suppose she was hoping for her support and advice. Angela is well known as a defender of women's rights, and she's damn good at what she does. Not that surprising after all, is it?'

Simon reaches for his jacket, which is hanging on a hook beneath the bar. He rummages in an inside pocket and eventually hands Emma a plastic sleeve holding several pieces of paper. On top, Emma recognizes the copy of a vehicle registration of a blue Honda Civic. She skims over the information. The vehicle owner's name is Andreas Kilic and, according to the registration office, he lives on Gustavslundsvägen in Alvik, less than half a mile from Jasmine's apartment. To Emma's delight, he carries multiple previous convictions including cybercrime, fraud and – most significantly – sexual abuse of a minor. Emma's palms begin to sweat. Sexual abuse of a minor! Suddenly, the stalker is highly relevant as a potential murderer. Someone capable of this is capable of anything. She leafs through the papers, checking the man's personal information and his passport photo. Everything matches the description Angela received from Jasmine – thirty-two years old, thin face with sunken cheeks, ash-blond hair.

Emma fixes her eyes on Simon. 'You have to take a closer look at Jasmine's phone. Search for messages from him, dick pics and the like. Including any deleted ones. You did confiscate her phone, didn't you?'

'Of course.'

'Did someone say dick pics?' The scent of freshly washed hair floods the space between Emma and Simon. 'I get several of those a day.'

Emma stares at her sister.

'Don't look so shocked.' There's a smile on Ester's bright-red lips. 'You said you were coming here, after all. I didn't know you were on a date.'

'I'm not.' Emma curses herself for calling Ester when she stopped at home to get changed. 'We work together.'

'So you're a lawyer?' Ester takes off a fluffy leopard-print jacket, flashing Simon a look that is both impressed and flirty.

'He's a cop,' says Emma.

'That's just as good.' Ester holds out her hand to Simon, turning the fact that she and Emma are twins into a farcical and somewhat embarrassing show.

''Course we look the same, but I've got more curves and my darling sister has got so skinny. And my hair is longer, as are my fingernails.' Ester holds up her hand, showing off tiny works of art with Christmas designs at the tips.

'And more Botox,' adds Emma.

'For sure. You should try it sometime.' Ester runs her index finger across Emma's forehead. 'Then you'd get rid of those worry lines. Anyway, what are you drinking?' She eyeballs Emma's and Simon's glasses, shakes her head and calls for the barman. 'A Cosmopolitan for me, please.' She turns back to Emma. 'But despite our differences, no one can tell us apart if we don't want them to.'

'Unfortunately.'

'I'm terribly sorry about the latest photo.' Ester grimaces apologetically. 'But that's my job.' She turns to Simon. 'Right? I can't help it if people can't tell us apart.'

She laughs when Simon gives her a blank look, digs through her handbag and fishes out her phone. 'I'll show you.'

'No, no, no.' Emma tries to grab the phone but Ester steps back.

'I think it's better if he sees it,' she says. 'Otherwise he might think it's you. And I am really proud of this photo.'

Emma's cheeks turn bright red when her sister holds her phone in Simon's face. It may not be her posing in scant underwear in the picture, but still.

'May I?' Simon takes the phone from Ester's hand and studies the photo more closely. 'Yes, I agree . . . the two of you look incredibly alike.'

Ester shakes her hips in some kind of exotic dance. 'I look pretty, don't I?'

'Absolutely.' When Simon looks up, his eyes aren't on Ester but on Emma.

Emma hides her glowing cheeks in her whiskey glass and takes a few sips, allowing the bourbon to dispel her embarrassment for a few moments. She feels exposed, even if she isn't the woman in the photograph. She holds out her hand for the phone.

'Have you had enough yet?'

Simon hands her the phone with a sympathetic expression, and Emma passes it to Ester. She would have liked to stamp on the thing, but what good would it do? Various pictures of Ester wearing barely anything will remain on the net for all eternity. And on people's retinas.

'You need to stop posting this crap online.'

'I'm sorry, sister dear, but I'm an influencer. It's my bread and butter.'

'Can't you post different things about yourself? Like vegetarian recipes, interior design tips or whatever?'

'Too much competition in those fields. I, on the other hand, am my own brand. I'm unique.'

'You're not. You look just like me, after all. Don't you get it?'

'Wow. No need to get all bitchy.'

Emma clenches her teeth, drains her whiskey and orders another. Apologizes to Simon. 'We should keep talking about the stalker.'

But Simon waves dismissively. Their unexpected visitor doesn't seem to bother him in the least. Patiently, he answers every question Ester poses about his work as a policeman. Have you ever shot anyone? What does it feel like to arrest a murderer? How many dead bodies have you seen?

Emma massages her temples. Christ, her sister sounds like a child. In order to bear the situation, she drinks some more. After a while Ester has finished her police questions, changing to a subject closer to her heart.

'Which body part has more nerve endings, the penis or the clitoris?'

Simon throws back his head and laughs loudly. 'I guess that would be the first one, since we men come more easily.'

'Ha! Wrong, wrong, wrong.' The alcohol makes Ester talk louder, waving her index finger through the air. 'You think you men come more easily. But you haven't got the faintest clue how a clitoris works. A penis has three thousand nerve endings, while a clitoris has—' Ester holds up eight fingers, 'eight thousand.'

'You don't say!'

'That's right. Eight thousand nerve endings that you men don't know how to operate. To you, a clitoris is either a doorbell or a scratch card. I mean, what the heck? What is it that you like?'

'Me?'

'Yes, you. If I go down on my knees for you, what do you want me to do?'

Simon pulls a face, incapable of uttering a word even though the alcohol should have loosened his tongue.

Ester kneels in front of him. 'You want me to give you a blow job, right? And that's how women work, too.'

'Stop it already!' Emma gets up and holds on to the bar when the ground shifts under her feet. 'I need to go to the loo. Keep an eye on my things?' She doesn't hear what the two of them reply, only hears them laugh. On her way to the toilet, she crashes against a table, apologizing to the two men whose beer spills on the table-top. When she walks on, she lifts her feet a little higher so she doesn't trip on anything.

In the toilets, she is struck by the smell of urine and a sweetish scented candle.

As she pees, crouching down, she hears a faint ringing in her ear. She ought to stop drinking now and go home.

A short while later she finds herself at the bar holding a fresh glass of whiskey, remembering that she meant to go home. But she's comfortable, and Ester's chatter no longer sounds quite as silly as earlier. Interesting, even – possibly aided by Emma's level of blood alcohol.

They chat and clink glasses with a few other customers, take selfies and sing karaoke on a raised platform. Someone shouts a round, they raise their glasses again and Emma's crashes to the floor. Simon helps the barman to sweep up the broken glass.

She feels sick.

Suddenly she is outside, and something is chafing in her back. Her eyelashes stick together. Why are they doing that?

She blinks up at the lamp on the ceiling and a bad feeling rolls over her like a wave. The lamp is a white ball with feathers. It is her lamp, the one from her bedroom.

What happened? How did I get home?

19

Through the doors of the Solna courthouse, Emma can see that Simon is already there. He's talking to John Hellberg and a man in a suit. Emma would have liked to avoid them – most of all Simon, strangely. The fear that is coursing through her body streams out through her pores, together with sweat and the alcohol she consumed last night. She still has no idea how she got home but suspects that Simon helped. She hasn't been able to reach Ester on her phone so far, and she didn't want to call Simon because she'd rather not talk about last night. The only positive: she didn't send Jens any messages.

Emma breathes deeply, pulls herself together, enters the building and nods at the trio. Simon returns the gesture while Hellberg merely stares at her. The third man, who turns out to be Stefan Hermansson, a prosecutor Emma came across a few times in her work, gives her a look of surprise, raising an eyebrow before shooting a puzzled glance at Hellberg.

You need to practise being more discreet, boys.

To avoid them, Emma walks straight to the information board to check in which room the bail hearing will take place. She can feel the men's eyes on her back and knows exactly what they're talking about – in Hellberg and Hermansson's case, at least. The two of them play floorball together after work, showering one other with undeserved deluges of praise.

Is she back? Didn't she quit the service after that guy bit the dust? Yes, but she's not with us, she's playing at being a lawyer.

Hopefully, Simon doesn't join in this old-boy circus.

A glance over her shoulder reveals that they are laughing about one of Hellberg's comments. Simon is laughing too.

Thanks for last night. Thank you very, very much.

Emma's back hurts and she fingers the scratch she discovered when she came to this morning. Did I fall or what? Whatever happened, she will never drink again. Not a chance.

The clock in the foyer shows five minutes to nine, and Emma wonders what's keeping Angela. Surely she doesn't believe I can handle the hearing without her? The thought alone makes Emma feel dizzy. What would I say? What strategy would I pursue?

She squares her shoulders when Hermansson steps away from the group and approaches her with a swaying gait.

'Emma Tapper. I heard you work for the Köhler office now.'

'Yes, as of two days ago,' she says from between dry lips.

'Look at that. Nice to see you back. I can't imagine what you must have been going through, but I can see you're back on your feet now.' He looks at her closely, evidently waiting for her to tell him what she's been up to. 'And where is Angela?' he asks when she doesn't oblige.

'She'll be here soon.'

'Aha . . . soon. The hearing starts in a few minutes.' Hermansson pulls his phone from his breast pocket, holding it in front of her face.

Emma takes a step back, answering with suppressed irritation in her voice: 'I know what time it is.' Then she takes another look at the display, recognizing Ester in cut-off jeans, bra and glittering Christmas decorations in her hair.

131

'You look lovely indeed.' Hermansson winks at her. He seems to believe he's twenty-five, even though he must be past fifty. He returns his attention to the picture, grunting so that his not insignificant stomach wobbles. Then he falls silent as the entrance opens and Angela struts in, wearing her usual high heels.

Hermansson's pockmarked face moves closer to Emma's. She inwardly recoils from his overpowering scent of aftershave. 'She's got four minutes left. She probably had to cover up all the bruises with make-up. You see, the woman likes it rough. That's why she always wears a neck scarf.' He wraps an imaginary scarf around his neck and pulls at it, grimacing as if he were being strangled. Then he turns away from Emma and returns to Hellberg and Simon.

Emma's eyes follow him. What was that? An attempt to put her off her stride before the hearing? To unsettle her with regard to Angela, the same woman he is currently greeting with a cordial handshake?

Emma wipes small beads of sweat off her upper lip while Angela frees herself from Hermansson's firm grip, walking over to her with a strained expression.

'Has the custody transport been?'

'Don't think so. At least, I haven't seen him.'

'Haven't seen him? It's part of your duties to let our client know we're here for him.'

'But I don't think he's arrived yet. If he had, I would—'

'And what are you even wearing?' says Angela, cutting her off. She studies the green T-shirt Emma has on under her jacket. 'You're a legal assistant now, not a policewoman.'

Emma opens her mouth to defend herself but closes it when Angela breaks into a smile. 'I had a hunch you'd show up wearing something like this, so I brought you a change of clothes.' She pats her handbag. 'Come on.'

Confused, Emma follows Angela to the corner near the entrance where a sign points towards toilets. In passing, she notices that the men are gathered around Hermansson, staring at his phone and laughing at something, Simon included.

The bastard!

In the ladies' room, Angela hands her a white tie-neck blouse. Emma thanks her and gets changed, casting furtive glances at Angela's neck to check for bruises – not an easy mission, considering the turtleneck emerging from the fur coat. It's not as if she believes Hermansson's idle gossip, but still. Now she thinks about it, she realizes that Angela always wears clothing that conceals her neck. Could Hermansson be right? Is Angela into sadomasochist sex games?

'I know who the stalker is,' she says, trying to stop her train of entirely inconsequential thoughts.

'Good. What was he doing on the night of the murder?'

'I don't know yet. I've only just found out who he is.'

'Then you have nothing. Get back to me once you know that he has no alibi.'

Angela pulls a packet of chewing gum from her handbag and hands one stick to Emma.

As she follows Angela out of the door, she guiltily pops the gum in her mouth. She's about to dish up a lie to her boss that she only had a couple of wines last night but is silenced by the sight of Vera Moretti. Nicolas's stepmother is jogging up the steps, light-footed as a ballerina, to the court room where the hearing is about to take place. Emma follows quickly and catches up with her when she sits down on a bench seat, taking off her grey coat and scarf.

'How are you?' asks Emma. After a moment of confusion, Vera seems to remember who Emma is. 'Did you not realize that . . . that the hearing is closed to the public?'

'Yes, but I wanted to come regardless. So that Nicolas sees that I'm here, in case—' Vera brushes a strand of hair behind her ear and plays with the knot in the nape of her neck. 'I've been thinking about what you said, you know. That he may not be the murderer . . . that it might have been someone else.'

'I understand. What about Giorgio?'

Vera shakes her head, her silence speaking volumes. Giorgio has not changed his mind about his son.

A voice informs them through speakers that the hearing is about to begin. Emma watches with relief as Nicolas is led into the room by two guards through a side door. Vera stands up and raises her hand to wave to her stepson, but stops halfway and lowers it.

Emma gives Vera a sympathetic look. 'We'll talk later. For now, we're going to do everything in our power in there.'

20

Nicolas sits down at the long, narrow table, resting his hands in his lap so that no one sees his handcuffs. Even though the judge knows, of course.

Angela Köhler and Emma Tapper sit to his left and right. Their scents collide in his nostrils – perfume and alcohol. The latter most likely stems from Emma, who is discreetly chewing gum.

Seriously? At least she looks somewhat more lawyer-like in her white blouse today, compared to the last time he saw her. But is she competent enough to defend him? He decides to give her a chance. If he understood it correctly, Emma performs all the dirty work in the streets while Angela represents him in court. Sounds plausible enough. Hopefully, the two of them complement each other and get him released. Even though he can see that his chances are slim, he has scarcely worried about it. Occupying his mind wholly has been the fact that Jasmine is dead. This realization, burrowing into his consciousness a little deeper each day, has rendered him apathetic. He is never going to see his sister again, the only person who understood him, who knew what he went through. Who is he supposed to share everything with now? He has no one left; only Douglas, but he doesn't see him very much.

When he entered the court room, he glimpsed Vera through the open door but not Giorgio, his own father. Nicolas can't tell which hurts more – that Jasmine is no longer alive or that Giorgio has abandoned him once more. Does he truly believe I could have killed her? And what does Douglas think? Nicolas wishes he could speak with him. But the day will come, and then he is going to tell his younger brother what happened in Jasmine's apartment, will admit that they did drugs. And he'll speak to Douglas about his drug abuse and his gambling addiction, will try to explain as best as he can how he managed to ruin his life so completely and what lay at the root of it.

Perhaps Douglas will understand.

The judge is a petite, plain woman whose make-up-free face probably hides a tough core that she was forced to grow over the years. He struggles with her hairstyle, as she reminds him of an old teacher in middle school – the hair cropped just above the shoulders and shaped in an unnatural arch towards the chin. That look ought to be forbidden these days.

Following some brief introductory words regarding the nature of the hearing, the judge gives the floor to the prosecutor.

The man Nicolas fleetingly noticed upon his arrival, Stefan Hermansson, gives a stretch at the table diagonally opposite. Seated next to him are the policemen Simon Weyler and John Hellberg.

The enemy. Those people want to lock him up for a murder he hasn't committed.

The prosecutor clears his throat. 'Since Nicolas Moretti is strongly suspected of the murder of his sister Jasmine Moretti, I see no alternative but to apply for the defendant to be remanded in custody. The main reason is the concern that the defendant could tamper with evidence. The investigation is still in an early stage and there is a risk that the suspect may remove evidence or interfere with the investigation some other way.'

Stefan Hermansson glances at his documents at perfectly regular intervals.

136

'On 25 December at 2.47 in the morning, Nicolas Moretti was taken into police custody on Ulvsundavägen for drunkenness in public, less than a mile away from the address where the victim was brutally murdered and later found with a slit throat. During a search, the defendant was found to have blood on his clothing as well as a Santa hat in the inside pocket of his coat. The hat also carried traces of blood. A bus driver stated that Nicolas Moretti got on his bus wearing said hat at 2.41 a.m. at Alviks Torg, only a few hundred yards from the murder victim's apartment. He disembarked at Ulvsundavägen, where a short while later he was taken into custody by police. At the same location, a bloodstained knife – the suspected murder weapon – was found in the bushes. The knife has been sent to the national forensic centre for analysis and we are awaiting results. And I would like to add that the timings correspond with the victim's time of death.'

Nicolas shuffles nervously in his seat, cursing his stupidity. Why did I take the knife with me? Why didn't I just call 112? At the same time, he remembers Angela's words: *You had just seen your near-decapitated sister. You were in shock.* As he listens to the prosecutor with one ear, images of the bloodbath he woke up to drift by in his mind's eye.

'There are several witnesses who saw the defendant outside the apartment in which the crime took place. Among those witnesses is one neighbour who saw him through her window with the murder victim. This witness also saw Roland Nilsson ringing the victim's doorbell at 22.15 p.m., dressed as a Santa Claus. According to her statement, there was a physical altercation between Mr Nilsson and the defendant, during which the former was pushed by the defendant and fell on to the road.'

Nicolas turns his hands so that his cuffs rub against his skin. That old bat again.

'With regard to this incident, a separate complaint of assault will be lodged against Mr Moretti. As you can see, there is still much to be examined in this case. Among other things DNA analysis is yet to be conducted on the knife, various items from the apartment of the murder victim, on the body, as well as on the defendant's clothing and body. A comprehensive autopsy is also yet to be completed. According to the first forensic findings, however, the victim died from a cut to her throat. The cut was the only recent injury on the victim, apart from bruising on the left middle finger. There is currently no explanation for the bruising. To all appearances there are no defensive injuries, indicating that the victim was asleep when the murderer inflicted the cut. These two observations on the body aside, there was an approximately one-week-old bruise on the right thigh.'

The judge notes something down on her pad of paper while the prosecutor informs the room that the defendant can be formally charged within two months. Nicolas is no longer able to concentrate, but he still grasps that the preliminary examinations shouldn't take long since the suspect was arrested while trying to run.

Nicolas closes his eyes, hoping to wake up soon from this nightmare that is worse than anything he's been through so far.

'I would like to state in no uncertain terms that I wholeheartedly disagree.'

When Angela's voice cuts through the room, Nicolas opens his eyes.

'My client pleads not guilty to murdering his sister, Jasmine Moretti. As the test results will show, he as well as Jasmine were under the influence of alcohol, cocaine and pills. What kind of pills precisely is unclear at this current point in time. The two of them spent the evening together and my client fell asleep on the sofa – or flaked out, to phrase it in his own words. At that point, Jasmine was still alive. But when he awoke several hours later, he was lying in her lap in a pool of blood. How did he react? What is a normal reaction in such a case? How would you have reacted?' One after the other, Angela looks at the trio at the other table – Simon Weyler, John Hellberg and Stefan Hermansson. Nicolas too is bestowed with a piercing stare, as well as Emma Tapper, the judge whose name escapes him, and even the court reporter, who is busily typing away on a computer keyboard.

'What is a normal reaction to an unusual event?' continues Angela. 'As you and I know, or should know, different persons react differently to stressful situations. Take a woman being raped, for example. She might scream and put up a fight, but it is just as likely that she is paralysed with fear, remaining completely still. Or perhaps she plays along because she sees no other option. She fears for her life. Nicolas reacted in a state of panic – he could see that he would be suspected of murder. Therefore, he tried to cover his tracks and took the knife. Did he act stupidly? Absolutely. But strangely? No.'

Angela pauses again and looks from person to person once more.

'There is evidence that suggests that Nicolas did not murder Jasmine and that the murder could have been committed by someone else.'

Nicolas watches as John Hellberg suppresses a yawn, but he believes in Angela – has to believe in her.

'The door to Jasmine's balcony was unlocked, and there are prints in the soil beneath the balcony that suggest the placement of a ladder. The ladder was found in the property's courtyard. Additionally, one of the forensic team secured a scrap of fabric caught on some steel beneath the balcony. The fabric could belong to clothing worn by the person who climbed the ladder and entered the apartment via the balcony. The colour of the fabric is purple with yellow dots.'

Angela pushes back her chair and rises to add emphasis to her next words.

'Who could the person be that murdered Jasmine Moretti? Who cut her throat in cold blood, practically executing her? Would a brother do something like that to his own sister? We aren't in Iraq, after all.' She pauses for effect, allowing the words to sink in.

Practically executed. A cold shiver runs down Nicolas's spine. Who murdered his sister so brutally, butchering her like an animal without giving her a chance to defend herself?

'I am now going to present you with two alternative suspects,' says Angela, holding up two fingers. 'For one, we have Timo Rantanen, who was provoked by Jasmine throwing a toilet brush at him in the toilets of the pub she visited with her brother shortly before her murder. Rantanen even attacked police inspector Simon Weyler one day later, clearly demonstrating his violent nature.' She fixes her eyes on Simon, and Nicolas wonders what she's talking about. Did the Finn pick a fight with a cop?

'A complaint has been filed accordingly. Furthermore, Rantanen carries multiple previous convictions for grievous bodily harm. In one case a man's spine was broken; he is now in a wheel-chair. Rantanen admits that he followed Jasmine and Nicolas on their way home from the bar in Traneberg. But what did he do next? So far, police have not managed to get hold of the friend at Telefonplan who Rantanen supposedly visited.'

Angela walks back and forth a few paces behind Nicolas's back, strengthening the seed of confidence that has sprouted inside him during her speech.

'Then we have Roland Nilsson, the so-called "Santa Claus", who got into an argument that turned physical when he rang the doorbell to ask for schnapps. Taking into consideration my client's statement, Roland Nilsson too can be accredited with a propensity for violence. He was home alone that evening and therefore had the opportunity to return to Jasmine's apartment, gain entry through the balcony and take revenge on those who had rejected him. It is possible that he murdered Jasmine and ensured that various evidence points towards Nicolas Moretti, who lay passed out on the couch.'

Angela pulls a face.

'Whether one of those two men committed the murder, or someone else – there is no reason to deny bail to my client.' She sits back down to signify that she has finished.

The judge asks for one minute of consideration before announcing her judgement.

Nicolas's confidence withers. One minute. She doesn't require any longer because she's obviously made up her mind.

21

Feathery snowflakes twirl through the air, landing on the cold asphalt outside the courthouse. Emma flips up the collar of her quilted jacket and scans the area for Vera Moretti to inform her of the result of the hearing. But the woman appears to have left already.

So, instead, she turns to Angela to touch base about where to go from here, but the lawyer is already on her way to a sky-blue Porsche, beside which a young man stands waiting for her.

Does Angela have a son? Emma dismisses the thought when the broad-shouldered youth grasps Angela by the waist and kisses her. Emma can't tear her eyes off them. The guy looks at least twenty years younger than Angela, a Stureplan yuppie in a trendy blouson. Why is she surprised? Perhaps because she imagined some kind of grey-haired businessman at Angela's side, not a young pup.

'What did I tell you?' The pungent smell of Hermansson's aftershave irritates Emma's nose when he walks past her with a grin, glancing in the same direction as she is. Asshole! She feels like shouting after him that Angela's personal life has nothing to do with her job, but decides against it. As she walks to her car, parked on the other side of the street, she watches the Porsche playfully swerving away through the slush and wonders where the pair are off to. Shouldn't Angela be on her way to the office to help her get Nicolas Moretti free?

The judge's decision to deny bail had not been unexpected, but it was a blow nonetheless.

'All according to plan,' Angela had said when they left the court room together. 'The judge would have failed in her duty if she had decided otherwise. But now we have two weeks until the next hearing, and we have much on our side.'

Emma had silently asked herself what Angela meant by 'much'. The stalker of whom they know a name but nothing else? Roland Nilsson, whose role in the whole story wouldn't be clear until the results from the Santa costume are back? Timo Rantanen, who supposedly has an alibi – the friend he allegedly visited?

The judge even ordered Nicolas to undergo a paragraph 7 examination, formerly known as a 'little psychological examination'. Emma feels some trepidation when she asks herself how such an examination would pan out. She doesn't want to think this thought to the end – Nicolas doesn't seem particularly stable.

She becomes aware of someone following her and turns around. Simon. He grabs her by the sleeve of her jacket.

'Are you sure you're fit to drive today?' He sounds serious but there's a cheeky glint in his eyes.

She continues to walk towards her car. 'How lovely that you're talking *to* me now and not just *about* me.'

'John doesn't like the two of us working together. He made it very plain.'

'We're working together? That's news to me.' Emma smiles grimly. 'What was Hermansson showing you on his phone?'

She snorts when Simon tries to get out of this by looking dumbfounded.

'Photos of my half-naked sister.' She arrives at her car and tries to open the door, but Simon pushes against it.

'Okay. I understand that you don't find that particularly funny, but John can be so bloody categoric. For him, everything is either black or white. I only meant to . . . ugh, dammit.'

Emma yanks open the door and climbs in, suppressing the urge to flare up even more. She knows Hellberg is a phoney everyone looks up to, and she knows how hard it is to swim against the current.

'Will you help me with the investigation of Andreas Kilic?' she asks in a calmer tone. 'I'm on my way there now.'

'To his home? No, I won't make it.'

'So much for working together.'

'That's not it. But I still have an interview report to write up and I need to catch up on a few other jobs that got left behind. And it's the holidays. Besides, Jasmine never reported the stalking – we have nothing on him. What exactly do you intend to do?'

'Don't worry about it. I'll go alone.'

Simon sighs. 'I promise I'll check Jasmine's phone for dick pics.' He smiles mischievously and gives her a nudge on the shoulder. 'Just like the ones your sister receives every day.'

Emma darts a glance at Simon. Evidently, he's trying to lighten the moment, but the thought of Ester and yesterday evening spoils her mood. She doesn't know why, only that something happened, something she can't remember. That's why she wants to get away from here, lock herself up in her car, with only the gap in her memory for company.

'It would be better if we found something on her phone first.' Simon seems to have cottoned on to the fact that she doesn't want to talk about last night. 'Pictures or threats of some kind. Then we could bring him in.'

'Of course. You do that.' Emma inserts the key in the ignition and turns it.

'Hang on.' Simon places his hand on her sleeve once again, gripping a little harder this time. 'Everything okay between us?'

His touch produces a panic-like reaction in her, making her shudder. 'Why wouldn't it be?' she replies, even though she has a hunch that he's referring to their boozy evening at the pub.

What happened there? Does she even want to know?

'Okay.' To her relief, Simon changes the subject. 'In that case, I've got something for you. We found the man who paid Jasmine's rent. However, we've already questioned him and consequently ruled him out as a suspect.'

'When did you question him?'

'Yesterday.'

'Before we met at the pub? Why are you only telling me now?'

'I couldn't risk you mentioning him at the hearing. Then John would have known that the info came from me.'

Emma shakes her head. Once again he withheld information from her.

'What did he say? Does he have an alibi?'

'He claims he was with his family. It was Christmas Eve, after all, so it's pretty plausible. Of course, I'll confirm with his wife. I promised to proceed as discreetly as possible. He said he and Jasmine were just friends and had no sexual relationship. Apparently, he paid her rent because he likes to help others.'

Emma rolls her eyes.

'I know what it sounds like,' says Simon. 'But even if he was sleeping with her, it doesn't automatically make him a murderer.'

'What's his name?'

'Christer Tillman.'

'Age? Address? Workplace?'

After seemingly battling with himself for a few moments, Simon reveals that Christer Tillman is fifty-three years of age and CEO of a temping agency with offices in Stockholm's city centre.

Emma slams her door shut and Simon manages to pull back his hand just in time.

She backs out of her parking space and pulls on to the lane. Fishes the hip flask from the glovebox, clamps it between her legs and unscrews the top with one hand. Curses her resolution never to drink again. She needs a sip – just one. But then she remembers the promise she made to herself. She can't go on like this, losing control and not remembering things. She curses Simon, screws the cap back on and puts the hip flask back. It's all his fault. And he should have told her about Tillman yesterday. Then again, she acted the same way when she didn't tell him about Rantanen. And then it all ended in the kerfuffle during which Simon got a toilet brush in the face.

Emma can't help but grin, softly singing Monty Python's 'Always Look on the Bright Side of Life' as she drives to the stalker's address in Alvik.

Once she arrives there, she searches the area for his Honda. When she doesn't find it, she parks her car and positions herself by the entrance to the underground parking garage beneath the multistorey building he lives in. She's in luck; after just a few minutes she manages to slip inside. She finds the Honda towards the back, between an Audi and a Saab.

How should she react if he turns up – merely observe or address him? She decides to hold back and see what he does and how he acts. Before confronting him, she must make absolutely certain that he's the right man. While she waits, she surfs the internet on her phone, but unwanted thoughts of last night distract her. What time did Ester go home? Why isn't she answering her phone? A door leading from the garage to the stairwell creaks several times as people come and go, but no one matches the description of Andreas Kilic. How long should she wait? An hour at most. She changes from sitting to standing, stretches, passes the time by counting the red cars, then sits back down.

The door creaks open again. Emma's eyes focus when a young couple enter the garage. The man is slim and could be Kilic's age. It's hard to tell whether he's ash blond because his skull is clean-shaven, but other than that he does look like the man in the passport photo Emma saw. She's slightly confused by the fact that the girlfriend is pushing a buggy. Angela never mentioned a child. She waits quietly as the family walks on. When the man unlocks the Honda with a remote, she knows that he is indeed the man she's looking for.

The couple store the buggy in the boot of the car – not an easy task, it seems. They fold it awkwardly and try to make room for it. Perhaps it's time to invest in a larger vehicle? But maybe a stalker needs a souped-up sports car with a large, wing-like spoiler?

The child is wearing a pink hat and appears to be a few months old. The woman buckles the child into a rear-facing car seat then climbs into the back seat herself.

As soon as the Honda is out of the garage, Emma calls Angela. While the phone rings, she realizes that she has nothing new to report. Emma merely saw the stalker with her own eyes but can't present any new facts as requested explicitly by her boss. The moment she decides to hang up, Angela answers the phone.

'I'm glad you called. I need you to attend Nicolas's interview at one o'clock today. I have just been informed of the time, but I can't make it. You can handle it, right?'

'Yes, sure.'

'And see to it that you're fit. Since the interview has been scheduled this hastily, I assume the police have new information they want to question Nicolas about. Better bring a pack of chewing gum. By the way, why are you calling?'

Emma smells her breath before telling Angela about the parking garage, Andreas Kilic and his family.

'He has a child that's only a few months old. Do you really believe it's him?'

'We can hardly ask Jasmine now,' says Angela. 'But she saw him with that car. And now that you mention it . . . she told me the young woman she saw with him looked pregnant. And the description matches him. Did you see his tattoos?'

'No, he was wearing a jacket.'

Silence at the other end. Emma can practically feel Angela's displeasure.

'I'll try to get closer next time,' she adds.

'Do that. If the tattoos match, we can be certain. And the newborn could explain why he hasn't been harassing Jasmine recently. His attention lay elsewhere, so to speak.'

'How do you know he wasn't stalking her recently?'

'She promised to contact me if it happened again. She didn't.'

'But if, as you said, he dedicated all his time to his child, then why should he kill Jasmine all of a sudden?'

Angela says nothing for a few moments, then replies: 'Answering that question is your job. Something must have happened, something that left him so desperate that he felt he had to kill her. We only need to find out what that was.'

22

Emma and Nicolas sit opposite one another in the interview room, both sweating in their clothes. He in a T-shirt that is too large for him and she wearing the blouse Angela lent her. It's too tight under her arms and she squirms in an attempt to shift the garment into a more comfortable position. But the blouse isn't really the problem. Emma needs the hip flask in the car outside, needs it so badly she can't think of anything else.

But why is Nicolas sweating? Emma suspects that, like her, he is undergoing withdrawal symptoms – not from alcohol, though, but drugs. He looks pale and struggles to sit still, shuffling around on his chair, running his nails across the tabletop, scratching his chin. The two of them have ten minutes alone before the start of the interview and Emma can't remember what she is supposed to say.

She tries, 'You did well during the hearing.'

'And you looked tired.'

Emma wraps a strand of hair around her finger, realizes that the gesture probably makes her look insecure, and stops. 'I was out last night. But not too late.'

Nicolas takes his hand off his chin and gives her an accusing look.

'Well, I met up with my sister.' Should she mention that Simon was with them? No, he probably wouldn't like that. 'She can be difficult at times. We're twins, you see, and I had to – never mind.'

'You have a twin sister too?' Something flashes across Nicolas's eyes as he seems to remember that he no longer has a twin sister.

'Oh, forgive me, I wasn't thinking . . .' Emma sheepishly lowers her eyes.

'It's all right,' says Nicolas.

Emma smiles as best she can and cuts the small talk. Neither of them is particularly good at it. 'I found Jasmine's stalker. His name is Andreas Kilic. Does the name ring any bells?'

Nicolas shakes his head. Emma describes him and mentions that he lives in Alvik, but Nicolas still doesn't recognize the man. And so she continues with Christer Tillman, the man who paid Jasmine's rent.

'I haven't spoken with him myself, but the police questioned him. He claims he and Jasmine were just friends.'

'Then that's probably how it was.'

Emma studies Nicolas's disinterested expression. The nonsense Christer Tillman fed them must sound unlikely even to him.

'I believe the two of them were sleeping together. What do you think?'

'That should be easy enough to find out.'

'Perhaps. But did you never ask yourself why someone would pay Jasmine's rent? Did you never ask your sister?'

'No.'

'But you said the two of you were close.'

'Yes, but we never spoke about such things.'

Emma stares at the bare walls, wondering if Nicolas has always been this taciturn. 'I visited your parents yesterday.' She hopes to inject some momentum into the faltering conversation.

Something changes in Nicolas's eyes then, and they seem warmer and more golden-brown. 'How is Douglas?'

'I got the impression that he was doing okay, given the circumstances. Only thing was, he had some kind of wound on his forearm that got infected.'

'What kind of wound?' asks Nicolas, more loudly this time.

'Your mother said it was just a scratch. Apparently, Douglas picked the scab until it became infected. Nothing to worry about.'

Nicolas swallows, his Adam's apple jumping up and down. 'Vera isn't my mother.'

'I know. May I ask how your real mother died?'

'She had a stroke.'

'I'm sorry. I don't really know what to say. Was that long ago?'

'Twenty-two years.' Nicolas leans across the table towards Emma. 'Can I ask a favour of you?'

'Of course.'

'Would you talk to Douglas sometime and tell him that I didn't—' He buries his face in his hands. Looking back up seems to demand a huge effort. 'Tell him that I'm innocent.'

Emma returns his stare, wanting to explain to him that she can't simply show up at the Morettis' for no good reason, but when she sees the panic in Nicolas's eyes, she stops herself.

'I might be able to. At some stage I'll need to speak with your father and Vera anyway, about certain things that have cropped up. Although I may not be able to tell your brother straight up that you are innocent, well, you know . . .'

'Thanks. Please tell him that I love him and . . . and to look after himself.'

Emma nods, even though she's probably promised too much. 'Speaking of— is there something else I should know about your family? I mean, it looks like you don't see one another too often.

151

You didn't spend Christmas Eve together, and no one knew that Jasmine owned a parrot.'

Nicolas stares into blank space and, just when it seems he's about to reply, the door opens and Simon walks in. He greets them both, shakes Emma's hand formally and sits down next to her. Then he places a folder on the table in front of him and makes a casual start by asking Nicolas if he's had a chance to rest up in his cell, if he's had lunch yet and if he'd like a coffee. Emma has to admit that Simon has a greater talent for small talk, even if Nicolas invariably replies by shaking his head.

'Let's make a start, then.' Simon pushes the button on a recording device and starts with the obligatory statements of time, place and date. 'Please describe to me the events of the evening of Jasmine's death, from the beginning and in as much detail as possible.'

'But I've already told you.'

'And I would like to hear it again.'

Nicolas breathes deeply. Then he tells them how it all began in the pub and how the rest of the evening unfolded.

In her mind, Emma compares Nicolas's story to the first time he told it and finds to her relief that the two versions still match. There are no divergent details nor any new persons.

Nicolas's statement takes a good half-hour. When he is finished, Simon takes a blank sheet of paper from the folder and places it in front of Nicolas, together with a ballpoint pen.

'Please write a sentence – any sentence.'

'Why?'

'Just do it.'

Nicolas scratches his chest and reaches for the pen, hovering its tip above the paper for a moment before starting to write.

Emma reads the words upside down and shudders.

The person who murdered my sister must be a psychopath.

He sets down the pen and pushes the paper to Simon.

'Thank you.' Simon files the sheet in the folder and carries on questioning Nicolas without mentioning the words on the page. 'You are a former football player. Do you miss it at all?'

Nicolas looks at Simon with disinterest. 'Definitely.'

'Are you better with one foot than the other? Right or left?'

'With my right foot.'

'Are you any good with your left foot as well?'

Nicolas glances at Emma, but she is just as confused by the strange questions.

'Does it make a difference?'

'I'm only curious. I for one am absolutely hopeless with my left foot. But I'm guessing as a professional player you can handle both feet.'

'Probably.'

'Okay, let's move on. Jasmine's post-mortem has been completed, and, as you just heard during the hearing, there was bruising on her left middle finger. I'd like to show you a photo, if that's okay?'

'On . . .'

'Only on her finger.' Simon slides a photograph towards Nicolas. Reluctantly, he leans forward.

Emma does the same. The finger in the picture is devoid of any colour except for three blueish lines that run parallel across the tip.

'Do you know how Jasmine came to have this bruise?' asks Simon.

Nicolas sinks back in his chair. 'No, no idea.'

'Did you notice whether she had this injury before you fell asleep?'

'I don't know. I didn't notice.'

Simon takes back the photograph, returns it to the folder and opens the top button on his polo shirt. 'Those yellow pills you and

153

your sister swallowed . . . You said you thought they were benzos. That is not true. The test results show that, among other substances, they contained MDPV. You know what that is?'

Nicolas's eyes widen a little, and Emma wonders whether it's because of surprise or shock. Probably both. Methylenediox – no, she can't remember what the abbreviation stands for, but the drug is mortally dangerous. In recent years it's cropped up in various forms – crystals, powder, pills. There have been several deaths resulting from the pills' effects; they triggered hallucinations so powerful that users thought they were Superman, trying to stop a train with their bare hands or something similar.

Who had Nicolas thought he was when he was inside Jasmine's apartment? What effect had the drug had on him?

Simon articulates Emma's thought out loud. 'How did you react to those pills?'

Nicolas's eyes dart from side to side nervously. 'Nothing special. I felt a little dizzy and then I nodded off.'

Emma senses that he's lying, that something else must have happened. But when Simon presses the point, Nicolas denies it, sticking to the version that he fell asleep and remembers nothing.

Simon flips a page in his folder. 'There is one more thing I need to mention.' He pauses for a moment. 'Jasmine was six weeks pregnant.'

Emma straightens up as if trying to make sure she heard right.

Simon eyes Nicolas closely. 'I can understand if this is difficult for you to hear right now, but I would still like to ask you if you have any idea who the father might be.'

Nicolas stares into the distance and gives an almost imperceptible shake of the head.

'Of course, we'll conduct a paternity test to find out who he is, but do you perhaps have an inkling?'

'No.'

A muddle of thoughts swirls through Emma's mind – the bourbon she drank last night, fragments of memories about how she got home, and the words Simon has just spoken.

Jasmine had been pregnant.

What if Andreas Kilic, the stalker, is the father? Then he would have a motive for killing Jasmine. He got her pregnant just when his first child by his girlfriend was on its way. In order to save the relationship with the young woman Emma saw down in the garage, he murders Jasmine. But no – according to Angela, Andreas and Jasmine probably had no physical relationship. But she wasn't a hundred per cent certain. 'We have to be open to all possibilities,' Angela had said. But the more plausible candidate for paternity was Christer Tillman – the man who allegedly only paid Jasmine's rent because he likes to help others. What a cliché. It's the same bromide you hear in interviews with applicants for police college: *I want to help people.*

Why not be honest and say: *I want to speed through town with flashing lights and chase criminals.*

Or, in the case of Christer Tillman: *I want to fuck.*

Emma finds it difficult to sit still for the remainder of the interview. It is time for her to burst Christer Tillman's Christmas bubble.

23

Christer Tillman's temping agency is situated on the fifth floor of a high-rise in Stockholm's city centre. When Emma exits the elevator, she finds herself directly in front of a receptionist who is sitting behind a desk of futuristic design. The young woman's blazer seems to blend into the mottled grey wall behind her.

'May I help you?'

Emma explains the reason for her visit and, after a brief conversation via intercom, a suit emerges from the fish-tank-like room beyond reception. Emma is surprised by how attractive the man is, surmising he is of southern European heritage. His dark hair and beard are dominated by grey.

Emma holds out her hand. 'I'm from Köhler Lawyers. As far as I'm aware, the police recently spoke with you about a case they are investigating.' She gives him a challenging look. She gets the impression he knows exactly what she's talking about.

'Please, come to my office,' he says with fake pleasantry, gesturing at the room he had emerged from.

The first thing that catches her eye is a framed photograph on the solid desk showing two playing children, an attractive wife and him.

How adorable. A proper family man.

They sit down in leather armchairs. Christer Tillman asks if she would like a glass of water, and when she says yes he pours her some from a carafe on his desk. Her mouth is so dry it feels dusty. She needs to moisten her tongue before beginning with the tactic she devised on the drive here.

'As you can probably imagine, I'm here about the murder of Jasmine Moretti.'

He smiles, but the furrow between his brows suggests that he isn't particularly pleased about her visit.

'You told the police that you and Jasmine did not have sexual relations. You and I both know that is not true.'

Christer Tillman reaches for his glass and drinks very slowly. Evidently, he is trying to gain time to gather his thoughts.

Emma too uses the opportunity to take a sip. Every word she speaks now needs to be correctly interpreted. 'The post-mortem results came through today. They tell us that Jasmine was six weeks pregnant.'

Water leaks from one corner of Christer Tillman's mouth. He wipes it off with the back of his hand, staring at the photograph on the desk. His eyes remain fixed on the picture for a long moment, giving Emma sufficient time to realize just how risky her bluff is. But when he turns back to her, she can tell by his face that it paid off.

'I can't afford to lose my family,' he says with glassy eyes. 'I'll tell you what you want to know – just keep them out of this.'

'Did you know she was pregnant?'

Christer Tillman nods. 'She told me a while ago. But I didn't kill her, I swear.'

'How long had you two been having sexual relations?'

'Since last summer. We met over the internet.'

'On which site?'

Christer Tillman loosens his tie. His forehead is now shiny with sweat. 'SugarDeLuxe.' His eyes search for his receptionist, as if he were trying to ask her telepathically to come in and remind him of an important appointment.

'Sugar as in—?' Emma gives him a questioning look.

'You know what it means.'

'No,' lies Emma. She wants to hear him say it.

'I was her . . . sugar daddy.'

'I see. So that was the reason you paid her rent?'

He nods.

'Can you explain to me how your relationship worked? What rules did you have?'

'Well, we met up a few times a week, went out for dinner, the theatre – the type of things a couple does. She was a student and strapped for cash, so I paid for things she wanted. Clothes, jewellery, beauty treatments, gym membership and the like.'

'And then she became pregnant. How did you react?'

'I was upset, of course. She told me she was taking the Pill. But then we talked about it, trying to figure out what to do. We had a beautiful relationship, believe it or not, and we agreed on a termination. She just needed a little more time to wrap her head around it.'

Emma gives a feeble smile. Suddenly she feels grateful for her own life, as miserable and sad as it may be.

'You think I killed her. But her brother has been arrested for the murder, hasn't he?'

'I only know that someone did it and I want to find out who.'

Christer Tillman runs his fingers across his stubble. Suddenly, he seems to grasp who he's speaking to. 'You are defending him. Of course you would try to throw suspicion on someone else.' He rises from the armchair, his tone harsher now. 'I think you'd better leave now.'

'Where were you on Christmas Eve?'

'I've already told the police.'

Emma gazes at him for a moment, accepting the fact that she won't get anything else out of him. And so she stands up and walks to the door he is holding open for her. Just as she's about to walk through, he closes it again.

'If there's anyone you ought to take a closer look at, it's that lunatic who attacked me outside Jasmine's apartment about a week ago. Some guy who went to uni with her – Philip something. Look at this.' Christer Tillman holds out the palms of both his hands. They are covered in scabbed-over grazes. 'I've got him to thank for these. He pushed me to the ground when I was about to get in my car. The bastard had been waiting for me outside.'

'What was it about?'

'I don't know. I guess he was in love with her or something like that. For some reason she told him about the pregnancy, even though she promised that it would remain between us.' Christer Tillman opens the door once more and holds out his hand to Emma in front of the receptionist, as if he had just completed a successful business meeting.

Emma shakes his hand, thanking him loudly and clearly for talking to her before rushing towards the elevator. The information she's received has turned out to be much more fruitful than she'd expected.

24

The moment Emma steps on to the street, she calls Angela. While the phone rings, her eyes go up to the roof-top bar on the opposite side of the road. Had Jasmine and Christer Tillman met there? It seems a typical location for a man trying to impress a young woman, and close to his office. Since Angela doesn't pick up, she tries Simon. Engaged.

With swift steps, she walks to her car, feeling slightly euphoric about what she has just learned. Christer Tillman was Jasmine's sugar daddy, got her pregnant and, for some reason, had been involved in a fight with Philip Stenhammar. She climbs into the car and leans back. I did it!

Christer Tillman fell for her bluff. She'd done nothing but list the facts, allowing him to believe that his paternity had already been proven.

Her phone rings and she answers. Simon. He is angry, she can tell right away.

'I've just had a call from Christer Tillman. Do you have any idea what you've done?'

'I got him to admit that he and Jasmine were sleeping together. He was her sugar daddy.'

'You told him he was the child's father. We don't even have the DNA results yet, dammit!'

'I told him no such thing. He came to that conclusion all by himself.' Emma watches the people walking past outside. They stare at their phones, looking stressed about the crowds or the cold wind lashing their faces. Meanwhile, Simon lectures her on sabotaging the investigation. Now, so he claims, it will be much more difficult during the impending interview to bring Christer Tillman to compromise himself by lying. *If* he indeed turns out to be the father.

'There is still a possibility that it's someone else,' he says in conclusion.

'In that case, we'd have another suspect,' replies Emma.

'We don't need any more suspects. We already have one, and his name is Nicolas Moretti.' Simon swears under his breath. 'Why am I even listening to you?'

'Because you too have a feeling that something is off.'

'You couldn't be more wrong. We have sufficient evidence to convict Nicolas of murder. The only reason I'm listening to you is that I want to know why. Why did he murder his twin sister? What was his motive?'

'I at least know what motive Christer Tillman could have had. Jasmine was pregnant by him and he was terrified of the consequences.'

'If he even is the father. *If.*'

Emma waits for a moment for Simon to calm down. 'Christer Tillman told me something else – something very interesting. Philip Stenhammar attacked him outside Jasmine's apartment about a week ago. He assumes it had something to do with the pregnancy. I'm going to drive there now to speak with him.'

'Her student buddy? You'll do no such thing.'

'Meet me outside his apartment if you want to be present.' She hangs up. On the drive to Gärdet, the suburb where Philip Stenhammar lives, she eyes her display each time Simon tries to get hold of her. Eventually, he leaves a voicemail: 'Wait for me. I'm on my way.'

When a resident opens the front door by chance, she slips inside but decides to wait downstairs. Better not to aggravate Simon any further.

A few minutes later, the Volvo appears on the other side of the street. Simon slams the door shut and looks around with a terse expression. When he spots her by the entrance, he walks towards her.

'It's high time you got a grip on yourself, Tapper.'

Emma lets go of the door, forcing Simon to run the last bit before it closes in his face. Then she hurries up the stairs, closely followed by Simon.

'You are walking on bloody thin ice. You've no idea of the trouble you're in for this stunt.'

Emma rings Philip's doorbell and hears footsteps. The spyhole grows dark when someone peers through it from the inside.

'Are you even listening to me?' hisses Simon in her ear.

'Be quiet.' When no one opens up, she hammers against the door. 'Philip, we only want to ask a few more questions.'

Again she hears footsteps. After a while Philip opens the door, a towel wrapped around his hips. Drops of water glisten in the fluff on his chest.

'I thought we'd discussed everything.'

Emma steps into the hall. 'Perhaps we will have this time, if you tell the truth.'

He leads them into the two-bedroom apartment, which is filled with high-tech gadgets. There's a huge television, 65-inch at least, a gaming console with a variety of controllers, a cross-trainer and other futuristic-looking appliances whose purpose Emma fails to discern.

'Studying clearly makes one rich.' Emma's eyes scan the rest of the living room, which is accented almost entirely in black. Leather sofa with a glass table. Two spinning armchairs that look horribly expensive; a designer shirt dropped across a cushion.

Philip leans against a column separating the lounge from the kitchen, crossing his arms on his chest. 'What do you want to know?'

'How do you know Christer Tillman?'

Philip looks down at his towel and tightens the knot. 'I assume he told you about our little altercation.'

Emma nods, waiting for him to carry on.

'The asshole put a bun in her oven and threatened her. He said she would have to pay back all the money he'd lent her if she didn't have an abortion.'

'And you are certain that it was his child?'

'That's what she said.'

'Maybe it was yours?'

'What are you talking about? We were just friends.'

'That's what Tillman said at the start, too. But, as you can imagine, we have conducted a paternity test.'

Simon purses his lips. Obviously it costs him some effort not to correct her.

Unlike Christer Tillman, Philip unfortunately doesn't step into her trap.

'The child is definitely not mine,' he says with a grin.

'I spoke with your father,' says Simon. 'He confirmed taking you home on Christmas Eve. However, not at ten o'clock like you claimed. It was eight o'clock.'

Suddenly a door opens and a bare-chested young man in boxer shorts emerges from the bedroom. Asian looks, tattoos on his chest. He too looks as if he's fresh out of the shower – heavy drops of water drip from his shoulder-length hair. 'Philip was with me the whole night,' he says, his eyes unwavering. 'He came to my place sometime after nine and stayed the night.'

Emma and Simon exchange a glance and sigh simultaneously. How could they have missed that Philip had company? His boyfriend, it appears, who had overheard them talking and now provides Philip with an alibi.

'I hope you realize that covering up a criminal offence is a serious matter?' says Emma.

'Philip murdered no one, and I'm not lying. He spent the whole night with me.'

Simon fixates Philip with his eyes. 'You met Jasmine outside ICA at Alviks Torg shortly before nine.'

Philip's eyes flick back and forth. His boyfriend gives him a puzzled look.

Emma, on the other hand, is not surprised. How many times has Simon kept information from her?

Simon steps closer to Philip until there is just an arm's length between them. 'CCTV at the cash machine filmed you both. The video shows Jasmine withdrawing money and handing it to you.'

Philip takes a step back. 'She owed me money from lunch, all right?'

'Lunch that cost two thousand kronor and needed to be paid back on Christmas Eve, of all times?' Simon grabs Philip's arm. 'It's no offence to owe someone money or sell something. But don't lie to me, or I will arrest you for assault on Christer Tillman and the murder of Jasmine Moretti.'

Philip yanks his arm free and starts pacing the room, kicking anything that's in his way – a bar stool, a sock that was dropped next to the couch, an electric guitar, which crashes to the ground. 'Okay, let me explain,' he says once the strings stop vibrating. 'I sold her some coke. That was why we met up. She wanted some every now and then, and I got it for her. But I had nothing to do with her death. I was at my parents' for the evening and then at Maximilian's.'

'And the yellow pills?' asks Emma, thinking of the MDPV in Nicolas's blood.

Philip gives her a blank look. 'What pills? I sold her cocaine and nothing else.'

Emma's phone rings. When she sees Angela's number on the display, she slinks into the stairwell, leaving Simon to carry on without her.

'How was Nicolas's interview?'

'Good, I think.'

'I hope so. What have you got?'

'The police have the post-mortem results. Jasmine was pregnant.'

'Who is the father?' asks Angela, not in the least surprised.

Strange. But that's just what she's like. Factual.

'They don't know yet. But I believe it's Christer Tillman.'

'Who?'

Emma remembers that she hasn't yet told Angela about the man who was paying Jasmine's rent. She outlines the most important points without going into the details of their conversation in his office.

'Does he have an alibi?' asks Angela, cutting her off.

Alibi. The only thing Angela is interested in. Evidently, all that matters to her is presenting the police with a new suspect.

'He claims he spent all of Christmas Eve with his family. Simon is still checking it out.'

'Simon. Sounds like you've become quite familiar. What else is Simon saying?'

Emma ignores the dig. 'Not much. It was a strange interview. He asked several questions about Nicolas's football career, like whether he kicked the ball with his right foot or his left. I got the impression he was trying to find out if Nicolas is right- or left-handed. Simon asked him to write something down on a piece of paper.'

Silence at the other end. When Angela speaks, Emma is annoyed at herself for failing to reach the obvious conclusion sooner.

'Perhaps the post-mortem showed that the person who cut Jasmine's throat was left-handed. That is less common than being right-handed and therefore a useful link in a chain of evidence. What is Nicolas?'

Emma thinks. He was sitting opposite her and picked up the pen with his . . .

'Right. He wrote with his right hand.'

'Good. But you need to get the post-mortem report so that we know for certain what the police found out.'

'But we won't get the report until they complete their preliminary investigation.'

'Our client shouldn't have to remain in custody that long. What do you think I hired you for? I want the report today. Find a way.'

Emma remains on the staircase for a while after Angela hangs up. How is she supposed to manage that? If she asks Simon outright and he says no, she's stuffed. She walks back into the apartment, stops in the doorway to the lounge and listens as Simon questions Philip about Jasmine's drug use. The two of them have sat down on the couch and Philip makes it sound as if it was an occasional thing, not a habit.

'She only took something when she was partying, not at any other time. Well, or if she had a difficult exam and needed to pull an all-nighter.'

Simon writes notes on a pad and casts a glance at Emma. 'I have all I need. Is there anything else you wanted to ask?'

'No. I have complete faith in you,' she says affectedly, hoping he gets her true meaning – namely that he is the last person on earth she trusts.

They thank Philip and walk down the stairs.

'When were you planning on telling me about the CCTV footage from Alviks Torg?' asks Emma as they step into the street.

Simon zips up his jacket to the top. 'You know I can't share everything with you. John is constantly on my back.'

'Hang on a moment. Wasn't it you who said we were working together?'

'Yes, but—'

'I understand. On your terms.'

'No, but—' Simon looks up at the heavy, overcast sky, as if he were hoping to find some superhuman strength up there. 'You have to understand that you are the defence and I'm a police officer. But since you won't give up . . . there is another video. CCTV shows Timo Rantanen at the main station on the night of the murder. His version of events following his visit to the pub checks out. He called at a friend's in Alvik but he wasn't home. He went back to the bar, changed his mind and took the underground to another mate's place.'

He shakes his head and walks to his Volvo. 'I'm sorry, but that's the end of your theory that Ranta murdered Jasmine.'

Emma feels a wave of disappointment crash over her head. Another potential suspect gone. But she doesn't wallow in self-pity for too long – after all, they still have Roland Nilsson, Christer Tillman and Andreas Kilic.

'Have you checked Jasmine's phone yet?' she calls out, walking after Simon. 'Did you find any explicit photos from the stalker?'

'Not a single one.' He unlocks the car with the push of a button, opens the door and turns to her, his arms on the door frame.

'There was nothing from Andreas Kilic. No texts, no pictures. Not even deleted ones.'

'Are you sure?'

'I went through everything. I'm just glad I didn't buy into your line of thinking and arrest him.'

Emma ignores the jibe. 'Strange. Do you think she might have owned several different mobile phones?'

'There were none in her apartment.'

Emma wipes a thin layer of ice off the windscreen with her hand, feverishly trying to figure out what doesn't add up. Jasmine told Angela about the messages – why isn't there anything on her phone?

'Could she have received messages and pictures on her computer, via email?'

Simon shakes his head. 'All her devices are synced. Whatever arrives on the computer also appears on the phone. But hopefully we'll know more on Monday. That's when forensics want to examine the computer.'

'Speaking of computers.' Emma takes a step towards Simon. 'Any chance we could do that right now? According to Christer Tillman, the two of them met through a platform called SugarDeLuxe, and I'd like to find out if that's true.'

'Now? My hands are full. I have to get back to the station and write up the complaint Christer Tillman has lodged against you.'

'What the hell – he's reporting me? What for?'

'The details of your offence haven't been established yet.'

Emma thinks rapidly. 'Then it's just as well if I come along. To clear things up, I mean.'

'Oh, really?'

Emma gives him a hard look. 'It's past five o'clock on a Friday, plus it's Christmas week. Not a soul is going to be there, least of all Hellberg. He probably knocked off at lunchtime.' She mimics Hellberg's low voice. 'I just need to go sort something. If you need me, you can reach me on my phone.'

Simon smiles. He's probably heard those lines plenty of times. Emma knows she is close to persuading him. Not that she's particularly keen to visit her former workplace. But she's keen to see the post-mortem report.

25

The first item Emma glimpses when entering the major crimes department is her old radio, the one that produces static noise when a mobile phone rings nearby. It's sitting on the windowsill next to her desk, which is now covered with Simon's things. Clearly, he is more fastidious than she is. Files and folders are neatly lined up on a rack with removable compartments; pens are lodged inside a penholder; hole punch and stapler are sitting next to one another at an angle, as if they were decorative ornaments. And, just as she predicted, no one is in the office except for a couple of narcotics detectives she saw when stepping out of the elevator at the other end of the floor.

'I could do with a coffee,' says Emma, casting a furtive glance at the filing cabinet under the desk. Is that where he keeps the prelim investigation folder for the Jasmine Moretti case?

'You know where to find the coffee machine.' Simon sits on his office chair. 'You can make me one, too, and I'll log on to Jasmine's computer in the meantime.'

Emma digs her nails into her palms. Shit. 'Do you know the password?'

'Nicolas gave it to me. *Twinsforever*. Cute.'

'There you have it. He gave you the password because he knows he has nothing to hide.'

Simon pulls a face but Emma doesn't give up.

'Have the results from the forensic examination of Roland Nilsson's Santa costume come back yet?'

'What do you think? The national centre for forensics only got it the day before yesterday, and it's Christmas.'

'Sorry, I was only curious. But have you had a chance to question Christer Tillman's wife?'

'Yes, and it's fair to say she wasn't best pleased with her husband. But she confirmed that they were together for all of Christmas Eve and that they drove from Vasastan to Upplands-Väsby shortly after 11 p.m. We're waiting for the video footage from the toll station at Norrtull. If the car is in it, you can cross him off your list too, regardless of whether he's the father or not.'

'He could have hired a killer,' says Emma.

'Sure. His secretary. Weren't you making coffee?'

'Yes, but it's not entirely inconceivable. It's happened before – completely normal people engaging a hitman. Well, "completely normal" might be a slight exaggeration, but you know what I mean. Take, for example, that lawyer who was shot. His ex-wife—' She stops mid-sentence when she realizes that Simon isn't listening as he's concentrating on typing something on the keyboard.

Frustrated, Emma makes her way to the kitchen. She can smell from the hallway that something is burning. Somebody must have forgotten to switch off the coffee machine again. When she enters the kitchen, she finds her suspicion confirmed. She drains the coffee dregs from the bottom of the pot and pours water into the machine. She's about to rinse the pot when she remembers that she doesn't have to do this crap any more. She puts down the pot and switches on the kettle. A short while later, she returns to Simon with two mugs of instant coffee, setting one down in front of him.

'You're welcome,' she says, noticing that he's managed to gain access to Jasmine's computer.

'Thanks. What was the name of the site where Tillman and Jasmine met?'

'SugarDeLuxe.'

Simon types the name into the search bar and clicks his way to the home page. Emma is surprised by the professional look of the site. There's an image of a woman wearing a suit in the background. The whole design radiates style and elegance.

Emma reads the banner at the top: Sweden's number one for extramarital affairs.

Simon scrolls down.

Get what you really want from a relationship. With a sugar daddy or sugar baby, you no longer have to dream – enjoy all the perks.

'A straight-up porn page, only with a nobler façade.' Emma blows on her coffee. 'Could you imagine something like that?'

'Me? Are you nuts? Anyone registering on this site knows that it's about the purchase of sexual services. That is plain criminal. On top of that, such sites are known for exploiting minors. I hardly believe the men subscribing to this site settle for buying Big Macs for those girls, or holding intelligent conversations.'

'Just like Tillman. He didn't settle for just paying Jasmine's rent. Try to log on – sometimes the username shows up automatically.'

Simon moves the cursor to the corresponding field and starts typing her name: *jas.* But nothing happens.

'Looks like this is as far as I get today, but the forensic IT guy will sort it on Monday.'

'And we're supposed to wait all weekend?' Emma points at the Outlook symbol. 'Why don't you check her emails?'

Simon clicks on the inbox and together they read through the list of senders: school of economics, various online shops, the department for educational grants, a nail salon. Nothing of interest. Emma skims through the remaining emails until her eye snags on a message. It sounds interesting: an abortion clinic on Sveavägen.

'Open this one.' She points her index finger at the screen.

They read the email together and learn that Jasmine had an appointment at the clinic on 3 January.

'This cancels Tillman's motive, if indeed he is the father,' says Simon.

'What are the clinic's opening hours? Is it open now?'

Simon goes to the home page. 'Too late. If you want to speak with them, you'll have to wait until Monday. Or perhaps you might want to schedule a consultation for yourself?' Something in his eyes changes. From a colleague to . . . to what? As if something significant had happened between them. He places a hand on her arm. The touch triggers a feeling of unease that burrows through her whole body.

What exactly happened at the pub?

Emma pulls back her arm, pretending not to have noticed anything. She points at the screen once more. 'Can you print this?'

'The email?' he asks with a hurt look in his eyes. 'What do you want it for?'

'I just want it.'

'Of course.' He clicks print, gets up and walks out into the hallway, where the printer is situated.

Just as she had hoped. The moment Simon leaves the room, she leafs through the folders on the desk but the file she's looking for isn't among them. Her temples throb with frustration. She replaces the folders and tries the filing cabinet. Locked. Where is the key? She used to keep hers by the paper clips. She picks up the container and rummages through its contents. No key. The moment she sets it back down, Simon returns.

'Here you go.' He hands her the printout. 'Are you happy now? Like I said, I still need to write up a report.' He turns his back to her, making it abundantly clear he's unhappy that she doesn't want to discuss what happened between them. But she just doesn't know what that was. A bad feeling festers inside her and lodges itself in her chest. Did they do something they shouldn't have? But then she should be remembering something – even a tiny detail.

'Okay,' she says, failing to come up with another excuse for hanging around his workplace. 'Then you'll have to come and let me out. I don't have an access card.'

The smile he gives her is difficult to interpret. She accepts that she could have handled things better – whatever it was she did.

He leads the way past the desks and Emma racks her brain. She must find a way to carry on searching, must play for time. Suddenly she notices the wall with the mug shots, showing predominantly young men putting on tough expressions. She grabs one of the photos in passing and stuffs it into the back pocket of her jeans.

'I just need to go to the loo,' she says when he holds open the glass door. She grimaces. 'Must be the coffee.'

Simon lifts his left arm to his face and stares pointedly at his watch.

'Why don't you go put away your gun?' she suggests in response to his blatant hint. 'So I don't take up your time unduly.'

'All right.' Simon, clearly annoyed, rolls his eyes.

He walks off towards the armoury, but Emma waits and catches the door before it shuts. She pulls the photo from her pocket, removes the sticky film from the back and fastens it across the latch, then shuts the door and catches up with Simon, hoping she hasn't triggered an alarm. But all remains silent. At the cloakroom, she waits for Simon to disappear into the armoury, then returns to the office. She exhales with relief when she pulls on the glass door and finds her trick with the sticky film has worked. Her heart is thumping loudly enough to be heard through the entire station as she walks back to Simon's desk, searching the penholder and the desk pad. Next, she runs her hand across the top of the filing cabinet and – *voilà* – there's the key. She unlocks the top drawer, searches it,

174

then tries the second drawer. Finally, in the third drawer she finds the folder labelled *Jasmine Moretti murder*. She glances at the door to make sure Simon isn't on his way back, then leafs through the pages until she finds the post-mortem report. She skims through it as fast as she can, eyeing the door once more. No Simon. Her finger runs along the lines and eventually stops at the section she was looking for.

The cut across the victim's neck runs from the right to the left, which, in conjunction with the forensic evidence suggesting the murderer was standing behind the sofa on which the victim was seated, leads us to the conclusion that the murderer was holding the knife (exhibit 4), which is also the murder weapon, in their left hand.

Emma pulls out her phone and takes a photo of the page, then she returns everything to the drawer and locks it. That moment, she hears voices in the hallway. A man and a woman are laughing about something. Emma freezes when she sees who is fumbling with their access card on the other side of the glass door.

John Hellberg. Standing next to him is a young woman in police uniform.

Emma keeps her eyes on the door as she slowly lowers herself, crawling under the desk. If she's lucky, Hellberg is wholly engrossed in his blonde company and won't notice that the door lock has been tampered with. If she's lucky, they're only here to fetch something and they'll leave soon after.

She makes herself as small as possible, one knee resting on a dusty multi-socket. She can no longer see the two of them, but can hear them all the better.

'What's it like having Ramberg for a boss? Is he still playing military?'

The policewoman laughs. 'You could say that. He can be a tad strict.'

'A tad? The man irons his underpants.'

The young woman laughs again, but sounds less self-assured. 'Where are the photos you told me about?'

'Oh, yes. Come with me, I'll show you.'

Emma gathers from the ensuing conversation that they're standing in front of the wall with the photographs, trying to identify a man the young policewoman recently pursued. It's about a robbery involving some guy who fled into a nature reserve.

Emma carefully peers out from her hiding place. Hellberg is standing behind the woman and pointing at a photo, leaning much closer to her than is appropriate.

Emma pulls back her head, her pulse racing. She knows exactly what Hellberg wants from the girl. An unpleasant tingling spreads through one leg, but she must keep still for a while longer and bear Hellberg's proximity. To Emma, it feels like she is the one Hellberg wants to fondle, push against the wall and—

A door opens. Footsteps echo across the room.

'Simon? Still at work?'

Emma holds her breath. Is Simon going to mention her? She breathes out soundlessly when he replies, 'I still had to write up the minutes from Nicolas Moretti's interview this afternoon.'

'Why? That can wait till Monday. The boy won't run away, after all. You don't seriously believe the prosecutor will consider letting him go just because Angela Köhler spins some fairy tale about a Spider-Man-like climber wearing purple-and-yellow clothing?'

'No, that's not why I—'

'The old bat's soft in the head, Simon. No wonder she and Tapper found each other. They're a good match, both as nutty as each other. Don't worry about it. Go home and enjoy the weekend.'

Emma sits frozen, listening as the young woman uses the opportunity to make herself scarce. Hellberg continues to bitch about the two 'witches' Köhler and Tapper, but his and Simon's voices fade as they leave the room. The moment the door falls shut behind them, Emma crawls out from under the desk and hurries out to the hallway as fast as her numb leg will let her, and on to the toilets. She locks herself in a cubicle and sits on the seat lid. The ebbing tension and all that she's just heard cause her hands to tremble violently. Or rather, all that she didn't hear. She is used to Hellberg's stupid lines – but Simon's silence? Why didn't he speak up in her defence?

She doesn't know how long she's been sitting here. After a while, someone knocks on the door. Simon.

She unlocks the door and steps out. She gives Simon a dramatic look, pretending she hasn't heard a word of Hellberg's verbal attack. 'Is he gone? I saw him when I came out of the toilets and went straight back in.'

'Well done. It's probably best we leave now.'

They leave the building and say goodbye with a non-committal 'catch you later'. Suits her fine. She has decided to visit the abortion clinic on Sveavägen on Monday. And she would rather do that without Simon.

26

The waiting room of the abortion clinic is furnished in the style of a cosy living room. Pastel-coloured couches, slat-backed chairs and side tables holding piles of glossy lifestyle magazines and frightening health brochures. Ten tips on how to lose weight after Christmas and get back in shape. An attempt to create a homely atmosphere so that the poor souls sitting here feel halfway comfortable, even though they must make a weighty and vital decision. To terminate or to keep. Death or life.

Emma had spent the weekend shadowing Andreas Kilic, Jasmine's stalker. Stood waiting outside his apartment in Alvik, freezing her arse off. Followed him and his family by car, only to learn that he was visiting his girlfriend's parents at a big house in Hässelby. There was no way she was able to make contact with him there. Her best chance to get close to him occurred on Saturday afternoon, when he left his apartment alone for once. She pursued him on foot to a tobacconist at Alviks Torg. She spotted her chance when he paid at the counter and turned to walk outside. But then some guy he knew appeared, foiling her plan.

After this failed mission she returned to her apartment in Mariehäll, spending the evening with Netflix and an ignoble longing for the bottle. But she resisted the temptation, instead making use of Einstein as an amateur psychologist, which turned out to be a stroke of genius: he listened patiently, only throwing in the occasional 'screw you'. Sunday passed in much the same way – she watched Andreas Kilic without getting near him. And in the evening, another therapy session with Einstein and a series on Netflix.

After she's read through the recipe for a bowel-cleansing smoothie, it's her turn. She walks up to reception, where a delicate young woman in a white lab coat gazes at her gently.

'How may I help you?'

Emma squares her shoulders and presents her request firmly but quietly, so the other two women in the waiting room can't hear her. 'I'm here as part of an investigation into a murder that occurred in Alvik on Christmas Eve. You may have heard about it.'

The receptionist's eyes betray interest. 'You mean that Nicolas Moretti, who's accused of killing his sister?'

'That's right. I need to ask you a few questions since it has come to light that Jasmine Moretti, the murder victim, had a termination scheduled with you. I need to confirm that this is correct and speak with the doctor she consulted.'

'Okay. Do you have her personal identity number?'

Emma recites the digits while the receptionist – Stina, according to her name badge – types them into her computer. Suddenly, her fingers pause on the keyboard. 'Oh, what was your name again, and who do you work for?'

Emma had been afraid that doctor–patient confidentiality could become a problem. Stina has probably just remembered that.

'Forgive me if I was unclear. Emma Tapper. Major crimes unit. You're welcome to view my warrant card.' She reaches into her handbag and touches her invalid warrant card, hesitant to draw it out. Does she really want to risk being charged with another offence – this time for false assumption of authority? A mere trifle compared to assault and all the other complaints filed against her by now, but still.

'Oh, just a moment.'

Emma watches Stina, whose eyes are glued to the screen. 'I've just noticed that Jasmine has not yet met with a doctor. She'd merely booked an appointment for an initial consultation, but then she cancelled it on the twenty-second of December.' Stina seems relieved, probably because now she is spared the awkwardness of obstructing a murder investigation due to formal confidentiality clauses. 'So, unfortunately, I can't help you.'

'So there's no one here she spoke with? Someone she might have told who the father of the child is?'

'No. She booked an appointment online and then cancelled it.'

Emma thanks her for her help and heads for the exit. Her hand is still in her bag, clutching the leather case holding her card.

Jasmine cancelled her appointment. It follows that she decided to keep the child, no matter what Christer Tillman, or whoever the father was, thought of it. A crystal-clear motive.

She calls Angela and tells her everything. The lawyer asks her to come to the office to discuss their next steps.

'You haven't even been here yet. Besides, we still need to sign your contract of employment and sort out a few other little inconveniences.'

Click.

On the way to her car, Emma stares at her phone. What other inconveniences?

27

Only a few people are out and about on Kungsgatan – not unusual for a capital city for the days between Christmas and New Year's. Passing cars splatter slushy snow on to the pavement, forcing the handful of pedestrians to inspect their clothing and move closer to the buildings, where signs in shop windows advertise price drops.

Köhler Lawyers turns out to be in an older building near the popular café Vete-Katten. When Angela opens the front door via the buzzer, Emma takes the wide stone steps to the first floor and enters the office. It consists of three large rooms with tall windows.

Emma immediately notices the ice-blue neck scarf Angela is wearing, secretly wondering if it conceals strangulation marks stemming from wild sex games involving leather whips and ball gags, or whatever else people use who are into that sort of thing. Not that Emma can imagine Angela partaking in such activities, but what is it they say? Still waters run deep. She swipes the thought aside, annoyed at herself. How could she allow Hermansson's cheap attempt at dragging Angela through the mud to affect her? The neck scarf is pretty and most likely nothing to do with concealing bruises. It goes well with the blue of Angela's figure-hugging dress.

They enter Angela's office, which is in the middle with connecting doors to the rooms on either side. As far as Emma can tell, they seem empty and unused. Will she perhaps get one of them as her own office?

'Is it just you here?' Emma wonders whether there shouldn't be an assistant of some description. As far as she remembers, Köhler Lawyers does not just consist of Angela.

'Yes.' Angela fetches a document and a ballpoint pen from her desk and hands them to Emma. 'Here's your contract. But before you sign, I'd like to know why I yet again had to defend you to John Hellberg.'

Emma tries to figure out what Angela is talking about.

'Don't look so surprised. He called to complain that you made certain allegations to Christer Tillman.'

Aha, that was the inconvenience – Emma's white lie. She excuses her transgression in the same way as she did with Simon.

'At least he admitted that he and Jasmine had a sexual relationship. And now we know that she cancelled her abortion. That gives him a motive.'

'We have nothing until we get the results of the paternity test.'

Emma chews on her bottom lip. 'But even if the child turns out to be someone else's, Tillman believed it could be his. And that terrified him.'

Angela steps closer to Emma and tilts her head. 'His wife confirmed that he spent the whole evening with his family.'

Emma exhales with frustration. 'We'll see if that's true when we get the video footage from the toll station.'

Angela's expression softens. 'I appreciate your dedication. There is still some drive left behind the broken façade.' She strokes Emma's cheek with two fingertips. 'You drink too much. You need to take better care of yourself.'

The touch makes Emma freeze. At the same time, she fights back tears. Angela worries about her – when was the last time anyone did that?

Angela's fingers arrive at her chin. She lifts Emma's head a little, forcing her to meet her eyes.

'Don't worry about the charges against you. I'll take care of it. Women must stick together. That's my motto.'

Emma nods without knowing why. She doesn't really understand what Angela means. But the support feels good. At least Angela doesn't leave her in the lurch.

Unlike John Hellberg.

Angela lets go of her and the moment of intimacy vanishes as abruptly as it arrived. 'We must present the court with a new suspect – someone with no alibi. Someone who creates doubts about Nicolas's guilt. Roland Nilsson is never going to do the trick, unless forensics finds some traces on his costume.'

As the two women continue to discuss the case, Angela walks up and down the room with her arms crossed. Emma reports in detail all that she's learned in the last few days. Once the formalities of her employment are sorted, Angela assigns Emma the room to the right of her office. It's as large as a hall, and when Emma moves around it there's an eerie echo. Probably because there's no carpet, though a dark rectangular area on the herringbone parquet suggests there used to be a rug beneath the desk. Suddenly, she imagines that someone was murdered in this room, rolled up in the rug and carried to a car waiting outside. Realizing she's been watching too much Netflix lately, she sits down on the orange plexiglass chair. The backrest makes a crunching sound when she leans back, and she finds that it's cracked. She asks Angela if she can have another chair.

'I'm afraid not.' Angela looks up from a stack of papers that she's reading with a highlighter in one hand. 'I sold some furniture recently because I ordered some new pieces. In the meantime, you'll have to make do.'

'Sure, no problem.' Emma returns to her new workspace, which feels incredibly luxurious even without a carpet and furniture – just because she has her own room with an adjustable desk. She sits down at the computer and tidies up the notes she has made on the case so far: the interviews with Timo Rantanen and Roland Nilsson, the visit to Nicolas's parents, the shadowing of Andreas Kilic and the conversation with Christer Tillman. When she is finished a few hours later, she pops into Angela's office.

'I thought you might want to grab some lunch. There's a decent sushi restaurant nearby.'

'Thank you, but I'm meeting with a client shortly.'

'Sure, perhaps another time. May I ask what about?'

Angela smiles but Emma can see in her eyes that she doesn't want to talk about it. 'We can go down together,' she says by way of reply. She stuffs a few things into her handbag, drapes her fur coat across her arm and strides past Emma without so much as glancing at her.

Okay, I get it. I'm just the assistant. She follows Angela into the stairwell, a feeling of inferiority in her chest.

Acting all posh, the old trout. High heels in the middle of winter; Louis Vuitton handbag; perfectly styled hair and perfect make-up; drenched in expensive perfume. The scent wafts up Emma's nose when Angela holds open the front door for her.

As she steps on to the street, Angela pulls on her arm suddenly and violently, making her stagger to the side. But when she regains her balance, she realizes that it wasn't Angela but a woman who is yelling right into her face.

'You killed my child! I need you to understand that you are responsible for my Oliver's death. Do you understand? You killed him!'

The woman's saliva sprays into Emma's face. She steps back and, after a moment of confusion, recognizes Oliver's mother. After another moment she remembers her name. Maria. Maria Sandgren. Emma met the woman several times during Oliver's interviews, but not after he took his own life. Maria is skinnier than Emma remembers, and she looks more tired. And then there's this crazed look in her eyes.

Emma wants to tear herself free, run away, get swallowed up by the ground just to escape Maria's rage. But she stands as if rooted to the spot – her legs refuse to move, her field of vision turns blurry, and all she can see is Maria's mouth as it moves.

'You killed him! You killed him!'

A car door slams shut and a lanky man crosses the street. Tom, Maria's husband. He grabs his wife from behind, trying to calm her. 'Come on. This isn't helping.'

'She killed our son! How can you allow her to live on as normal? And you!' Maria spins to Angela. 'You said the police conducted their investigation contemptibly and that Emma Tapper should have been prosecuted for breach of duty – at least! But now you suddenly work together – she is an assistant in your disgusting firm!'

Angela takes a few steps towards Tom and Maria, pointing her outstretched arm at their BMW.

'Take her away! Right now!'

'And you're a racist to boot!' Maria hangs in Tom's arms and spits at Angela's grey pumps.

Angela glances at her shoes before she shoos the couple with determined gestures. 'Get in the car before this situation escalates!'

Finally, Tom manages to manoeuvre Maria into the car. Emma doubles over, gasping for breath. She just wants to get away from all the people who have stopped to stare at them, from the man filming her on his phone. She staggers towards the door and feels Angela's hand supporting her back, directing her into the hallway. Inside, she leans against the directory sign, closes her eyes and breathes deeply. She tries to wrap her head around what's just happened – what Maria said. That she should have been prosecuted. Finally, she looks at Angela, who is sitting on the steps, cleaning her shoe with a tissue.

'When you hired me, you said you were impressed by my work. You said it was Hellberg's and the prosecutor's fault what happened to Oliver.'

Angela pauses and meets Emma's eyes. 'And I meant it. But you must understand that Oliver Sandgren was my client. I said what his parents wanted to hear – what they needed to hear, having just lost their son.'

'And the easiest way was to blame me?'

'Hang on! I never bad-mouthed you internally. You have Hellberg to thank for that. Whatever I said to my clients is between me and my clients. From Maria and Tom's point of view, it was all the police's fault, and in this case, you were the police. You were the one they met, and you were the one who interviewed Oliver.'

Emma digs her nails into her palms. Yes, she interviewed Oliver. The charge was suspected rape of a minor. The sex was consensual, but at the time the girl had only been fourteen years old. One year younger than Oliver.

'I should have objected,' says Emma pathetically, fighting back tears. 'After all, I had the feeling that it wasn't rape in the true sense of the word.'

'I'm sure the girl's parents were aware of that. But still they decided to press charges when they found that their darling daughter had had sex. They were the ones who got the ball rolling. Hellberg kept it rolling, and when the going got tough he made sure you were the one to take the fall. All you did was follow orders from above.' Angela places the tissue on the stairs with a look of disgust. 'Our legislature with regard to rape is truly appalling when love-struck teenagers are at play. If I had a son, this is the first thing

186

I would teach him. Keep your pants on until you're of legal age, and ideally still then.'

Emma tries to smile, but at the thought of Maria's hateful tirade she barely manages to twitch the corner of her mouth.

Oliver is dead, and in the eyes of Maria and Tom, Emma will always carry the guilt. She was the one who had wreaked havoc in his room, searching for used condoms and other evidence of rape. And she repeatedly urged him in the presence of his parents to describe the highly intimate moment with his girlfriend in great detail. How he fumbled around with the condom with nerves. How his girlfriend helped him. How he came too quickly and how they laughed it off. Details no fifteen-year-old wants to discuss, least of all with his parents.

'Stop dwelling on it.' Angela rises and brushes down her dress. 'It's an awfully tragic story, but we both know that the prosecutor decided what you should do. And he was the one who didn't object to Hellberg's demands.'

Emma nods. She isn't entirely convinced, but it still feels good that Angela is taking her side. Even if she evidently told Oliver's parents something else.

'Anyway,' says Angela, 'the sushi restaurant you mentioned. Is it any good?'

'Yes, but weren't you on your way to a client?'

Angela unties her neck scarf, which had slipped out of place during the melee. 'He can wait.' She smiles and fastens the scarf as she walks to the door.

Emma stares at her, unable to take her eyes off the bruise that appeared beneath the fabric: a longish purple stripe around the neck.

So, Hermansson was right. Next question: how does he know?

28

Since her windscreen is again fogged up from the inside, Emma wipes a peephole with her glove. After all, she needs to see if Andreas Kilic leaves his apartment.

She drove here straight from her lunch with Angela, because she didn't know where else to go. She didn't feel like going home and lying on the couch while the thing with Oliver was still buzzing around her mind. Better to do something constructive and stake someone out.

She's been sitting here for two hours. Thankfully, she's managed to resist the temptation to call in at the liquor store around the corner. Enough of that nonsense. The fact that she's just experienced physical assault is no excuse, even though that is precisely what her brain has tried to tell her repeatedly.

Emma clenches the steering wheel to stop her hands from shaking. The thought that Angela sacrificed her to make herself look better before Maria and Tom won't let go of her. Sure, they didn't know each other well at that point, and Emma can see that Angela needs to build long-term relationships with her clients. She spoke about it a lot over lunch.

'You have to remember one thing. One must build a good rapport with one's clients and create an us-against-them feeling. That is the only way people keep coming back to you and recommend your firm to others.'

Emma had nodded, stuffed a salmon sushi roll with wasabi into her mouth and internalized Angela's words. But still she can't shake the feeling that she was duped somehow. And what did Maria mean with her comment about Angela being a racist? Was that to do with the social media post about the children of refugees? Emma didn't want to ask Angela about it. Maria must have just burst out with it in her rage and hysteria.

Emma wipes her glove across the windscreen again and peers outside. No Andreas Kilic. Her thoughts return to Angela, to the neck scarf and the suspicious bruise. Could Stefan Hermansson actually be right? Does Angela like it rough? Strangulation games. Is that what she and her young lover get up to?

Emma switches to a different radio station, one that's not playing ads at the moment. Does it even matter what Angela does in her free time? Emma concludes that her boss's activities are neither criminal nor inappropriate, but strictly private. So, the answer is no. The bruises merely shocked her, and she ought to banish them from her memory, along with the question of how Hermansson apparently knows.

When the door in front of her opens, she leans closer to her peephole.

Come on. Yes!

Andreas Kilic emerges, a duffle bag across his shoulder, and disappears around a corner. Emma jumps out of her car and walks after him. Her target heads in the direction of the old Alvik industrial area. Darkness has settled across the city, and on the other side of the water the lights of Fredhäll sparkle above the cliffs.

Where is he going? The answer appears shortly after. Shining above an entranceway a little further on is the logo of World Class, a chain of gyms, and Kilic takes the entrance.

Emma pauses on the pavement. This could be her best chance, but she doesn't have workout clothes with her. Never mind. She waits a couple of minutes so he can make his way to the changing room, then follows him inside. She picks a black top and some leggings from a shelf labelled 'sale' and heads to the reception desk, where she pays for the clothes and a trial membership. She changes in the women's room and wipes the worst of the slush off her trainers. Then she walks down the rows of weightlifting musclemen, spotting Andreas Kilic warming up on a rowing machine. Unfortunately, he's wearing a long-sleeved sweatshirt so she can't tell if he has tattoos on his right arm. Emma sits down on the rowing machine next to him, inserts her feet in the loops and activates the menu on the display to enter the desired distance and calories. After just a few minutes at a high speed, she's dripping with sweat and puffing like an old chain-smoker. Her last training session was probably a year ago, but this feels good. The more she pushes, the more effectively she dispels the thoughts of the attack on her and Angela.

Ten minutes later, she is completely puffed. She takes a brief break, then climbs off the machine and goes to a nearby mat to continue exercising as she waits for Andreas Kilic to finish his training. Hopefully, he'll take off his sweatshirt; it's the only way for her to ascertain that she's after the right person. She studies him more closely from her vantage point. He is no muscleman, his physique more reminiscent of a long-distance runner. His face is dotted with moles. When Emma feels like her stomach muscles have reached their limit, he finally climbs off the rowing machine and pulls off his sweatshirt. Underneath, he's wearing a white T-shirt. Emma eyes his arms, searching in vain for a skull and a spider web. She gets up from the mat and moves closer. Negative.

Frustrated, she sits down on a bench. It would seem that Andreas Kilic is the wrong man. According to Jasmine's description, her stalker had tattoos. Dammit!

Emma's eyes follow him as he drinks water from a bottle, wipes the sweat off his forehead and fetches some weights for a leg press. Suddenly, she notices something else about his arm – pale scars.

Emma thinks feverishly. The scars are on his right arm where the tattoos ought to have been.

Clearly, he's had them lasered. Now she sees it. The scars are pale outlines of a spider web and a skull.

Next conclusion: he must have had them removed quite recently. How else could Jasmine have known about them?

Filled with genuine curiosity, Emma walks up to Andreas Kilic. 'Hi, excuse me.'

He turns.

'I happened to notice that you've had tattoos removed. I'm thinking about doing the same with this one.' She pulls up one leg of her leggings, revealing a blueish-black dolphin on her ankle that she'd had done during a holiday in Cyprus. Back then, she'd been in her late teens, and these days she'd rather be without the tattoo. 'I've been wondering, does it hurt?'

'No, not particularly,' he replies, more kindly than she expected. 'No worse than snapping a rubber band against your skin. And you get a numbing ointment.'

'Oh, that doesn't sound so bad. How long until the area has healed?'

'A few weeks after each treatment.'

Emma grimaces. 'Does it take several treatments?'

'Three for me.'

She leans forward, inspecting the scars more closely. 'Doesn't look too bad. How long ago was your last treatment?'

'That was in the spring – eight or nine months ago?'

'Okay.' Emma scrutinizes him, trying to figure out if he's lying – but why should he? He doesn't know what she's up to.

'Would you recommend the place where you got the treatment done?'

'Definitely. It's on Götgatan. I don't recall the name, but there shouldn't be too many places like that.'

'Thanks, that's where I'll go.' Should she ask if he knows Jasmine Moretti to see what he says and how he reacts? She decides against it, now that she knows he's had the tattoos removed. Something is off. Jasmine couldn't possibly have seen the tattoos six months ago, like she claimed, because Andreas Kilic no longer had them at that point.

29

'She lied. Jasmine must have fabricated the story about Andreas Kilic, but why? I don't get it.'

Emma and Simon sit opposite each other in a cramped café on Södermalm, sipping their lattes. Behind the counter, two hip baristas prepare the orders, moving to the beat of the Christmas music and serving the requested coffee creations with flirty, tip-fishing looks.

Andreas Kilic had been telling the truth with regard to his tattoos. The laser clinic on Götgatan, which Emma visited straight after the gym, had confirmed this. His last treatment had taken place nine months ago. Emma had immediately called Angela and passed on the information, but she too had been unable to come up with a plausible explanation as to why Jasmine might have lied.

'She must have seen the tattoos,' Angela had said. 'But if he had them removed as you say, then she had known him for much longer.'

Simon stirs his spoon around his glass and occasionally blows the hot coffee. 'I think Angela is on the right track. The two of them must have met more than nine months ago, when he still had the tattoos. But then something must have happened that really ticked her off.'

Emma nods. 'Maybe she wanted to hurt him somehow.'

'He broke up with her,' says Simon, thinking out loud. 'Didn't you say he recently became a father? He simply chose another woman.'

'But then why bother to contact a defence lawyer and claim he harassed her? If revenge was what she was after, like the chick in *Fatal Attraction*, she could have just gone to the police.'

Simon places his elbows on the table and rubs his cheeks. 'I completely agree, but it's still not the truth. Everything suggests that the two of them didn't know each other. There's no digital trail between them, no messages, no nude pictures, nothing. But, as you say – why did she lie?'

'Unless they were extremely discreet,' says Emma. 'He was probably cheating, and when his girlfriend became pregnant he ended things with Jasmine. And when Jasmine turned out to be pregnant too, he panicked.'

'But she was only six weeks pregnant,' Simon points out. 'If Jasmine had met up with him six weeks ago, she would have seen that the tattoos were gone. Especially if they had sex.'

Emma rests her chin in her hands and accepts that Simon is right. 'Maybe she simply forgot to tell Angela. They weren't in contact for a while,' she says, even though she doesn't really believe it herself. Something is wrong about the whole story; she just doesn't know what.

'We'll have to wait for the results of the paternity test before pursuing this line of evidence any further,' says Simon. 'And besides, until recently you were convinced Christer Tillman is the father.'

'Yes, true. But it could actually be anyone at all – we don't know who she met with. Have you found nothing interesting on her computer?'

'Who knows? Maybe we have.' Simon leans back with a contented grin, folding his hands on his chest.

'What now? Aren't you going to tell me?'

He shrugs and dons a lofty expression. She knows she shouldn't allow herself to get wound up, shouldn't enter into this game. But she's finding it hard to forget what happened at the police station on Friday – that Simon didn't stick up for her when John Hellberg let rip about her and Angela.

'So, your boss thinks Angela and I are witches,' she says, knowing full well that her timing isn't great. But she's been stewing on this the whole weekend. 'Why didn't you say anything? Why did you allow Hellberg to carry on like that?'

Simon looks confused for a moment, then straightens up, contemplating her. The penny drops and she realizes that she has exposed herself somehow.

'How do you know what Hellberg and I talked about? I thought you were in the toilet?'

'I was,' she says, recognizing her mistake. 'But I didn't go right away. I overheard the first part.'

'How curious. I've been wondering why I can't find the key to the filing cabinet containing the Jasmine Moretti case file. And then Åsa noticed that someone had placed sticky tape on the door to the office.' Simon rests his chin on his hands. 'It caused a huge fuss among my colleagues. There was speculation about a break-in and all sorts. But no one is missing anything. Except for me, right?'

Emma picks nervously at a scab on her hand. How could she have been so clumsy? With flushed cheeks, she pulls the key from her jacket pocket and places it on the table.

Simon picks it up and holds it up to his eyes. 'I'm not going to ask why you wanted to read the files of the prelim investigation. I'm fully aware that they are of interest to you and Angela. But don't do anything like this again, or else I will report you.'

'Thanks,' she murmurs.

'You don't have to thank me. I kept mum for my own sake. How do you think Hellberg would have reacted if he'd learned that I let you into the office? The ugly duckling, so to speak. Or rather—' he says, trying to correct himself. 'I'm not saying that you're ugly. Only that—' There is panic in his eyes as he gropes for the right words.

'That I'm an outcast,' says Emma.

'Exactly. You are definitely not ugly.'

He says it so loudly that the guy and the young woman at the next table glance at them. And a voice in her head tells her that his strange demeanour has nothing to do with his slip of the tongue but rather with the evening they drank together at the pub. She has not failed to notice the way he looks at her – looks that are not strictly those of a colleague. Or perhaps she's just imagining things. Who is she to judge whether someone is acting strangely? After all, she was the one who used Simon to get her hands on the post-mortem report.

'We found her profile on SugarDeLuxe,' he says a little later when she reminds him of Jasmine's computer. 'Her username is *Sunflower* and she's been a member for nearly two years. In recent months, she's been in contact with four men on the page. One of them apparently met with her the day before Christmas Eve. Someone calling himself Mr Goal.'

'The day before the murder,' Emma observes.

'Yes, but we don't know for certain if the meeting actually took place. We only know they had arranged to meet at three o'clock that day at the lounge of the Radisson Hotel on Vasagatan.'

'Can we find out who's behind the profile?'

'We can trace the IP address, but that'll take a while, especially now, during the holidays. He paid the membership in bitcoin, which means we can't trace him that way.'

'I have an idea.' Emma sips her latte and asks herself whether her plan is really such a good one. But – what the heck. 'I'm going to sign up on the site and become a sugar baby. Then I'll get in touch with Mr Goal and arrange a date with him. Then we've got him.'

Simon gapes at her. 'You will do no such thing.'

Emma pulls out her phone and navigates to SugarDeLuxe. 'Why not? It's hardly illegal.'

'No, but inappropriate. And possibly dangerous. We don't know what kind of idiot he is.'

'Exactly, and that's what we need to find out. What should I call myself? Hot Mama? No. Mr Goal prefers more spiritual names. How about . . . Kissing Butterfly?'

Simon opens his mouth in protest but has his hands full trying to save his latte from a mob of teenagers who are pushing past with their backpacks. Once the danger has passed, he leans forward and gazes at Emma with a serious face. 'Are you sure you've thought this through?'

'Yes, and it didn't take me more than a minute. And when the time comes, you will follow me inconspicuously.'

Simon snorts. 'Then let's hope he doesn't reply. Anyway, what photos will you upload?'

Photos? She hadn't thought of that. Men like that don't want just any photos. If Mr Goal is to take the bait, she'll have to show a little more. Selfies in revealing outfits, ideally with one shoulder strap slipping off and – then she has an idea. 'I'll steal some off my sister.' She blocks Simon's renewed objections by pointing out that Ester probably doesn't mind, and that she owes her a few favours anyhow. Emma registers as a new member and fills in her profile while Simon reveals another detail from Jasmine's computer.

'We found something else. Jasmine was a member of an ACA group, if you know what that means.'

'No, never heard of it.'

'Me neither, but I googled it. ACA stands for Adult Children of Alcoholics. If I understand it correctly, they follow the twelve-step programme of Alcoholics Anonymous and apply it to other areas as well. So, their groups are not just about alcohol and drug dependency. Jasmine was in the "sexual abuse" group.'

Emma looks up from her smartphone. 'Sexual abuse. Do you think she was affected?'

'She hardly would have joined such a group otherwise. I'm sure sugar babies encounter all kinds of pigs.'

'Probably.' Emma allows this new information to sink in. She needs to discuss this with Angela. She continues with her profile, frowning at one question. She looks at Simon. 'What kind of figure do I have?'

'I'd rather not answer that one. I fear it may be used against me at some point. Didn't you want to use your sister's photos?'

'Yes, but just one close-up of her boobs or something like that. In this bit, I have to describe myself in words. By the way, what did Jasmine look like? Mr Goal probably has a type. I guess she was slim but still had curves.'

'I suppose so.'

'That'll do.' Emma enters the rest of the information and composes her first message to Mr Goal. Hi. You seem nice. Tell me more about you. She reads the text a few times, erases it and starts again: Hi Daddy. You sound like an interesting man and I believe the two of us could have a lot of fun. Message me. X

'Do you have plans for this evening?' asks Simon once she's sent the message.

'It already is evening,' she says with a look at the dark street outside.

'I need to borrow you for a while. Just say yes or no.'

'Borrow me?' Emma slips her phone into her pocket. She doesn't usually like surprises, but perhaps he wants to make things right between them – invite her to dinner or something of that kind. Should she give him this chance?

30

They stroll through Södermalm, killing time until 8 p.m.

Night has fallen outside, and Emma feels like she's inside a snow globe with all the other people who are shopping, admiring glittering window displays and stopping in cosy cafés. A fairy-tale land.

Emma still doesn't know where they're going. Simon refuses to give anything away, and for a moment she considers packing it in and driving home. But she knows how that would end – with a battle against the bottle and another therapy session with Einstein. She might as well have fun elsewhere.

A while later, Simon stops at a crossing and gestures at the entrance to some sort of basement bar a little further on.

'That's it. I'm going in first and you follow in five minutes.'

'Why can't we go in together?' she asks, surprised and irritated at the same time.

'You'll see.' He holds up one hand, his fingers spread. 'Five minutes.'

Emma conveys her annoyance with a loud sigh. 'I only hope they have alcohol in there,' she says, without thinking. It's so easy to forget good intentions.

He aims for the basement bar, walking past a pizzeria, down some steps and finally vanishing through a door. Five minutes.

Emma checks the clock on her phone and finds that she's just received a message.

Mr Goal has replied on SugarDeLuxe.

Excitement floods her body. She opens the message with trembling fingers. Sure, we can meet and have some fun. How about champagne lunch tomorrow 1pm at the Riche?

Emma stares at the text. Tomorrow? Tomorrow is New Year's. Never mind. She can't miss this chance. She writes a reply: Love to. I will sit at the bar in a sequin dress.

She puts her phone away. Can she still fit into the dress? She'll figure it out. Now she must tell Simon about it. She rushes towards the basement door, clinging to the handrail as she climbs down the slippery steps. Once she has entered the place, she tries to get her bearings and figure out where she is. A group of people sit in a circle in the middle of the room. All are still and staring at her. What is this? Emma had expected a bar, maybe a restaurant. She's about to turn back around when she spots Simon on one of the chairs. He, too, is looking at her, but gives no indication of knowing her.

A woman clad in bright clothing and radiating a spiritual aura approaches her. Narrow shoulders, light step.

'Welcome. I can see you're new. Please take a seat – I'll fetch you a chair.'

'Er, no, thanks. I think I'm in the wrong place.'

'Don't be afraid.' The woman places a hand on Emma's shoulder. 'The first time is hard for everyone. Sit with us. You don't need to tell us anything if you don't want to. You can just listen.' The woman's eyes gleam with kindness, which has the opposite effect on Emma. She feels like running away.

What has Simon dragged her into? An AA meeting? What an asshole!

I don't drink any more, dammit!

She gives him a hard look but he stubbornly averts his gaze.

All right then, if that's how you want to play it.

Emma sits on the chair the woman has placed between a dark-skinned woman in her twenties with afro hair and a man around forty. The group comprises a colourful mix of eleven participants. There's a man with a comb-over in a suit, a haggard man with a goatee, a plain woman in a flowery dress, and a guy with a cap whose leg trembles uncontrollably. Old and young. But that's just what alcoholism is like – it can strike anyone. The woman in bright clothes appears to be the group leader. She opens the meeting after double-checking that it is 8 p.m. and that everyone is present, except for Lina, who is otherwise engaged today.

'I would like to welcome you two once more.' Her eyes move between Simon and Emma, who sit four chairs apart. 'Since you found us, you've probably read about our twelve steps. I would like to remind you all that confidentiality and anonymity form our spiritual foundation. Whatever is said in here remains confidential, and we all of us carry responsibility that nothing is shared outside this room. You may give your first name or make one up. My name is Charlotta.' She looks at Simon, who introduces himself with his real name, then at Emma, who also decides against an alias. Still, she does not intend to speak or come back.

'I will begin with an excerpt from the first book of Moses, chapter 19, verses 4–8.' Charlotta reads from a loose sheet of paper in her hand. 'But before they retired for the night, all the men of Sodom, young and old, came from all over the city and surrounded the house. They shouted to Lot, "Where are the men who came to spend the night with you? Bring them out to us so we can have sex with them!" So Lot stepped outside to talk to them, shutting the door behind him. "Please, my brothers," he begged, "don't do such a wicked thing. Look, I have two daughters who have never slept with a man. Let me bring them out to you, and you can do what you like with them. But don't do anything to these men, for they have come under the protection of my roof."'

When Charlotta falls silent, placing the sheet under her chair, Emma glances about. Tries to figure out what all this is about, but no one takes any notice of her. Most participants are staring into blank space, some of them listlessly, one of them wiping away tears.

Charlotta's tone sharpens. 'We all of us sitting here have experienced sexual abuse at home. What can we do to help one another?'

Emma fixes her eyes on Simon again. Sexual abuse. She feels like walking over to him and giving him a shove, and asking him what the hell he's playing at? But then it dawns on her that this isn't about her but about Jasmine. They spoke about it in the café earlier. Jasmine was a member of an ACA group entitled 'sexual abuse'. This must be the group. She listens to Charlotta with renewed interest and attention.

'If you want to give someone a gift for the moment, ease their pain. If you want to give them a gift for life, help them to confront and accept the pain.' Charlotta looks around the participants. 'Who wants to make a start?'

A rotund woman with grey hair raises her hand. Emma guesses her to be around sixty. Her hands are rough and wrinkled, and her teeth the yellowest Emma has ever seen. The woman's name is Tuja.

'I visited my brother last week like I said I would. But I couldn't bring myself to confront him. I just couldn't do it, and now it's probably too late.' She looks around the room, her expression suggesting that she is seeking encouragement, but no one says anything.

Is that how the group works? No one butts in or gets involved.

Instead, Tuja introspects, placing her hands in her lap and twiddling her thumbs. 'The whole thing was probably my fault too. I never fought him, just let it happen. Again and again. And every time I thought, he must know that I don't want it. I mean,

203

why did he want it? We were siblings. Who wants sex with their sister? I don't get it.' She tries to hold in a sob with the back of her hand, pulls out a tissue and wipes tears from her eyes while several group members nod sympathetically.

Emma lowers her gaze and stares at her dirt- and salt-stained trainers. What am I doing here? By what right am I voyeuristically partaking in these people's honest revelations and traumas? She studies their faces. The guy with the cap stares straight ahead, while a man with glasses rocks his body back and forth. All of them carry heavy burdens of grief, guilt and shame, etched into their DNA.

Just like she does, because of the story with Oliver. The memory gives her a pang to the chest, and she dispels the pain by focusing on what is being said in the room.

The man with glasses speaks next. He can't bring himself to visit the grave of his sister because he failed to protect her from their father's sexual assaults. When he is finished, the woman with the afro lifts her hand. She always wakes up at midnight, the time her grandfather used to enter her room whenever her parents were away and the grandparents looked after her. She leaves it at that, and next in line is the man with the cap. He does not wish to say anything today, and the others in the room nod respectfully. Instead, a man with an athletic build takes heart and clears his throat. He is thinking about taking his own life or killing the man who raped him – his athletics coach. But he is struggling to make up his mind.

Emma begins to feel ill at ease and she hopes the meeting will soon be over. But then another person lifts their hand.

Simon.

He hunches over on his chair, closes his eyes and begins to speak haltingly. 'I was seven years old the first time it happened. My father took me in the car, saying he wanted me to accompany him for something special. I thought we were going to buy a puppy – I had wished for one for a long while. Instead, he took me to a villa full of men. They were friends, he told me, and he would be having lunch with them. I was asked to wait in a bedroom. Then one man after the other came to me and . . .' His voice breaks. He rests his forehead on his folded hands. 'I had to do things with them I didn't understand then. But today . . .' He looks up, his eyes filled with tears, his breathing heavy. 'When we drove home, he said this was our secret. I remember the feeling well, the chaos of emotions. Everything seemed wrong, but at the same time I was so proud. Papa and I had a secret.'

Emma feels a rushing in her head, and it takes her a while to realize that the others have stood up. Charlotta declares the meeting closed, but anyone who wishes may stay and drink coffee. Tuja has swapped chairs, now sitting next to Simon and silently placing a hand on his shoulder.

With wobbly knees, Emma walks to a table at the room's long side and waits until the young woman with the afro pours coffee from a flask for herself.

'How did you find the meeting?' she asks, glancing at Emma while filling her cup.

'I'm not sure.'

'You never get used to it. It's just a matter of taking the plunge and facing your demons.' The woman smiles. 'Would you like some?' Without waiting for a reply, she pours a cup for Emma. 'Help yourself to carrot cake. Ruben made it.'

'No thanks, I'm not hungry.'

'Then I will have your piece.' The woman winks at Emma, takes two pieces of cake and meanders to one of the standing tables.

Emma looks at Simon again, but he's still busy with Tuja. She sips on her coffee and considers driving home. But at the same time, she knows that Simon brought her here for a reason. They are here to fish for information about Jasmine – to find out what happened to her. Someone in this room might know something.

Hesitantly, she joins the woman with the afro, setting down her mug on the table.

'Your name is Jina, right?'

The woman tugs at the bottom edge of her jumper. 'Yes, that's what they call me. Beautiful name, isn't it?'

'It is.' Emma blows on her coffee. 'Well, there was this woman who told me about this group. I thought she'd be here tonight, but . . .' Her eyes scan the room. 'Perhaps she didn't feel like coming.'

'What's her name?'

'I don't know, but she's of Italian descent, with long dark hair.'

Jina narrows her eyes. 'Italian, you say? Pretty?'

Emma nods.

'There's only one woman who comes here matching that description.' Jina suddenly sounds harsh. 'How do you know her?'

'I don't really know her personally. We met in an online forum on the same subject as this group. I was too scared to come at first, but she promised she'd be here. Something must have come up.'

'How do you know what she looks like if you've only been in contact through a forum?'

Emma takes a sip of her coffee, squirming. 'She had a profile picture.'

'Are you a policewoman?'

The question takes her by surprise, but she replies truthfully: 'No. What makes you say that?'

'Because the woman you ask about has been murdered by her brother.' Jina's face hardens. 'It's probably best if you leave now. And don't ever come back. I'm going to tell the others that you were here to spy. Show some respect.' She turns on her heel, drops her slices of cake in a rubbish bin and disappears among a few other participants, who shortly thereafter turn to Emma, staring daggers at her.

With an apologetic expression, she goes to her chair, fetches her jacket from the backrest and rushes out of the room. Before she can pull the door shut, she hears someone call after her: 'How disrespectful! Disgusting.'

Emma agrees. But she didn't ask to come to this meeting – Simon tricked her.

Outside, the wind has picked up. Snowflakes swirl in Emma's face, and she shivers with cold. The pizzeria catches her eye, luring her with its warm smells. She enters the restaurant, orders a pizza cacciatore and mineral water at the counter, sits down at a free table and texts Simon to let him know where she is. Then she calls Angela, telling her about the ACA group and her suspicion that Jasmine was sexually abused.

'Jeepers!' Angela sounds stunned. 'Did they say who by?'

'No. Like I said, I was thrown out, but the group is about sexual abuse within the family.'

In the ensuing pause, Angela asks a man in the background to be quiet when he calls out for her to hurry up. Emma feels bad. Had she interrupted Angela during something? Perhaps the two of them are in the middle of some role play with ropes and handcuffs. She forces the involuntary thoughts aside when Angela continues to speak. 'This could be good for us. The person who abused her could also have a motive for killing her. You need to speak with Nicolas and ask him if he knows anything.'

'Okay.' Emma considers Angela's words. Her conclusion might be rash, but then again she might be right. Maybe Jasmine had begun talking about the abuse and someone had silenced her. They agree that Emma will visit Nicolas in the morning. Angela can't come because she has to be present at another client's questioning.

They finish their conversation when Emma's pizza arrives. In the middle of her meal, Simon arrives. He sits down opposite her and shakes his head.

'You caused a mighty stir in there. You should have heard the noise when people realized – when people thought they realized – you were police. The dark-skinned woman wanted to report you, and someone else wanted to call a friend at the *Aftonbladet*. Another woman stood around crying. I can tell you, I only got out by the skin of my teeth.'

'Yes, you put on a right show down there.'

Something dies in Simon's eyes. He stares at the menu that is hanging on the wall behind the pizza bakers, his face stony.

'Or . . . was that . . .' Emma puts down the cutlery and dabs her mouth with the napkin. 'Did that really happen?'

Simon turns his face to her and looks serious, but after a while his expression lightens and he starts to grin. 'Did I tell you that I wanted to become an actor before I applied to police college?'

Emma bundles up the napkin and throws it at him. 'That is not okay, especially not in front of those people.'

'Perhaps not. But I had to lay it on thick to appear believable.'

'Did you learn anything? Did anyone say anything about Jasmine?'

'Nothing that helps us. But unlike you, I am taking things slowly.'

Emma eats another forkful of pizza. 'Maybe I wasn't as prepared as you.'

Simon smiles. 'I'm sorry. But still – it was a little bit funny.'

Emma swallows and smiles back. 'About as funny as your reaction when I tell you what I'm about to say. I have a date with Mr Goal at 1 p.m. at the Riche tomorrow.'

'You're kidding!'

'Not at all. Are you with me or do I have to pull this off by myself?'

'Hang on.' Simon reaches for her can of mineral water and opens it. 'Are you saying he replied to you and you're actually planning to go?'

'Definitely. Hey, that's my drink.'

Ignoring her rebuke, he mutters in between sips: 'Emma Tapper. You will be the death of me.'

31

In the interview room of the remand prison, Emma sits down opposite Nicolas. His violently trembling legs make the table vibrate. He sweats, looks pale and his eyelids sag like wet teabags.

'We need to talk.' Emma gets straight to the point, wants to see how he reacts. 'Jasmine was a member of an ACA group about sexual abuse within the family. Why?'

Nicolas withdraws into himself, where – presumably – thoughts and emotions rage in chaos.

'This is about your life. I'm trying to save you from a conviction for murder. If you know anything, you need to tell me urgently. What happened to Jasmine?'

'Where is Angela?' Clearly, he's trying to play for time.

'She's busy with another client,' Emma replies truthfully, although it doesn't seem fair to Nicolas. But neither does she want to lie. 'Tell me about Jasmine,' she asks again.

Nicolas snorts. 'She had a sugar daddy. You should be taking a closer look at him.'

'The police already have. But as I said, this support group is designated for people who were exposed to sexual abuse in some form within their own family. And if Jasmine was in therapy as an adult for something like that, I suspect that you know something. Who are you protecting?'

A tougher version of Nicolas emerges. 'It's New Year's. Don't you have anything better to do?'

'No.' Emma is surprised at his new self. Doesn't he give a damn about what happened to his sister? Suddenly she shudders. What if— She finds it difficult to finish the thought but forces herself to. What if Nicolas was the one who abused Jasmine sexually? Tuja described a similar situation last night. Her brother slept with her and she could never bring herself to fight him.

Were Nicolas and Jasmine having sex?

In the back of her mind, Emma's thoughts circle around the results of the paternity test they are waiting for. What if Nicolas is the father? That would have given him a motive for killing her. A rather powerful motive.

'I'd like to talk some more about Andreas Kilic, the stalker.' Emma's voice sounds less confident now. 'You really have no idea who he is?'

Nicolas replies with a shake of his head and a smacking sound. Irritating.

'I've received information that suggests Jasmine might have been lying with regard to Kilic. She'd probably known him for longer. Why, do you think, would she lie in this matter?'

A shrug for an answer.

Emma braces her elbows on the table, glares at him and fills her voice with as much confidence as she can muster. 'All the evidence points to you as the murderer and still you are keeping something from me.'

No reaction.

She had to make him talk. But how can you get someone to talk about a sexual assault they might have committed themselves? She doesn't want to make allegations, but . . . Then she remembers something – Nicolas's fear for his younger brother. What is it founded on?

'Douglas. Why are you so concerned for him?'

'Jasmine is dead and I stand accused of her murder. The fact that I worry about how he's doing shouldn't come as a surprise.' Nicolas again withdraws into himself, and this time not only his legs tremble but his entire body.

'How are you doing?' Emma asks herself whether she has gone too far. At the same time, she feels she's getting close to something – she has doubtless hit a nerve. 'Is there anything going on in your family that . . .' She searches for the right words. How do you ask such a question? 'Is Douglas in any danger of getting sexually ab—'

'No!' Nicolas jumps up from his chair, gasping for breath and looking about as if he doesn't know which way is up.

Emma eyes the door and is about to shout for the guard when Nicolas walks around the table and grabs her arm.

'I need something badly. Please. You need to get me something. I can't take it any longer.'

Emma decides to hold still, breathing as calmly as she can. There is despair in Nicolas's eyes, and desperate people are capable of anything if they don't get their way. 'What are you talking about?' she asks, even though she knows what he means.

'Cocaine. Speed. I don't care what. Please. You have to get me something.'

'Me?' Emma frees herself from his grasp, feeling somewhat irritated by his demand. Sure, there are lawyers who provide their clients with this or that, but what makes him think she would do something like that?

'I'm afraid I can't.' Emma relaxes a little when the door opens and a guard looks inside.

'Everything all right in here?'

Emma nods and asks him to take Nicolas back to his cell since their conversation is finished. The guard doesn't seem convinced, and she can see why. Nicolas is towering over her, his jaws and fists clenched. But the man does as she asks, and when he disappears into the corridor with Nicolas, she buries her face in her hands and breathes deeply, feeling annoyed at herself for ruining yet another interview.

She was so close and still knows nothing, except that Jasmine could have been sexually abused by someone in her family and that Nicolas is deeply worried about Douglas. The whole thing stinks, and she is determined to get to the bottom of it. But first she needs to go home and get dolled up as a sugar baby – her date with Mr Goal awaits.

32

When Emma approaches the bar at the restaurant Riche in her sequinned dress, she feels like a disco ball. The dress sits more loosely than she expected. Apparently, nearly a year of emotional darkness with whiskey, anxiety and depression has been good for her weight. Sure, vegetating on the couch has also caused her skin to slacken and her muscles to dwindle, but nothing that couldn't soon be fixed with a little exercise. In the meantime, her tall stiletto heels help with her calves.

She orders a bourbon even though she doesn't want to drink alcohol under any circumstances. But it would seem strange if she sat without a drink on New Year's Eve. Around her, the lunch crowd mingle in elegant dress – suits, cocktail dresses, little black numbers. Everyone in the room radiates upper crust and festive mood.

Is one of them Mr Goal?

She glances at Simon, who is sitting at the other end of the bar. After protesting initially, he agreed to come in support.

'I can hardly let you go there alone,' he'd said.

Emma suspects John Hellberg is on his back, and that he's afraid of getting into trouble. But now he's playing along with the blind date too, dressed elegantly in a tuxedo to blend in with all the dandies and spruced-up bimbos toasting with champagne and greeting one another with kisses on the cheek.

How can all these people bear it?

Emma thanks the young barman when he serves her the glass of whiskey. She closes her eyes and inhales, her body instinctively responding to the burning, sweet smell, her brain screaming out to drain the contents in one gulp. But she only ordered the drink as a prop. She can easily imagine that Nicolas feels similarly – this desperate longing for something that eases the loneliness and pain. She wonders what triggered his drug abuse, turning a former pro-fessional football player into a gambler and a junkie. Since the last interview, she's been thinking a lot about how she could win his trust. Perhaps the easiest way would be by granting his wish and giving him what he wants, something she can't do without either – drugs. She can see now that she is an alcoholic, that she seriously needs to quit drinking. But today she has to play her role as a sugar baby. She smiles at herself, moistening her lips with whiskey. I am a sugar baby. Come on, Mr Goal, buy me an apartment and new fingernails, then you can shag me as much as you like.

Just ridiculous.

She glances at Simon – a second too late to realize that he is trying to warn her about something.

'Kissing Butterfly?' The speaker has chosen an intonation that is supposed to sound seductive.

Emma turns around, conscious of the subtle scent of eau de cologne. Blinks a few times before she realizes who the man is standing behind her, and how she knows him. The grey, trimmed beard, the hazel eyes, gleaming differently now than they did at their previous encounter.

Giorgio Moretti. Jasmine and Nicolas's father.

His smile dies abruptly. They stare at each other for a while before he utters from between clenched teeth: 'What is this?'

'A date,' Emma replies as calmly and firmly as she can. 'I wanted to know who Mr Goal is and now I do.'

Giorgio's chest rises under his suit jacket and white shirt. 'What are you talking about?'

'Kissing Butterfly.'

'This is a mistake.' He turns to leave, but Simon blocks his way.

'If you wish to make a scene, please, be my guest. If not, sit down and act as if we're having a splendid conversation.'

One of Giorgio's eyes twitches, accentuating his fine wrinkles. He looks about, seemingly debating with himself what sort of impression a scuffle would make on the other guests. Eventually, he sits down beside Emma.

Simon sits on the other side of him and leans on the bar so he can better see Giorgio's face. 'We know you are Mr Goal and that you had a date with a sugar baby named Sunflower the day before Christmas Eve at the Radisson Hotel. We have the evidence on Jasmine's computer, so don't try to deny it.'

Giorgio stares at the countertop. 'That was a mistake.'

'That too?' asks Emma.

'Jasmine tricked me into coming. She wanted to confront me and find out if I meet women that way.'

'Why didn't she simply call you?'

'I asked her the same question, but she reckoned she wanted to catch me in the act. And she was right – my clever daughter was right – I never would have admitted to it otherwise.'

Emma and Simon exchange a glance across Giorgio's hung head. Simon looks as though he doesn't believe the man's words either.

Simon takes over. 'Were you aware that Jasmine allowed herself to be kept as a sugar baby?'

'No, but I suspected as much following our encounter at the Radisson. How else would she have found me on the platform if she wasn't using it herself? But I didn't ask her, and now it's too late.'

'How did she know you were Mr Goal? You don't have a profile picture.'

Giorgio loosens his bow tie. 'She said she recognized me by certain details I mentioned in my description. And then she saw a picture of my Tesla I'd uploaded. Apparently, part of my house was visible in the background.'

Emma plays with her glass. A picture of his Tesla. Are the kind of girls engaging with such platforms impressed by fancy cars?

'And what happened when you met at the hotel?' she asks.

'I already told you. She wanted to confront me.'

'It's just that it sounds a little strange. Like we said, she herself profited from such an arrangement. She couldn't have been completely opposed to it.'

'How should I know.' Giorgio loosens his tie even more, as if he were struggling to breathe. 'She probably thought I shouldn't be doing such a thing because I'm married. But all I can say is that Vera and I have an open relationship. We allow each other certain liberties.'

'What exactly do you mean?'

'You know exactly what I mean. And now I don't feel like discussing this any longer.' Giorgio makes to stand up, but Simon places a hand on his arm.

'Hold on, just a few more questions. How did the conversation at the Radisson go? Did you argue or did you get on well?'

Giorgio gives Simon an intent look. 'Am I being accused of something?'

'No, not at all. We are merely investigating the murder of your daughter, and I would like to understand what motive your son might have had for killing his sister.'

'You'll have to ask him that.' Giorgio rises from his seat and puts on a smile. 'Right, I'm leaving now, and if you have a problem with that you'll have to arrest me.' He nods at them, turns on his heel and pushes through the crowd towards the exit.

'I don't get it,' says Emma when she has recovered sufficiently to remember her untouched whiskey.

'Giorgio Moretti met his own daughter on a blind date,' says Simon. 'That much I understand. And in hindsight it makes perfect sense that he's called Mr Goal – a football coach.'

'And apparently he's bloody good at scoring,' says Emma with a grin, realizing in the same moment that she hasn't entirely lost her police humour. 'But it can't be right that Jasmine wanted to confront him on account of cheating on Vera. She wasn't in contact with her parents much, they didn't celebrate Christmas together, and they didn't even know that Jasmine owned a parrot. Why would Jasmine give a damn? Besides, I saw a pink flamingo in Giorgio and Vera's garden.'

Simon looks at her blankly.

'Swingers,' she explains. 'Couples who are open to sex with other couples display this through flamingos. And it matches what he told us – that he and Vera have an open relationship.'

'I own a pair of swimming shorts with pink flamingos.'

Emma suppresses a laugh. Images she would rather not see form in her mind's eye. 'Okay, not everyone knows that, but Jasmine most definitely did. That's why I don't believe for one moment that she wanted to appeal to her father's conscience for straying. Trust me – something is up in that family.'

'I share that feeling.'

Emma waves at the barman and asks for the bill.

'Already?' asks Simon, and for some reason the disappointment in his voice feels good to Emma.

'Yes. Because we need to go to the Radisson.'

33

Emma stamps the snow off her shoes before she and Simon enter the hotel. She'd swapped her heels for a pair of boots, otherwise they would have had to take the underground.

The Radisson is notably quieter than the Riche. Just a handful of guests with suitcases checking in at reception, and a few small groups sitting in the armchairs in the lobby, talking. Emma and Simon walk up to the deserted bar, where Simon flashes his warrant card at the Barbie-like young woman on the other side. He explains the reason for their visit – that they want to speak with anyone who might have seen Giorgio and Jasmine Moretti the day before Christmas Eve.

'I was working that day.' The young woman taps herself on the chest. 'And I was truly shocked when I saw in the news that she had been murdered.'

'So you recognized her?' Emma feels relieved as well as astonished that they've hit the bullseye first go. 'Countless people come and go here, don't they?'

'Yes, but she stood out from the crowd, all dolled up. I have an eye for these things. I've been working here for a while, after all. I've seen many women sitting around and waiting. At some point a man shows up and they disappear to a room that he pays for.' She laughs, looking proud of her powers of observation. Then she goes on: 'But she seemed nervous. That's not uncommon, but with her it was extreme. She looked as if she were on the verge of passing out, and I asked her if she wanted a glass of water. And then the man she was meeting turned up. It was strange, somehow – instead of saying hello and going through the usual introductions, it seemed they already knew each other.'

'Did you hear what they said?'

'No, I was standing here and they were sitting over there.' She nods at some sofas in the corner. 'But I got that he was angry, that they were arguing about something. The only thing I caught was that they were talking about someone called Douglas.'

'What were they saying about him?' asks Emma.

'I'm not sure. It was as he was leaving, she called something after him. Something like "Don't you dare do that to Douglas!"'

Once they are satisfied that the young woman has told them everything she knows, Emma and Simon shift to a table by the window, where some waning daylight finds its way in from the slush-covered street outside.

'Something's up with Douglas,' says Emma, sitting in one of the armchairs. She tells Simon that Nicolas is worried about his younger brother and that he flared up when she asked him about it.

'Don't make assumptions,' says Simon. 'Jasmine was probably abused, but we don't know who by. It wasn't necessarily someone from her immediate family – it could have been a teacher or a neighbour.'

'But Nicolas knows something – I could tell. And now that Giorgio turned up . . .' She shakes her head. 'I need to speak with him again.'

'With Giorgio?'

'No, with Nicolas.' She checks the time. 'I'll go from here, it's not far. Why don't you take a closer look at Giorgio in the meantime, see if you can find anything of interest.'

'Do you really believe he—?'

'I don't believe anything. But I want to know why he had a date with his own daughter. The story he tried to sell us at the bar was nothing but nonsense.'

Simon rolls his eyes. 'Okay, it's only New Year's Eve, after all. Who would have other plans?'

34

Nicolas visibly raises his eyebrows when he sees Emma waiting for him in the interview room once again. And just a few hours after her last visit.

'Are you on your way to a New Year's party?' he asks, taking the same chair as last time.

Emma looks down at the sequinned dress shimmering through the unbuttoned coat with the zebra pattern she had borrowed from Ester.

'No. I've been playing sugar baby, and that's why I'm back.' She waits for a reaction, but when there is none she tries again. 'I arranged a date with a sugar daddy, and guess who showed up? Giorgio. Your father.'

Nicolas says nothing.

Emma raises her voice. 'Do you understand what I'm telling you? Jasmine met with Giorgio on a date. According to him, she lured him there to confront him about his lifestyle. But I don't believe him. I believe it was about something else.'

Nicolas sits perfectly upright and stock-still on his chair. Emma can't even tell that he's breathing.

'Say something. You must have some sort of opinion about the fact that your father meets women online and pays them money. And that he met with Jasmine. Did you know about that or is this news to you?' She waits for a reply. How is he handling this information? How does he process it, sort it, file it in his mind? She folds her hands on her stomach and changes tack.

'A young woman who saw them together claims they were arguing about Douglas. Do you know why?'

'No. What were they saying?'

Finally, a reaction. A physical one, even – his eyes flicker, there is sweat on his forehead. Emma is more convinced than ever that Nicolas is keeping something from them with regard to Douglas. But why? What had happened that he would rather keep mum than save himself from a life sentence in prison for murder?

'He's your younger brother. If he's in trouble, you need to tell me.'

Nicolas stares at her, his face devoid of any expression. Perhaps she's wrong; perhaps she's read too many stories about paedophiles. The topic isn't as taboo as it used to be. More and more often, headlines appear in the media about some celebrity or other who was abused as a child. But that doesn't mean that this is the case here. She doesn't press the point, instead asking him questions about Giorgio – about his open relationship with Vera, and what Jasmine might have wanted from him on their blind date. But Nicolas merely scratches his arms and grinds his jaw from side to side – typical withdrawal symptoms.

Emma packs up and walks to the door. Only then does Nicolas open his mouth. 'Have you thought about what I asked you earlier?'

Emma stops and looks at him over her shoulder. She'd hoped he'd forgotten. At the same time, she knows how it goes. The brain never forgets a missed high.

'You know I can't.' She takes a few steps back. 'But if I were to get you something – what do I get in return?'

Renewed energy flares up in his eyes, the longing for what she is offering, the hope that he might soon receive what he craves. 'What do you want from me?'

223

'I want you to come clean with us. I can feel that you're keeping something back. Since I work for your lawyer, everything you say stays between us. Just so you know.' She studies him with an increasingly bad conscience. How can she make promises to him she already knows she can't keep? She has no contacts in that scene. But next time she sees him she can tell him she has something lined up, that it's just a matter of days. Maybe then he would . . .

'Do we have a deal?' she asks, placing one hand on the door handle. She doesn't know how to interpret his answer. It is a shrug.

35

'Why doesn't he even try to defend himself?' asks Emma when she meets Simon about half an hour later outside the police station in Solna. 'He just sits there and doesn't make a peep. The only time he showed any reaction was when I told him that Giorgio and Jasmine argued because of Douglas.'

'Well, perhaps that's simply because he actually did what he's accused of.'

Emma stamps snow off her boots and pulls up her collar as they cross a street that is gritted with salt. The sun has disappeared and cold creeps into her every bone. 'But why should he want to kill Jasmine?'

'That's what I'd like to know.'

'But I really don't think it was him.'

Simon smiles. 'You only say that because he's your boss's client. Angela's turned your head. Where have your police instincts gone?'

She decides against commenting, resolving instead that she's going to prove she's right. Nicolas is innocent. She repeats those words in her mind over and over as they walk towards the Solna Centrum underground station. Nicolas is innocent. Nicolas is innocent. At the same time, worry about the paternity test gnaws at her. Doubt has crept into her mind – doubt that the police and the prosecution ought to cultivate. They are the ones who should be asking themselves if the right person is being remanded in custody, with all the new suspects she and Angela have presented them with and with all the dirt that has come to the surface thanks to her investigations. Instead, she is the one doubting Nicolas.

'May I ask what measures you and your colleagues are taking to ensure you are leading this investigation objectively?' asks Emma. 'Are you truly open to the possibility that someone other than Nicolas slit Jasmine's throat when you collect evidence and question witnesses and so on?'

'I can only answer for myself. I honestly try, but in view of the overwhelming evidence, combined with his behaviour during the night of the murder, it's like claiming the Earth isn't a sphere.'

Emma is tempted to mention the post-mortem report, which states that the murderer held the knife in their left hand. She would like to remind Simon that Nicolas is right-handed, but for some reason she remains silent. It's bad enough that she admitted snooping around in his office. He doesn't need to know that she actually found something useful.

'Let's talk about Giorgio,' she says instead, curious as to whether Simon learned anything. On the way here, she had spoken with Angela. Her boss had been thrilled to hear about the blind date – especially when she heard who showed up.

'You need to keep digging,' she'd said. 'The more irregularities and wrongdoings we can find among the Morettis, the more doubts we'll raise in the jury.'

'As you know, Giorgio doesn't have any prior convictions,' says Simon, startling her from her thoughts. 'But I googled him and checked him out on social media.' Simon fishes his phone from his pocket and taps the screen. 'I didn't really find anything in particular, but bearing in mind all that we've learned, several things stand out. Take a look.' He hands her the phone and Emma sees that he is on Giorgio's Facebook profile. When snowflakes land on the screen, she seeks shelter beneath the awning of a building, scrolling down the posts. Below one photo, taken outside a public swimming pool on the Bosön peninsula, Giorgio writes that he visited with Douglas. Another image shows Giorgio wearing a tracksuit, one arm placed around the shoulders of a young footballer. Several postings are about driving boys from his team home after training.

'He's got a heap of boy pics.'

'I know,' says Simon. 'Even normal things suddenly appear damn suspicious.'

Emma scrolls on. A common theme seems to connect his postings – Giorgio with boys. Always in the combination trainer/player, of course, but still. There are hardly any photos showing Giorgio with other adults, the few exceptions having to do with business occasions.

Emma follows a link Giorgio shared to an article about a cup match. She skims through it and tells Simon: 'Giorgio has organized a cup match taking place in Spånga tomorrow.'

'I saw that.'

'The tournament is aimed at football-crazy youths who don't belong to a club. Listen.' She lifts one index finger. 'There are children and adolescents who don't have any plans at weekends – who may not be able to celebrate Christmas and New Year's. To them, football offers a welcome diversion.'

'At least you can't complain about his lack of community involvement.'

Emma looks at him. 'Ugh, yuck, I shudder at the thought. What if that was why Jasmine confronted him? "Don't you dare do that to Douglas!" she told him.'

'Don't forgot that this is pure speculation.'

'That Giorgio is a paedophile, you mean?'

'Your words.'

'Why has no other adult spoken up? His Facebook friends, for example. He has many. And all those parents who've been allowing him to drive their children home.'

'Because people don't think like that right away. And that's good. Most youth coaches are all right. But we're sitting on some quite different information.'

'And what are we going to do with it?'

Simon shrugs. 'Firstly, we don't know if it's true. And if it were true, we still don't know if it had any connection to Jasmine's death.'

'Does it matter?'

'I'm investigating a murder. Hellberg would never allow me to pursue this other story. Without solid evidence, we can't charge Giorgio.'

Emma snorts and hands the phone back to Simon. 'Now you sound like those parents who close their eyes to the facts.'

'I'm not saying I don't care. But I don't have the time to—'

'Whatever.' Emma waves one hand dismissively and hurries on towards Solna Centrum. She can't bear to listen to such nonsense any longer. Hellberg this, Hellberg that. What if everyone cowered before that man? What would the world look like then?

'You do realize why Hellberg took the young policewoman into his office? Certainly not to show her some photographs.'

'What have you got against him this time?' calls Simon after her, gasping. 'You were the one who used me to get your hands on information about the investigation.'

'Sure, you're right. But I've had some experiences with Hellberg you don't know about. Perhaps before you defend him you ought to know that one time he held me down on the bonnet of a patrol car. When I refused to let him touch me, he became furious. The rejection hurt his pride so much that he threatened to spread rumours about what a slut I was.' Emma walks faster, maybe to evade Simon's look of suspicion, or maybe to escape from herself.

She doesn't mind which of these two reasons applies – so long as she said it.

'Wait!' Simon calls out, and he pulls her by the arm. 'Are you serious?'

'No, of course not. I just made it up because I have a vivid imagination. And also I'm a hysterical psycho, just like all women who report such incidents. Or else a boring spoilsport. I can well imagine Hellberg still saying such things about me today.' She pulls herself free and carries on towards the underground.

'Hold on, wait. We can talk about this. What are you doing tonight? Are you going to a New Year's party?'

'No, I am going to look for solid evidence.'

This time he doesn't follow her. Emma isn't certain whether to feel pleased or not. She only knows it feels good to have spoken out. Liberating. Simon may not believe her, but perhaps she has sown a seed of doubt in him, something that will grow until one day he realizes what kind of man the boss he looks up to truly is.

36

Back at home, Emma pulls off her boots and fetches a bottle of whiskey from the pantry. An adamant voice in the back of her head warns her not to touch the stuff, but it's New Year's. If she really sets her mind to it, she can control her alcohol consumption. She pours herself a glass, shaking the last few drops from the bottle and cursing the pathetic amount, scarcely covering the bottom of the glass. She rummages through the cupboard, pulling aside flour, rolled oats and a whole bunch of other bags and packages, but can't find another bottle. With a twinge of panic, she empties the glass and checks the fridge. There should still be a few bottles of bubbly, including one that Ester gave her as a gift. Her sister had wanted to celebrate her six hundred thousandth follower on Instagram.

She finds one bottle of cava, one of Prosecco, and a few bottles of beer. She decides on the latter and opens one just as the beeping of her phone announces receipt of a text message. Ester. She invites Emma to join her at 'the most wicked party with a bunch of awesome people'. Kissing emoji, red heart, red heart. Emma takes a sip of her beer, swipes the message away and is about to put down her phone when she changes her mind. There's one thing she's been wanting to do since speaking with Nicolas this morning. She opens Facebook Messenger, types *Douglas Moretti* in the search field and checks the profiles until she finds his picture. He is wearing a blue striped football jersey. Then she composes a message.

I spoke with Nicolas today. He asked me to wish you a happy new year. Best wishes, Emma (Köhler Lawyers)

Her finger hovers above the 'send' symbol, hesitating. Is this inappropriate in any way? Probably. But she desperately needs to get in touch with Douglas, and so she sends the message and fetches another beer. Before she can open the bottle, she receives a reply.

Okay. How is Pelle?

Pelle? she replies with a question mark. What Pelle?

Three dots move in Douglas's reply field, and Emma keeps her eyes on them until the reply comes through.

Jasmine's parrot.

Emma stares at the message. So, Douglas knew that his sister owned a parrot after all. In front of his parents, he had acted as if he had no idea.

She paces slowly up and down the room, wondering what this means. Did he write this message because he's worried about the parrot, or because he's trying to tell her that he secretly met up with Jasmine? But why wouldn't he want his parents to know?

She writes back: I see. I call him Einstein. He's doing fine. How about you?

She can hear loud music and cheerful voices from the apartment next door. She glances out of her balcony door. Two young women stand smoking on the neighbouring balcony, taking a break from the hustle and bustle inside.

When Douglas's reply comes through, she closes the door. I feel like shit. Trying to block everything out with Fortnite.

Way to celebrate the new year, she'd like to write, but who is she to judge how he spends New Year's Eve? She looks in the mirror on the wall behind the sofa and raises her bottle to herself.

'Happy New Year, Emma. I'm glad you could make it. Wow, you look so fit. Thanks, I've been working out lately.' She smiles at her reflection, brings the bottle to her mouth and cuts her lip on the lid, which is still on.

Oh, that's right. She fetches the bottle opener from the kitchen and pauses by the birdcage, holding her face close to it.

'I'm not lonely at all, am I? I've got you. Happy New Year, Pelle. No, Pelle doesn't suit you. You're an Einstein. Then why don't you tell me what happened when your owner got killed? Pretty please.'

The parrot stares at her, and Emma stares back.

Power play.

Damn bird! You aren't going to help me.

She fills a bowl with crisps and lies on the couch to watch the fifth episode from the first season of *How to Get Away with Murder*.

Perhaps she might learn something from the series. What would the main character, defence attorney Annalise Keating, have done to achieve Nicolas's acquittal? Emma likes Annalise. The way the woman squashes her opponents in court appeals to her. The attorney would do anything to reach her goal. The expression 'to operate in the grey zone' comes to mind.

Emma binges one episode after another, until fireworks bang and crack outside her window and the sky is lit up vibrantly. She picks up the bottle of cava she opened earlier and which still has a little left in it, carries it to the balcony and inhales the fresh air. The party next door is cranking up. Men in tuxedos and women in dresses crowd on to the balcony, pushing from behind so that one guy half hangs across the railing. When he spots Emma, he raises his champagne glass to her and shouts over the noise: 'Happy New Year!'

Emma returns the toast.

'Are you on your own?'

232

She gestures affirmatively, whereupon he puts on an expression of concern.

'It's New Year's. You shouldn't be celebrating on your own.'

'I'm not celebrating. Besides, I have a parrot in here. He's enough for me.'

'A parrot? May I come over and chat with him?'

'What? No.'

'Then come over here. There are so many people here, one more or less won't matter.' He is pushed again and spills his champagne on the sleeve of his shirt. A woman inside the apartment yells: 'Let's get this party started! Come on! Whoop whoop!'

The crowd joins in with her shouts of joy and the people out on the balcony push back inside through the narrow door.

Emma too returns to her apartment. Not in a million years would she consider partying with those people. She picks up her phone when the screen lights up, indicating the arrival of a message. There are two, in fact – one from her mother and one from Simon. It hurts to find no message from Jens, but stuff him. She opens Simon's message.

Happy New Year! How much longer are we going to act as if nothing happened?

As she reads the text over and over, a growing sense of unease permeates the fringes of her drunkenness. Is Simon hinting at their last conversation? No, it must have something to do with their night at the pub. Something must have happened that shouldn't have.

Shit, shit, shit! That is precisely why she has to quit drinking. She refrains from answering and returns to the couch, but just as she reaches for the remote, the doorbell rings.

She has a hunch who it might be and is tempted to shout 'Buzz off!' The guy from the balcony. But then she remembers what the woman had shouted: 'Let's get this party started.'

She walks to the hallway, opens up and finds herself looking at the man, his face oozing confidence.

'I thought you might have changed your mind,' he says. There are dimples around his mouth when he smiles.

Emma puts on the most seductive smile she can muster in her alcoholized state and brings her face up close to his. 'Depends what you have on offer.'

'Ah, that's how the wind blows. What does my lady desire?'

'A little extra fun.' Emma smiles as a voice of warning echoes through her mind, asking her if she knows what she's getting herself into. But she might just have found a solution to the promise she made to Nicolas.

He takes her over to the party, where they squeeze past sweaty suits and skin-tight dresses. Arms and legs sway to the rhythm of the music on a Persian rug where the dining table had presumably been. Pointy heels twist and turn on the parquet flooring. One guy moves his hips back and forth suggestively as he dances towards her. Emma stops him with a gesture.

'Who the hell was that clown?' she asks her new friend, who on closer inspection turns out to be rather attractive. Friendly smile, sexy eyes. The dimples are the deciding factor, of course.

'No idea.' He leads her to a corner of the room where two blondes are leaning over a glass table, snorting lines of coke. A little off to the side stands a guy with gelled-back hair, and Dimples approaches him. Some banknotes and a small ziplock bag change hands.

Emma reminds herself that she is no longer a policewoman and that she set this transaction in motion. She's made up her mind – she cannot risk Nicolas's disappointment because then he might close off even more. That is why she has to get him what she promised.

Pangs of conscience with regard to her intentions churn in her stomach, along with the cava. She is planning to smuggle drugs into the remand prison, just like those black sheep among the defence lawyers she sometimes reads about in the paper. But she has to do it in order to progress in her investigation. And most of all, she has to do it for Douglas.

Dimples returns to her and hands her the ziplock bag together with a kiss. At first she only pretends to play along, but the more their tongues explore one another, the more she relaxes, pushing against him and running her hand through his wavy hair.

What is she doing? She twists herself out of his arms before this goes too far and heads for the bathroom, claiming she prefers to be alone while doing coke. Inside, she hides the bag in her bra, fixes her smudged eyeshadow and adds volume to her hair with some spray she finds in one of the cupboards. Not too bad.

Someone rattles on the door handle. She leaves the bathroom and is caught immediately by Dimples, who drags her to the make-shift dance floor.

And why not? Just for a few minutes.

They dance and drink champagne, then go outside on the balcony and talk to some other guests, of whom Emma only sees mouths with big red lips. On the sofa, a young woman sits with her dress hitched around her waist astride two legs wearing suit pants. Next to them, some guys bounce to the beat of the music as if they were on a trampoline.

Emma and Dimples twirl around the dance floor, laughing more exuberantly by the minute. At some point, she drinks from a glass she finds on a windowsill. They stagger through the apartment, groping each other and making out.

When Emma wakes up the next morning, she can't remember going to bed but figures out what must have happened.

Dimples is lying next to her, naked and on his back. Realization strikes her like a lightning bolt and she feels instantly sobered. Damn! She covers him, props herself up on her elbows and scans the room. The sequinned dress is lying in a pile on the floor, her shoes next to it, and her knickers hang from the door handle. Great. Suddenly she remembers something else – the cocaine. She slaps her palm to her forehead. How could she be so stupid?

She kneels beside the bed and peers under it. Finds her bra and a sock she's been missing for a while, but no ziplock bag. Increasingly nervous, she looks around until her eyes come to rest on the dresser next to the door and the glass bowl on top of it. She vaguely remembers poking around in the pebbles in that bowl. She walks over to it, sticks two fingers inside and fishes out the small bag, eyeing the white powder inside. She asks herself again how she could have been so stupid. She must get rid of the damn stuff as soon as possible.

Snoring sounds from the bed reach her ears. She buries the bag again and studies the white buttocks now facing her. High time she got rid of the guy. She glances at her kitchen clock through the doorway. Quarter to ten.

What time was the cup match at Spånga, the one organized by Giorgio Moretti? Eleven?

She walks back to the bed and nudges the sleeping prince.

'Hey, wake up!'

37

The noise level inside the Spånga gymnasium is high. The place is bustling with youths wearing football jerseys, with team captains and coaches as well as parents there to root for their teenagers. Emma wishes she had swallowed a couple of paracetamols before coming here. But with all the fuss of kicking out her nocturnal visitor, she hadn't thought of it. What was the guy's name again? Or rather, had he even mentioned his name? Doesn't matter. At least she got rid of him.

With a thumping headache, she meanders along the edge of two football pitches marked out with orange cones on the artificial turf, keeping an eye out for Giorgio and Douglas. She spots both after a few minutes. Giorgio is wearing a blue tracksuit top and is talking to the captains of the various teams. A little further along she finds Douglas, who is practising tricks with some friends, all of them wearing identical black jerseys. He still wears the bandage on his arm, but apparently it doesn't prevent him from playing.

She buys a coffee at the makeshift kiosk and positions herself next to a group of adults watching one of the matches. From here, she can see Giorgio as well as Douglas. She tries not to think of last night, but the truth is difficult to deny. She went to bed with some guy and can't remember anything. Perhaps she shouldn't give herself a hard time about it – she is single, after all, and doesn't have to justify herself to anyone. But she knows that's not the issue. The issue is that she has lost control.

I must quit drinking. I have a new job and responsibilities, new possibilities . . . what possibilities, to be exact? Is she finally going to sort out her life just because she has a task? Yes, she'd like to think so, at least. But if she wants to continue to work for Angela, she'll have to show her what she's capable of.

A few minutes later, Douglas's match kicks off. They are playing a team in green, and Emma watches Giorgio, how he asks his substitute players to get ready, how he speaks to them, pointing his finger, encouraging them.

Can it be true – is he in fact a paedophile?

A voice in the back of her mind reminds her of Simon's words: *Don't forget this is pure speculation.* Now, watching Giorgio on the other side of the field, she struggles to imagine him abusing children. A respected football coach who, in his spare time, organizes cup matches for disadvantaged youth.

At the same time, she knows that this is precisely how it goes. The power he holds over these adolescents. Who can play? Who can skip a match? Who will be allowed to attend try-outs for a higher team? Who will the talent scouts pick? What if there are some boys on the pitch here feeling sick to their stomach for fear of getting trapped alone in the changing room with their coach?

Emma takes a long sip from her plastic cup. It is her goddam duty to find out what this man is up to, regardless of its relevance to Jasmine's murder.

While the match continues, Emma combs her phone with a sense of trepidation. She needs to check if she sent any messages during the night. To her relief, she finds there are none to Jens, only some Happy New Year messages to friends and family.

When the full-time whistle blows, she walks closer to the team with the black jerseys, keeping her eyes on Giorgio and Douglas.

Giorgio stops by a man wearing a camera around his neck and scribbling notes on a pad during their conversation. A journalist. Emma tosses her empty cup into a rubbish bin and watches as Douglas heads towards the kiosk. Keeping a watchful eye on Giorgio, she follows Douglas. The boy is about to squirt tomato sauce on a sausage inside a bread roll while pinning an open can of drink under his arm.

'Shall I hold that for you?' Emma nods at the can.

Douglas gives her a blank look, then after a moment he exclaims, 'Oh, it's you.'

Emma smiles. 'How was *Fortnite* last night?'

Despite the watchfulness in his hazel eyes, she senses the boy has built up a need to talk. 'I came second. But I nearly won.'

'Cool.' Emma reaches for the can, and after a moment's hesitation he allows her to take it. 'Is your arm any better?' She nods at the bandage. 'Is the graze healing as it should now?'

'Yes.'

'Glad to hear it. Not very nice for you, having to take antibiotics. Did you get dirt in the wound?'

'No, it just wouldn't heal.' He takes a bite of his sausage and glances at Giorgio and the journalist. 'What are you doing here?'

'My nephew is in one of the matches.' Emma is prepared for this question. 'And then I saw you and thought I'd say hi. Nicolas is awfully worried about you. Every time I see him, he talks about you.'

A smile scurries across Douglas's face but vanishes quickly. Emma considers giving in to Nicolas's demand and telling the boy that his big brother is innocent. But what if he isn't?

Emma feels bad for having doubts. But how can anyone be certain?

She decides against saying any such thing. If it turns out that Nicolas is putting on an act for them all, she doesn't want to be the one who lied to Douglas's face.

'Do you know why he worries about you?' she asks instead.

Something flashes in Douglas's eyes. Emma doesn't know what it is, but she senses that the subject touches him deeply.

'How should I know?' he replies.

'I thought perhaps you talked about something before the thing with Jasmine. Problems at school or at home, or something like that.'

Douglas snorts, holding out his hand for his can. 'Can I have my drink, please?'

'Sure.' She hands him the can. As he gulps a few mouthfuls, some boys from his team walk past and ask if he wants to hang out and play ball.

'Just one more thing,' Emma says before he disappears. 'Why can't your parents find out that you know about Jasmine's parrot?'

He gives her a puzzled look. Then he smiles faintly and walks after his mates.

'You can contact me any time if you want to talk,' she calls after him. 'We're connected on Messenger now.'

Uncertainty washes over her, and she asks herself once more if she is misreading the situation completely.

When she looks back for Giorgio, he has vanished. She rises on the balls of her feet, peering across the heads of the crowd, and spots him as he's about to leave the gym, one arm slung around the shoulders of a boy from his team. She rushes after him and turns the corner to the changing rooms. In the same moment, a door shuts further down the corridor. Is that where they went? Emma looks around and sees people coming and going through the entrance, parents sipping on coffee, teenagers tapping on their smartphones or eating chocolate balls, but no sign of Giorgio with a boy in a black jersey. She walks up to the door. The sign reads *Storeroom*. She holds one ear against the door, trying to hear what might be going on inside, but the buzz of voices from the changing rooms makes it impossible. Anger and frustration grapple with reason. Part of her wants to burst into the room and interrupt whatever is going on inside, while the other part is screaming at her to wait. What if she's mistaken? She positions herself in front of a noticeboard, pretending to read the messages as she waits for what feels like an eternity. Several times she has to stop herself from tearing open the door. Four or five minutes later they emerge, and the boy shuffles off towards the gym. Giorgio pauses outside the door, straightens up, raises his hands over his head and stretches his upper body.

What on earth had he been doing in there?

Emma's eyes return to the boy and register that the jersey is untucked at the back. Surely it was tucked in earlier, wasn't it?

38

In the waiting room of the Lidingö medical centre, people sit scattered across the chairs. Some are engrossed in newspapers while others fiddle around on their phones or try to keep an eye on their children, who are clambering on the furniture. Whenever a beep sounds, everyone casts a glance at the queue number display.

Emma and Simon are sitting on a sofa together, waiting for Martin Lund to spare them a few minutes. He is the doctor who treated Douglas's arm and prescribed the antibiotics. They tried their luck at this medical centre since it's the closest to the Morettis' home, and the man at reception helped them without hesitation once Simon flashed his warrant card. That's the reason Emma had asked Simon to accompany her – she wanted to avoid using her own invalid card and risk adding another charge to her list. She would have preferred to come alone otherwise. With regard to Simon, everything feels weird since he sent her that message on New Year's Eve. *How much longer are we going to act as if nothing happened?*

The implication of these words runs between them like viscous oil. He hasn't mentioned anything so far.

Nor has she. Instead, she told him about the football tournament yesterday and how Giorgio vanished inside a storeroom for several minutes with a boy from his team.

'A few minutes is all it takes,' Simon replied, but he soon turned serious when he realized that his joke had fallen on deaf ears. Yes, Emma is used to police humour, but just the thought that Giorgio Moretti sexually assaulted a teenager while she stood outside the door and did nothing made her feel so ill at ease that she hadn't even managed to drink the entire bottle of Prosecco last night. Although that might also have had something to do with her sense of failure at drinking again, and with her fear because of her blackout with that guy from the New Year's party. This fear still envelops her like an invisible blanket, making her sweat profusely even though she has taken off her jacket and draped it across her legs. She is clutching the jacket as hard as she can, telling herself to hang in there. Just a brief conversation with the doctor and then she can hop in her car, drive to the booze store and stock up on the only thing that can ease her pain.

Ten minutes later, they follow Martin Lund to an exam room. The man strikes Emma as more of a hipster with his own backyard brewery than a doctor. That's probably because of the tattooed forearms she glimpses under the white sleeves, and the man bun. He sits down on an office chair behind his desk and leans back, tapping the tips of his fingers together rhythmically.

'I am told you want to talk about Douglas Moretti. I hope nothing's happened to him?'

'Why would you ask that?' asks Emma.

Martin Lund's bearded face pulls a grimace of resignation. 'If the police want to speak to me about one of my patients, I assume it's not about a trifle. And I've been worried about Douglas for a while. So, if you tell me what you know, I will tell you what I know.'

Emma has to hand it to him – he gets straight to the point. No palaver about doctor–patient confidentiality or the like. Emma likes him already, even if he does look like a hipster.

243

'We have reason to believe he may suffer abuse at home,' she says. 'We have no proof, only some indications. That's why we want to ask you about the wound on his arm. He claims it's a graze that doesn't want to heal.'

'A graze.' Martin Lund shakes his head. 'That's not correct. It's a burn that, in my opinion, he inflicted on himself with a candle, a lighter or something similar. Since then, he has burned himself repeatedly. It's a form of self-harm. I've already spoken with the parents and advised them to consult a specialist in children's and youth psychiatry, but they didn't want to hear.'

Emma exchanges a look with Simon before asking: 'Did they say why?'

'No, but I'm guessing the father is of the opinion that such nonsense isn't necessary. The mother is more open to offers of help, but if you ask me, I get the impression that he wears the trousers.'

'Did you speak with Douglas alone about it?'

'No, one of his parents was always with him. But regardless, it's rare for a teenager to open up like that to a stranger. That takes professional conversations with a psychologist or someone who is truly in their confidence.'

'Do you have any suspicions as to the cause of his self-harming behaviour?'

Martin Lund activates his computer screen and scrolls down a document. 'According to his patient file, he was treated two years ago for a similar injury. And considering what's just happened in his family, one can hardly ignore his behaviour. I don't want to speculate any further – the causes can be manifold. These days, children experience dangers from so many sides.' He looks back at Emma and Simon. 'But there's definitely some traumatic experience behind his behaviour.'

'If you had to guess, what could such an experience have been, in your opinion?'

'I never guess out loud. To find the root of the cause is your task, and that's why you're here.'

'Yes.' Emma had hoped for a bombproof theory that matched her own. But most people don't accuse others of such things without solid proof, and Martin Lund seems to agree. And, like he said, a multitude of reasons could lie behind Douglas's self-harm.

But in this case, Emma knows more than Douglas's doctor: Giorgio Moretti met his daughter on a blind date shortly before she was murdered; Jasmine was a member of a self-help group for victims of sexual abuse within the family; Nicolas is deeply worried about his younger brother. She needs to speak with someone who is close to Douglas, who sees him every day and ought to be able to gauge his well-being.

'His class teacher,' says Emma to Simon on their way to their cars, having thanked Martin Lund for his help. 'We need to speak with Douglas's class teacher.'

'Which school does he attend?'

'I don't know, but that shouldn't be difficult to find out. Worst case, we ask Nicolas.' She pulls out her phone and types in Douglas's name together with the words 'school' and 'Lidingö' and hits enter.

'By the way, did you have a good New Year's?' asks Simon as he pulls a beanie from the pocket of his jacket and puts it on.

She doesn't reply immediately, wondering whether he knows about her accidental visitor. But how could he?

'I just stayed in and had a relaxed evening.' She taps her screen again, cursing the miserable reception. 'Well, seems to me that Giorgio Moretti is quite stubborn when it comes to his children. He doesn't want Douglas to see a psychiatrist and didn't want to get Nicolas a lawyer. Why would that be?'

'Hmm,' mutters Simon closely behind Emma. 'So you spent New Year's all by yourself?'

Emma inhales the cold air. Can't he stop already? 'Yes, just me and Einstein.'

She focuses on the search results, not wishing to be reminded of the fact that she awoke with a man in her bed whose name she doesn't know. She can see from the corner of her eye that Simon is scrutinizing her. His intent stare makes her lower her face even more. Is it that obvious?

'Here we go. Torsvik school.'

'Who's his teacher?'

'Doesn't say. This is an article about an athletics competition where Douglas came second in the 100-metre race, but I'll keep searching in the car. I'm about to freeze out here.'

'Wait.' Simon catches her by the jacket, forcing her to look at him. 'Are we okay?'

'How do you mean? Is something wrong?'

Simon lets go of her and folds his hands behind his head. 'You know, Hellberg is constantly on my back, asking me what I'm doing.'

'You're investigating a murder.'

'Is that all?'

'Isn't that enough? I thought that's what cops do.'

Simon snorts, spreading his arms. 'Okay, I give up. Let's look for that teacher now, and then I have to go back to the station.' He turns around, walks to his Volvo, opens the driver's door and shoots her a look before climbing in. 'We'll talk on the phone if we find anything. And by the way, keep your hands off the flask in your glovebox. I'm a cop, remember?' He slams his door shut, starts the engine and swerves out of his parking space with spinning tyres.

What was that? Emma walks to her car and gets in. Cranks up the heater, holding her stiff fingers in front of the vents and staring at the glove compartment. Oh God. Her whole body screams for alcohol. During their conversation with Martin Lund, she had fantasized about driving to the booze store afterwards and granting herself one sip. Just a tiny one, nothing that would cause her any trouble in a traffic stop.

But now Simon has gone and ruined everything, making her feel bad.

What a tyrant!

39

Half an hour later, a woman in her sixties invites Emma and Simon into her apartment at Hjorthagen. Her name is Monica Hammergren and she is Douglas's class teacher, and she gesticulates as she speaks as if she were standing in front of a blackboard. Simon had contacted her through the school's office, and she'd said they were welcome to call round since she was at home doing her post-Christmas clean. They sit down at a pine table in the kitchen. Monica serves coffee in a blue-rimmed set and home-made cake on a silver tray as they talk about the terrible fate that has befallen Douglas's older sister.

'I phoned his mother a few days ago to ask how he's doing. Dear God, it must be so awful for the whole family.'

Emma nods in agreement. 'Does Douglas have a lot of friends? Would you say that he gets along well with others?'

'Well, in the class he only really spends time with one other boy. Other than that, he's very quiet and difficult to get close to. Sometimes I think how lucky it is that he plays football, where he's forced to act as part of the team. His father coaches.'

'Yes, I know,' says Emma. And I know other things too. She doesn't say that, as much as she'd like to. 'We suspect that something may be wrong with Douglas. We believe he burns himself. Self-harming. Were you aware of that?'

Monica clutches her chest, fiddling with a pendant dangling from a thin gold chain around her neck. 'God, no. Otherwise I'd have spoken with the school's social worker a long time ago. When did he start, do you know?'

'Possibly two years ago, but we don't know for certain.'

'Poor child. And after everything that's happened, it's unlikely to get any better. Darling Jasmine, I just don't understand it.'

'Did you know Jasmine?' asks Simon, helping himself to a caramel slice.

'Oh yes, I was her and Nicolas's teacher also. That was many years ago now, but I remember them both well.'

'I see. When was that?' Simon takes a bite of the cake.

'About fifteen years ago, from seventh to ninth grade. The murder came as a huge shock to me. Still, I'm not surprised – or rather, I am surprised, but in hindsight I should have recognized the warning signs.' Monica rubs her hands together.

Emma and Simon wait for her to go on.

'Yes, Jasmine was a loud and loquacious girl, while Nicolas was quiet and withdrawn. In that regard, he and Douglas are alike – both are somewhat unapproachable. You know, there was an incident once where I and several other teachers had to pull Nicolas and Jasmine apart. It was during breaktime, and she had evidently ticked him off. It's not unusual for siblings to argue, but this went beyond that. They were fourteen or fifteen at the time and he went completely berserk, throwing her to the ground and throttling her. When we dragged him off her, she was blue in the face.'

'What was the argument about?' asks Emma, worried. Such a witness statement is not going to be to Nicolas's advantage in court. On top of that, she's found out that on the day of his arrest, he tried to run from the custody suite's reception area. And she herself has experienced Nicolas's aggressive side when he asked her to get him drugs. Hopefully, no one is going to find out about that one, but this latest development is discouraging.

'And you know,' continues Monica, 'the other thing is, neither of them had a decent explanation for what happened. But if my memory serves me right, their fellow students said that Nicolas was angry because of something Jasmine had said. Something she was supposed to keep to herself. Like I said, she liked to talk, so I can well imagine that it was about some girl or other.'

Emma shifts uncomfortably on her chair. A girl. Would Nicolas have throttled his sister because she blabbed something about a girl he was seeing? Boys that age can be sensitive, but not this sensitive.

'Did you report the incident to the police?' asks Simon.

'No. After much toing and froing, we agreed with the father to leave it be. They were siblings, after all.'

Emma folds her hands on her stomach. 'What was Vera's opinion?'

'She wasn't there. She isn't their real mother, you know. Not that it makes a difference, but he was always the one who attended parent–teacher meetings and all that. She rarely came to school. I think I only met her once Douglas joined us.'

'I see,' says Emma, realizing she's forgotten about her coffee. As she sips the now cold liquid, a thought takes shape in her mind. If Giorgio sexually abused Jasmine and perhaps Douglas too, could it be that Nicolas . . . ? She glances at Simon, wishing to share her thoughts with him, but he is wholly engrossed in his caramel slice. So she thinks it through by herself. Could Giorgio also have abused Nicolas? She imagines the broad-shouldered man, how he cracks open the door to Nicolas's room, slips in bed with him and places a finger on his lips, reminding him to keep quiet.

That would be a more plausible explanation for Nicolas's behaviour with Jasmine. Maybe she found out and told someone.

'Did Nicolas and Jasmine often argue like that?' she asks, setting down her cup a little too hard.

Monica casts a worried glance at the rattling china. 'No. They held back after that event, and then they went off to senior school. But I do wonder what would have happened that time if we hadn't been close by. It could have ended very badly indeed.'

Emma steers the conversation back to Douglas. According to Monica, he is good at sports but has gone downhill in other subjects lately. In hindsight, not all that surprising. Emma only half listens. She wants to be alone with Simon and tell him about her latest theory. As soon as they are in the stairwell, she bursts out with it.

Simon stops by a window on the first landing and turns to her. 'Stop throwing around wild allegations. We've got nothing on Giorgio.'

'Yes, we have a whole lot, but you're closing your eyes to the facts.'

'No, or else I wouldn't have come with you today. But like I said—'

'We need solid evidence,' says Emma, finishing the sentence for him.

Simon sighs.

'You said yourself some of his behaviour was suspect,' she continues. 'And you saw all his pictures on Facebook. And then there's the boy he disappeared into the storeroom with.'

'I know.' Simon runs his hands through his hair.

'"But Hellberg",' she says, parroting Simon.

'No, it's not about him. But – well – I don't know.' He grabs Emma by the shoulders. 'If Nicolas were to talk about the abuse – provided it actually happened – that would change everything. That's all I can say about the subject at the moment.'

Emma draws squiggles in the dust on the windowsill with her finger. Considering how closed off Nicolas is, she has little hope of extracting useful information from him, least of all on such a sensitive subject. On the other hand, she has something he desperately wants, at home in a bowl on her dresser – the ziplock bag she still hasn't disposed of. It all depends on building a good rapport with one's clients, Angela had explained to her after the incident with Oliver's mother. It is important to create a sense of us-versus-them.

'This afternoon, Nicolas is meeting with the psychologist about the paragraph 7 examination,' she calls after Simon, who has let go of her and is walking down the stairs. 'I'll go and speak with him afterwards.'

40

The blonde woman rises when Nicolas enters the visitors' room. He is astonished how utterly normal a psychologist can look. Jeans and black leather jacket. Long, curly hair with a frizzy fringe; somewhat unkempt, like you sometimes see on middle-aged women who don't want to accept the fact that they shouldn't wear their hair in the same style as thirty years ago.

'Kerstin Thor, lead psychologist at the National Board of Forensic Medicine.'

As he shakes her hand, he feels weaker and more fragile than ever. It seems to him the woman can already see right through him with her piercing blue eyes.

Can she see what I've done? Who I really am?

He avoids her gaze and sits down on the green wooden armchair the psychologist points to before sitting down diagonally opposite him. Between them is a coffee table holding a carafe of water and two glasses. He fills one glass for himself and drinks, his hand shaking, trying to delay the start of the conversation. He doesn't want to be here, does not want to be questioned by a psychologist trying to dissect his life. A little psychological examination, or whatever it's called. As if he were mental. He snorts inwardly. But perhaps he really is. Damaged for life after all the crap he's gone through.

She begins with small talk and explains that their conversation is going to take about an hour. Following that, she will compile an assessment for the court, elaborating whether a more comprehensive examination, a so-called forensic psychological examination, is going to be necessary.

Nicolas sets down the glass and traces a scratch in the wooden armrest with his index finger, reminding himself of the strategy he's decided on: don't say too much, but just enough to satisfy her.

'Let us start on the night your sister was murdered. From your interview notes I gather that you went to sleep in your sister's lap, experiencing a kind of blackout. Later you woke up with blood on your clothes. Is that true?'

'Yes.'

'Do you often experience such gaps in your memory?'

Nicolas focuses his eyes on her mouth. Then he looks up at her, but his thoughts are somewhere else. Curses himself about those yellow pills he took with Jasmine. He thought they were benzos, Rohypnol at best. But not MDPV, the zombie drug. He knows that is what the stuff is called, as well as monkey dust, bath salts and other names. And he knows that people go nuts on it, and not just a little. Not in the sense that they feel extremely good. No, they lose the plot. Jump off balconies, hack off body parts they believe are poisoned, see their own faces distorted beyond recognition. He himself had the feeling he was on the sinking *Titanic*. What had happened between the sinking of the ship and the moment he awoke in Jasmine's lap?

'I wouldn't call it a memory gap,' he says with as much composure as he can muster. 'I flaked out and must have slept very deeply from all the stuff we swallowed.'

'I see. Can you tell me about your first experience with drugs? How old were you and how did you come into contact with them?'

'It was at a party. I think I was around twenty. There was a guy who had cocaine with him, and I tried some.'

'At twenty you were in the middle of your football career.'

Nicolas feels a pang in his chest. He remembers how angry Giorgio had been when Nicolas turned up hungover at the match the next day. How his father had threatened to kick him off the team. 'Yes. But I only did it the once. Then it was many years before I took anything again. That was when I came back from Russia.'

'And if I read it correctly, you quit playing football after your career in Russia. Is that right?'

'Yes.'

'What was that like for you, when you came home to Sweden and no longer played football? What did you do?'

'That was a tough time. I had money, but I was never really happy. I felt as if I wasn't at home anywhere.'

'And you came back into contact with drugs during that time?'

'Yes, that's roughly how it was.'

'And then you started to gamble. Poker, horse racing and other stuff. Why?'

Nicolas looks up, meeting her eyes properly for the first time. 'It was awesome. Well, at first it was. I had the feeling I was alive again, but then things spun out of control.'

'Yes, as far as I know you gambled away all the money you earned as a football player. What, do you think, caused you to end up in such a situation?'

He shrugs. 'I just sort of slid into it.'

'But what were you feeling?'

'I don't know. Panic, perhaps. But sometimes it felt like it wasn't really about me, as if it was all some kind of game.'

'Can you explain that some more?'

Nicolas moves nervously in his seat. He doesn't know how to explain it. Does he even understand it himself?

'Take football, for example,' he tries, kneading his hands. 'When you're at the top, it's difficult to comprehend that you're indeed one of Sweden's top players. You live in a vacuum, so to speak. It was the same with the gambling – I simply went on and on.'

'Have you always liked playing football?'

'I grew up with it. I don't know anything else.'

'What was it like to have your father for a coach?'

'Practically made no difference.'

'Did you feel like he treated you differently because you were his son?'

'Sometimes, maybe. He yelled at me in a way he never would have with the other players. But it didn't bother me. Back then, I didn't give a damn.'

Nicolas reaches for his glass again and sips on his water, trying to blank out everything else. He doesn't want to think of his father, of the half-hour car rides to and from training during which he never knew what his father wanted to talk about and he used to stare out of the window without seeing anything, just wanting to arrive as quickly as possible.

Kerstin Thor crosses her legs, leans forward and folds her hands on one knee. 'What did the two of you talk about?'

'I don't know. He's my father – we talked about different stuff.'

'You mean, you talked about things you wouldn't have talked about with other people?'

'Pretty much.'

'Do you like your father?'

Nicolas's cheeks flush and he hears a beeping sound in the distance that comes closer and eventually fills his whole head. This is the second time that's happened to him. The noise. The feeling of being rooted to the spot when everything is about to blow up. There are things he doesn't want to talk about – things that must never reach the light of day. And still she continues to probe, deeper and deeper.

'Your mother died when you were eight years old.'

He blinks a few times, realizing that she has changed the subject.

'Tell me what you remember in connection with her. The first thing that comes to your mind.'

Nicolas opens his mouth, stares at her, and thinks about her question until the noise in his head subsides. 'She used to cook pancakes for me after school. She was always in a happy mood. We used to play Monopoly for hours, Jasmine too.'

'How did you feel when your father married again and Vera became your stepmother?'

'It was okay. My father was much better.'

'But what did you think of it?'

'It worked.'

'What did Vera mean to you? I mean, a new person coming into your family must have changed things a bit.'

'Yes, but I wasn't really interested.' Nicolas focuses once more on the psychologist's mouth, noticing the fine lines around her lips when she speaks.

'Why not?'

'I was too busy. Friends, football and things like that.'

'I see. Did you and Vera get on well?'

More shrugging. 'All right.'

'What was it like for you when the family received a new addition? Douglas is a bit of a latecomer.'

He asks himself what kind of an answer she expects. Would anyone admit to hating their brother or sister? That's what it was like at the start. He had felt pure hatred, wanted nothing to do with Douglas, hadn't wanted to be near him when Vera and his

257

father cuddled the baby. But that had passed in time, and eventually Douglas had come to mean the world to him.

'Vera is younger than my father, and it was totally normal that they would have a child together.' He hopes she doesn't keep pressing him about his feelings with regard to his brother.

'Were you pleased?'

He sighs. 'Yes, I was.'

'Do you see much of him?'

'Reasonably.'

'And what do you do when you meet?'

'Grab a coffee in town and the like.'

'He plays football, just like you. Do you go to watch his matches?'

A large hand digs itself into Nicolas's guts, grabs his innards and twists them. Bloody woman! You know perfectly well that I never go to watch. I bet you read it in some file or other. And I bet you guessed why.

'No, not really,' he says as calmly as he can manage.

'Why?'

Nicolas presses his lips together and starts chewing on them.

'I can see that it's difficult for you to talk about this. Did something happen between you and Douglas that damaged your relationship?'

Nicolas fidgets with the scratch on the armrest, squeezing the tip of his finger against a wooden splinter until his skin breaks. He stares at the dark red drop of blood. It's only small, but he quickly wipes it on his trouser leg nonetheless. He must get rid of it – there's so much blood, Jasmine's blood, and he is covered in it.

Pull yourself together, warns a voice in his head. Pull yourself together.

He props his elbows on his knees and buries his face in his hands, hoping she hasn't noticed anything. What if she thinks it

258

was me? That I murdered Jasmine? Did I? Who else could have done it? The front door was locked.

'Okay. Let's talk about you and Jasmine. How was your relationship with her?'

He looks up, peers through his fingers, brushing them across his face and leaving a smear on his skin. 'We hung out regularly.'

'And has it always been that way?'

'Sometimes more, sometimes less.'

'When was it more, when less?'

Nicolas stifles a yawn. What a load of rubbish.

'We were just like any normal siblings. Sometimes we had more contact, sometimes less.'

'I see. But if we start with your childhood, did you play together much as children?'

Nicolas stares at her. If the woman says 'I see' one more time, he is going to kill her. He smiles weakly. 'Yes, I guess we did.'

'I see. And as teenagers?'

He clutches the armrests until his knuckles stick out white.

'I mostly played football then.'

'And later, as adults? Were you much in contact?'

'Every now and then.'

'Did she meet up with the rest of the family much?'

'Not really.'

'Do you know why?'

'She probably didn't feel like it.'

'I see.'

Nicolas grips the armrests hard. No, you don't see anything, you stupid cow. You haven't the faintest clue, dammit.

Maybe it was me. Maybe I'm the one who slit Jasmine's throat.

41

In the elevator up to the remand prison, Emma stands crammed between two uniforms and a man in handcuffs. Sweat runs down her back, and she unbuttons the collar of the elegant new black coat she's acquired to fit better into her new role. Unfortunately, she feels less like a legal assistant than a drug dealer. She has hidden the cocaine in her bra. Crossing her arms on her chest, she smiles at the policemen as confidently as she can and tells herself that it will go without a hitch. It must go without a hitch.

At the entrance to the prison, she lets the others go first. When it's her turn, she hands the guard at the counter her ID. The man informs her that the conversation between Nicolas and the psychologist should be nearly finished, and that she is welcome to wait outside the visitors' room.

Thank you. Thank you for not searching me. But I guess you don't do that with lawyers? A sudden feeling of uncertainty overwhelms her. What is she doing? But it's too late to turn back. She has no choice but to carry on and act normal.

Two guards walk towards her in the corridor, one Japanese in appearance while the other is a large Viking, taking her in with narrowed eyes. Emma clenches her jaw, feverishly trying to figure out what to do in case the pair stop her and find the coke.

'Hi,' says the big one in passing.

Emma stops and returns his stare.

'Miss Secret, right?' He whistles with appreciation, beaming at her.

Relief floods her and she moistens the roof of her mouth. 'Shouldn't you fill your time with more intelligent activities?'

He winks at her. 'Look who's talking.'

'It's my twin sister. So don't go making me the object of your dirty fantasies.' Emma winks back and carries on towards the visitors' room. The guy shouts after her: 'If you say so. But you looked damn good in that bikini.'

She waves her hand dismissively. The moment she turns a corner, she leans against the wall, bent forward and breathing deeply. Shouldn't she just go home and forget about this? No, not now that she's come this far. She squares her shoulders and checks her phone while she waits for her meeting with Nicolas. Angela has sent her a message – a reply to Emma's daily report.

Good work. Good luck with Nicolas. One statement from him and we've got Giorgio.

Emma closes the message when the door to the visitors' room opens and a woman with a smart leather jacket and a voluminous head of hair emerges. Emma guesses she is lead psychologist Kerstin Thor and immediately approaches her.

'I represent Nicolas Moretti and thought perhaps you'd give me an indication with regard to your assessment for the court?'

Kerstin Thor stops. She doesn't have much choice, since Emma is standing in the middle of the corridor. 'Wow, you spare no effort.'

A nearby guard signals Kerstin Thor with a nod of his head that Emma is who she claims to be.

'I was coming to speak with Nicolas anyway. How did it go?'

'Good, thank you. But I do believe a forensic psychological examination will be necessary. There are too many question marks in connection with his childhood and the underlying factors for his drug abuse.'

'So you will apply for the examination?'

'Yes. I suspect he may be suffering from a chronic dissociative disorder, and that he experienced some kind of traumatic event that he can't process.'

'In his childhood?' asks Emma.

'It's too soon to say. But it's obvious that he's shielding himself from something that happened in his past.' Kerstin Thor indicates with a glance at her watch that she's in a rush.

Emma asks one more question. 'Do you mean he's repressing something?'

Kerstin looks up from her watch. 'Simply put, he is aware of the trauma but suppresses it so successfully that he sometimes believes it's someone else's. But as I said, a diagnosis requires a much more thorough evaluation. What I told you is merely my spontaneous first impression.'

'Thank you,' says Emma, and she lets the psychologist go.

She enters the visitors' room, takes off her coat and drapes it across the armrest of an empty chair. Nicolas takes no notice of her, staring straight ahead apathetically.

Emma takes a seat and begins cautiously. 'I met the psychologist outside the door. Apparently, all went well.' She kneads her hands, wishing she could leave. She doesn't feel comfortable around Nicolas today. His jaw is clenched and he fidgets, unable to sit still.

'I spoke with Monica Hammergren, your former teacher. She told me about an incident during which you throttled Jasmine. Do you remember it?'

Nicolas lifts his chin slightly.

'What was it about?' she asks.

Something flashes through his empty eyes, as if he were debating with himself whether to say something or not. 'She never could keep her trap shut,' he bursts out eventually.

A sour taste fills Emma's mouth. 'Keep her trap shut about what?'

'I don't remember.'

'Is that what happened at her apartment? Did Jasmine say something she wasn't supposed to say?' Too late does Emma realize what she's just hinted at – that Nicolas is the murderer, that he lost control over something Jasmine said and killed his sister. But the most frightening part is that he doesn't react.

'Maybe,' he says. 'She never could keep anything to herself.'

Emma swallows down the bile, pours herself a glass of water and drinks. She would rather leave right now, but she needs to question Nicolas about Giorgio, has to find out whether her suspicion is correct. Was he too abused by his father?

'Douglas is inflicting burns on himself,' she says. 'I spoke with his doctor. He believes Douglas is unwell and that he displays self-harming behaviour. And since Jasmine was evidently sexually abused by a family member, this could be the case for Douglas too.'

Nicolas closes his eyes. The idiot just sits there and closes his eyes. Doesn't give a toss about his younger brother just so he doesn't have to talk about whatever it is he is suppressing.

'Could it be that your father . . .'

Nicolas slowly opens his eyes, and this time they are no longer empty. Something menacing flashes in them, as if he were about to pounce on her. Emma peers at the door, wondering if a guard is nearby. Nevertheless, she makes another attempt, asking outright: 'Did Giorgio sexually abuse you and Jasmine? If so, you have to tell me. Partly because it's important for our investigation, and partly because of Douglas. He could be the next victim.'

Nicolas's knuckles are white, and Emma glances at the door again. Not to call for help, though. Instead, she reaches down the neck of her jumper and pulls out the ziplock bag.

'This is for you. But you only get it if you give me something. Tell me about Giorgio.'

No reaction.

'I saw him two days ago at a football tournament with a boy. He went into a storeroom alone with him. I don't know what happened inside, but I worry that he is laying hands on more victims. If you tell me what you know, we can put an end to his doings.'

Nicolas leans forward, his eyes fixed on the pouch, looking as though he's fighting an inner battle. Finally, he opens his mouth. 'Someone told Jasmine that one of us would die before we turned thirty.'

Disappointment fills Emma's chest. 'What are you talking about? Don't try to sell me some nonsense now. Do you want the coke or not?'

'I know it sounds strange, but a fortune teller foretold that one of us would die, and then it happened. Are you slow or something?'

Emma considers this new information for a moment. Is it relevant? She doesn't for one moment believe in fortune tellers and the like. But at the same time, she can't dismiss this. Jasmine was murdered just before midnight, so close to her birthday. If Emma has learned one thing in her years as a policewoman, it's this: never believe in coincidence.

'Who foretold that?' she asks.

'Some old bat in Bromma, I think.'

'Did any other predictions come true?'

'Not as far as I know.'

A knock on the door reminds Emma of what she's holding in her hand. In reflex, she throws the bag at Nicolas. He tries to catch it but Emma watches how, as if in slow motion, the pouch hits his chest, slides down his T-shirt and drops to the floor.

The door opens and the guard who thought Emma was Miss Secret enters, followed by Simon and Hellberg.

A drop of sweat runs down her forehead and catches in her eyebrow. She forces herself not to stare at the pouch, but notices from the corner of her eye that it's lying beside the table leg nearest to Nicolas.

'The police are here to interview Nicolas Moretti.' She hears the guard's voice from somewhere on the fringes of her panic. 'Perfect timing, now that you're already here.'

Emma tries to pull herself together. 'Now? Why did no one call ahead?'

'We did,' says Hellberg. 'But Angela didn't deign to answer her phone.' He walks into the room, bringing with him the smell of recently smoked cigarettes.

'May I have a word with you outside first? So I know what this is about?'

Hellberg pulls a chair next to Emma and slumps into it. 'Why? We aren't obliged to inform you of the questions we want to ask a suspect.'

Emma looks beseechingly at Simon, but he completely ignores her, fetching the last remaining chair from a corner of the room and placing it between Hellberg and Nicolas, less than a metre away from the ziplock bag.

Panic streams through Emma's entire body. That's her new job gone – she is off to prison with a drug conviction.

She looks at Nicolas. He gave her a nod, didn't he? Or is she imagining things? She glances about, unsure of what to do. But then she decides to interpret what she thinks she saw as some kind of signal.

She presses one hand to her mouth, coughing and squeezing tears to her eyes. She doesn't know if that's going to help, but she'll try anything to gain time.

'Water,' she gasps. 'May I have some water, please?' She waves at Simon, who reaches for the carafe on the table. While he fills her glass, she notices Nicolas lifting one slippered foot, placing it on the pouch and dragging it towards himself.

Emma drinks slowly and thumps her chest. 'God, what a terrible cough.'

'Can we begin already?' Hellberg doesn't bother to hide his impatience.

Emma nods, her mouth full of water.

'Good,' says Hellberg. 'Because we received the results of the paternity test of Jasmine's child.'

42

That bloody Santa Claus!

Nicolas walks into his cell and stops in the middle of the tiny room.

I should have finished him off when I had the chance. Smashed his thick skull on the tarmac. Rammed an icicle in his eye.

The guard slams the door shut behind him. Never before has Nicolas appreciated the sound of a lock clicking shut as much as in this moment. His sister allowed a pisshead to get her pregnant, and by the looks of it she wanted to keep the child. How is this possible?

His hand travels to his waistband, and he uses two fingers to fish the ziplock bag from between his butt cheeks, where he managed to hide the powder when the interview came to an end and everyone stood up. At first he was going to pretend he was tying his shoelaces, but then he remembered that he was wearing slippers. And so he adjusted his socks instead, slipping the pouch into his hand while Emma distracted the two cops with a thousand questions about Roland Nilsson, that goddam Santa. Have you already spoken with him? What did he say? Is he being treated as a suspect in the murder of Jasmine? Nicolas is asking himself the same question, but most of all he's wondering why Jasmine went to bed with a man like Roland Nilsson. Would she do anything for money? Had she been that screwed up? Worse than himself?

He pours the white powder on the foldable table on the wall, feeling a little proud of his and Emma's teamwork. He and his defender led the cops on a merry old dance. The thrill of victory he felt is still boosting his confidence. He arranges the powder in two lines. They are bigger than normal, probably twice as much. Usually he'd save some for later, but in here – impossible. He snorts the stuff up both nostrils and brushes the rest aside with his hand. As he waits for the drugs to kick in, part of him wonders why Emma changed her mind about smuggling the stuff into prison. She took a huge risk. Perhaps it was because she is stuck down a deep hole, just like him. Her glassy eyes and the smell of alcohol speak volumes. You don't get rid of that smell by sucking on a mint – you only make a fool of yourself.

He flexes his arm and chest muscles, relishing the high and the feeling of freedom it gives him. No accusing glares judging him; no boring questions he doesn't feel like answering. Did you know that Jasmine was pregnant? What did Roland Nilsson want when he rang your sister's doorbell? What was your argument about?

In small steps, Nicolas walks in circles around the narrow room. Once, twice, three times . . .

Did you know that your father is a sugar daddy? How often do you see Douglas? What was your relationship with Jasmine like? Were you close? How close? Why didn't you immediately call the police when you woke up and found Jasmine dead? Are you aware how that looks? Various evidence points to you as the culprit.

He stares at the ceiling, seeing Emma in his mind's eye, the suspicion in her look as the meaning of the prophecy dawns on her. He curses his stupidity as he realizes he's got himself even deeper in the shit. Fortune tellers are con artists, and their predictions don't come true unless someone decides to make them come true. And who knew that either he or Jasmine were supposed to die before their thirtieth birthday? That's right – he and Jasmine. And she was the one who died.

He holds one hand in front of his mouth and pretends he's holding a microphone.

'Lake and beach lay glistening, oh distant star . . .'

Jasmine sang that song at the apartment. But what had happened next? Did she tell him about her pregnancy? And that the damn Santa was the father? He wants to know, wants to remember, wants to understand what happened.

Suddenly he loses his balance, staggers, holds on to the wall and closes his eyes. He needs to remember what happened. He knows he drank beer and talked to the parrot. Then he was lying in Jasmine's arms, looking at the knife on the coffee table, the one they used to crack nuts. And then his eyes fell shut. At some point during his slumber, he half heard something creak. Where had the noise come from? From a door? If so, who had entered the apartment and walked to the couch? He clenches his fists, wants to smash the face of the bastard who is sneaking up on them to cut Jasmine's throat. Through his closed eyelids, he makes out the dark shape of a person stopping in front of him. Nicolas has no time to waste. The instant he opens his eyes, he strikes.

43

Angela's heels clip-clop on the herringbone parquet as she paces in front of her desk, her hair flying about as agitatedly as she is speaking.

'He struck down a guard yesterday. Do you understand what that means?'

Emma wipes her damp hands on her trousers, feeling like a badly behaved pupil awaiting her punishment.

'He completely flipped out. How could you give him cocaine?' Angela stops, bracing her hands on her hips. 'You do realize that everyone knows you smuggled the stuff inside? And now Nicolas has proved how violent he can become on drugs. How do you think this is going to look in court? What were you thinking?'

Emma swallows, wishing she had drunk a little more this morning. Perhaps then she would be brave enough to speak up in her defence. But there is no justification. She made a mistake, a terrible mistake, committed a crime, even.

'I'm sorry. I thought I could make him talk.'

'And look how that worked out.' Angela presses her lips into a thin line and walks towards Emma, who, despite the situation, can't help but peer at Angela's silver neck scarf. She waits for the next telling-off, but instead her boss places one hand on her arm, switching to gentle Angela.

'Don't worry. I've already taken care of our problem. Neither the prison management nor the police are going to press charges. That would only reflect poorly on them, since any of them could have slipped Nicolas the drugs.'

Emma tries to process what she's just heard. Did Angela threaten the prison staff, Simon and Hellberg? Did she claim one of them had smuggled drugs into prison for Nicolas? Damn, she likes this woman!

'Thanks,' she mumbles.

Angela places her index finger under Emma's chin, forcing her to meet her eyes. 'You don't need to thank me. Women must stick together. It's the only way for us to survive among all these men. Am I not right?'

Emma nods. She has the best employer in the world. Angela defends not only her clients but also her staff.

'What are we going to do about Roland Nilsson?' asks Emma. She shudders, like she did during the interview when she first heard that this man was the father of Jasmine's child. That means Jasmine and he . . . No, she doesn't want to picture it.

Angela lets go of Emma's chin, walks to her desk and searches for something in her handbag. 'The police are going to question him today. Hopefully, the national forensic centre will expedite the examination of the Santa costume. We'll have to wait for those results, but if it contains traces of Jasmine, even just a single hair, Stefan Hermansson is going to engage in some serious comfort eating after the next court hearing.' She pulls off the cap of her lipstick, touches up her lips and returns the stick to her bag. 'The way things look at the moment, the Christmas gnome is our best chance. Christer Tillman's alibi is difficult to refute. Around the time of the murder, he was driving home with his family from celebrating Christmas. The surveillance footage from the Norrtull toll station confirms it.'

'Okay.' Emma isn't particularly disappointed, now that they are focusing on Roland Nilsson. 'Um, there's one more thing,' she says a little sheepishly while Angela sorts some papers on her desk. 'Nicolas told me yesterday that Jasmine was told by a fortune teller that one of them would die before their thirtieth birthday. Isn't it strange how the prediction came true just a few minutes before?'

Angela pauses mid-movement and meets Emma's eyes. 'When did he say that? Before or after you gave him the cocaine?'

Emma swallows at the pointed remark and feels her stomach turn sour. 'Before.'

'Who was the clairvoyant?'

'He didn't know. Only that it was some woman in Bromma.'

'Do you believe in that sort of thing? Do you believe there are people who can predict the future?'

'No. I went to a fortune teller myself once. I believed it at first, because some of the predictions seemed to come true. But afterwards I realized that her statements were quite broad, easily interpreted in different ways. But in this case – the prediction being that either Jasmine or Nicolas would die before their thirtieth birthday – the interpretation possibilities aren't endless.'

'You're trying to say that the murderer must have known about the prediction?'

'Yes, unless we believe in clairvoyants or coincidence.'

'Did anyone else know?'

'I couldn't ask him. That's when Hellberg and Simon came in.'

'If we want to use this in court, we need to find out who this fortune teller is and who else knew of it.' Angela sits down on the edge of her desk, tapping her thigh with a pen. 'The problem is that it's not helping our client. At this point in time, we know of no one else who knew about the prophecy.'

Emma kneads her hands. 'I thought the same. What if Jasmine told Roland Nilsson about it?'

Angela holds the pen to her freshly made-up lips. 'No, that's too far-fetched. No matter which way we look at it, it'll fall back on Nicolas. What do you think the prosecutor is going to claim if we mention the prophecy?'

Emma shrugs.

'That Nicolas took it very seriously,' says Angela. 'One of them was going to die, and he made sure it wasn't him.'

Unease grows in Emma when she realizes that Angela is right. Stefan Hermansson was bound to use the story to his advantage. But something else bothers her even more – Angela has just provided Nicolas with a motive for killing his sister. She forces the thought aside, focusing on Angela, who continues to talk about the clairvoyant without any trace of the kind of turmoil raging inside Emma.

'If we run this esoteric angle in court, it'll sound like we have nothing better in store. Roland Nilsson, on the other hand, was mentally unstable. He's just gone through a divorce and impregnated a prostitute slash sugar baby. On the night of the murder, he got drunk and rang Jasmine's doorbell to persuade her to have an abortion. But then he found another man with her – someone he could pin the murder on. He went back home, gathered his courage, returned to Jasmine's and killed her. That sounds much better.'

'Perhaps,' says Emma hesitantly. 'But he doesn't really strike me as clever enough to come up with such a plan. I see him more as someone who might act in the heat of the moment, out of jealousy because of the other man.'

'We can fine-tune the motive,' Angela says decisively. 'But let's forget about the fortune teller for now. Make sure Nicolas doesn't mention it in front of John and Simon. That would only be grist to their mill.' She slides off the desk and her expression tells Emma that the subject is closed. She adjusts her dress and disappears into the next room. 'And now I must go see a client who was arrested for aggravated robbery in Flemingsberg.'

Emma walks to the window and watches the snowflakes land on the parked cars down in the street. She wishes she too had thick skin like Angela. Then she wouldn't have to stew over the question of Nicolas's innocence, because the only thing that mattered would be winning. But she feels torn. Even though, thanks to Roland Nilsson, victory seems to lie within their grasp for the first time, she is still on the fence when it comes to Nicolas. At this stage, there is more evidence against him than against Roland. Does she want to help a murderer be acquitted? Can a terrible childhood and possible sexual abuse by the father justify murder? She argues with herself and reaches the conclusion that the answer is both yes and no. It depends on what exactly happened, and she still doesn't know.

Her phone rings and she checks the screen. Unknown number. No thanks, I don't want to buy anything and I don't want to change mobile providers. She dismisses the call and, from the corner of her eye, notices Angela in the next room. Emma moves closer to the cracked door, focusing on the neck scarf. Her boss fascinates her in a strange way. The tough, professional lawyer, who at night – well, what does the woman do at night?

Angela Köhler, the kinky boss lady.

Emma clasps a hand to her mouth to stop herself from giggling and continues to think about her elegant employer. Angela packs a pink toilet bag and a hairbrush into her Louis Vuitton handbag, slings it across her shoulder and walks to a wooden door that is propped open. Apparently, there's some kind of storeroom on the other side. Angela pushes against something that prevents the door from shutting – a mattress with blue and white bedding.

When her mobile phone rings again, Emma fishes it out of her bag and picks up, mostly so that she doesn't have to explain to Angela why she was spying on her.

The caller is Jina, the young woman from the ACA group.

'There's something I need to tell you about Jasmine. Can we meet up?'

Emma presses the phone harder to her ear and takes a couple of steps away from the door when she notices that Angela has seen her. 'Definitely. Are you free now?'

44

Emma stands outside the Åhléns City department store and watches people as they crowd down the steps to the underground, pushing and shoving their way through the store entrances, and others who, laden with computer or shopping bags, take the shortcut between Mäster Samuelsgatan and Drottninggatan. A mecca for pickpocket gangs. The policewoman in Emma wants to call out to the lady over there to watch her handbag. And the guy with the backpack – clearly you don't have any valuables in the outer pocket? Don't tempt those assholes unnecessarily; at least make it hard for them.

Her eyes scan the crowds, searching for Jina, who'd said she would meet her at ten. Now it is five past.

Emma can't wait to hear what Jina has to say, hasn't stopped thinking about it since the phone call. Perhaps she's accepted the fact that solving a murder is more important than confidentiality. But will whatever she is going to tell Emma exonerate Nicolas or bring him down?

From the corner of her eye, she spots a security guard making his rounds through one of the shops, stopping to chat with the young saleswomen in the cosmetics department, both of them pouting with fat, Botoxed lips. By the look of it, neither of them has had a customer yet today. Perhaps Emma should go to see one of them and allow herself to get beautified once her meeting is finished. She could badly do with it, even if she doesn't want to look like a copy of those bimbos. She studies her reflection in the window, and even though the pane is dirty it is obvious how run-down she looks. Straggly hair, dark lines under her eyes, some red pimples on her face. Repulsed, she turns away and goes back to focusing on the crowd rather than her appearance. Suddenly, her thoughts drift to the storeroom in Angela's office. Was what she saw really a mattress with bedding? Is Angela sleeping in the office? Maybe she does when she works late into the night. That wouldn't be so strange. As far as Emma knows, Angela has no family, only her young lover. Have they perhaps broken up? Did he throttle her too hard? Emma stops those thoughts before they run wild. Cut it out. That is Angela's life. Keep out of it.

A few minutes later, Jina comes up the escalator. She's wearing a knee-length yellow quilted jacket, a pink neck scarf and a purple hat – a burst of colour amid a mass of people in winter clothing. Her big brown eyes look around searchingly. Emma waves at her, wondering if she should greet the woman with a hug, but abandons the thought when she remembers how their last conversation ended. And besides, Jina looks grimly determined, going on the attack the moment she arrives.

'This is not okay. I don't even know what to think.'

Emma gives her a baffled look.

'Angela Köhler. You work for her. I read everything on the murder of Jasmine and saw a photo of the two of you together in the *Aftonbladet*. Why did you come to spy on our group, then? Angela already knows everything about Jasmine.'

'I don't follow.' Emma takes a step back. 'Did you know that Jasmine was stalked by someone?'

'What? No. What's that got to do with anything?'

'Jasmine turned to Angela for help because of a stalker. When you said Angela already knows everything about Jasmine – I thought that's what you meant.'

Jina wipes her nose with her glove and purses her light-blue-painted lips. 'You don't know.' She laughs drily. 'So, you don't know. Angela was a member of the ACA group. She started about a year ago and attended regularly, but then she stopped from one meeting to the next. And now she's defending Jasmine's killer – that's utter madness. Angela and Jasmine were practically best friends. They always stayed after the meetings and talked.'

'Now you've completely lost me. Angela was a member of the ACA group? As an active participant?'

'Didn't you hear me the first time? Yes, Angela came several times and told us how—' Jina presses her lips together. She looks as if she is reformulating the sentence in her mind. 'What she experienced. And it wasn't a pretty tale, I can tell you that. The woman has been through a lot. That's why I don't understand how she can defend Jasmine's murderer. She of all people should be on Jasmine's side, even in her death. Women have to stick together, she used to say all the time.'

A shiver runs down Emma's spine. She had not expected this. She tightens the collar of her jacket around her neck and tries to sort out her thoughts. 'Forgive me if I seem confused, but this is complete news to me.'

'I have a theory.' Jina comes one step closer. 'Angela wants to make one hundred per cent certain that Jasmine's brother gets put away. That's why she's defending him. It's the only plausible explanation I can think of. Like I said, Angela and Jasmine liked each other. They always had coffee and so on after the meetings.'

Emma gazes out at the crowd of people again, trying to make sense of things. But the new information bounces around her head in cartwheels.

'Why should Angela want to see Nicolas convicted?' she asks.

'Because she was friends with Jasmine. Don't you see? She wants to ensure that Jasmine's killer goes to prison.'

Emma nods, even though she doesn't understand it at all. It kind of sounds logical, but then again it doesn't. A defence lawyer wants to see their clients acquitted, not convicted. Angela employed her specifically for the purpose of winning this case and gave her the info about the stalker, the man who might even be her murderer.

'So, Jasmine never said anything about a stalker? For example, that he was standing in her courtyard, staring at her window?'

'No, I already said.'

'Okay. Did she mention a fortune teller who predicted that either she or her brother would die before their thirtieth birthday?'

Jina frowns. 'No, I'd remember that. Shit, that's insane.'

'So you don't know this story? Jasmine never spoke about it in the group?'

'I never heard her talk about any fortune teller, like I said. Right, I must get going, but promise me you'll get that psycho killer brother of hers behind bars. Jasmine didn't deserve this.'

Emma grabs Jina by the arm. 'Wait. Then you must help me. What do you know about Jasmine? Why was she in the group?'

Jina presses her made-up lips together and seems to fight a battle with herself. 'You'll find the reason in her family,' she says after a while. 'I don't want to say anything else on the subject. That would be a betrayal of the whole group.'

'But what about Angela? Do you think she attended because she was also sexually abused, or did she come as some kind of expert?'

'She came for the same reasons as the rest of us.' Jina accentuates her reply with a raised eyebrow. Then she throws up her hands in resignation. 'All right, then. Since Angela is a damn traitor, I'll tell you. There's an old newspaper article online that I found after Angela told us about an utterly bizarre incident. And since the article is available to anyone . . .' Jina gives a shrug. 'She told us her grandfather used to . . . well, you can fill in the blank. Anyway, the article says that Angela's mother cut off his dick with a pair of secateurs and soon after hanged herself in prison. But to be totally honest, I wonder whether it really was the mother who maimed him.'

Emma stares at Jina, unsure what to believe.

'How do I find the article?'

'Search for Vanessa Köhler. That's Angela's mother.'

Emma slowly raises her hands to her mouth and blows on her frozen fingers while everything she's just heard buzzes around in her head. Suddenly, a thought pops into her mind and she blurts it out: 'So that's why Angela likes strangulation games. I saw the bruises myself, and she always wears a neck scarf. That's her method of regaining control of her sex life and processing the memory of the abuse. And her mother hanged herself, therefore she's fixated on the neck. Right? That's how it works . . . one relives the trauma.'

Jina brings her face close to Emma's, and Emma can smell the fruity scent of her lipstick. 'You don't understand a thing.'

45

Twenty minutes later, Emma is back at the office. She pulls off her wet boots and sneaks into Angela's office. The wooden flooring creaks, and when she steps up to the desk to take a look around, she feels like a burglar. But then she tells herself that she has no reason to feel bad. Angela has lied to her, withheld from her the fact that she knew Jasmine in quite a different way than through the stalker Andreas Kilic. She and Jasmine were members of the same ACA group and, according to Jina, something like best friends. Why hadn't Angela said something?

A thought has formed in Emma's head since she and Jina parted ways. What if Jina's theory is true? What if Angela really is working towards a conviction for Nicolas? If that were the case, then she only employed Emma for show. An incompetent former policewoman who will have to take the fall if they lose the case – a defeat Angela has been planning from the beginning. She hasn't really participated actively in the investigation, instead dumping the whole affair on Emma – a broken ex-cop who drove a fifteen-year-old boy to commit suicide.

Tears well in Emma's eyes.

Dammit! She liked Angela, looked up to her. The power woman. Part of her even believed she could become just like Angela, a respected lawyer in high demand.

You naïve fool.

Anger pushes more tears to her eyes. Very well. Angela seems to believe Emma is weak, someone to use and sacrifice.

She scans the desk, determined to find something that corroborates Jina's claims. A folder labelled *Theft* catches her eye. She picks it up and finds another folder below, this one labelled *Minor Drug Possession*.

Trifles. Nothing worthy of a celebrity lawyer.

Emma puts the folders aside and opens the top drawer. Pens, paper clips, a charger cord. She checks the second drawer. Envelopes and stamps. A camera and an old recording device. Third drawer. A blue-and-yellow carton of pills labelled Valdoxan. Emma opens it and pulls out one of the blister strips. Several hollowed-out eyes stare at her. She googles the pills on her phone – antidepressants.

Is Angela depressed? If so, she doesn't show it. Then again, few people brag about how poorly they feel. And besides – if Angela really was raped by her grandfather, she probably has a lot to process.

Then she remembers the article. She searches for Vanessa Köhler, Angela's mother, and clicks on the headline that reads She murdered her own father. Even though Jina has already told her what happened, Emma's jaw drops as she reads. Part of her thought Jina might have exaggerated, but she hadn't. When Vanessa Köhler found out that her father had raped his granddaughter throughout her entire childhood, she cut off his penis and left him to bleed out. And it was true that she hanged herself soon after in prison. The feeling of guilt for failing to protect her daughter had been too powerful.

Emma looks up from the screen when she hears a door open and close, but soon realizes that the sound came from somewhere else in the building. Her heart beating loudly, she tries to get all the new information in some sort of order. But nothing makes sense; it's all one big muddle. She calls Angela, needs to hear her say that it's just a misunderstanding, but only gets her voicemail. Yes, she has a meeting with a client in Flemingsberg, but she needs to answer her phone now. This is important. Emma curses her phone, curses Angela, who brought Nicolas Moretti into her life. Why is the woman using her? Why did she lie about the nature of her acquaintance with Jasmine? Anger festers in her. Is the whole thing some kind of test? Has Angela forced an impossible case on her, wanting to see how she copes and if she's worth employing full-time at the oh-so-posh Köhler office?

Emma feels as though she's growing horns. She resolutely dials the number of police headquarters and demands to be put through to the chief at Flemingsberg station. The process takes several minutes and several times, while she waits with her phone pressed to her ear, she comes close to changing her mind. Should she really confront Angela in this manner, question her motives over the phone?

Before she can make up her mind, a woman answers.

'Hanne Adolfsson. How can I help?'

Emma introduces herself in a firm tone as a legal assistant for Köhler Lawyers. 'My colleague, Angela Köhler, was going to see a client who is being detained at your station for aggravated robbery. She asked me to look out some information for her, but now she's not answering her phone. I know she's been having problems with her phone lately, so I thought I'd try to get hold of her this way.'

'Uh-huh. I haven't seen her. What's the prisoner's name?'

Emma hesitates. 'I'm afraid I don't know. But he's being held for aggravated robbery.'

'We have no one here for aggravated robbery.' There's a sigh at the other end. 'Hang on, I'll go and double-check.'

Emma thanks her and paces the room as she waits for Hanne Adolfsson to return.

'Yes, I was right,' she says when she's back. 'We have no one here who has been arrested for aggravated robbery. You must have the wrong station.'

'Probably,' says Emma, and she apologizes for troubling her. Unease grows in her chest like a tumour. Why had Angela said she was seeing a client when he doesn't exist? What is she playing at?

Or did she just mention the wrong station to Emma?

Her eyes return to the desk and she remembers that she hasn't checked the bottom-most drawer. She opens it and finds a folder bearing Jasmine Moretti's name. She lifts it out and leafs through the files: the charge for murder, minutes of the arrest, application for custody awaiting trial, Angela's notes on Jasmine's stalker. They are the same documents Emma has already received. *Blue sports car, Honda Civic with an R at the start of the plate number and a 2 in the middle. The stalker is around thirty, of slender build with ash-blond hair. He carries tattoos of a skull and a spider web on his right arm.*

The text was written on a computer, but one sentence has been added by hand.

The stalker's girlfriend is pregnant.

Emma stares at the blue ink. She knows the sentence means something, but she can't quite put her finger on it. *The stalker's girlfriend is pregnant.*

The text was written on a computer, the additional sentence by hand.

Suddenly, a strangled gasp escapes her. She was the one who told Angela that the couple had a child. Angela then added the information by hand. Emma still doesn't have the answer to every question, but what she does know now is how Andreas Kilic's lasered tattoos add up.

It wasn't Jasmine who fabricated the story about the stalker, but Angela.

46

Emma is standing outside the door to an apartment, her jacket soaked through with snow and her hair damp. Her finger hovers over the doorbell. The name on the sign reads Benjamin Wikander. Angela's toy boy. She's been searching for Angela the entire afternoon, tried in vain to reach her on the phone, and drove to her penthouse apartment on Kungsholmen. A man in his forties opened the door and looked surprised when she asked about Angela. He explained that Angela had rented out the apartment to him a year ago. Didn't Emma know? No, she'd replied. On the way out, the man had run after her with a bundle of letters.

'Could you please give these to Angela?'

Emma had taken the letters and glanced through the senders. Enforcement authority, enforcement authority, enforcement authority. It seemed absurd. Is that why Angela sleeps in the office?

With her hip flask for company, she had sat in the car, conducting online research until she found Benjamin's address on Östermalm. An eminent old three-storey building with wide stone steps and an old-fashioned cage elevator.

Her index finger is on the doorbell, but still she hesitates. She wants to minimize the risk of Angela simply refusing to open. Instead, she calls her boss on the phone. Moments later, she can hear it ring on the other side of the solid timber door. Angela is in there.

Now she rings the doorbell. The shrill sound gives her a start. Why is she so nervous? She has a right to demand answers from the person who is using her. Or has she got it all wrong? Some part of her still doesn't want to believe that she has been duped, that Angela could be so calculating.

To Emma's surprise, Angela opens the door almost immediately. Even though she's dressed in casual clothing – a grey turtleneck sweater and matching trousers – she frightens Emma with a grim, almost lunatic look in her eyes.

'Why are you calling my mobile when you're standing outside the door?'

It takes considerable effort for Emma to speak calmly. 'I wanted to double-check that you're here.'

Silence. The only sound in the background is Danny Saucedo, that melody that makes your chest ache.

Finally, Angela takes a step to the side and asks Emma in with a put-on smile. 'Since you've come to find me here, I assume it's about something important.'

'You could say that.' Emma takes her boots off inside, hangs her jacket on an empty coat hook, and follows Angela to a living room decorated with masculine colours, straight lines and minimalist details.

'Would you like a glass of red wine?'

'No, thanks.'

Angela walks to a dining table, on which sits an open bottle of Ripasso. She pours a glass and holds it out to Emma.

'You don't have to pretend for my sake. This is much better than the swill in your flask.' Angela swirls the wine around the glass. Emma can smell the aroma.

She takes the glass and samples the wine while Angela fills a glass for herself. The lawyer strolls to a brown leather lounger and sits, nodding at Emma to take the lounger beside it. Emma reluctantly lowers herself into the chair, twisting her body into a half-sitting position as if she were sunbathing. She feels as though she and Angela are best friends at a wellness weekend. This is not how she had imagined the confrontation.

'How was the meeting with your client in Flemingsberg?' Emma sticks to the interview strategy she's prepared over the last few hours.

'You know I wasn't there. Get to the point.'

'Okay.' Emma feels increasingly certain that Angela knows why she's here. 'There is no stalker. You made him up.'

Angela brings her glass to her lips, signalling to Emma with a nod that she wants to hear more.

'I found the documents you put together about Jasmine. Various information you gave me about Andreas Kilic – his vehicle, his description and so on – can be found in the police register. But then you added at a later point that the girlfriend was pregnant – after I told you about the couple's child. You couldn't have seen that in the police register.'

Angela sips on her wine. 'I must say, impressive.'

'And then we have the stalker's tattoos I told you about. In his description it reads just as you told me, that he has a skull and a spider web. But, as you now know, he had them removed through laser treatment nine months ago. Jasmine couldn't have seen them, or at least not at the point in time you told me.'

Angela twists the glass on her lap. She seems genuinely proud. 'This is why I hired you. I knew you were a talented investigator.'

'But why? Do you know how many hours I spent on that stalker? You even tried to tell me Jasmine was the one who lied, when in truth it was you. And you lied with regard to the ACA group. You were a member yourself, and that's how you knew Jasmine.'

Angela smiles as if she pities Emma. 'The thing is: I used to be Sweden's hottest lawyer. I was a TV legal expert with a team of incredibly hard-working people. And what happened next? I happened to publish a post on Facebook using the term "sons of beards". Of course, you can't say that in our politically correct country, and all hell broke loose.' Angela empties her glass, the muscles in her neck tense. 'It seems that people *want* women to get raped by those cute, innocent boys. I cannot comprehend how they can be so naïve. But people like you or me – people who are clued-up on such matters – aren't permitted to say it out loud, because then we are racists.'

Emma opens her mouth to ask whether her boss is referring to the controversial entry about immigrant children she read about, but closes it when Angela raises her voice.

'One post was enough – one single post – to lose everything. That is the state of freedom of speech in Sweden. My clients jumped ship, commissions dwindled, I moved to a smaller office, sold my furniture, rented out my apartment.' Angela presses her lips together for a moment, then carries on more calmly. 'I know you were there – he called. You can throw the letters in the bin. I don't want to see them.'

'I'm sorry,' says Emma lamely.

'Me too. But—' Angela holds her index finger in the air. 'I still have the firm, a firm that I built up over fifteen years. I am going to do everything to keep it, whatever it takes, even if it's risky. I promised it to myself from the start. And when Jasmine's brother was arrested for murder, my chance came.'

Emma suddenly has the hiccups and presses her fist to her mouth to hold back the next one. She focuses on Angela.

'I was with a client in police custody when I heard what had happened. Of course I was upset by Jasmine's death, but then I accepted that I couldn't change that, no matter who committed the crime. But if I succeeded in getting the person towards whom all the evidence pointed acquitted, I would restore my good reputation, and everyone in need of a good defender would hire me. Absolutely everyone.'

Emma's doubts flare up once more. 'So, you do believe Nicolas is the murderer?'

'That doesn't interest me. I'm a defence lawyer. I do all I can to get my client off, no matter what they've done. That is my job, and that counts for you too.'

Emma nods, even though she's no longer certain whether she wants to keep this job.

'But why invent the story with the stalker?' she asks, since she still doesn't get it.

'I'm sorry about that, but I really needed this case. To convince Nicolas to engage me, I had to let him believe there was a stalker we could deflect suspicion on to.' Angela moves her feet up and down, and her fluffy slippers look like two frolicking bunnies. 'It was easier than I thought. He swallowed the story immediately.'

Emma tries to organize her thoughts. Angela invented the story with the stalker to win Nicolas as her client. A case with a huge media buzz, which – if all goes according to her plan – will lead to an acquittal and new clients. What can she say? That there's a devil inside Angela the like of which the world has never seen before? Or that she is completely insane?

Angela puts on an expression of innocence. 'There is still too much of the policewoman inside you, Tapper. Forget it. In our judicial system, everyone has the right to a defence lawyer, and we are going to save the Köhler firm.' She raises her glass in a toast, but Emma can't bring herself to raise hers. Even though she feels some sympathy for Angela's situation – one single Facebook post destroying her career seems unfair – all the lies weigh heavy in her stomach.

'I should go now.' Emma rises inelegantly from the lounger.

Angela lowers her glass. 'You aren't going to drink with me? Are you going to quit, just like that?'

'You lied about the stalker, and you lied about the ACA group.'

Angela deposits her glass on the floor with a thud, stands up and points an accusing finger at Emma. 'You judge me. You of all people, who drove a fifteen-year-old to jump in front of a train, you come here and dare judge me.'

Emma summons all her strength. 'How am I supposed to do a good job when you don't tell me everything you know? You knew Jasmine, and Jina told me you and Jasmine always stayed and talked after the meetings. You knew Jasmine was being sexually abused. Don't you think that is relevant to the investigation?'

'Jina!' Angela laughs. 'I had a feeling it was she who blabbed.' Suddenly she falls silent, a shadow of fear passing across her face. 'What did she say about me?'

'Nothing. She has a deep respect for the confidentiality agreement.' Emma doesn't want to discuss Angela's mother and grandfather right now. That doesn't belong here.

Angela seems to crumple with relief. But somehow she remains collected, lifting her chin. 'I do too. No one in an ACA group gives out names. But now that you know I was a member, I can tell you that you were right. Jasmine was sexually abused, but she never said who by. The trauma was so deep-seated that she was never able to talk about it, not even after several years of therapy. But believe me, I was glad when you told me what you found out about Giorgio. Perhaps Jasmine's tormentor will finally receive what he deserves.'

Without answering, Emma walks to the hallway. Angela follows close behind.

'Don't forget that you have me to thank for having a job once more. I believe in you and I'm convinced we can win this case.'

Emma spins around. 'Not if you keep withholding information from me. And it would be nice if you showed some commitment. I've seen very little of you thus far.'

Angela folds her hands, seemingly considering this allegation. 'Okay, I want to be completely honest with you. It all became too much for me. The shitstorm online, my firm on the verge of bankruptcy. I was totally burned out.' She shakes her head. 'What, do you think, was that like for me? As a workaholic? And so I hired you – for three reasons. Partly because I could no longer handle everything on my own. Partly because I knew how you had been treated, but most of all because I had a feeling you and I could become a strong team.'

Emma slips into her jacket, feeling torn. Should she stay a little longer, despite everything? Angela has just bared her innermost feelings to her. Is it okay for her to simply up and leave? Can one leave a person alone in that state of mind? Chaos of thoughts and emotions. But her disappointment about the lies sits deeply. Not even whiskey and wine can flush it away.

Emma pulls the letters from the government enforcement authority from her inside pocket, places them on a stool by the wall and leaves the apartment.

'After everything I've done for you!' roars Angela down the staircase. 'After everything I've done for you!'

47

Emma leaps into her car, slams the door shut, rests her head against the steering wheel and breathes deeply, trying to sort out her thoughts. What should she do? Drive home and tell the world to go fuck itself? Quit her job and register with the unemployment office once more?

She reaches for the flask in her glovebox and drinks. But it's not helping; the chaos in her head remains. Even though she condemns Angela's dirty tricks, she can't help but admire her too. Emma has never before met a person who fights with such determination to save her firm, her career and her reputation.

She looks up at Angela's window on the third floor, where two large candles emit soft light. Should she go back up there and tell Angela that despite everything she will help her get Nicolas Moretti free?

Emma's moral compass spins wildly in all directions. Angela doesn't give a damn whether Nicolas murdered Jasmine or not. Emma does. At the same time, she wants to win the case and prove Hellberg wrong. In that regard, she and Angela are alike – each wants to restore their reputation and their career.

Emma pulls out her phone and dials Simon's number. He answers on the third ring.

'No, thanks. I don't need drugs.'

Emma holds the phone away from her ear, wondering what he means.

'You must realize that this wasn't particularly helpful for Nicolas,' he goes on. 'Striking down a guard and all that.'

When Emma realizes why Simon is being so cold, she rubs her hand across her face. After everything that's happened in the last few hours, she'd completely forgotten about the incident with the cocaine. And that Angela had accused Simon and Hellberg of smuggling the drugs into the remand prison.

'No, that wasn't ideal,' she mumbles. 'I wonder how he got his hands on the stuff.'

'Listen, Tapper, I've got work to do. What do you want?'

'Have you questioned Roland Nilsson?'

'Yes.'

'How'd it go? What did he say?'

'You can cross him off your list. The forensics results from the Santa costume are back. They found no trace of Jasmine.'

'Really?' Emma wipes the windscreen, which has already fogged up again, and tries not to let her frustration show. 'But didn't you find anything else in the apartment? Perhaps he got changed before he went back to Jasmine's. The fabric on the steel bar below the balcony was purple and yellow.'

Simon snorts. 'We did not search his apartment. At that point, we had nothing on the man. The only crime he's guilty of is adultery, but as you know he and his wife are going through a divorce. He has no motive. Forget him as a suspect; it wasn't him. First of all, he was far too drunk to climb up a ladder, and second, he seemed genuinely surprised when we told him that Jasmine was expecting his child. He had no idea she was pregnant. Listen – I must go.'

'Hang on, just one more thing.'

A sigh at the other end.

'Can I have a copy of Jasmine's phone records? I need to check something.'

Another sigh. 'I don't have time for this game any longer. Tell me why you want it, or else this conversation is over.'

Emma considers telling Simon about Angela's lies. But how would that help? They would probably take the case off Angela, which might not be the worst idea. The way things look at the moment, they'll lose anyway. They have nothing left against Roland Nilsson. They'll have to start from scratch, and Nicolas is the most plausible suspect.

Even if Emma doesn't want to believe that he did it, she is this close to agreeing with her former colleagues. All evidence points to Nicolas. Furthermore, he didn't react when she indirectly accused him of the murder, and he is prone to violent behaviour under the influence of drugs. The night of the murder he had consumed MDPV, a drug well known for inducing excessive violence. And then there's the issue with the prophecy.

'I want to see if I—' She breaks off mid-sentence. She can't possibly tell Simon that she's looking for a fortune teller in Bromma whom Jasmine supposedly visited, and that the woman's phone number might be on the list. Angela had explicitly advised her against mentioning this to the police. Still, she has to find out if anyone else knew about the prediction. She refuses to believe that Nicolas is the only one.

'If I may give you a piece of advice,' says Simon, 'lay off the booze. Later, Tapper.'

The line crackles. Simon has hung up.

Emma starts the engine, cranks up the heater and begins a discussion with herself. Does she want to continue to work for Angela? Does she want to get Nicolas off even though he might be the murderer?

Eventually, she drives off. 'There is still too much of the policewoman in you,' Angela had told her, and perhaps she's right. But she had also said she was glad about what Emma had found out about Giorgio Moretti. Even if Nicolas is guilty, there is still a fourteen-year-old boy who needs help.

His little brother.

An hour and a half later, Emma is sitting in her car on Dagsverksvägen in Spånga, observing the entrance of a grey multi-storey building where Adam Ballin lives with his mother and three siblings. He is the boy Giorgio took into the storeroom during the football tournament.

She found him online. On the tournament home page there was a team photo, together with the names of players and a few newspaper articles praising Giorgio's dedication and commitment to make football accessible to all youth, regardless of their background or social class.

One of the articles quoted him as follows: 'Several of the youths have shown interest in joining a club, a circumstance that gives me particular joy.'

'Yeah, right,' Emma had muttered. More boys for him to abuse.

She drains her flask. What would a fourteen-year-old boy do on a Friday night in Spånga in the middle of winter? Hang out at some school grounds? Too cold. At a youth centre? Possible. In that case, he might be home late. Or is he gaming on the computer with a friend?

Emma is stretching when the front door of the house suddenly opens. It's probably the tenth time since she's been sitting here. This time, however, two lanky teenagers emerge, burying their faces in the hoods of their warm puffa jackets so that Emma can't make them out. But when they cross the street in front of her car, one of them looks up.

Adam Ballin.

Emma gets out of the car and follows them, smells the nicotine wafting through the brisk chill and sees the glow between their fingers as they share a brotherly cigarette. They cross another road and walk through the car park towards a Lidl supermarket. Adam throws away the cigarette before they enter the shop.

Emma watches from a distance. The pair stock up on lemonade and energy drinks, debate whether to select crisps or cheese puffs, and fill a paper bag with loose confectionery. While his friend lines up at the checkout, Adam slinks back outside and tries to light a smoke, but the lighter doesn't want to work in the strong breeze. Emma snatches the opportunity and rushes over to him.

'Not happening, is it?' She smiles at him. 'Hang on, let me try with mine.'

'Awesome.' He sticks his hands in his pockets while he waits.

Emma pretends to rummage through her handbag, all the while keeping an eye on the checkout. The friend is paying for his things, so she has to hurry. 'Oh, now I remember where I've seen you before. You were at the cup match here at the stadium the other day, right?'

'Um, yeah,' he mumbles, his lanky teenage body squirming.

'I thought so – I always remember a face. Your trainer is Giorgio Moretti.'

'Yes. You know him or what?'

'A little.' Emma takes one step closer to Adam, staggering a little. 'Shit, slippery!' She laughs as she studies the boy's face more closely. So young and vulnerable, so blurry. She squints in an attempt to focus her sight, but it's no use. 'I have a pretty serious que . . . que . . .' She clears her throat and focuses on her voice, trying not to slur her speech. 'A serious question. I saw that you went into a storeroom with him. I know what he's up to – you are not to blame. This is not your fault whatsoever, you're just a child. But if no one speaks up, he'll find new victims.'

'What the hell are you talking about?' Adam glances at the exit, and Emma's eyes follow his. The friend is walking towards the large glass doors, carrying a shopping bag.

'Did he want you to do something with him? I mean, something sexual.'

Adams eyes widen as if she were completely insane, and then he walks over to his friend.

'Who was that?' asks the other boy, laughing loudly once they've started walking away.

'No idea. Some crazy old drunk.'

Emma suppresses the urge to run after them. What on earth was she thinking, stalking a boy outside a supermarket and asking him if he was raped? That's not how it works. A teenager doesn't tell anyone just like that. Least of all a crazy old drunk.

Did he really call her that?

With a dry mouth and a sudden craving for greasy junk food, she walks back to her car the long way. She wants to avoid giving the impression that she's following the boys. She's not quite that crazy. This certainly wasn't her smartest move – that much she realizes, even if she's a little drunk. She laughs at herself. The idea to drive here seemed brilliant at the time.

At a petrol station nearby, she buys a bratwurst with bread and a double serving of mashed potato, stuffing her face as she walks back to her car. Her phone rings. She tries to get it out of her bag, succeeding only once she sets the paper plate down on the ground.

Angela's name is on the screen.

Emma considers hanging up, but then changes her mind. An apology from her employer would suit her just fine.

'We lost Roland Nilsson. The Santa costume was worthless.'

'Yes, I heard,' says Emma. 'I spoke with Si—'

'I want you to clear your things from the office. Right now. When I come into work tomorrow morning, I want to see no trace of your junk.'

'But shouldn't we—'

'Right now!'

Emma staggers back in alarm. In the same moment she realizes Angela has ended the call, she steps into her mound of mash.

48

Emma mutters expletives as she walks up the steps to the office, sometimes louder, sometimes under her breath. Then she stops to write the word *bitch* on the pale-yellow wall with her index finger. Bloody hyena! But perhaps this is for the best. Who wants to work for a psychopath like Angela Köhler? Emma trips on the topmost step, catches herself and fishes her keys from her bag. Suddenly she hears someone running up the stairs behind her. She glances over her shoulder.

Angela's toy boy.

'Out of my way!' he shouts breathlessly and pushes her away from the door. He pulls at the door handle, tries a key that doesn't fit, then searches for another. 'Damn!'

'What's going on?' Emma rubs the spot on her shoulder where she hit the wall. Instead of irritation, worry begins stabbing at her. Something is wrong, she can tell by Benjamin's flickering eyes and his panicked body language.

'She's hanging herself!' he yells, trying another key. 'We need to get in! She's dying!'

The pain in Emma's shoulder vanishes. Has she heard right?

'Let me,' she says, taking the bundle of keys from his hand.

'Go on, hurry up!'

Emma pulls herself together, shakes the key ring until she identifies the right key, sticks it into the lock and turns it. Then she yanks open the door and rushes in.

The room straight ahead is empty. Emma pauses, turns her head in the direction of Angela's office, then races to the door and storms in. Her eyes immediately fall on Angela, who is hanging from a lamp hook with a noose around her neck. Her bare feet twitch beside the desk.

Benjamin reaches her first, wrapping his arms around Angela's legs and lifting her up. 'Find something to cut the rope!'

Emma tears open the top drawer and cuts herself on something. Never mind! There are scissors in the second drawer. She jumps up on the desk and starts sawing at the rope.

The scissors won't cut properly. 'Come on!'

Another few attempts and she's done it. Angela tumbles head first on to the desk. With Benjamin's help, Emma lowers her to the floor and tugs at the noose, which has dug itself into Angela's skin, battling with the knot until it comes undone. Angela's chest isn't moving, and when Emma places two fingers at her neck, she feels no pulse.

'Call an ambulance!'

Emma positions her hands in the centre of Angela's chest and counts each push out loud. One, two, three, four. On number fifteen, she glances at Benjamin to see if he's called the ambulance yet. But his hand holding the phone hangs limply, his eyes staring blankly.

'Make the call!' She keeps pumping up and down, breathes air into Angela's mouth twice, keeps pushing. A rib cracks, but Emma ignores the sound. Six, seven, eight, nine. Another glance at Benjamin. 'Why won't you make the call?'

Next to her, an arm twitches. Emma stops and studies Angela. Small muscle cramps, her lips not as blue as before.

Emma slaps her cheek. 'Angela, wake up! You need to wake up!' She slaps her harder and shakes her.

Angela's hands shoot up all of a sudden, her eyes darting from side to side searchingly, lids flickering.

'Angela, it's me, Emma. Look at me. Look at me!'

After a while, Angela's eyes focus on her with a look that Emma can't read. But Angela is alive. She reaches for her throat and wheezes as if the noose were still there.

Emma gets up and plants herself in front of Benjamin, who is even paler than Angela. 'What's the matter with you?' She rips the phone from his hand. 'Have you forgotten the number? One – one – two.'

'Don't call. She'll go berserk.'

'What the heck . . . ? She could have died.'

Benjamin wipes the sweat off his forehead. 'You don't understand. She . . .' His shoulders droop. 'She does this regularly.'

Emma gapes first at Benjamin then at Angela. The latter is sitting up now and trying to remove the rope, which has become entangled in her hair.

Benjamin helps her, then tosses the rope aside and wraps his arms around her. He cradles her like a small child, rocking from side to side and stroking her hair.

In the middle of all this upheaval, Emma's phone rings. She tries to fish it out as quickly as possible so as not to disturb this surreal moment. It's Douglas, calling via Facebook Messenger. Emma accepts the call, but all she can hear is whistling and rushing sounds.

'Hello?' She walks to the next room. 'Douglas? Are you there?'

'You said I could call you,' he stammers eventually.

'Yes, for sure. Has something happened?'

Silence. Emma listens intently, trying to identify the background noise. Engines, tyres on asphalt. Cars driving at high speed.

Then Douglas speaks again. 'I'm on the pedestrian bridge at Frösundaleden. I can't go on. I'm sorry.'

49

There is little traffic on Birger Jarlsgatan. When a traffic light switches to red, Emma punches the steering wheel with her fist and looks around the darkness. No headlights, no approaching vehicles. She hits the accelerator. Someone toots at her, but she doesn't care. She's in a hurry, has to get to her destination in time to prevent Douglas from jumping off the bridge. The boy must not end like Oliver.

All happening at once. First Angela, now Douglas.

Her hands tighten around the steering wheel. She can't stop thinking about Benjamin's refusal to dial 112. Angela will go berserk – she does this regularly, he said. What the hell is that about?

Hangs herself, just like that.

Emma can't understand it. At the same time, it dawns on her that she has very few problems compared to certain other people. The setback with Roland Nilsson must have been a tough blow for Angela. Is she on the verge of losing the case and with it her firm? Is that why she tried to hang herself?

On the E4 she passes a Saab that's plodding along in no hurry, then flashes her lights at two idiots driving side by side, zooming past them once the one on the left realizes that he's in the way. Further ahead, a truck approaches the pedestrian bridge at Frösunda on which Douglas is standing.

Emma's pulse races out of control.

If only he hasn't climbed the railing yet. If only he's not jumping.

Emma has decided against alerting the police. She doesn't want to stress the boy out, doesn't wish to destroy the newly built trust. He called her, after all, wants to speak with her, not with some officials in uniform. Besides, she too is a policewoman – no longer on paper, perhaps, but in her heart.

She can make out the bridge up ahead now but can't tell whether there's someone on it. She glimpses something red – clothing, perhaps.

A sign announces the exit in 400 metres. Emma speeds up even more and takes the exit to Hagapark. Her car fishtails, slushy snow splattering around it like a fountain. She's driving too fast. The road is slippery, much too slippery. She tries to steer in the opposite direction, desperately trying to regain control of the vehicle. A copse of trees. Too close.

This is going to end badly.

Emma takes a few seconds to realize where the bang came from. The airbag.

Gaspy breath. Flashing headlights. Her head thumping, she tries to open the door but it's jammed. She leans in with her shoulder, hits and hammers at the door with her fists until she tumbles out of the car. She scrambles to her feet and runs towards the pedestrian bridge, sliding on the icy asphalt.

When some traffic lights switch from amber to green, Emma spots the red object again. It's Douglas's puffa jacket. He's sitting on the handrail, his legs dangling above the highway, where cars and trucks thunder past. Emma cautiously walks down the steps, stopping a few yards away from him.

'Douglas! Whatever happened – this is not worth it. Come down from there, then we can talk.' She holds out her hand, but he only stares at it.

'There's nothing you can do. It's over.'

'There is always something one can do. Even if everything seems hopeless right at this moment.'

Douglas gazes down at the vehicles speeding past and leans forward.

'Don't let go!' Emma calls, squinting in the headlights. 'Please, talk to me!'

He leans forward even more, his arms stretched out fully now. All that's holding him are his fingers around the rail. 'I wanted to get out to say hi to them, but Mum wouldn't let me.'

'Say hi to who?'

'Dad and Jasmine.' Douglas looks at her with tears in his eyes. 'We saw them outside a hotel in the city, and now she's dead. And that's my fault, just because I told her something.'

'You told Jasmine something?'

Douglas nods.

'What?'

'Everything. And she knew exactly what I meant. She was videoed and photographed too.'

Something trickles into Emma's eyes. She wipes it off and looks at her hand. Blood. 'Who videoed and photographed you?' she asks, fingering the bruise on her forehead. It must have happened on impact.

'I can't say. If I do, it'll all land online and everyone will find out. I was—' Douglas hides his mouth inside his collar, murmuring through the down filling. 'Naked.'

'Douglas.' Emma takes one step closer. 'You have done nothing wrong. Those who threaten you are in the wrong. They're even committing a crime. No one is going to accuse you of anything.

Please, come down. Everything feels awful right now. I don't know exactly what it is that you've got involved in, but from now on things can only get better.'

'You don't understand. You have no idea.'

'Then come down and explain it to me.' She extends her hand a little more. 'Please, come.'

Relief floods her when she finally feels his hand in hers. They both collapse next to the railing. What if he had jumped? What if he had taken his life, just like Oliver?

In the distance, Emma hears sirens. She peers towards Hagalund and makes out blue lights among the high-rise buildings.

'Did you call the cops?' Douglas gives her an accusatory look.

'No, someone else must have. Probably a driver who saw you.' She looks around, vaguely recognizing a dark silhouette by the small woods where she had the accident. Then she looks back towards Hagalund. The blue lights are coming closer, reflecting in the windows of the nearby houses.

'I don't want to talk to the police.' Douglas's voice switches to falsetto. 'That's impossible, I can't.'

'Don't worry. I'll stay with you the whole time.'

A patrol car stops by the bridge, and Emma pulls Douglas closer. Two uniforms climb out and approach them slowly, as if they are afraid of rekindling a situation that has evidently calmed down.

'What happened outside the hotel?' she asks Douglas as her stress level rises. She must get something out of him, a trail for her to pursue. 'Why were you there?'

'I don't know – it was really weird. My mother was upset about something, and I had to stay in the car. She was supposed to take me to a friend's place, but then she drove after my father instead. And then we saw that he was meeting Jasmine.'

'Which hotel?'

'Something with an R; I don't remember. It's close to the main station.'

'When was that?'

'Um, one day before Christmas, I think.'

Emma straightens up when the cops arrive, an older man with glasses and a woman with two plaits under her cap. She doesn't know them from before and introduces herself, one hand on Douglas's shoulder. 'I'm a policewoman. Emma Tapper. Former policewoman, I mean. I assume someone called in a potential jumper?'

'That's right,' says the woman, nodding at Douglas. 'Is that him? Do you know him?'

'Yes. He called me. I work for Köhler Lawyers. We represent Nicolas Moretti. I don't know if you're familiar with the case, but Douglas is his brother.'

'Yes, I've heard of it,' says the man. He bends down to Douglas and tries to speak with him. When he receives no reply, he asks who he can call. The mother or father?

'No one,' says Douglas, his voice laced with panic. 'You can't call either of them.'

'But we must. You're under-age, and they need to know what happened.'

Douglas pleads with Emma. 'They can't call them.'

Emma swallows. Her throat feels as if a noose were tightening around it. She knows the police officers are going to contact the parents and hand Douglas over to them, no matter what he says. The only way to prevent this would be for Douglas to give them clear signals that all is not well at home. 'Why can't we call your parents?' she asks in an attempt to nudge him in the right direction. 'You have to tell us what happened.'

Douglas breathes heavily and buries his face between his knees.

Emma squeezes his shoulder and keeps trying to make him talk, even though she knows it's pointless. She has witnessed a similar reaction with Nicolas. Both are equally withdrawn.

She gets up reluctantly and follows the policewoman a few steps to the side because she wants to hear more about the incident on the bridge. As they talk, two more patrol cars arrive. One of them stops in front of her wrecked Ford. Unease grows inside her. She fishes a mint from the pocket of her jacket and pops it in her mouth. While she answers the police officer's questions, she keeps an eye on the uniforms who are now walking around her car, shining into it with torches.

Her teeth chatter as she talks, but not from the cold.

Meanwhile, the policeman has draped a yellow blanket around Douglas's shoulders and is leading him to one of the patrol cars. Before climbing in, Douglas shoots a frightened glance at Emma. Or is that disappointment in his eyes? The thought of the police taking him to Giorgio gives her heart a painful twinge. But still she holds up a thumb to him.

'Excuse me.'

The rough tone makes her spin around. She is looking at a uniformed chest and tilts her head back so she can see the police officer who has approached her. Square chin, serious eyes.

'Is that your vehicle?'

Emma nods. He's probably already run her plates. If not, he will do so shortly.

'Then I must ask you to blow in here.' He attaches a mouthpiece to the breathalyser. 'We have a witness who saw you driving recklessly.'

Sweat forms on her forehead. In a daze, she thinks over the events of the past day. How much has she had to drink? A few sips of whiskey in the car, a glass of wine at Angela's, then a dram of – no, she should be fine.

She takes a deep breath, closes her lips around the mouthpiece and exhales until the tester has the required information.

Then she awaits the result as impatiently as the tall policeman.

50

This time, the roles are switched. In the interview room, Emma finds herself on the side of the table where the suspect usually sits. Today she is neither a policewoman nor a legal representative, but just a pathetic creature who got behind the wheel with alcohol in her blood. But worst of all – sitting opposite her is John Hellberg. He fidgets with a ballpoint pen, skimming over the transcript of her interview following the alcohol test.

He groans with distress but the glee in his eyes is obvious. 'Point 11 per cent blood alcohol. Jesus, Tapper.'

Emma clenches her fists under the table as hard as she can. The last thing she wants is to break down in front of Hellberg. She knows how much he is enjoying the situation.

On her arrival at the station, she had heard him whisper to the patrol officer, 'Make sure you take her blood too so she can't claim she only started drinking after the accident.'

Anything to make this as difficult as possible for her.

'Point 11 per cent,' he says with a chuckle. 'That's about two bottles of wine. Although . . .' His eyes travel downwards and come to halt around chest level. 'You're quite small and probably can't handle much. Maybe it was just one bottle.'

Emma spreads her fingers to avoid cramping up. It takes a huge effort for her to sit up straight on the chair.

A wide grin spreads across his face but quickly vanishes. 'So, you admit to serious intoxication behind the wheel and reckless driving.' He looks at the transcript in front of him. 'You don't remember exactly how much you drank. Some whiskey, wine, some more whiskey. Then you decided to drive.' He clicks his tongue. 'Not your smartest move. Think of your client, Tapper. What will he think? This is damaging for him, too, after all. However, I do have to praise you for admitting you have a problem with alcohol. Not everyone does that. But of course, you know how it works with mitigation and all that.'

Suddenly, there's a knock on the door. Both are equally surprised to see who enters.

Angela.

A wedge in Hellberg's mockery, liberation for Emma. Or . . . She straightens up a little more, feeling rattled. What's Angela doing here?

Just a few hours ago, she was dangling from a rope above her desk in her office. Nothing about her suggests any such event now, merely the ultramarine blouse with the upturned collar, around which Angela wears a pretty bow.

'Hello, Emma,' she greets her curtly, and turns to Hellberg. 'I hope you're not trying to interview my client without the presence of her lawyer? You do remember that tiny rule, don't you?'

The glee drains from Hellberg's face. He glowers at Angela as she scurries over to the table on her high heels and sits on the wooden chair next to Emma.

'We were only chatting. Old memories and all that.'

'I can imagine. But now that I'm here, you may start.'

Emma tries to express gratitude with a smile, but her mouth is on strike.

'Well, we've already discussed the matter of drink-driving . . .' Hellberg sorts his papers. 'So, Emma Tapper, I am informing you—'

'One moment,' says Angela, cutting him off. 'I know that Emma admitted to driving under the influence. But a boy was standing on a bridge and was about to jump. She was forced to get there as quickly as possible. It was about life and death, and Emma saved him. And that is only down to the fact that she took the car.'

Hellberg sets the pen down on the desk and touches his chin, fingering a cut he probably gave himself while shaving. 'And what are you trying to say?'

'That the charges against Emma of serious intoxication behind the wheel are going to be dropped. She wishes to change her statement.'

With a strained expression, he picks the pen back up. 'Understood. I am noting it down.'

'And I want permission to drive in the next forty-eight hours,' Emma throws in, now that Angela has hit her stride.

'Forget it.'

'Oh, really?' says Angela. 'I haven't forgotten that you threatened to destroy my career if I didn't go to bed with you.'

Hellberg stares at her. 'I was only joking. Are you still hung up on that?'

'No. But your wife might be, or all the others who follow me on social media.'

A vein on Hellberg's forehead bulges. 'You probably don't have many of those followers left.'

'I still have enough. Do you want to take the risk?'

'Okay,' Hellberg says after a while. 'Who gives a shit? Can we continue now?'

Angela nods.

'Then let's move on to the previous reports. Emma Tapper, you are suspected of assault. You forcibly removed a can of pepper spray from police officer Simon Weyler and sprayed it in Timo Rantanen's face, resulting in stinging and pain. How do you respond?'

Emma breathes in, trying to moisten her tongue with saliva, but her mouth is dry. 'I confirm having acted in this way, but I deny having committed a criminal offence.'

'Can you please explain that a little more? Help me understand.'

'In my view of the situation, Simon was at a disadvantage when he was attacked by Rantanen. And so I did what was necessary.'

'She pleads self-defence,' interjects Angela.

Hellberg glares at her. 'Legal assistance may be present during an interview, but ought to keep their mouth shut and let the lead interviewer do the talking. You do remember that tiny rule, don't you?' He smiles insincerely, and Angela responds with a smile that looks even more fake.

Emma bounces her knee nervously. 'How is Douglas? Does anyone know?'

'He's with his parents and meeting with a psychologist,' replies Hellberg without taking his eyes off Angela. 'There's no need for you to be concerned about him.'

Quite the opposite, she feels like saying. But what use would that be? Someone like Hellberg would dismiss her fears as nonsense and ask her if she has any evidence against Giorgio. No, she doesn't, only the panic in Douglas's eyes when he told her that there were films and photos of him. Something he's hardly going to talk about with Giorgio sitting beside him.

Eventually, Hellberg forfeits the staring contest with Angela and asks Emma to relate the incident with Rantanen in detail.

She starts again from the beginning, emphasizing once more that she had no choice but to intervene.

'The prosecutor is going to drop the charges,' Angela whispers into Emma's ear when she has finished talking.

Hellberg looks up from his notepad. 'I heard that.'

'You were meant to.'

Emma massages her aching temples with her fingers. 'Could I please have some water?'

'We're nearly done,' replies Hellberg. 'I want to talk about the incident with Christer Tillman. You contacted him and led him to believe he was the father of Jasmine Moretti's unborn child. He has decided to withdraw his complaint, but regarding your unethical conduct in this matter – I'm leaving that to the disciplinary committee of the Bar Association.'

'You do that,' says Angela. 'Anything else?'

Hellberg throws the pen on the table and picks up his smartphone, tapping at it. 'You might think you can get away with anything, but if I were you, I would—' He pauses dramatically, studying Angela as if he were genuinely concerned for her. '—cut loose your employee as soon as possible. Emma's conduct damages your good reputation as a lawyer – provided you still have such a thing. She drink-drives, breaks the rules of ethical conduct of your profession, and also—' He places the phone on the table and slides it in front of Emma and Angela. 'And also, she is shagging the man investigating the case of your client.'

Emma and Angela lean forward to see what Hellberg is referring to. When Emma sees the picture of her and Simon outside the pub at Traneberg, she feels as though she's floating away through the air. The image is blurred and taken from a distance, but it's clear enough to make it obvious what they are doing. She is lying on her back on a table, and Simon is bending over her. Their winter jackets conceal most of it, but not everything. Suddenly, she knows where the scratch on her back came from. She didn't fall after all.

She hovers back on to her chair, meets Hellberg's eyes and shrugs her shoulders. 'That's not me. That's Ester, my twin sister.'

51

Emma lowers her nose into the glass and sniffs the dash of whiskey left in the bottom before knocking it back. Nudges the glass towards the barman waiting on the other side of the counter. He'd asked her how the investigation into the Moretti murder was going and whether they'd get Nicolas Moretti off. She'd muttered 'Maybe' in reply, adding that there were several things afoot that might influence the verdict. She doesn't feel like talking about it. Right now, she has other problems.

For example, has she lost her job? She doesn't know. Following the interview, Angela had merely said 'Bye' and disappeared without even waiting until Emma was given back her personal belongings. She squeezes her eyes shut at the memory of the humiliation she was forced to swallow.

Former colleagues, staring at her. The station chief despairing of her, and all the while Hellberg grinning happily in the background.

Suddenly, someone speaks behind her. 'I only hope you didn't come by car?'

She turns her head. Simon. He's sitting on the bar stool next to her.

'What are you doing here?'

'I thought I couldn't really let you face this evening by yourself.'

Emma gazes aimlessly into the distance, mostly because she's too ashamed to meet his eyes. 'Very considerate of you.' Then something dawns on her. 'You called Angela?'

He answers with a shrug.

'Thanks,' she murmurs, noticing that he's eyeballing her glass. Her conscience is instantly pricked. Why is she drinking again? Why didn't she just drive home?

'Quite a lot going on lately,' he says after a few moments of silence.

'Yes.'

'For example, me sleeping with your sister, apparently?'

Emma pulls an apologetic face. 'Well, I had to . . .' She spreads her hands, knocking her glass in the process but catching it in time. 'You understand.'

'I do. But maybe Ester didn't have to lay it on quite so thick.'

Emma frowns.

'You don't know?' Simon pulls out his phone and holds it up for her. The display shows Ester's Instagram profile with a photo of her and Simon from the night at the pub. Two faces close together, smiling into the camera. The text suggests that Simon Weyler is Ester's new beau: *The man in my life.* Love heart, love heart.

'She even tagged me.' Simon puts the phone away. 'Now half of Sweden believes that I'm with Miss Secret.'

'What the—' Emma rubs her forehead. 'I am so sorry. I didn't know she'd do anything like that. I asked her to say that she's the woman in the photo, but only if anyone asks.' She tilts back her head and stares at the ceiling. 'This is so typical of her.'

Simon drums his fingers on the bar. 'I'm sure she meant well.'

Emma snorts. 'How did Hellberg get his hands on the picture in the first place? Did you ask him?'

'Some colleague from another team saw us. They were in the area to question residents.' Simon leans closer to Emma. 'He really

316

wants to finish you off, Tapper. The fact that you quit the service evidently isn't enough for him.'

'And now he's got it in for you too. You made out with the enemy, so to speak. That's what Hellberg is like.'

'Made out with.' Simon straightens back up. 'So that's how you see it.'

Emma focuses on a crack in her thumbnail, playing with it while her thoughts gather momentum. Did they really have sex on an icy table outside the pub? Asking Simon is out of the question. That would be admitting that she can't remember anything.

'Hellberg is a pig,' says Simon, and he orders a Coke and a bowl of peanuts. He too seems eager to change the subject.

'Did you get the phone records I asked you about?' asks Emma once Simon is served his order.

'What records?'

'Jasmine's. I need them to check something.'

'That's right.' Simon stuffs a few nuts in his mouth. 'No, you never told me what you needed the list for, and to be quite honest, we can't carry on like this. Too many things happen with you all the time.'

'But—' Emma begins to reply, but she closes her mouth when she realizes that it no longer matters. Her career at Köhler Lawyers is bound to be finished, and so it is no longer her job to locate the fortune teller. But she must tell Simon about Douglas's situation.

'You have to do something about Giorgio Moretti,' she says. Simon shoots her a doubtful look, but she ignores it. 'Douglas told me that someone took nude photos and videos of him. But he's too scared to say who.'

'And you believe it's Giorgio?'

'Who else? The boy is miserable. I hate to think about what's going on at his home.'

Simon places his fingers at the bridge of his nose, massaging the spot between his eyes. 'The prosecutor is never going to issue a search warrant based on those circumstances. Douglas will have to tell us, not someone who at the same time is arrested for drink-driving.'

'Then speak with him. Do something!'

'Like I said – I'm not sure there's anything else I can do for you, Emma. You have to understand – you made a fool of yourself. I know that you used to be a good cop, and I also know that there are many among our colleagues who believe you were treated unfairly, but—' He doesn't finish the sentence, looking instead at the door when someone enters.

Timo Rantanen, as always barefoot in wooden clogs. He scans the room for an empty table, his eyes catching on Emma and Simon. He trudges over to them, panting into Emma's face. She steels herself for an attack but relaxes a little when Ranta grins broadly.

'You damn ratbags. Here again, knocking back the hard stuff?'

'Um, whiskey,' says Emma.

'Coke,' adds Simon.

Ranta grimaces, baring teeth that are stained from chewing tobacco. 'And when are you growing into a real man, huh?' He pushes between them, placing his arms around their shoulders and leaning in with all his weight, forcing Emma to put one foot on the ground to stop herself from falling off her bar stool.

'I'm glad you're here. I generally try to avoid contact with the pigs whenever I can, but now that I'm meeting you here in peace, I need to tell you something you might want to know.' He gazes from one to the other. Even though Emma has drunk more than enough herself, she is repulsed by his permanent state of drunkenness.

'The chick you thought I killed,' he carries on. 'She dropped her scarf when she left here with her brother.' He nods towards the exit. 'Out here in the car park. I tried to catch up with them to tell them, but they ran away. They must have been shit-scared of something. Maybe of me.' He laughs at his own joke.

'Where is the scarf now?' asks Emma.

'I don't know. When I came back, it was gone. I thought you ought to know.'

Emma tries to understand why Rantanen has told them what he just did. Jasmine lost her scarf, that much is clear. And someone must have found it. Who?

'Why did you come back?' she asks.

'I went to Berra's place, down at Alviks Torg, but he didn't open up.'

'That's right.' Emma remembers him mentioning this during his interview. 'What did the scarf look like? What colour was it?'

'I think it was purple with yellow spots or something like that.'

For a moment, everything around her goes still, and Ranta blends into the background as a blurry mass. But her memory is crystal clear.

She is back outside Jasmine's apartment, standing below the balcony, gazing up at the green façade and pointing at the reinforcing steel from which flutters a scrap of fabric. Purple and yellow.

52

The grey parrot paces around his cage, pecking at the bars and flapping his wings. Emma feels like tossing a blanket over the cage. Goodnight, be so kind as to shut up. But it's probably time to get up. Rays of sunlight creep through the blinds, making her blink.

'Yes, yes, yes,' she mutters, folding back her duvet. Then she walks to the kitchen table and leans over the cage. 'What use are you to me? You are our star witness, and yet you don't want to talk.'

The parrot tilts his head.

Emma mimics the bird's voice. 'Who murdered Jasmine? Nicolas or Giorgio? Timo Rantanen or Roland Nilsson? Or someone else?'

No point. She walks to the sink and fills a glass with water. Her head feels like stodgy mush, and yesterday's events – the drink-driving, the humiliating interview and the subsequent pub visit – eat at her from the inside as if she had swallowed acid.

What time did she get home? At least she can assert that Simon merely hugged her at the end of their pub visit – no more, no less. She might have been a tad disappointed, but she can understand it. He probably saw through her memory lapse and didn't want to go to bed with someone who doesn't know what she's doing. The term 'rape' flashes through her mind. Not that she views it as such, but others might claim something like that if they knew the state

Emma had been in. The poor man! She's probably scared him off for good.

With shaking hands, she opens the pantry door and reaches for the bottle of whiskey. As she fiddles around with it, memories from yesterday's interview come back to her. What was it she had said? What promises had she made? 'Yes, I accept that I have a drinking problem. Yes, I am ready to seek counselling.'

Does she want to prove Hellberg right? Were her promises just hollow words?

She puts the bottle back and shuts the cupboard door. Fetches a jumper from her bedroom and pulls it on, walking back to the living room. Switches on the TV and the coffee machine, lingers in the middle of the room, wondering what to do today. Nothing. Vegetate on the sofa and binge-watch a series. Her eyes return to the pantry door. What the heck. She takes the bottle back out of the cupboard and opens it, but then her doorbell rings, foiling her plans. She stares into the hallway, reluctantly sets down the bottle on the kitchen bench and tiptoes to the peephole.

Strangely, she isn't surprised when she sees who's on the other side. The woman seems to pop up everywhere. Emma opens up, astonished at how normal Angela looks today, dressed in casual clothing and trainers. Well, the white windcheater looks horribly expensive, but still. No make-up, not even lipstick, hair in a pony-tail, wide headband with ear warmers.

'I thought some fresh air wouldn't hurt you. Get dressed and we'll go for a walk.'

No way, Emma would like to reply, but instead hears herself say, 'Okay, sounds good.' She invites Angela in before noticing that the bottle is still on the kitchen bench. She lunges over to it and manages to lay it flat in the sink before Angela appears in the doorway. 'Dress warmly. It's freezing outside.'

Emma smiles. Did Angela see the bottle? Probably, because she glances towards the sink as Emma goes to the bedroom.

She takes off her clothes and picks out some thermal underwear and warm trousers. When she closes her wardrobe door, she remembers something. Holding her jumper in front of her chest, she leans out of the door.

'Listen, Angela. There's something I found out last night.'

Angela closes an old police newspaper she was browsing through.

'I happened across Timo Rantanen at the pub in Traneberg. He told me Jasmine lost a purple scarf with yellow spots on her way home. But when he came back from Alviks Torg, it was gone.'

Angela touches her chin. 'Interesting. So you went back to the pub.'

Emma curses her mistake, but then pushes it aside. This is more important.

'If the scarf matches the fabric on the steel bar, that would mean the murderer picked it up on his way, then followed Jasmine and climbed to her apartment via the balcony.'

'But until we find the scarf on a suspect, we can't prove anything,' Angela replies.

'That's true. But still, it's evidence in favour of Nicolas's innocence.'

'I don't know. Rantanen is hardly a reliable witness, with his drinking problem. Let me think about it for a while.'

Emma disappears back in her bedroom. While she gets dressed, she feels slightly confused about Angela's feeble reaction. This could be the breakthrough they have been waiting for. What are the odds of Jasmine losing a purple scarf with yellow dots, and a scrap of fabric underneath her balcony being the same colour? But Angela is right. They would have to find the scarf on a suspect, and thus far they haven't.

When they emerge into bright sunlight a few minutes later, Emma is annoyed that she didn't bring sunglasses. Angela leads the way down the hill into the centre of Sundbyberg, then across the small river Bällstaån, lined with new multistorey builds. Along the jetties, the moorings lie deserted and frozen over at this time of year.

'I owe you an apology—' Emma falls silent when Angela starts to speak at the same moment, something sounding like the start of an explanation. The two of them look at each other and smile.

'You first,' says Angela.

Emma takes a deep breath of the crisp air. 'I am deeply ashamed of everything I've done. And for leaving you on your own last night. I had no idea how badly you were doing. I feel like an absolute moron.'

'You don't need to apologize. I'm doing fine.'

'But you tried to kill yourself.'

'Not at all. I called you and Benjamin because I knew you would cut me down.'

Emma glances at her, remembering Benjamin's words after they managed to get Angela to the floor. *She does this regularly.* What did he mean by that? Is hanging oneself something ordinary to him, some kind of bizarre game?

'You could have died. Don't you get it? Imagine we hadn't come in on time.'

'Emma, I know exactly what I'm doing. Of course I have my own little issues, but I know how to handle them and I have them under complete control. Try to view it as another form of healing. Some do yoga, others drink alcohol, and I—' Angela pushes the button on a pedestrian crossing. 'Perhaps I need somewhat more drastic measures to relax.'

'So this had nothing to do with your firm and the case? Because you thought we were losing?'

'Losing? We are losing nothing.'

Emma swallows. She doesn't want to say it, least of all now that it looks as if Angela might not fire her after all. But still she opens her mouth. 'I think it might be a good idea for you to talk to someone. Like a psychologist.'

Angela seems unfazed. 'I've been carrying these problems around since my childhood. No shrink can help me. Trust me, I've tried often enough. The only things that help me are pain and cheating death. No therapy in the world compares. I'm sorry if I frightened you. Benjamin has become used to it.'

'I see,' says Emma, with enough presence of mind not to scream, even though that was her natural reaction. Stefan Hermansson had said Angela likes it rough, and Emma in her stupidity had assumed her boss engaged in strangulation games in bed as a form of self-healing. But now she sees that the reality is much worse. Angela hangs herself, just like her mother did.

There's a rattle next to her, and she realizes that the red traffic light man has switched to green. She hurries after Angela, who is already halfway across the road.

'Enough about me,' says Angela when Emma catches up with her. 'How are you feeling after the drink-driving incident? You'll see that all will be well. Exigent circumstances weigh more heavily than a little blood alcohol. As soon as the matter goes to court, I'll talk to the prosecutor.'

'But I had point 1—'

Angela cuts her off by raising a hand. 'It was my fault too. I forced wine on you when you didn't want any. Just leave this matter to me. Please. I owe you as much. All right?'

Emma nods as she tries to keep pace with Angela. The more she thinks about last night, the more she agrees with her boss. It was an emergency situation. And besides, she has no drinking problem. She didn't drink this morning, and if she wants to, she can control herself. From now on, she's going to be an anti-alcoholic. She's got work to do, after all, and a case to win. At least, it seems that way, even if Angela hasn't explicitly said she can keep her job.

She listens with half an ear to Angela, who, following her dangerous move yesterday, seems to have undergone some kind of awakening or mystical personality change. Apologies about the stalker and the ACA group gush from her as they walk through a pedestrian underpass and then up to Sturegatan, which is still swathed in festive glitter.

'I acted terribly unfairly towards you, and I understand why you reacted the way you did. It was all my fault.'

'Forget it,' says Emma, pleased that in the end she didn't tell Simon about what had happened with Angela. That would have been difficult to take back.

'Come with me.' Angela drags her to a clothing store whose windows are stuffed with Santas and reindeer.

A small bell jingles when they enter the store. A circle rack hung with jackets near the entrance exudes the smell of leather. Further back, Angela finds a corner to her taste – formal and businesslike.

'Well, you and Simon,' she says, winking at Emma as they move among the racks, feeling fabrics between their fingers. 'I had a hunch something was going on, but that you were so keen on each other you didn't even manage . . .' She laughs, picks out a blouse and holds it against herself. 'How do you like this one? I'm going to try it on.'

'Do that.' Emma is relieved that Angela doesn't pursue the topic of her and Simon. Apparently, she isn't bothered that Emma lied about the woman in the picture being Ester. Thinking about it some more, Emma concludes that to Angela, the truth is of no import. To her, all that matters is proof.

Emma is filled with a certain sense of pride. Perhaps Angela isn't so bad a defence lawyer after all.

Absent-mindedly, Emma browses the shelves while Angela disappears into one of the changing rooms. After a while she waves Emma over, asking for her opinion.

Emma pokes her head around the heavy curtain and tries not to stare at Angela, who is only wearing her bra. Least of all she wants to stare at the bruises on her neck. Even though they've only recently had an intimate conversation, Emma struggles with the new girlfriend role.

'Looks lovely,' she says when Angela fastens the last button on the blouse.

'Good.' Angela unbuttons the garment. 'I've been thinking about what we spoke about earlier. Unfortunately, Ranta's story about the scarf doesn't help us. Bearing in mind this wretched prophecy and the fact that Nicolas punched a guard, we'll have to change our strategy. We're going to make use of the psychological assessment, according to which he suffers from a trauma that he cannot escape from and that causes him to believe it's about another person.'

'So, you believe he murdered Jasmine? Despite the scrap of fabric under the balcony?'

'It's getting difficult to prove anything else, don't you think?' Angela places the blouse on a stool and searches for something in her jacket, which she has hung on a hook. 'If we can prove, however, that Giorgio abused him sexually as a child, and if we can connect this trauma to the murder, he may receive a more lenient sentence.'

'But why in this case would he want to kill his sister? Shouldn't he cut Giorgio's throat?'

'Yes, you'd think so. But who can tell what's going on inside such a broken brain? Maybe Jasmine started talking more and more about the abuse, and Nicolas was terrified that it might become public knowledge.'

'Did she talk about it in the ACA group?'

Angela pulls back the corners of her mouth in a hard-to-read expression. 'No details. She was extremely cautious, but I still had the feeling she was on her way to opening up. Perhaps Nicolas noticed it too.'

Emma shifts her weight to the other leg. Could Angela's new theory be true? She doesn't want to believe it, doesn't like the idea that Nicolas committed the murder. At the same time, she is forced to acknowledge that the evidence suggests he did. Even if Giorgio is a swine, there's nothing to suggest that he climbed Jasmine's balcony on Christmas Eve. If Jasmine owned a purple scarf with yellow dots, she might even have climbed up the balcony at an earlier point in time – for example, if she had locked herself out.

'Douglas claims he was filmed and photographed. On the bridge, he told me that he was threatened with exposure on the internet.'

'Who threatened him?'

'He didn't say.'

Angela snorts. 'Sounds just like Jasmine. They cry for help but can't bring themselves to tell the truth about their father. The great Giorgio Moretti. Let's go get him. Try to find something that will lead to a search warrant for the house.' She bends over the stool and presses something to the blouse. Emma can't believe her eyes. Angela is removing the security tag with a gadget she carries with her.

'What are you doing?' Emma quickly glances over her shoulder. 'You aren't stealing the blouse, are you?'

Angela dresses, slipping into her jumper and jacket. 'Is it better to take the wheel drunk at the risk of running someone over?' she asks, zipping up her jacket to the neck.

Before Emma has a chance to reply, Angela strides past her and smiles at the saleswoman, who has approached them like a predator.

The woman smiles back, but Emma sees her glancing towards the changing room.

'Hang on, what are you doing?' demands Emma when she catches up with Angela near the till. 'This is theft.'

'Calm down. You don't want to be caught.'

'Me?' Emma huffs, but then she realizes that she's trapped. In court, it would look like they worked as a team – Angela removed the security tag while Emma kept a lookout.

Damn!

The little bell by the door jingles and Emma is struck by the cold air when they step on to the pavement.

'Hey, you!'

Emma looks back. The saleswoman is leaning out of the door, calling after them.

In a split-second decision, she rushes after Angela, who is already running.

53

Giorgio Moretti is tall and of a naturally strong build. And yet his drooping shoulders beneath his coat are obvious as he enters the funeral home at the edge of Lidingö centre.

Emma is standing in an entranceway diagonally across the street, wiggling her toes to prevent them from freezing. She has been following Giorgio for more than an hour, first by car when he left his Lidingö villa, and then on foot as he ran some errands at a tobacconist and a pharmacy. Perhaps he bought more antibiotics for Douglas – antibiotics his son requires for burns he inflicted on himself.

How could it have come to this? Why hadn't Douglas's teacher noticed anything? His friends, other grown-ups? But Emma knows how it goes. Some issues are so incomprehensible and complex that people can't handle them. Does this apply to Vera, Douglas's mother? Does she close her eyes to things happening right in front of her? Her husband raping her child? Emma can't even begin to imagine how such a suspicion would feel. Would she too block out the truth?

She apologizes to a man trying to get into the house. She steps aside so he can open the door, then glances back at the funeral home. Giorgio has turned around and is standing in one of the windows. Emma ducks into the entranceway and presses herself against the rough surface of the wall.

Did he see her? Hopefully not. The street is busy with people trying to get their shopping done before Saturday evening. They carry bags, swipe their phones or lift their purchases into their cars. Why should he notice her, of all people?

Emma massages her aching elbow. Their escape from the sales-woman had ended with Emma slipping on ice. Luckily, they had managed to shake off their pursuer.

'There we go, all went well,' Angela had said.

'Don't you dare drag me into anything like this ever again!'

Angela had lain down on her back, making a snow angel with her arms and legs, shrieking with laughter. At some point, Emma had become infected, and she had laughed so hard for so long that her stomach hurt. In truth, she hadn't felt this alive in a very long time.

Nevertheless, she is still mad at Angela, and definitely non-plussed. In the last few days, Angela has shown sides of herself that don't at all go with the image of the successful defence lawyer she upholds in public. Emma is undecided what to make of it. In some ways, it feels liberating. Who is she to judge? At the same time, the lies about the stalker and the ACA group continue to bother her. Sure, Angela wants to save her firm at any cost – that much Emma can understand. But what about Emma herself? Is she capable of defending a client who is suspected of murder? Is she doing right by Nicolas?

Emma pulls out her phone and searches for 'self-harming' in combination with 'hanging', skimming through the information appearing on the screen.

Those affected often feel an alleviation or relief from their psy-chological torments when they are replaced by physical or perhaps more comprehensible pain. Self-harming behaviour is not a failed suicide attempt, but rather a survival strategy.

Before she reads on, she glances at the funeral home, recognizing Giorgio's outline.

It isn't uncommon for self-harming to coincide with other self-destructive behaviours, for example eating disorders or certain personality disorders. Hanging oneself is the most extreme form of self-harm. In contrast to other forms of self-harming, there is a high risk of involuntary suicide.

Thanks very much. What if she and Benjamin hadn't turned up in time, or if neither of them had had the right key? It sounded like Angela had already been waiting on top of the desk with the noose around her neck until she heard someone outside her door.

Emma has never heard anything like it before, has never met anyone who risked their life in such a manner.

Is there even a diagnosis for this kind of personality disorder?

The door to the funeral home opens and Giorgio emerges. Emma tries to make herself as invisible as possible as he walks to his Tesla. But instead of climbing in, he walks past it and carries on away from the town centre. Strange. He isn't really dressed for a stroll outdoors – he is wearing neither boots nor hat, scarf nor gloves.

Emma pulls up her hood and follows him at a safe distance.

They follow a straight road lined by villas set on sprawling properties until Giorgio turns down a footpath. Emma speeds up so she doesn't lose him. The path leads to a small park, where she spots Giorgio behind a tree with his phone pressed to his ear. The conversation only takes a few seconds. Then he walks deeper into the park, meandering along aimlessly, to all appearances.

Emma wraps her arms around herself, shivering as she seeks shelter behind a stone statue. She is close to abandoning the pursuit when a boy with a backpack approaches Giorgio. They exchange a few words. Then they carry on together and eventually disappear behind some bushes. Emma speeds up, trying not to breathe loudly, but when she reaches the other side of the bushes the two of them are gone. Maybe they went up those stairs? She runs over there, taking several steps at a time, and peers around. The path at the top is deserted save for an elderly woman pulling a shopping trolley along. Emma climbs back down the steps. Are the two of them hiding somewhere? Have they sneaked off to a cosy rendez-vous al fresco?

Damn creep!

Even though Emma is stiff with cold, sweat runs down her spine.

She rounds another bush and searches around randomly. They must be somewhere; they couldn't have got that far.

Without warning, a shadow looms behind her, clamps an arm around her neck and pulls her back until only the tips of her toes touch the ground. Emma doesn't need to turn her head to know who it is.

Giorgio Moretti.

'You are damaging my reputation. Don't you get it?'

Emma pulls at his arm, fighting for air and struggling to hold on to the little bit of ground beneath her feet. 'Let me go!'

'Adam's mother called me. Apparently, some drunk woman outside Lidl claimed I sexually abused her son during the football tournament. Do you have any idea where such accusations can lead? Huh? Do you?' He squeezes his arm harder. Emma staggers, fighting his tightening grip.

Her feet lift off the ground and now she can scarcely breathe. Summoning her last strength, she tries to punch his sides with her fists, aiming for his kidneys, but her own body is in her way. Instead, she strikes something hard in his coat pocket and reaches inside to pull the object out. To her surprise, he suddenly lets go of her, and she tumbles to the ground. She puts a hand to her throat, gasping for air and trying to stand up, but her legs refuse to play.

Where did he go? Emma shuffles about in the snow, turns her head and sees Giorgio disappear along the path in the same direction they came from. The boy has vanished into thin air. Tears fill her eyes and she blinks quickly to dispel them, but also so that she can see what it was she pulled out of Giorgio's coat pocket.

A mobile phone in a black leather case.

Still gasping, she taps the screen and clenches her fist victoriously when the phone unlocks. She checks the last number he dialled.

Vera Moretti. Disappointment rises up in her. She had hoped it would be the boy with the backpack, hoped to identify him and bring him in to make a witness statement against Giorgio Moretti. She scrolls down the list of calls. Douglas Moretti, Erik Svensson, Petter Lund. Several names she will have to check. She taps her way to the email inbox and reads the first message from one Staffan Wiklander. It's about the new training times at the Lidingö ice rink. The next email is from a car insurance company regarding a claim for some parking damage that occurred outside the Friggavägen Coop between 8 and 8.20 on the morning of 25 December. Emma recalls the broken headlight she noticed during her visit to the Morettis on the day after Christmas Day. So the claim rings true, but something nags at her nonetheless. Hadn't Giorgio and Vera stated in their interview with Simon that they had stayed at home all of Christmas Day? She will have to ask him. The next few emails don't look as if they are from the boy Giorgio just met.

Emma lowers the phone to her lap, only to pick it back up quickly when she remembers what Douglas had told her on the bridge. That he was photographed, videoed and threatened by someone.

She opens the gallery and finds to her surprise and shock that the last photo Giorgio took shows Douglas on a bed. He eyes the camera with bemusement, posing naked in a way that is probably supposed to be sexy.

Emma doesn't know whether to laugh or cry. But one thing she knows for certain.

Giorgio Moretti is finished.

54

Early on Sunday morning, Giorgio Moretti is led out of his Lidingö villa in handcuffs by Simon and another officer in plain clothes to a car parked outside his property. He hangs his head, staring hard at the ground. It is quiet in this part of town; only a man walking his Rottweiler glances furtively at the hushed kerfuffle. Judging by his expression, he is wondering what is going on here this early in the morning.

Emma watches everything from the other side of the street, feeling frustrated. She would have liked to be part of the action, would have liked to arrest the man who abused his son. And she wants to search the house for further evidence they could use in court against Giorgio Moretti. After all, it's thanks to her that the major crimes unit can make this arrest. And what does she get? To stand around and freeze her toes off. Hellberg had even doubted her version of how she came into possession of Giorgio's phone. He hadn't wanted to believe Simon when he reported that Moretti had attacked her and gripped her in a chokehold. After some persuasion, though, he had accepted that an arrest by police would result in a huge and long-lasting media frenzy. Well-known football coach arrested for suspected paedophilia – sounded rather like Patrik Sjöberg, the athlete and former world record holder in the high jump, whose stepfather had sexually abused him for years.

And besides, it makes no difference to the Nicolas Moretti case. He is still suspected of murdering his sister.

A broken family. What a tragedy.

Emma looks out for ice as she crosses the road, waiting until Giorgio is sitting behind the tinted window of the Volvo before catching Simon's attention.

'Find anything?'

He turns to her, lowering the volume of the radio on his belt. 'We're still searching. And it'll take a while. This place is huge.'

'But what do you think?'

'He hasn't said anything, but it almost seemed to me as if he knew we would come.'

'He must have known that I'd find the picture on his phone.'

'Maybe. In that case, he may have successfully destroyed evidence at home. But on computers and the like, you can always find something. Let's keep our fingers crossed.'

Emma nods, overcome by the uncanny feeling that she's being watched. She instinctively glances at the tinted car window and shudders when she sees that Giorgio is looking at her. She turns her back to him.

'Have you checked out the damage on the Tesla?'

'No, I haven't had a chance. Listen, we need to go.' Simon opens the driver's door and places one foot in the car.

'Can't you do it now?' Emma holds on to the door frame and lowers her voice. 'I only want to know if it was Giorgio or Vera who was using the car. During their interview, they said they were home all morning on Christmas Day. Something doesn't add up. Give headquarters a call, won't take long.'

With forced calmness, Simon closes the door behind him. 'Maybe one of them popped out to get bread rolls for breakfast or something. That hardly means anything. It was the day after the murder.'

'It might, because neither of them mentioned it. Make the call.'

He shakes his head but takes a few steps to the side and does as she asked.

In the meantime, Emma moves closer to the house, noticing movement behind one of the windows. Is it Vera, or maybe Douglas? She would like to go inside and talk to him, make it very clear to him that he is not to blame for any of this, that his father alone is at fault. But her former colleagues would never allow her in; she has no business there.

She curses under her breath when John Hellberg, yawning, emerges from a garage beside the house. But she stays put, waiting. Let him try to tell her to bugger off – this is a public area, and besides, she hasn't crossed any cordons. Because there are none.

'Tapper,' he says briskly when he spots her. 'Where's your camera? One could almost think you've turned journalist.'

Emma ignores him, focusing instead on Simon, who is walking back towards her after making the phone call.

'I've just learned something rather interesting. There are two reports for the parking damage. One from Vera Moretti and one from a member of the public who contacted the police online. The problem is that, according to Vera's statement, the accident happened outside the Lidingö Coop around eight o'clock in the morning on Christmas Day, while the witness claims it occurred at 11.55 p.m. on Christmas Eve. Guess where?' He's struggling to contain his excitement and answers his own question before Emma and Hellberg get a chance to say anything. 'At Runda Vägen in Alvik, a side street right around the corner from Jasmine's apartment. Right at the time of her murder.'

'Hold on.' Hellberg braces his hands on his hips. 'There is someone who can testify seeing the Tesla near the apartment at the time of the murder?'

'Yes. One Anna Karlsson, resident of Runda Vägen, heard a bang outside her window. When she looked, she saw someone climb into the Tesla and drive off.'

'Description?' Hellberg and Emma say simultaneously.

'Well, that's a little vague. A person in dark clothing. We'll have to go there and question her.'

Hellberg swipes his hand across his forehead. 'And why the hell did you only find that out now?'

Simon pulls a face. 'Like I said, the woman reported the incident online. And you know how it goes. Our colleagues at the contact centre write a report if they have time, and haven't a clue that a few hundred yards away we're investigating a murder.'

Red blotches form on Hellberg's cheeks. 'All right. Let's assume this is true. Giorgio visited Jasmine just before the time of the murder and became upset about something. He was so stressed that he drove his car into something. Next thing, Vera reports an accident that occurred the following morning at a different address. What can we take from that?'

'She's covering for him,' says Emma.

Hellberg glowers at her, places an arm around Simon's shoulders and leads him to the side. 'Check out what Vera is doing inside, but don't let on that we . . .' His voice trails off. Emma breathes deeply to force down her growing frustration, but it's not helping.

She isn't welcome here. It's time for her to swing by Anna Karlsson's at Runda Vägen and extract a witness statement from her that will exonerate Nicolas.

She hurries to her car, jumps in and leaves the posh quarter. She can hear a rattling on one of the wheels – a reminder of her drunken drive and the accident. She needs to get the damage repaired. She doesn't even want to think of all the other things she also needs to fix. Still, she feels a nagging shame about the fact that she's been drink-driving for a long while now. Of course, she hadn't mentioned that when they questioned her. Why should she admit to more than they can prove? But everyone knows that it wasn't her first time. She simply had the bad luck to get caught. Or was it lucky after all? Because now she is forced to tackle her problems, can't get away with telling her counsellor that she doesn't really drink that much and isn't hurting anyone. And the excuse that she's only drinking to fill an inner void has turned stale. She has been forced to take responsibility for her actions and face the truth that she could actually have harmed someone else.

She takes the major thoroughfares, not yet busy at this time of the morning. An almost empty underground train thunders alongside her on Tranebergsbron, only a handful of passengers scattered through the carriages. The water under the bridge is covered with a layer of ice and snow; an old boat lies frozen in place between some bare trees. Suddenly, she notices movement in her rear-view mirror and leans to the side so she can see better.

What the . . . A green Audi is following her close behind. Hellberg's car. She looks from the road to her rear-view mirror and back. What does he want? A moment later, he winds down his window, attaches the flashing light to the roof, switches it on and blows his horn, demanding she pull over and stop.

Her body tenses as old memories of Hellberg pass through her mind. Him, leaning over her at her desk, rubbing his crotch against her chair. The chase for a burglar that ended with Hellberg driving into the woods and holding her down on the bonnet. 'I was only joking,' he'd said afterwards. 'I just wanted to see how you'd react. What, now you're mad at me?'

A few hundred yards further on she can see the Traneberg exit. Emma clicks on the indicator and slows down. Another glance into the rear-view mirror. She takes a deep breath, reaches for her phone in its holder on the dashboard, pulls it out a little and points the camera lens at the driver's door. When it's time for her to turn off, she puts her foot on the brake and adjusts her phone once more. Ready.

Hellberg toots at her again. Following the exit, she turns right at the first opportunity and finds herself on a street lined with trees and shrubs. A little further on lie tennis courts, closed for the winter. Emma winds down the window by an inch or two and climbs out, waiting by the driver's door while Hellberg walks over to her, holding a breathalyser.

'You're not driving to Alvik, are you?'

'What makes you think that?'

He gives a snort, removes the plastic cap from the tube and attaches it to the reader.

'Blow in here, Tapper. I hope for your own sake that you're sober.'

For your own sake. If only he were always this thoughtful.

Emma breathes deeply and bends down to the tube he is holding out for her.

'Not so fast.' He withdraws his hand. Inspects the tube, holding it so close to his face that he's going cross-eyed. Twists and turns it before inserting it in his own mouth and sucking on it like . . . Like in the wet dream he seems to be experiencing right now. She feels sick, staring at the tube he is once more holding out to her, saliva dripping from its end.

'Well then, show me you're not drink-driving.'

'What's this about?'

Hellberg grins a crooked grin. 'Do I have to take you down to the station? Is that what you want?' He brings his hand closer to her, rubbing the tube against her bottom lip.

Emma's temples throb. She twists her head to the side and shoves his chest.

'Ah, assault of an officer in the line of duty.'

Before she knows what's happening, Hellberg spins her around so she's facing the car, pressing his entire body weight against her back and stuffing the tube between her lips.

'Right, baby, blow!'

The plastic attachment pushes into the roof of her mouth. Emma tries to blow but all she can manage is a wheeze. One of her arms is jammed between her chest and the car door. With the other, she tugs at Hellberg's jacket. He grabs hold of her wrist and twists her arm on to her back. Her shoulder cracks, but at this moment she scarcely feels the pain.

'Let's try this again,' says Hellberg cheerily, rummaging in his trouser pocket for something.

'Let me go!' Emma isn't sure if he's being serious. Is he going to handcuff her? Or is this just some grotesque jest? Something he will later play down with words like 'I was only joking.'

'Let me go!' she shouts again, repeating the phrase louder and louder. When Hellberg shoves the tube further down her throat, her screams turn into indistinct retching sounds. Suddenly she feels something that silences her. At first she wonders whether she's only imagined it. But then there is no doubt – his hand is moving up and down in a fast rhythm, thumping against her backside. When he begins to moan, she knows for certain. What he pulled out of his trousers wasn't handcuffs.

He groans into her ear. 'Damn, Tapper. This is what you've been waiting for, right?'

Emma squirms in his grip and looks around searchingly. Not a soul to be seen who might be able to help her. Only the rushing of traffic over on the bridge.

'Don't worry, I'm not going to rape you. Do you think I'm stupid enough to leave my DNA on you?'

Her eyes fill with tears but she refuses to let them go. Instead, she focuses on the red flashing light in her car. But how can that help her now?

Hellberg moves his hand faster, gasping words he must have heard in porn movies. A few moments later his body convulses and his sounds become longer. Finally he says, 'You little whore!' and lets go of her.

Emma coughs when he pulls the tube out of her mouth, feels for the door handle, hurls herself into her car and locks the door while Hellberg is busy wiping his sperm on his underpants.

After all, he can't leave any DNA at the scene of the crime.

55

She can't drive on, can't see the road or other road users, almost hit a cyclist before. She stops eventually at Tranebergsplan. All she can hear is Hellberg's panting in her ear. 'How many colleagues have you shagged, Tapper? You and your sister, you are so cheap. You want my cock inside you, am I right, Tapper? Admit it.'

With trembling hands, she opens the video on her phone, forcing herself to watch it. To her simultaneous relief and horror, the film clearly shows her and Hellberg. It shows his contorted grimace when he pushes her against the car, shows what he does and that he forces her. And through the gap in her window, it's possible to hear everything that's being said.

She waits for the feeling of triumph in her chest, but all that is smouldering inside her is a deep sense of shame. How could she have allowed this to happen? She hadn't expected such an extreme turn of events when she prepared her phone. She'd thought Hellberg would come out with his usual arrogant bullshit. '*You do know your new career lies in my hands? People like you must be kept on a short leash, Tapper. You shag anything that moves.*' At most, he would try to hit on her, perhaps rub himself against her like he used to, but not . . .

She closes the video.

. . . not go this far. She grabs a packet of wipes from the glovebox and pulls one out, washing her hands, forearms and cheeks. Then she pulls out another and scrubs the inside of her mouth so hard that the saliva she spits on the street tastes of blood. She gazes at the red slime, clenching her teeth as Hellberg's actions begin to sink in.

That bastard!

She pulls the door shut, locks her hands around the steering wheel and heads towards Anna Karlsson's address with only one thought on her mind.

He's going to be sorry for this.

On Runda Vägen, she spots Hellberg's Audi, drives past it and turns at the next intersection. She parks so that she can keep an eye on his vehicle. Let him question Anna Karlsson – Emma has other things to worry about now.

Ten minutes later he comes out and strides with an irritating bounce in his step to his car. He seems relaxed, as if today were the best day of his life.

Emma follows him at some distance when he takes off swiftly, waiting for the Audi's rear end to disappear behind the hedge of a property before turning the corner herself. Along Alviksvägen, he drives exactly the way she knew he would – far above the appropriate speed in these icy conditions. Emma puts her foot down while two opposing thoughts wrestle in her mind.

Don't do it! Come on, drive, dammit! No, this could end really badly. Who gives a fuck?

She catches up to him, then overtakes at breakneck speed. She breathes deeply before cutting in ahead of the Audi and hitting the brakes. She holds the wheel firmly as she fishtails, hearing her tyres screech, but not only hers. In her mirror she sees the Audi swerving to the left, bursting through a snowdrift and knocking over a traffic sign before crashing into a huge oak tree.

She hears a dull bang. Snow tumbles from the branches on to the green paint.

Emma pulls over and climbs out. Crosses the road and runs to the Audi, whose bonnet is crumpled like a concertina. Through the broken windscreen she can see Hellberg hanging in the seat belt with a wound on his forehead. Blood is dripping on to the inflated airbag. He whimpers as he tries to straighten up.

'Hellberg!' She smacks his cheek. 'What the hell happened?'

He turns his face to her. His pupils flicker from side to side.

'You had an accident and need help. But first you should take a look at this.' Emma pulls out her phone, starts the video and holds it through the shattered glass in front of his face. Even though adrenaline is pumping through her veins, she shudders with disgust at having to listen to this shit again. Hellberg's eyes widen as he realizes what the video contains. Once she has achieved her goal, Emma withdraws her hand, lifts Hellberg's chin and waits for his eyes to focus.

'One wrong word about this accident and the video goes public. If I want to return to the police, you will give me glowing references. The photo showing me, or rather my sister, and Simon disappears. Yes, you know what I mean. Oh, and the matter of Oliver Sandgren. His suicide was tragic, but not my fault. You will assume full responsibility. Shall I go on?'

Hellberg shakes his head and utters with gargling breath: 'Ambulance.'

'Certainly, it'll get here soon. But first I need to . . .' Emma opens the buckled door as far as it will go, reaches for his jammed legs and feels for his fly.

'What are you doing?' The fear in Hellberg's eyes fills her with a surprising amount of pleasure.

'Just one more small detail. Hold still.' She grimaces at the thought of what she has to do, but she has gloves with her to make it more bearable.

The moment she's done it, her phone rings. It's Simon.

'Where are you? You just vanished.'

'Yes, I left to talk to that witness, Anna Karlsson.'

'Forget it. Hellberg is on his way there. I need you here. We can't get anything out of Douglas. He says he'll only talk to you. He really needs to tell us something about the picture on Giorgio's phone. How it was taken, whether they were home alone, and so on.'

Muttering sounds from the car. Emma presses a hand to Hellberg's mouth, smothering his whining for an ambulance with her glove.

'You mean, you want me to do the job of the police?'

Brief silence at the other end. 'Yes. Will you help us out? It might be useful for Nicolas in the end.'

From the corner of her eye, Emma notices a man dressed in grey approaching from the direction of a bus shelter. She bends over Hellberg and casts one last warning stare at him. Then she takes her hand off his mouth and moves around the car in a hunched position.

'I'm on my way,' she tells Simon. 'Give me twenty minutes.'

56

When Emma arrives at the Moretti villa, all is still quiet on the street. But on closer inspection, she spots a few inquisitive faces behind the curtains across the road, and one neighbour is shovelling snow in his driveway even though he could easily drive over the few millimetres of fresh snow that fell last night.

Simon is waiting for her on the steps outside the front door, absent-mindedly playing with the pink flamingo.

'Hellberg was in a car crash. I just heard from headquarters. Apparently, he drove head-on into a large tree.'

'Oh dear,' says Emma, opening her eyes wide enough to give the impression of being surprised by the news. 'How is he?'

'His condition is serious, I believe. The paramedics are cutting him out as we speak. Evidently, he's conscious.'

'Wow. I read that the department for transport is warning of black ice. Let's hope he got through it okay, despite everything.'

Simon nods. Then he opens a paper bag he's holding in his hand, inviting Emma to look inside. She leans forward and sees a silver nutcracker with an elaborate handle.

'We found it in the garage. It was rolled up inside a yoga mat that was hanging on the wall. Do you follow? Jasmine had some bruising on her finger that the pathologist struggled to explain. And on the night she was murdered, they were eating nuts but we never found a nutcracker.' He jiggles the bag in front of her eyes. 'So now the Tesla was seen not far from Jasmine's apartment on the night of the murder, and we've found a hidden nutcracker. If Jasmine's fingerprints are on this, Giorgio not only sexually abused his children but also murdered Jasmine. His own daughter.'

'But why?' asks Emma.

'Well, I don't believe she confronted him about being a sugar daddy, as he tried to tell us. I believe their meeting was about the abuse she was subjected to as a child. She wanted to speak with him about it, wanted him to apologize, heal old wounds and so on. I don't know. But of course, he couldn't tell us that. He was terrified that Jasmine would expose him by, for example, writing a book or talking about it on TV or something like that.'

Emma tries to make sense of everything. 'But then why would he remove the nutcracker from the crime scene and not the knife?'

'To deflect suspicion on to Nicolas.'

Emma considers this for a moment but fails to see the logic behind it. Leaving a murder weapon behind at the crime scene in order to incriminate someone else makes sense. But his own son? And the nutcracker. Why go to the trouble of making it disappear?

'It was inside a yoga mat, you say?'

'Yes, in the garage.'

'Is Giorgio right- or left-handed?'

Simon opens his mouth to reply but then closes it, gazing at her pensively. 'Now I see. When you broke into my filing cabinet, you were after the post-mortem.'

'Broke in? Me?' says Emma with a smile that equals a confession. 'You were trying to find out during the interview whether Nicolas is right- or left-handed. It doesn't take a post-mortem report to tell me that you're suspecting someone left-handed. So, which is Giorgio?'

'I don't know, but I'll have it checked out.'

'Do that. Not that you and your team seemed to care much about the fact that Nicolas is right-handed.' Emma winks at him. 'But still.'

'Of course we discussed it. But it isn't conclusive evidence. The murderer could have used his other hand on purpose. There are plenty of people who watch *CSI*.'

'Sure.' Emma gives up, can't be bothered pointing out to Simon that the police were wrong once again. She peers through the crack in the door Simon left open. 'Okay. Where is Douglas? I'm sure he'll be able to tell us which hand Giorgio uses to write.'

Simon invites her into the hallway, where Åsa, a former colleague, nods at Emma before carrying on with her search of the coat stand.

Vera is standing by the extractor fan in the kitchen, smoking. She's wearing leggings and an oversized knitted jumper. They greet each other across the room, and Emma walks over to Douglas, who is sitting on a corner sofa with a laptop on his knees.

'How are you?'

A vampire movie flickers on the screen, but Douglas looks as if he is on another planet.

'Come on, let's go to your room,' says Emma.

'Hang on.' Vera taps the ash from her cigarette into the sink and walks over to Douglas, stroking his hair. 'Want me to come with, darling?'

Douglas looks up at his mother slowly and nods.

'Then we might as well stay here,' says Vera with red-rimmed eyes. 'It's utterly absurd. You have to understand that we're both in shock and that Douglas needs me. If it's true . . .' She touches a silver amulet on her chest. '. . . which I don't believe for one minute. Where did you get all this from, anyway? You are destroying Giorgio's life. Our life. Don't you see?'

The tension in the room is palpable. 'Yes, I can see that this must be extremely difficult for you. But I have to speak with Douglas alone. He asked me to. I'm sure it's in your best interests for him to tell us freely and openly what happened.'

'But what exactly is supposed to have happened? Why did you arrest my husband? What are you accusing him of? He can't . . .' Vera's eyes dart back and forth between Emma and Simon, who is standing a little off to the side.

'Douglas,' says Emma. 'Why don't you go ahead to your room? I need to speak with your mother first.'

Without a sound in reply, Douglas folds shut the laptop, dragging his feet as he walks off.

Emma turns back to Vera, frantically searching for the right words. But what do you say to a mother whose husband has raped their child?

'Like I said, I can't even begin to imagine how difficult this must be for you,' she begins softly. 'But there is evidence that suggests we are correct, or else we – er, the police wouldn't be here. And they never would have arrested Giorgio and searched the house otherwise. So, if you know something, or if you have the feeling that something is wrong, tell us.' Vera turns pale and Emma senses that her mind is working in overdrive. Perhaps she'll relent soon. 'Remember that this is about your son,' she carries on. 'He's still a child, and if it's true that Giorgio . . . well, then your husband carries full responsibility.'

Vera takes a few swaying steps and clings on to the backrest of the couch. 'No, no,' is all she can manage.

'We know Douglas burns himself. And if I understand it correctly, you were willing to take him to a youth psychiatrist, but Giorgio wouldn't let you.'

Vera stares into blank space. 'No, that's not right, that's not possible, it can't be.'

Emma places a hand on Vera's arm. 'I'm going to speak with Douglas now. In the meantime, try to get some rest.'

Vera walks around the sofa in a daze and lowers herself on to it.

Emma shoots a glance at Simon. He nods his assent, taking over Vera's supervision.

Douglas's room is decorated in dark-blue tones and suggests that football and video games are his two great hobbies. CD cases lay strewn on the ground, a large screen is attached above a desk. Douglas is sitting in a swivel chair, and mounted on the wall behind him are several posters of well-known football players. One of them shows Nicolas, making a gesture of victory in a blue-striped jersey – a moment of happiness when he had no idea of the trials ahead. Emma shifts a few remote controls on the two-seater couch so she can sit down. She asks him what he's playing, gradually getting him to thaw a little. They talk about *FIFA* and about which of the players is Douglas. After he's explained the game for a few minutes, the atmosphere is relaxed enough for her to dare broach the subject.

'Douglas, as I mentioned last time, no part of this is your fault. Remember, the responsibility always lies with the adult.'

He avoids her gaze and stares at the chequered carpet.

'Up on the bridge, you said someone took pictures and videos of you. And that someone threatened you. Can you tell me who that was?'

Silence. The only sound is the squeaking of the swivel chair as Douglas swings from side to side.

Emma moistens her lips. 'The police found a nude photo of you on your father's mobile phone. So you don't need to worry that you're betraying him in some way. We already know that it's him. Okay?'

Douglas freezes and stares at her as if she's lost the plot. 'No, it's not him. You're completely wrong. It's not him.'

'But . . .' Emma hesitates. Is the boy lying? Is he trying to protect his father? 'He had a picture of you. A picture of you naked on a bed.'

'Yes, because he found it on my phone. And he was furious and sent it to himself. And then he told me that if I didn't stop this, he would show everyone on the team what I do.'

'Stop what?'

'Taking pictures like that. I told him a friend and I mucked around, swapping pics with some girls and so on. I couldn't . . .' He rubs his thumb against the bandage on his arm, tearing it open at the edge.

Emma asks as calmly as she can: 'You couldn't what?'

Douglas stares at her from wide eyes, his breathing fast and shallow.

Emma slides forward on the edge of the sofa, preparing herself to catch him in case he passes out and falls off the chair.

'Who is taking nude photos of you?' she asks again.

Douglas rips a piece off the bandage and, with his fingertips on his palm, rolls it into a small ball. 'My parents had an argument on Christmas Eve. My father wanted to go and meet some chick. They think I don't notice anything, but I know he sees other women. And my mother went nuts, took the car and drove after him.'

Emma tries to understand what Douglas is saying, what he's hinting at. 'You mean, both Giorgio and Vera drove somewhere on Christmas Eve?'

'Yes, once we came home from visiting Grandma and Grandpa. They thought I'd gone to sleep, but I was awake and . . .' He swallows, then stammers feebly. 'They both went out but told the police they were at home.' He gives Emma a puzzled look. 'Why did they lie? Why did they lie about what they were doing on the night that Jasmine was murdered?'

Emma stands up and goes over to Douglas, taking his hands in hers.

'I don't know, but I'm going to find out,' she says, uncertainty nagging at her.

Has she overlooked something? Has Vera done more than just cover for Giorgio?

Suddenly, something that has been bothering her deep down comes bursting to the surface, and she lets go of Douglas's hands. The yoga mat! The nutcracker was hidden inside a yoga mat in the garage, but she hardly imagines the mat belongs to Giorgio. More like Vera. Why would Giorgio hide the nutcracker in a place where his wife was likely to find it?

'Is your father right-handed or left-handed?'

'Um, right-handed.'

'And your mother?'

'She's left-handed.'

Emma can scarcely conceal her excitement. Her thoughts tumble in cartwheels. How far is a woman prepared to go to protect her husband, and to prevent the unspeakable thing she's been suppressing for so long from coming to light? Did Vera drive to Jasmine's on Christmas Eve and . . .

Emma gives Douglas an urgent look. 'I have one more question, and it's an important one. Who took the Tesla that evening – Giorgio or Vera?'

57

Nicolas shuffles along the corridor, sensing the aggression and the testosterone radiating from the guard beside him. It's the same man he knocked down a few days ago. Chill, he wants to tell him. I'm all good today, haven't taken anything.

When they arrive at the interview room, the guard opens the door and Nicolas peers inside to see who's waiting for him. Emma and the cop, Simon Weyler. His eyes search Emma's. He would like to apologize to her for his little glitch, and for making her risk her job for him. But that will have to wait until he's alone with her.

He sits down on the empty chair. Emma sits beside him, and Simon on the other side of the table. He wonders what they want from him. More questions, the guard had told him. But he can see by their body language that there's more to it. They are tense, bent forward as if they are burdened by bad news.

'Is this about Douglas?' He remembers Emma's last visit. 'Has something happened to him?'

'Yes and yes,' replies Simon. 'He's doing relatively well. But a few things did happen.' He touches his chin, pausing for effect, and Nicolas shudders. 'Your father has been arrested for sexually abusing Douglas, and we conducted a search of your parents' house. In the course of that, we found some things we would like to ask you a few questions about to help us understand.'

Nicolas's stomach cramps up, and he feels a pain in his chest and a roaring in his ears.

'Why? What did you find?'

'I can't go into detail. But as you know, Douglas hasn't been doing well for a while. Two days ago, he tried to jump off a bridge across the E4, and I believe you know why. It's high time you told us the truth – if not for your sake, then for Douglas's.'

Fear overwhelms him, choking him. Douglas has tried to take his own life, that's how bad things have got. Of course he knew, but still. Somewhere deep down he'd hoped only he and Jasmine had been victims, not Douglas too.

Not his Douglas.

Nicolas clenches his fists while Simon's mouth moves as if he has just suffered a stroke.

'I'm certain that your sister's murder is connected to this sexual abuse. I just don't know how. Please help me out.'

Nicolas's skull feels like it's about to burst; lightning bolts flash before his eyes. Memories trying to break out with violent force and him fighting them back, again and again.

'Nicolas,' someone says, touching him. He turns his head. It's Emma.

'Where is Angela?' he asks. 'My real defence lawyer.'

'She was unable to come today, but I'm here. I know you didn't murder Jasmine. It was someone else, someone who didn't want her to make public what you two went through during your childhood. The same that Douglas is going through now. Am I right?'

Nicolas glares at her. The woman thinks she knows what's going on, but she hasn't a clue. 'What has Douglas said?' He becomes louder. 'What has he actually said?'

Emma starts back. 'Not much. And I understand him – he's fourteen and all alone in this matter. As long as you don't talk.'

Nicolas feels like punching her in the face, chucking her and the cop against the wall. He knows why. Because they are right. They're trying to tell him nicely that he's a coward, that he ought to be there for Douglas. And yes, he should be, he should have been for a long time. But it's impossible, absolutely impossible. Not a single person in the world would understand why he hadn't done something about it. He calms down, tries to breathe normally again.

'Why was my father arrested?' He looks straight at Emma and Simon, genuinely baffled. Why Giorgio?

'Because we have evidence against him,' replies Emma, but she doesn't sound as convinced as before. 'Douglas, on the other hand, claims that it wasn't Giorgio who abused him but someone else. But we get the feeling he's too afraid to say who.'

Nicolas focuses on a line someone has drawn on the table with a felt pen, fighting the images that come crashing over him unstoppably, like a wave. How they used to drive in the car when he was younger, how he had to undress, how he was photographed and filmed, how he was forced to do things he knew deep down were wrong. Every night he was terrified of closing his eyes, not wanting to fall asleep, not wanting to be awakened by someone lying beside him, reaching between his legs and arousing him.

It was his fault, he must have wanted it, or else his penis wouldn't have become hard.

He wanted it, just like . . . like . . .

'Think of Douglas.' He hears Emma's admonishing words while his head is filled with the disgusting sounds of panting and moaning, and he can feel the body rubbing against his. 'Think of your little brother. He needs you now. He can't do this on his own.'

Nicolas puts a fist into his mouth and bites it as hard as he can.

Think of Douglas, think of your little brother. Think of Douglas, think of your little brother.

Something explodes in his chest. The repulsion he has been suppressing for all these years. The fear he has suffered that one day it would all come out and everyone would know. He wonders who is screaming, and realizes that it's the feeling of shame and guilt inside him that has finally had enough.

'He is not my little brother! He is my son. He is my little brother and my son.'

58

The words circle around Emma's head like a mantra as she and Simon walk to the exit after handing Nicolas back to the guard.

He is my little brother and my son. He is my little brother and my son.

How is this possible? How are humans created on this planet?

In the reception area, they run into Angela, who has hurried here, brushing snowflakes off her coat.

'Did you get anything out of him? How did he react to his father's arrest?'

'Come on.' Emma opens the door to the staircase. 'Let's talk outside.'

When Angela raises an eyebrow, Emma shoots a sidelong glance at two guards who are chatting a few yards away. What she has to tell her boss is a delicate matter and not meant for their ears.

Excitement crosses Angela's face when she understands that Emma must have something interesting to report. They step out and close the door behind them. Emma waits until a man in a suit with a briefcase vanishes into the elevator. Then she drops the bombshell.

'Douglas is Nicolas's son.'

Angela stares at her and Simon, uncomprehending.

'Nicolas is the father of Douglas,' Emma says, trying to make it clearer. It still hasn't sunk in properly for her either, even though she's had half an hour to digest the news. 'Vera Moretti raped Nicolas and had a child by him. Douglas. It wasn't Giorgio who sexually abused his children, but Vera.'

Angela looks blank for a few more moments, but when the penny finally drops she laughs so loudly that the guards behind the glass door turn to stare at them.

'Seems like we aren't the only ones who've got a screw loose,' she gasps, holding a hand to her mouth.

Emma and Simon exchange a baffled look. Before they can say anything, Angela's outburst ends as abruptly as it began. She raises her chin, dons a professional expression and turns to Simon.

'Then I suggest you immediately contact the prosecutor and order an arrest warrant for Vera Moretti as well as a paternity test for Douglas. The statute of limitations for rape of a minor has only recently changed. Previously it was fifteen years from the time the victim came of legal age. Now there is no limit at all, because it has become accepted that sexual abuse can result in lifelong trauma.'

'Vera probably also murdered Jasmine,' says Emma. 'A witness saw the Morettis' Tesla not far from Jasmine's apartment around the time of the murder. And Douglas told us that Giorgio and Vera left the house late on Christmas Eve in separate vehicles, and that it was Vera who took the Tesla.'

Angela folds her hands and wiggles her fingers as if they were tentacles. 'Douglas can testify that Vera drove the Tesla, and we have a witness who can place the vehicle at Runda Vägen, just a stone's throw from Jasmine's apartment. But she only saw the car – no driver?'

'She did,' says Simon. 'She saw a person, but her report was made online, so we would have to question her again. Hellberg was on his way to her, but perhaps you've heard—'

'I have indeed.' Angela's face is priceless. 'I just spoke with a fireman I know. He was there, cutting through the roof. Apparently, Hellberg was wanking off while driving. His fly was undone and his pants were . . .' She pulls a face and moves her hand back and forth in front of her hips. 'Sticky. He must have come and lost control of his vehicle.'

Simon's eyes grow wide, and he looks like he is debating with himself whether to believe this story or not.

'You're kidding,' says Emma, wondering whether her glee is obvious. Her stunt worked better than expected.

'Not at all,' replies Angela. 'But he deserves at least some recognition. At least he had an explosive orgasm.'

'So, it's really true?'

Angela acts offended. 'You can bet your bottom dollar. My source is highly reliable. He would never joke about such a serious matter. After all, this might damage Hellberg's reputation.' She drips with sarcasm, adding quietly: 'And about time too.'

Emma feels strangely proud. The story with Hellberg is her work. She's managed to take revenge discreetly. Hard and merciless. Not by blowing off his skull with a bullet or by maiming him like you see in movies. Nor by reporting him and dragging him into a long and gruelling court trial with her compromising video evidence. She's managed without such measures. She is holding Hellberg in the palm of her hand, can demand of him whatever she wishes. Karma, and all that.

'Call him,' Angela says to Simon. 'No, not because of that,' she clarifies when Simon looks at her sceptically. 'It would be useful to know if he made it to the eyewitness and collected a description of the person driving the Tesla.'

'Yes, but—'

'Call him. Either everything's all right and he answers, or he's in intensive care and doesn't.'

Simon opens his mouth, then closes it and walks a few steps to the side.

'Anything else?' asks Angela once she's certain Simon really is making the call.

Emma thinks. Anything else? She feels as if a whole lot has happened in the last few days. Angela tried to hang herself, Douglas came close to jumping off a bridge, she herself was caught drink-driving and nearly for theft, even though the latter is on Angela. And Giorgio tried to choke her and Hellberg pinned her against a car and . . . But the best or the worst thing, depending on how you look at it, is that Nicolas finally opened up about his trauma – that Douglas is his son and that he's spent half his life living in fear of Giorgio and others finding out. Anything else?

'The nutcracker,' she suddenly remembers. 'The police found a nutcracker in the Morettis' garage, which may have caused the bruises on Jasmine's finger.'

'What nutcracker?'

'You might remember that there were nuts and nutshells on Jasmine's coffee table. But no one realized that the nutcracker was missing. Now the police have found one. It was rolled up inside a yoga mat in the garage. Vera's yoga mat.'

Angela frowns, and Emma guesses she is following the same train of thought as she did earlier. Why would Vera take the nutcracker but not the murder weapon? To cast suspicion on Nicolas? But then – why take the nutcracker?

'Odd, no doubt.' Angela taps her index finger against her chin. 'But good for us. Before the day is over, Nicolas will be released from prison. We're defending him, not Vera Moretti.'

They turn to Simon when he comes back with his phone in his hand.

'I got hold of Hellberg. He spoke with the witness. The Tesla was driven by a woman with pinned-up hair.'

'Bingo,' says Angela. 'Could it have been Vera?'

'Probably, but the witness only saw the woman from a distance. That means we probably won't be able to do a photo array with her. But the witness picked up a piece of the broken headlight that fell on the road in the accident. Which means we can definitely prove that the Tesla was near the scene of the crime.' Simon looks at each of them in turn. He appears to be waiting for something else.

'Don't you want to know how Hellberg is doing?' he asks when nothing is forthcoming.

Emma and Angela exchange a look and reply at once: 'No.'

59

Emma tears the plastic wrapping off the new office chair and places it in front of the desk that was delivered a few days ago. She looks around contentedly. The Köhler firm has come back to life. Angela has replaced the furniture she sold with items from an auction house. 'Won't hurt for them to look a little used,' she'd said. She bought back the hand-knotted carpet from the same person she had sold it to. Green indoor plants in large clay pots stand dotted across the herringbone parquet in all three office rooms.

In the little more than three weeks since Nicolas's release from remand prison, Angela's phones have been ringing non-stop, and her desk pad is covered with pink and yellow arrest notices. Reminders to call this person and that. Names of new clients with times and dates of appointments.

The law office is booming, thanks to Angela's and Emma's successful efforts to stop proceedings against Nicolas. It's probably mainly Emma's achievement, but she is happy to share the win with her boss.

While Emma unboxes the next chair and removes the plastic wrap, she glances over at the brand-new TV. The main focus of the show airing at the moment is Vera Moretti, who is in remand custody. A reporter in the lobby of the police station holds out the microphone to a person Emma has seen a lot of lately. It's Simon, well known to the media by now.

'Is it true that Vera Moretti is also suspected of the murder of her stepdaughter, Jasmine Moretti?'

'Yes, that is true.'

'On what grounds?'

'I can't go into detail here, but we have evidence and witnesses that support our theory. Vera Moretti is a strong suspect.'

'But in the beginning the police were relatively certain that Nicolas Moretti was the murderer. How do you know you've got it right this time?'

'In the course of the ongoing investigation, new results, evidence and circumstances emerged that invalidated the suspicion against him and led to the charges being dropped. But as I said, I can't go into details.'

'New circumstances, you say. Are you referring to the sexual abuse Vera Moretti committed on her own and Giorgio Moretti's children?'

'Yes, among others.'

'Did she abuse all three children?'

'Yes, that is what the evidence suggests. But we are still at the beginning of the preliminary investigation, and there is still a lot of material for us to work through and evaluate.'

Simon indicates with a nod that he will say no more.

'Just one more question.' Someone holds a microphone under Simon's nose. 'A paternity test confirmed that Nicolas is the father of Douglas. What do you say to that?'

'Well, it must have been a huge shock for everyone. It is an enormous family tragedy, and we must be considerate of all involved. The whole thing is going to be extremely difficult for them, even without the attention of the media.'

Emma focuses back on the chair, removing the last of the plastic. An enormous family tragedy. Yes, that's probably the least one can say. And sadly the media haven't been considerate at all of those involved. Each headline is worse than the last:

Nicolas Moretti is the father of his little brother; She raped her stepson and bore his child; Giorgio Moretti's betrayal of his children – he must have known.

And of course, self-proclaimed experts put in their ten cents' worth, analysing and debating this controversial topic to death, which is difficult to understand, let alone rationalize. How can a mother rape her children? Only a man would do such a thing.

Emma too had shared this view to begin with, but that was because various pieces of evidence pointed to Giorgio. It wasn't just that he was a sugar daddy and met his own daughter on a date. In addition, he was a youth coach who had sneaked into a storeroom with Adam Ballin and saved a nude picture of Douglas on his phone. What else had she been supposed to think?

Vera refused to explain what everyone wanted to know. Why? How can anyone do such a thing to their children? The only statement she made in her defence was that she was abused herself – an almost cliché excuse offenders use in an attempt to justify their behaviour.

Her comments about the murder of Jasmine are equally sparse. Yes, she drove to her stepdaughter's on Christmas Eve for fear Jasmine might blab. But she never went up to her apartment and she definitely did not cut Jasmine's throat. Instead, she had remained in the car and, after mulling it over for a while, decided not to 'wake any sleeping dogs'.

And then the classic blackmail number, which Emma grudgingly recognizes in herself. Vera admitted to this because there is proof, digital evidence of the abuse, among other things. Vera's computer and mobile phone contained a lot of pornographic material, especially involving Nicolas, Jasmine and Douglas. There were pictures and videos she deleted but which the IT forensics managed to recover. Material she held over the children's heads to threaten them into silence.

'In case you're thinking about saying something to Papa – I'll show him this. And then I'll just say you took those photos and posted them online to make money.'

She threatened Nicolas with something that would have been extremely difficult to cope with as a teenager: 'What do you think Giorgio is going to think of you when he finds out that you are Douglas's father?'

Vera eventually admitted to raping Nicolas, because she could hardly talk herself out of the DNA test results. And at this point of the investigation, no one would believe her if she had claimed Nicolas had wanted it too.

She denied, however, having anything to do with the nut-cracker. 'Someone else must have hidden it in the yoga mat. Why should I do such a thing? If I were the murderer, I would have taken the actual murder weapon, the knife, with me.'

Emma had been thinking along the same lines and in the course of conversations with Angela and Simon had reached the conclusion that Vera had needed a scapegoat. She had left the knife behind to pin the murder on Nicolas. Then the police wouldn't be looking for an alternative suspect.

But the whole thing still nags at her. Why had Vera taken the nutcracker in the first place? As some kind of trophy? Emma can't think of a plausible explanation. Then again, people sometimes do strange things, especially under pressure.

Her phone beeps. A text from Simon. He asks if she wants to grab a coffee this afternoon. She replies with *yes* and a smiley. Then she finds that she also has a message from Jens.

Haven't heard in a while. Congratulations on your success. Want to catch up one of these days? ♥

Emma switches off the display. Not a chance. Why does he contact her now, after all those months of silence when she needed him? She looks at her phone and snorts with contempt. Turns her head towards the front door as it opens.

Angela breezes in wearing hot-pink boots and a tiger-print coat that Emma has never seen before. In passing, she waves a folded-up Ikea bag at Emma.

'I'm moving back into my apartment. The guy has finally gone.'

Even though Emma feels a little sorry for Angela's tenant, she can't help but smile. Evidently, he's decided not to pick a fight with a lawyer who wants her apartment back – least of all one who recently won an impossible case. Smart choice.

'By the way.' Angela pauses in the door frame. 'The wanker is back on his feet, apparently. Perhaps we ought to go visit, see how he's doing.' She winks at Emma and carries on to her office.

The smile on Emma's lips widens.

The wanker. Angela isn't the only one who's been calling Hellberg by that name lately. The nickname has spread through the police station like the coronavirus.

Couldn't have ended better than that.

Emma gathers up the packaging and carries it to the hallway. Suddenly she hears Angela swear about something and walks over to her. Her boss is red in the face, struggling with a moving carton that's about to slip out of her grasp.

'I'll take it,' says Emma, catching it. 'Shit. What have you got in there?'

'Books. It needs to go down to the car.'

'All right.' Emma lugs the box to the exit, bracing it with one thigh so she can open the door. With careful steps she climbs down the stairs, peering past the carton to see where she's going.

Nevertheless, at the point where the stairs go round the corner, she missteps, teeters, then manages to catch herself but not the box. It crashes down the stairs and finally comes to rest upside down. Books and various other objects fall out. A toilet bag, a blow-dryer, a bottle of shampoo. And something else. Emma steps closer to get a better look, and tugs at the fabric sticking out from the box.

It is purple with yellow dots. A scarf.

Emma freezes. What was it Rantanen said? That Jasmine lost a purple scarf with yellow spots and that a quarter of an hour later it was no longer on the pavement.

Emma and Angela had reached the conclusion that someone must have picked it up – someone who might have followed Jasmine and Nicolas.

With a growing sense of unease, she realizes she has made an unwelcome discovery. She examines the scarf more closely, and *voilà*, there is a tear at one end.

The steel bar below Jasmine's balcony. Somebody probably climbed up there and got caught on it with an item of clothing.

Alarm bells go off in Emma's head as the truth sinks in that she is holding said item of clothing in her hands.

But why is it in a box in Angela's possession? If she'd found it somehow, she would have had to hand it over to the police. She knows that this is an important piece in the puzzle of the murder investigation.

If only the scarf was found on a suspect . . . Angela had said something like that to her. If . . .

Was it . . . No. The thought is so morbid that she doesn't want to think it through. Angela couldn't have . . . On the other hand, she had withheld an important piece of evidence that would have connected the murderer to the scene of the crime.

As realization slowly sinks in, Emma continues this train of thought.

Had Angela been the one who followed Nicolas and Jasmine home from the pub? Had she picked up the scarf? And had she got caught on the reinforcing steel when she climbed up to Jasmine's apartment?

Footsteps in the stairwell. Emma looks up and sees Angela in her pink boots walk towards her. She tries to sort out the chaos in her head.

The prediction that came true. Why hadn't she thought of that sooner? Vera could hardly have known about it since she and Jasmine weren't in contact. Angela, on the other hand, had seen Jasmine frequently at the ACA meetings and most likely had known what Jasmine was afraid of – that either she or Nicolas would die before their thirtieth birthday. Perhaps she had even been inspired by the prophecy. She would have known that Nicolas in connection with a murder scandal would guarantee huge headlines.

Had Angela produced this scandal herself? Had she made sure Nicolas would hire her as his defender?

Yes, Angela had already admitted as much when Emma confronted her about the made-up stalker.

'I'm sorry about that, but I really needed this case. To convince Nicolas to engage me, I had to let him believe there was a stalker we could deflect suspicion on to.'

It was no accident that she had appeared at the police station the same night that Nicolas was arrested for suspected murder. She had known the overwhelming evidence against him and that he would be charged with murder.

'It was you!' says Emma when Angela stops in front of her. 'And then you took the nutcracker and hid it in Vera's yoga mat. That's why you were so keen for me to find something on Giorgio that would lead to a search warrant. But you didn't take the knife. It had to stay at the crime scene to throw suspicion on Nicolas. You orchestrated your own impossible case.'

Angela bends down, reaches for the scarf and runs her fingertips over the soft fabric. Then she fixes Emma with her eyes.

'Remember – women must stick together.'

ABOUT THE AUTHOR

Photo © Johan Almblad

With fifteen years of experience in law enforcement, Anna Karolina is perfectly equipped to write crime fiction. Having made the jump from working in the Swedish police's Robbery Unit to being an author, Anna was keen to write more than mere procedurals. Setting out to portray her antiheroes and their complex relationships with an authenticity matching her knowledge of policing, she quickly became one of Sweden's most notable crime writers. Her first novel, *Savage Congress*, the first in a series following notorious policewoman Amanda Paller, was met with high praise from both critics and readers.

She continues to craft stories that depict criminals in as much detail as they do investigators, drawing on her own experiences to create a compellingly detailed and accurate, albeit fictional, world of crime and punishment.

ABOUT THE TRANSLATOR

Lisa Reinhardt studied English and linguistics at the University of Otago and lives with her family on the beautiful West Coast of New Zealand. Her recent work includes Hangman's Daughter Tales author Oliver Pötzsch's *The Master's Apprentice*.

Made in the USA
Monee, IL
24 August 2022

12357286R00225